MARY BLANDY

'. . . All I know is there's a strangeness in you.'

'Tonight?'

'Tonight more than usual. Nearer the surface, shining out of your eyes, trembling at the tips of your fingers. You may damp down the fires within you. But not for always. Not for always, Mary Blandy. You're born out of your time. This sceptical age has no use for powers such as yours.'

'I have no powers, I tell you. None – none.' Trembling gripped her stomach like cramp.

'You have, I tell you. You have! A century ago they would have burned you . . .'

MARY BLANDY

first published as
THE HANGING WOOD

Joan Morgan

A STAR BOOK
published by
the Paperback Division of
W. H. ALLEN & Co. Ltd

A Star Book
Published in 1980
by the Paperback Division of
W. H. Allen & Co. Ltd
A Howard and Wyndham Company
44 Hill Street, London W1X 8LB
This edition reprinted 1980

First published in Great Britain by Macdonald & Co.
(Publishers) Ltd, in 1950 under the title 'The Hanging Wood'

Printed in Great Britain by
Hazell Watson & Viney Ltd, Aylesbury, Bucks

ISBN 0 352 30436 7

BIBLIOGRAPHY

Miss Mary Blandy's Own Account (A. Millar, in the Strand, 1752).

The Authentick Tryals of John Swan and Elizabeth Jeffryes, With the Tryal of Mary Blandy (Oxford, 1752).

The Fair Parricide, A Tragedy in 3 Acts (Fetter Lane, 1752).

*The * * * * * * Packet Broke Open* (Paternoster Row, 1752).

Captain Cranstoun's Own Account (Holborn, 1753).

The Letters of Horace Walpole (1746–52).

Park Place (Percy Noble).

Also the *Victoria County History of Berkshire,* numerous contemporary letters and reports, and privately printed books on the Henley district.

AUTHOR'S NOTE

I HAVE wanted for a number of years to tell the strange story of Mary Blandy. I first tried it in play form, but a mere Georgian pastiche emerged. Through studying most of the available Blandyana, both at the British Museum and in privately-printed books on the Henley district so kindly lent me by Captain Eric Noble—until recently owner of Park Place—the story gradually took possession of me.

It was not an easy one to reconstruct; much of the contemporary material is apocryphal and there is a certain amount of conflict even in established fact, but a general picture began to form when seen against a background that has changed so little in two centuries.

I have not deviated in any material way from history; the Trial is authentic, as is some of the dialogue. No character or incident is entirely imaginary. A minor liberty has been taken in the introduction of the celebrated Jack Fletcher, and where no portrait existed of minor characters in the drama I have had to fill one in. In making Mary the central figure of a novel I have added just that element of fiction that makes truth less strange.

J.M.

Lake Cottage
October 1949.

"If Love, in deep distress, can aught prevail,
You'll prove attentive to our tragic Tale,
Our well-known Tale:—The base Deluder's fled,
And the too-fond, too-credulous Fair is dead.
Guilty or guiltless, who can surely tell?
A spotless Angel, or a Fiend of Hell?
To heaven alone we'll leave her dubious Case,
And strive to mend the World through her Disgrace."

The Fair Parricide.

CONTENTS

PART ONE 1747-8

CHAPTER ONE

At this hour the air had an edge, as though already summer held a premonition of autumn. The sky was swept clean by the rain of the night before and the pavements on the north side of the street were still wet.

Closing the door carefully, she glanced up the street. It was empty of life, broad and straight and formal as a street in a print, the smooth red façades of the houses broken here and there by an oversailing half-timbered gable of earlier date. The flint and chalk chessboard of the church tower struck a note of cold strength above the warm domestic glow of plunging roofs.

Ten minutes past six. Ten minutes past six on an August morning in the year of our Lord 1747.

Soon now the street would be awake: dogs would be let out, mats shaken, windows thrown up, fires raked, hot water carried in gleaming cans; ostlers would be grooming horses for the early start of the London coach and serving maids calling reluctant travellers at the Lion and the Bell, the Catherine Wheel and the White Hart. The shutters would be taken down at the butcher's in the market-place, and in the chemist's window the slanting sun would discover emeralds and rubies and sapphires imprisoned in great bottles, bringing even to the leeches in their jars the news that a fresh day had begun. Soon now the chair-mender would be taking up his position on the kerb and the knife-grinder setting out from his cottage in Friday Street, but for the moment the town was empty of life.

The heels of her shoes echoed off the pavement as she walked quickly in the direction of the river. All her movements were swift and decisive, giving an illusion of purpose to her most random gestures. She was not, by the standards of her day, beautiful, but her long limbs, her grace, and a certain arrogance of bearing gave her distinction. Her face was oval, with a fine straight nose and unsmiling lips, and her eyes glowed darkly below the wonderful arch of her brows. She was not young. She had never been young. Even at eighteen no one would have spoken of Mary Blandy as a girl. Now, at twenty-seven, she had the indefinable agelessness of the intelligent spinster. She was not warm, not soft, not gay, yet—as she hurried across the bridge before the world was awake—her figure was a disturbing one, carrying with it an uneasy suggestion of curbed force, of banked-down fires.

She paused for a moment to watch the river's downward flow. Swollen by the rains of a bad summer, the waters were brown and swift as they churned round the piers of the old bridge. Something in her answered the power of the current, and her long fingers grew taut on the parapet.

There was a legend that never at any hour had Henley Bridge been empty of passengers. She had never quite believed it, yet even as she started to move on she could hear the clip of hooves as a farm-hand led a splendid Shire—descendant of the old English war-horse—across from the Berkshire bank.

Ahead of her the London road swept to the crest of the hill, a road cut deep through chalk. Leaving it, she followed the line of the river. A film of water lay over the meadowland on either side. Plover rose up crying as she passed. Iris and purple spikes of loosestrife raised their heads above the water, and tall dry teazle grew on the higher ground. The air was very still and clear, and even the leaves of the great elms were motionless.

This was the hour she loved, this hour before the day—with all it might or might not bring—had begun. Here, alone in the neutrality of dawn, she was conscious of a sense of lightness, as though she had been set free of her identity; a woman alone, swift of foot and mind, in a world new-born with each dawn, a world without hope, fear, regret or even memory, a world of infinite possibilities, as yet untested. Here she was no longer Miss Blandy, spinster of this parish. She was of no parish, of no time; ageless, free; herself.

The sun was clearing the hills now and almost at once the air lost its suggestion of autumn. The pale golden light caught the hurrying river and singled out each blade of grass for flattery. The withies on the long island swayed gently as a small breeze sprang up, and a heron passed overhead, flying lazily upstream from the heronry at Fawley.

Leaving the Wargrave road, she turned in at a small gate, taking a path that led up to the hanging woods of Park Place. Of tall beech, the woods rode the hill for several miles, following the line of the Thames. In spring the trees stood knee-deep in a sea of bluebells and in autumn the hillside burned with the dark flame of their leaves. It was here that she had first heard the nightingale. Above her head now she could distinguish the soft secret song of a young blackbird, and in the distance a robin scattered a cascade of small notes.

Paths intersected the woods, and clumps of dark yew robbed them of uniformity. Beyond the crest of the hill the trees gave way to formal parkland dominated by a rather ugly mansion. The house would be rebulit many times, but never with charm. It was only the land that was beautiful, a thousand acres of it enclosed by six miles of road, rich in timber and close-cropped turf, in orchard and river-meadow, wild flower and wild fowl and in every gift nature could bring to it and wealth conserve.

Since her father was trustee for the estate, the privilege of walking its paths had been Mary's from her early youth. The privilege would, she supposed, continue when the house once again changed hands; it was unlikely that mere nobility would withhold what royalty had conceded.

These trappings—a coronet on a coach or three feathers above a stable gate—had, she supposed, a meaning for her father. For her these woods, part of a forest that had diverted the tide of conquest and settlement, held a deeper, more primitive meaning, something that transcended the snobberies of a country town. Her father, Town Clerk of Henley; her mother, the former Miss Stevens of Culham Court; her uncles, Mr. Serjeant Stevens of Doctor's Commons and the Rector of Fawley; herself, the reputed heiress; the respected position the Blandys enjoyed in this small corner of the world, and their acquaintance among the neighbouring gentry; the cap-touching and the limitless credit from the tradespeople; the family pew in church and the houseful of servants; the silk gowns her maid laid out for her, and her own elegant accomplishments—needlework and elocution and dancing; these things had always been hers, were as much part of her as the air she breathed. It would only be if one or many of them were stripped from her that she would be consciously aware of them. They were hers, part of the entity that was Miss Blandy, spinster of this parish.

And yet—and yet——!

The age in which she lived presented paradoxes disturbing to a heightened sensibility: on the one hand coarse, ruthless, bestial, insanitary, vicious and amoral; on the other, cultured, elegant, honourable and well-mannered; an age that could accept the brutalities of 'Butcher' Cumberland and—in a London where masques and scavenging ravens co-existed—flock to Tower Hill to see the heads of the Scottish Rebel Lords exposed; an age which—for all the scepticism of the wits—had only recently repealed the laws against witchcraft and in which love-philtres were still advertised. It was a day in which the lusty heart of an earlier England still beat thickly beneath a sprigged waistcoat—when an inheritance might be wagered on the turn of a card, guts rotted by wine in Bristol glass and pock-marked bodies clothed in Lyons silk; a day which brought a certain regularity to its relationships by recognising its mistresses and acknowledging it bastards; a day in which political corruption was lent dignity by the high places in which it flourished; an age which was to leave an unsurpassed legacy in art, in letters, in all the graces of living; an age when aristocracy was the apex round which revolved the painters, the wits, the architects, the cabinet-makers, an aristocracy climbing to the summit of that hill which led down to prudery and pig-iron, an age in which the sky was not yet blackened, the countryside not yet scarred, when no ugliness existed save in the hearts of men.

Something of which—instinctively rather than intellectually—Mary sensed, sensed in a vague uneasiness, a prescience of the ferment below the bland surface of her daily life.

The woods ended and the glade called Happy Valley flowed in all its smooth perfection to the water's edge. Across the gleaming line of the river, Oxfordshire lay like a map, and she could trace the line of the Chilterns, petering out towards Shiplake, then rising in layer upon layer of beech-wood to sweep across the county boundary into Buckinghamshire. Henley lay in a hollow, its red roofs already hazed over with smoke as countless breakfasts were being cooked. Here on the hillside no sound disturbed the peace of the lovely morning, and the sight of so much activity in the town below was curiously unreal; the daily chores of Lilliput.

She breathed deeply, drawing the clean air into her lungs until her head swam. Then quite without warning, as so often before, the feeling of exultancy left her. Turning back, she realised she was hungry, with a cold hollow void, that her back ached, that her thin shoes were wet with dew, and that she was more than two miles walk from the familiar faces round the breakfast table.

The mood that had sent her out had ebbed away. The woods no longer filled her with a sense of lightness and freedom; they were oppressive in their loneliness. It was not here that she would find the answer to the unformulated question that lay at the back of her mind, that core of emptiness that nothing in her pleasant well-ordered life could fill. A quest; was that what life was? But for what? What, in the last analysis, was this fret, this hunger?

She started to hurry now, the thought of her parents, the servants, the cat, the dog and all warm living things drawing her with a longing so intense that it seemed almost as though some premonition of instability had entered her mind.

As she drew near the town, her pace slackened and she walked with circumspection. A curious disordered figure loped ahead of her over the bridge. She recognised it for that of Jack Fletcher, the Wargrave Fool.

She could never see the poor creature without disquiet. Abnormality was to her infinitely sad, infinitely horrible. In a way she could not have explained, he was a link with that undercurrent of darkness of which she was at times almost morbidly aware. There was no one in whom she could confide her thoughts without fear of ridicule. At times it seemed to her her generation protested its scepticism a shade too much.

A greeting from a man on horseback recalled her to the bright morning. "You're up with the lark, Miss Blandy!"

She returned the greeting with a slow smile which gave her an air of complicity, as though she shared with the horseman the secret of some early tryst.

Hart Street rang now to the hooves of horses. It was Friday, and gentlemen from the surrounding countryside were meeting at the Bell for their weekly game of bowls. The street, so empty when she left it, was now filled with animation: the Oxford coach was pulling briskly out of the yard of the White Hart, a pair of terriers in hot pursuit, and a brewer's dray stood outside the Lion, its splendid horses groomed and prinked like court beauties.

The pavements were thronged with women, their dissembling faces shaded from the morning sun by flat straw hats, their talk as empty as their baskets. A haywain moved slowly up the street, leaving behind a trail of wisps, eagerly investigated by a flock of sparrows in watch for just such a windfall. The coffee-house was taking down its shutters; heavy-eyed and sluggish as its customers, it was the last shop to open.

When Mary reached her house, Ned Hearne was out on the pavement polishing the brass plate. At one time the plate had said: MR. FRANCIS BLANDY, ATTORNEY-AT-LAW, but years of Ned's industry had worn the letters flat until little could be read. No matter; the brass shone gaily, and with half the important families of the district in his pocket, the lawyer had no need to advertise.

Ned's plain face lit up. "Good morning, Miss Mary!" Coming to the house when she was thirteen, he saw Mary still as a young girl, and the bond of affection between them was a warm one. Literate and loyal, Ned Hearne was something more than a footman; whether with the silver or a confidential message, implicit trust was placed in him by all the family.

"Good morning, Ned. Isn't it a lovely day?"

"Good to be alive, miss!"

Breakfast was over, and she could hear the murmur of her father's voice through the closed door of the study, punctuated now and then by the clerk Littleton's jerky assents. There was no sign of her mother. A place had been left for her at table, and there was some bacon in the chafing-dish. She took two or three rashers and cut herself a slice of bread. They baked twice a week, and the loaf was moist and close, with a deep black crust. The butter—set in a mould used for the Blandys for nearly thirty years—was kingcup yellow and beaded with moisture. From the same farm came the jars of thick cream, the great geese at Christmas and the fat capons when there was company. Mr. Blandy liked it to be known that he kept a good table; an innocent enough vanity.

Mary rang for her chocolate. After what seemed to her a considerable time, the cook-maid, Elizabeth Binfield, came into the room and, in silence, put the small silver pot at her side.

"Good morning, Betty," she said. Even to her own ears her voice rang false off the flat surface of the maid's hostility.

Something in the girl's smouldering good looks filled Mary with uneasiness. There was an animal element in her which seemed an intrusion among so much smooth mahogany. In the year she had been with the Blandys, Betty's conduct and industry had been beyond criticism; her references from the rector of Fawley—in whose employ she had been since early girlhood—had been excellent. There was nothing to be said about her, Mary knew. Yet the doubt remained. Harvest of some chance sowing, Betty had been given the name of the village where she had been abandoned in infancy. She was, the Reverend John Stevens said, more than usually in need of kindness. Mary had not at the time been able to resist the retort: "My dear uncle, no one is more charitably inclined than myself, but I really cannot help feeling that a doorstep twenty years ago does not completely justify the sullen acceptance of every subsequent benefit!"

The fear, so insistently repeated, of what would become of Betty Binfield if she were to be turned out seemed to Mary to take on the elements of a subtly-levied blackmail. "I assure you I shall not have it on *my* conscience if Betty goes the way of her mother," she once commented. Pretty Mrs. Blandy was deliciously shocked. Secretly, she had a great admiration for her daughter's sharp tongue.

Through some keyhole or other, the words got back to Betty, to be added to her store-house of grievances. All Mary's trinkets were in the store-house: her laces and her ribbons and her caps and the row of narrow shoes in her cupboard; her petticoats and sacks as well, the bombazines and the muslins and the tabbies and the paduasoys and the cashmeres. Every note that came for Mary, every caller, every rumour of the fortune to which the only child was heiress, went to feed the foundling's resentment. There was in Mary a core of aloofness that did little to make her loved.

The church clock began to strike the four quarters, then the hour of ten. These same chimes had punctuated almost every moment of Mary's life, cutting her days and nights into twelve, her hours into four. Penetrating to every room in the house, they had become part of the fabric of familiar things. Once when, in a severe frost, the clock stopped for a time, it was as though she could no longer hear the sound of her own breathing. When on rare occasions she went to town, the sound of the chimes on her return would strike a note of welcome that was warming as the bark of a devoted dog. Her life, revolving on a small orbit, was made up of small things.

She sat for a time drinking her chocolate, no longer aware of the spiritual emptiness of an hour earlier.

Were there any letters for her? The posts were the warp that held together the fabric of polite life, and the highly dangerous accomplishment of letter-writing was in this day reaching maturity. Not that Mary had any correspondence among the wits; such letters as she received would be notes from ensigns met at a ball, or the boasts of school-friends, all now it seemed not only *successfully,* but *happily* married.

She glanced at the hall table: an invitation to a garden-party at Paradise House. She smiled faintly. So General Lord Mark Ker had decided to extend his purely professional acquaintance with his lawyer! Mrs. and Miss Blandy, for the fourteenth of September. The fourteenth. That would mean postponing their visit to Bath by a week. If, of course, her mother thought the invitation sufficient reason for postponement. After all, a garden-party——!

On the other hand, Lord Mark—an old man, older than her father—was a link with the great world, and neither of her parents despised links, even links so fragile as a mere garden-party.

What, she wondered, should she wear? The lawns would be cool and smooth in the shade of the great dark trees. She had visited the house called Paradise several times in Mr. Blunt's day. Her father had, she knew, arranged its leasing to Lord Mark. How restless these people were! Estate management and conveyancing were by far the most profitable side of her father's practice. Mr. Blandy had once threatened to adopt as his motto old Fuller's comment that "The lands of Berkshire are skittish and apt to cast their owners". In her own short lifetime, Park Place had cast both Lord Archibald Hamilton and Frederick, Prince of Wales, not without profit to the attorney of Hart Street. Who would be the next?

Card in hand, she went in search of her mother. At this hour she would probably be in the kitchen planning the day's meals.

The great stone-flagged kitchen seemed as usual full of people: Ned Hearne; her mother's maid, Mrs. Deane; Betty Binfield; Susannah Gunnel, who had been with Mr. Blandy since before his marriage; the two washerwomen, Mary Banks and Ann James; Dame Emmet, the charwoman and, as Mary had expected, Mad Jack Fletcher.

The Wargrave Fool had made of the kitchen table a pulpit and was mimicking her uncle, the Rector of Fawley, with that uncanny fidelity which was his one gift. The accomplishment opened the doors of half the kitchens in the town to him, and she had no doubt he exploited it, but she had never been able to join in the laughter it provoked.

Gathered round the poor clown, the domestics were turned by Mary's entrance into pillars of salt. She paused in the doorway. "I was looking for my mother." Now, as always upon catching the servants out, she found herself seeking to put them at their ease, saying "my mother" rather than "your mistress".

Dame Emmet—a good humoured old creature, tough of fibre—was the first to come to life. "Madam's in the garden, miss, getting the flowers."

"Thank you, Dame." Mary smiled. She was fond of the old charwoman. Closing the door, she shut in the too-warm smell of dough rising by the fire, of cats and domestics.

The garden, hemmed in on all sides by a chaos of red roofs, was long and narrow. Ropes of wistaria ran the length of the flint walls, and grass paths cut between the beds with their massing of colour and scent. It was curiously homely: borders of pinks, wallflowers and sweet william, stocks and phlox, moss roses and primulas, each in its season. It was almost as though, in revolt against the wide formal gardens that surrounded the Wren mansion of her girlhood, Mrs. Blandy had sought something wholly her own: a woman's garden, personal and fragrant. From the valley of the Tamar she had brought big purple violets, from Westmorland the scattering of tiny daffodils beneath the walnut tree, and from a Somerset lane hart's tongues for a shady corner. She would beg roots and cuttings from friends everywhere: a knot of shamrock from a cousin in Kerry, dark gentians from a friend doing the Grand Tour, a sprig of myrtle from the gardens of the Alcazar in Seville. Few of these exotics survived, but the pleasure they gave her was almost as great as the trouble they gave her acquaintances.

She moved quietly along the border, her delicate skin protected from the sun by a hat that flapped with every step, her hands protected by loose gloves. Almost in the shadow of her hooped skirts trotted her adored pug, Dandy. Minute and smooth as porcelain, the little dog gave no trouble, content always to sit on his cushion or perch under an arm—black mask alert, tiny paws taut—or, as now, to pad up and down in a confusion of petticoats. The China Dog, Mr. Blandy called him.

Mrs. Blandy avoided exertion, snipping only those flowers which were within easy reach. "I have to be a little careful," she would say. Mary could never be sure whether or not her mother was delicate. On occasion she had taken to her bed for a few days, but her manners were so perfect, her good humour and self-control so complete and her appearance—by the time Mrs. Deane had done her work—so charming, that no impression of illness remained. No one—Mary least of all—knew what lay behind these infrequent withdrawals from the everyday round; the secret of the pain endured, and its cause, was one the pretty woman shared with none. Gay and affectionate, she had in her day been a skilful flirt; she had early acquired the gift of taking life lightly. It was with regret that she came to realise her only daughter had not inherited her temperament. Mary was, she thought with a touch of apprehension, in danger of developing into that most undesirable of things: an intelligent woman.

"Good morning, mama," Mary called.

"Molly dear!" Mrs. Blandy lightly kissed the girl's cheek. Mary was aware of the scent of violet powder. "Where have you been?"

"In the hanging woods."

"You've been gone hours, dear. We were quite worried!"

Mary gave one of her rare laughs. "Did you think I had a rendezvous?"

"I only wish I could, darling!" An echo of the old archness awoke for a moment. "There's something so morbid about walking in the woods alone. I'm sure no one would have done it in my day!"

Mary took the trug from her mother, burying her face in its conflict of fragrance.

Pausing at his study window, Mr. Blandy thought he had never seen a prettier picture than the one his eyes held at this moment; the two figures in print gowns set in a sunlit garden. His garden. His wife, his daughter. His.

Pride in possession warmed him and fed him and gave meaning to his existence. He was never too tired, never too perplexed by his work to draw strength from the sight of his possessions: the splendid freehold house in the principal street of the town; the rich deep carpets; the fine furniture, made by the best craftsmen of the day; his prints, fresh from the hand of Hogarth himself; his books, first editions of the poetry of Pope and the satires of Swift; the parcels of land, rising in value with the growth of the town; his silver, his Bristol glass, his china—Worcester and Rockingham; his wife's linen and his daughter's gowns; the wines in his cellar, and the ham smoking in the chimney corner. All his——

"You were saying, sir——" Littleton's voice jerked him back to the work in hand. Littleton was not a treasured possession. A pent-up fellow. He detested pent-up fellows. Fond of good living himself, with the bloom of it on him, he held in contempt the secret cocoa-bibbers and burners of midnight oil.

Thin of hair and flank, Littleton had the movements of a puppet in impatient fingers. His neck jerked, his bony hands and ill-shod feet jerked; his words were blurted rather than spoken. He had a trick of dropping his eyes—perhaps from shyness—which gave him a furtive air. Not born to the sphere from which articled clerks are drawn, he worked conscientiously for a meagre wage. If Mr. Blandy could have found a clerk willing to contribute as much for as little, he would probably have been rid of him. This, Littleton guessed. In making himself indispensible he showed fidelity and cupidity in about equal measure.

"You were saying, sir——" he jerked again, with a kind of grovelling impatience.

Mr. Blandy took a pinch of snuff. He did not particularly enjoy snuff, but there was nothing like a good vehement sniff to drive home a point. And even with the negligible Littleton he liked his points to be driven home. The clerk had an uneasy suspicion that he was the dog on whom Mr. Blandy's most telling effects were tried.

"Now about this parcel of land I intend to settle upon my daughter——"

The door opened and Mary crossed the room with swift long strides. "Good morning, papa." She kissed the plump cheek.

"Good morning, my dear child. Did you enjoy your walk?"

"Very much," she said briskly, anxious not to be called upon to elaborate. Her father had a disconcerting trick of withdrawing casual approval of her actions when given time to reconsider them. She had learned even as a child to circumvent his second thoughts. She turned. "Oh, good morning Mr. Littleton. I didn't notice you lurking in the shadows!"

Littleton coloured wretchedly, averting eyes that had covertly followed her every movement. "Good morning, Miss Blandy."

"Aren't you warm in here with the windows closed?"

"Not particularly, my dear."

"You look it. At least, Mr. Littleton does!" Closing the door quietly behind her, she ran up the wide shallow stairs to her own room.

Mrs. Blandy suffered from a curious terror of being taken ill in the night and being unable to make anyone hear, and for a considerable time now Mary had slept in her mother's former dressing-room, sometimes even sharing her mother's bed. The door connecting the two rooms was always left ajar. Mary's room was a small one looking down on the narrow courtyard that ran along the west side of the house. Its hangings were of apple-green chintz, the quilting of which had taken her an entire winter. The little room had a rather childish charm which did not seem to emanate from its owner. It was almost as though the room wore a disguise, was, in some way, a defence against curious eyes. The tiny walnut bureau had a quite spurious air of innocence; it was not in these 'secret' drawers that you would expect to find a private diary or notes from proscribed lovers. The flounced dressing-table awaited a girl in her first ball gown; the rustling silks and pale gauzes in the cupboard had been made for just such a girl. But—the shield shaped looking-glass told her—Mary was not that girl.

She stood at the window staring down into the yard. From the laundry she could hear the voices of the two washerwomen, and old Dame Emmet's bawdy laugh. A feeling she could not analyse stirred in her.

Life. Those three women—coarse, strong, old—had known birth and death and mating; had worked all their days, eaten and drunk lustily, loved man and child with their instincts. Life; the raw, crude, hot life of the body, the life Betty Binfield's mother had known, that the girl herself would know as surely as the vixen and the doe knows it, untutored, uncontrolled, violent; not tempered and polished and veneered like the life Mary herself knew, that life of schools and books and the courtesies of the ballroom.

She swung away from the window, leaning against the wall. Her long pale face was without expression, her inviolate body rigid and still.

The church clock was striking eleven.

Eleven o'clock. Twelve hours to be filled before she would return to this narrow bed with its fine chill linen—the door half-open to a nervous woman's room, and sleep, as always, elusive. Twelve hours to be filled. Useless to go to the circulating library; she had changed her books the day before. The work of the house was done by the domestics; her mother did the flowers, Mrs. Deane the mending. She had already taken a walk.

Twelve hours, stretching ahead like a bale of pallid silk.

The lines of her jaw tautened.

No matter. In ten days' time there would be the garden-party at Paradise House.

CHAPTER TWO

THE CARRIAGE was at the door. It had stood there for nearly half an hour, advertising to the world that Mrs. and Miss Blandy had been invited to Lord Mark Ker's garden-party.

A client went into the lawyer's house and came out again, and still there was no sign of the ladies.

The sun was beating down on the street without pity, that last despairing blaze of a September afternoon. The hills across the bridge were misty with heat and dogs lay panting in what little shade the yards afforded. The horses were tormented by flies and the postillion from the livery-stables little less uncomfortable in his smart tight cloth.

At last Ned Hearne opened the door and the ladies appeared on the step, but even now, it seemed, a start could not be made; Mrs. Blandy appeared to have forgotten something. Her maid ran panting up the stairs and Mr. Blandy came into the hall to tell his wife and daughter for the second time how charming they looked.

Mary stood on the top step, a tall white figure, white of hooped muslin, white of dipping straw hat, white of skin, white, even, of the roses she wore. For compensation, Mrs. Blandy had brought to herself all the colour of her borders, a flutter of pinks and mauves and hyacinth blues that was only a little absurd. As they crossed to the carriage, the pavement beat hotly through the thin soles of their slippers.

The drive, for which horse and man had waited so long, was over in a matter of minutes. Mrs. Blandy had scarcely time to acknowledge the Rector and fail to see the mercer's wife when they had pulled up the steep road to the outskirts of the town. Other equipages—chaises, a coach or two—were turning awkwardly in the confined space in front of the gracious house, and even from the road the chatter of voices could be heard, formless and excited as the flocking of starlings at dusk.

Inside the gardens the scene was one of pure enchantment, possessed of all the arch prettiness inherent to the *fête champêtre*. The great dark trees—ilex and yew and cypress and cedar of Lebanon—seemed no more than a painter's trick to balance light with shade. The lawns had been nursed to perfection by a century's care, the flowers brought on, held back for just such an occasion, while the petticoats and sprigged waistcoats of the guests were gayer than the roses themselves. Here and there the delicate pastel was broken by the violence of military scarlet, but Mary's eyes lingered no longer on one group than another. There were always young officers in Henley on some pretext or other; alike as two pins, her little bureau was filled with their messages of courtesy. Courtesy; no more. One, it was true, had for a short season shared her walks, and her mother's hopes had run high, but he had rejoined his regiment and nothing more had been heard of him. Perhaps her stride had been too long for him.

Standing a little apart, she was conscious that Lord Mark was making his way in her direction. He had not the slightest idea who she was, but she made a pretty picture standing there under the magnolia.

"Is no one getting you any refreshment, ma'am?"

She curtseyed. "No, milord."

"I'm sure I don't know what these young gentlemen are made of! In my day such a thing would have been unthinkable."

"This is scarcely an age of chivalry, milord."

"Chivalry, by George! We had eyes then for a pretty face!" He turned, searching the nearby groups. "Willie!" he called. "Willie!"

Willie was, it appeared, a Captain of Marines whose uniform Mary had not till this moment noticed. A rather unimpressive figure, she did not watch him approach with particular interest.

"Willie—come here and do your duty!" Lord Mark cried

as he drew near. "Allow me to present my nephew, Captain Cranstoun, ma'am. Miss—Miss—you must forgive an old man's memory——"

"Blandy."

"Miss Blandy, of course. Mr. Blandy's daughter! I don't see your good father anywhere."

"Unfortunately he had to attend a meeting at the Town Hall," she said smoothly. The invitation had not, she knew, been extended to the lawyer.

"A busy man—a busy man," Lord Mark murmured.

Willie waited, cocked hat in hand. A man in his thirties, he was not above average height. As Mary turned to him, he bowed low. His hair was red and tightly coiled as rusted springs. She waited for the conventional speech: the honour she was conferring on her humble servant, his delight to be of service, and the rest. It did not come. The man raised his head and, still without speaking, met and held her eyes. An old enough trick, in all conscience, she told herself, yet she was aware of a curious feeling of faintness, as though these hot blue eyes alone were real and all else a shimmering illusion.

After what seemed an intolerable pause, he said: "In what way can I serve Mr. Blandy's daughter?" He spoke the English of Edinburgh.

She must, she knew, speak now, or at least move, or look away. The situation was becoming absurd, the man's insolence insufferable.

"His lordship suggested that——"

"Yes?"

"My lord, you thought——" She turned to find herself deserted by her host.

Cranstoun's laugh, with its subtle note of triumph, startled her. "My uncle's a very remarkable old man."

For answer she began to move away from him, as swiftly as the crowded lawns would permit. The blood was coursing through her veins as though she had awoken from a trance. She was conscious of Cranstoun a pace or two behind her, his walk oddly supple and soft for a soldier. Or, rather, a marine.

"You cover a lot of ground, Miss Blandy."

"I'm more accustomed to hills than lawns, sir."

"I, too."

"Yes?"

"The glens and mountains of my native Scotland."

"Oh."

The grounds, confined as they were by high flint walls, were not extensive. Leaving the lawns, they descended a flight of steps between hedges of clipped box. Their feet now rang off the stone walks of an old herb garden and the air was sweet with the scent of lavender, loud with the hum of bees.

As Mary paused to read the hour by the sundial, Cranstoun stood a little apart. "I'd not have thought you a young lady to live by the clock."

"I was born in the shadow of one, sir."

"A tyranny!"

Realising the implication of intimacy this quiet part of the gardens lent, Mary turned once more up the steps, pausing at the top to search the scattered groups for her mother. The sight of her—a bright figure surrounded by clerical black—was irresistibly comic. "Mama seems to have drawn to herself all the clergy in Bucks, Berks and Oxon."

"And you, one poor Captain of Marines!"

She evaded his eyes, but there was no mistaking the laughter in his voice. "Your uncle suggested, sir, that you might get me some refreshment," she said formally. Her social experience was conventional and she had no weapons with which to deal with a voiceless assumption of familiarity which seemed to her—for all that the man was Lord Mark's nephew—a little impertinent.

Cranstoun found her a seat in the shade of an ilex, and made his way towards the marquee. She watched him dispassionately, forced to admit he carried himself well. He would be in his element with pipes and a kilt, she thought derisively, the stocky, strutting Scotsman! Now, she knew, was her chance to give him the slip, joining her mother's covey of rectors. Perhaps, on the other hand, it would not be wise to offend a kinsman of one of her father's best clients. Also, the afternoon was extremely hot and her feet, in their too-narrow slippers, cried out for rest. Also, it was very pleasant in the deep shade of the tree, pleasant, too, the thought of refreshment.

No, on balance the arguments for flight did not seem very potent.

Cranstoun returned with some peaches and an excellent syllabub, taking his place unasked on the seat at her side.

Their talk now ran on the safe lines convention demanded.

"How fortunate Lord Mark has been with the weather."

"The old boy always had the luck of the deuce."

A pause, then, "Have you been in town lately, Captain?"

"On my last leave."

"Did you go to the play?"

"Why yes, ma'am."

"They say Mr. Garrick it very fine."

"As an actor, yes. I'd not say the same for him as a dramatist." A quick smile, then, "But sure, ma'am, doubtless you know more of these matters than I."

"You forget how out of the world we are here, sir."

"You *live* in Henley?"

"Yes. And you? Are you quartered here?"

"No. For my sins, Southampton."

"Sir Andrew Agnew's regiment?"

He laughed, the laugh of flattery. "So Miss has already broken hearts among my brother officers!"

Mary smiled her enigmatic smile.

"And shall we have the pleasure of seeing you at my uncle's dinner-party on the twenty-seventh, ma'am?"

"I'm afraid not, Captain. We leave for Bath in two days' time."

He expressed his dismay with all the excess of a beau.

Fellow guests joined them, pausing for a time, then making way for others. As Mary watched the comedy of her small social triumph she was aware of Cranstoun only as Lord Mark's nephew. Her sudden popularity among the ladies of Henley amused her keenly. That these new-found friendships would not be followed up when next they met in haberdashers or library, she knew from experience. Suffice that, for the moment, her own wide acquaintance in Captain Cranstoun's eyes and his assumption of familiarity with her in the eyes of other women were curiously pleasant.

When at last the shadows lengthened and her mother came in search of her, she was content to leave. Sufficient for the day. Etiquette demanded that Cranstoun should call to pay his respects tomorrow. Should she, or should she not be at home to him? The problem occupied her through most of the hours of the night.

CHAPTER THREE

THE PROBLEM did not however arise. The Captain did not call. Separated by less than half a mile—downhill all the way—he did not trouble to pay her that small, that minimum formal tribute. In other circumstances she would have dismissed the lapse as evidence of lack of breeding, but in the case of Lord Mark's nephew the excuse was scarcely valid. Ride roughshod over the conventions as he might, he would know that the common rules of courtesy demand he at least send a footman to pay his respects to Mrs. and Miss Blandy.

Useless to delude herself he had been recalled to his regiment; he was, she knew, in Henley drumming up recruits to fill the gaps left by Culloden.

The incident was an irritating one. It was not that the Captain of Marines was in himself of particular interest—he was mediocre enough in all conscience. If he was memorable at all, it was for audacity. Had he behaved better, she told herself, she would have remembered him less.

But he had not behaved better, either at their meeting or since. As she made her final preparations for tomorrow's journey, something of her original uneasiness returned. His conduct with her mother and with his uncle's other guests had been conventional enough. It was only with herself that the barriers were down. Why? What was there in her that conveyed an impression of—there was only one word for it—accessibility to this man?

The augury, on the eve of their departure for Bath—that season of which, she knew, her mother expected so much—was not a happy one. If she could be humiliated in Henley, where her family had been respected for generations, what was she to expect of that city dominated by wealth and rank and wit and beauty which was the magnet of half the unmarried girls in the kingdom?

Disquiet travelled with her along the road to Newbury, lodged with her at Marlborough, whispered at the back of her mind as—rising in tier upon tier like a Roman city in a dream—Bath drew clear of its amphitheatre of hills.

In the weeks that followed she found herself inside the citadel, that lightly-defended inner city to which grace and social accomplishment were the pass-word, and in which poverty and war and political strife had no existence. The voice of doubt was soon stilled in the heady illusion that here in this wider scene she was more completely herself than ever before, in the fullness of her powers such as they were. A fresh face among fresh faces, there was no previous knowledge of her to limit an implication of accomplishment. This easy assumption of equality was, she knew, peculiar to Bath; it was only here that—one among a dozen partners on one of a dozen nights—Frederick, Prince of Wales, would choose Miss Blandy for his partner.

It could not last, she knew. No matter. Transience had its value; the players in this comedy were not called upon to sustain their rôles beyond the limit of their abilities. Suffice that for a short period the best her day had to offer was hers for the taking.

Making her curtsey to the heir to the throne under a thousand candles and half as many eyes, the defection of one Captain of Marines was unimportant indeed, and it was not until the last night—Mrs. Deane packing and her mother in bed—that the thought of Cranstoun returned to her. The memory was sharp and clear-cut; the memory of his eyes, blue as a kingfisher's wing, holding her own as though—suddenly she understood—as though she were a compliant serving-maid at a tavern.

Her nerves awakened by the realisation, she snatched a cloak and hurried out, to walk with swift strides through the deserted streets of the city. The harvest moon was rising clear of Sham Castle and the pale squares and crescents took on a breathless beauty.

The night met her mood, sublimating her restlessness. Until now she had moved with the crowd on the surface, but now, alone for the first time, she became aware of Bath instinctively, sensing it with the beat of her pulses.

The waters!

The waters. They were everywhere. Not confined in the baths of wealthy *malades imaginaires*; not flowing obediently through pipes and away through conduits; not only in the Pump Room—to be sipped, flat and warm and insipid, as part of a fashionable morning ritual—but everywhere, pulsing up out of the earth, warmed by Sul-Minerva alone knew what subterranean fires, pulsing up through the centuries, since the beginning of time, unexpended, inexhaustible.

Her excitement gave place to awe; awe of nature, of the force and mystery of nature. She had from the moment of arrival been conscious of a sense of urgency, of energy, mistaking it for the puissance of the city itself. She knew herself wrong; it was this; this artery, this life-force at the core of the earth, throbbing beneath the suave surface; timeless, immutable, unknowable.

CHAPTER FOUR

Mr. Francis Blandy sat at his writing-table watching the rain that streamed down the casements. In the cold light, his face lacked something of its customary gloss; the freshness of the cheeks had a hint of purple, their roundness sagging a little over the submerged bone-structure.

November was an unpleasant month. A sudden warm spell, following swift on the heels of a long period of rain and fog, had brought with it a sickly humidity that blurred the mirrors, tarnished the silver, streaked the walls, and collected above the doorways in beads of moisture. Everything he touched was damp: banisters, latches, chairs; the very papers on his table were damp, the ink blurring, the parchments giving off a sour smell. The fires that blazed in the grates were powerless against this insidious season, seeming only to bring out the dampness. Even his clothes felt moist to the touch, the velvet jacket sticky, the smoking-cap limp. Linen taken from the presses steamed when it was aired, catching his throat when he went to the kitchen to be shaved in the morning. His silk hose seemed to cling to his shapely legs and the ivory of his meerschaum to slip through his fingers.

It was as though for all the care and thought and money lavished on it, his house had been caught out. Others, he knew, were worse off than he; there were floods everywhere, mile upon square mile of them where the swift Lodden met the Thames. The mischievous Assendon spring was in spate, flooding the cellars of Mrs. Mounteney and other of his friends in New Street. Some had not tasted wine for a month, their precious vintages awash in brown water in which the rats swam.

Yes, things could certainly be more uncomfortable than they were, but, on the other hand, he could not help admitting, they could be a lot better.

It was not only the weather. Rising to look out on his wife's bedraggled garden, he allowed himself one of those fits of depression which, descending on him at times, made up for their rarity by their intensity.

His head ached. It usually ached after a night at the coffee house. His bilious irritability at breakfast was a thing his wife and daughter had long since learned to negotiate. But in extenuation he would not, he told himself, have stayed so late if he had not already felt the depression coming on.

He returned to his chair. The broad expanse of the writing-table seemed white with bills: bills from wine-merchants, bills from livery-stables, bills from the farm, bills from the grocers in the market-place; bills from chandlers and stationers and butchers and bakers; bills for oil, for candles, for fuel; tithe demands on parcels of land; taxes of various sorts; small accounts for the repair of clocks and the reseating of chairs. It seemed fantastic how many items went to keep three middle-class people in reasonable comfort.

Then, added to these habitual household expenses, were others less reasonable. Surely two women could not need so many pairs of slippers, so many caps and petticoats and sacks and gloves and scarves, even for a successful season at Bath!

At the time, the trip to Bath had seemed to justify its cost, and he had not quibbled at the expense; Mary's encounter with the Prince would long be remembered locally. But as the weeks passed, and the only tangible dividend appeared to be the passion she had inspired in the heart of a young apothecary in Cheap Street, Mr. Blandy began to have second thoughts. An apothecary! At such a cost!

The acquaintance she had formed in high places had not been renewed. Her circle had not widened; even the neighbouring families she had encountered in Bath had not extended any friendship to her. She had, she assured him, her memories. But memories! The word had a faintly ominous ring on the lips of a spinster of twenty-seven.

In an age dominated by wealth and rank, Mr. Blandy was ambitious. While himself only a handsome young lawyer on the make, he had carried off the pretty Miss Stevens of Culham Court. It was not without pride that he would casually mention "my brother-in-law, Mr. Serjeant Stevens". To embellish a conversation with: "As Milord Camoys was telling me——" gave him a glow of pride that more than compensated for the longest hours spent straining his eyes over faded parchments. To be able to say with truth: "His Royal Highness was telling my daughter——" was, perhaps, the crown of a life spent in honourable pursuit of success.

"Mary," he would say, with a nice touch of deprecation, "is an heiress in a small way." The sum—it was allowed to be understood—was somewhere in the neighbourhood of ten thousand pounds.

The rumour was two-edged. Where a certain number of fortune-hunting young officers were attracted, as many more were scared off; the sum had an unpleasant taste of bait.

In this Mr. Blandy's motives were misconstrued. For his daughter to be regarded as an heiress was a single brick in the structure of prosperity and stability he was building, one with the Rockingham and the Chippendale. He was not out to catch a husband for Mary. Where Mrs. Blandy waited, sentimentally, to see her girl married, Blandy temporised. Yes, of course, Mary should marry when the right man came along, a man in all ways worthy of her. But where, he demanded, was such a man to be found? Mary was an heiress; more, she was a woman of distinguished mind; cultured, studious, thoughtful. She had grace and elegance and wit. It would take a very remarkable man to match these attributes.

This, for the world, the surface picture of a proud parent. The truth no one, not his wife, not his friends, certainly not Mary herself, would ever know.

Mary was his life; the centre and core of his being, the meaning of everything. His cataloguing of her merits might smack of pride or vanity, but it no more than scratched the surface of his true feeling for her. His love for the girl was a thing apart, touching a depth unsuspected by anyone. Seeing him, handsome even in middle-age, glazed over with good living, complacent, a little self-important, something of a snob, something even of a toad-eater, none among his acquaintance would have guessed at this core of deep, almost primitive feeling. For his pretty, inconsequent wife he had affection; for his friends, a warm toleration; Mary, he loved.

Her light step on the stairs, the brush of her lips against his cheek, the lilt of her low voice, the swiftness of her movements, even her rather astringent tongue delighted him, a delight all the keener for being secret. He might be moody with her—over-strict and over-indulgent by turn—but he knew in his innermost heart that for him she could do no wrong.

CHAPTER FIVE

LIFE FOR Mrs. Blandy ran its smooth course, jolted only faintly by those small crises arising out of what she called 'Mr. Blandy's meanness'.

Brought up herself in a large prosperous household, she had no idea of the value of money. Her own portion was not large, but she had always blithely assumed it adequate to any of her small demands. Retrenchment she loathed. Her confidence was based on an ability to order everything she wanted, secure in the knowledge that the tradespeople would wait till the end of time for their money. It was not in her generation that this same town would coin the sobriquet 'snobs and debtors'.

Mr. Blandy would indulge her to the limit of his patience then, with a suddenness that seemed to her unreasonable, a halt would be called. His limited complacency was dangerously misleading. He would allow a servant to pilfer for months on end, then, without a reproach or a warning word, turn him over to the law. He would suffer all sorts of familiarities from his inferiors, only to annihilate them with his tongue at the last. A tippler would be permitted to drink at his table, and not until the poor wretch had been fooled to the top of his bent would the Blandy door be closed to him.

In a day when the nation could be roughly divided into those who had no money and those who could never get enough of it, money lay at the root of most domestic discord, but with the advent of Christmas, a truce was called at the house in Hart Street. "Your father's quite recovered from his meanness," Mrs. Blandy told Mary delightedly when he returned from town with a pineapple for which he had paid a guinea.

With curtains drawn against the early winter dusk, candle-light lent the table something of the overripe beauty of a Paulo Veronese: deep rich colours of china, jewel darkness of glass; mounds of peaches and pears—caught in the narrow moment between perfection and dissolution—luminous purple grapes and, climax of all, the fabulous pineapple.

The faces round the table, warmed by good food, blurred by good wine, reflected the room's mood; even the Rector of Fawley looked as though his cloth had not quite severed its link with a richer, more jocund order. Mr. Blandy and his brother-in-law, Mr. Serjeant Stevens, vindicated the geniality and broad tolerance of the law, while Mr. Pocock of Turville Court and St. James's Square brought fashion to the feast.

Of the ladies, Lavinia Pocock alone was in the tradition, with her gurgling laughter and her insolent bosom. For her Mrs. Blandy had all the awed admiration of antithesis. Bright-eyed as a child, the pretty little woman was given up to pure pleasure in her guests.

Mary, lulled and relaxed, her cheeks faintly flushed, looked —in her father's eyes at least—almost beautiful. The talk flowed over her, talk such as she had heard for as long as she could remember, enlivened now and then with a flash of scandal *á la môde* from the Pococks.

A minor note was struck by Mary's godmother, Mrs. Mounteney, a long-backed woman who, in Mr. Blandy's words, 'indulged widowhood to excess'. Her eyes would catch Mary's occasionally and for a moment her face would light up. The two had an affection for each other neither was volatile enough to express.

The dinner dragged its length through an endless dessert like a python through a lush and decomposing jungle. Mary was aware that her father was toasting Mrs. Pocock. Mr. Blandy's flirtation with his wife's oldest friend was a family jest of long-standing.

"Your glass, Mary——"

"No more, papa."

"Nonsense—you're not a child," Mr. Serjeant Stevens cried.

"Do you good, Molly dear," Mrs. Blandy said comfortably.

"The vine was put into the world——" the rector murmured, unsure of chapter and verse.

Candlelight caught at the turbid crimson stream of wine and soon the talk moved to Bath, evoking a faint echo of Mary's triumph.

Lavinia claimed Frederick's acquaintance. "I always find Norfolk House so much more amusing than St. James's," she cried. "I can't help thinking what a remarkable woman Lady Archibald Hamilton is—she contrives with equal tact to be mistress both of the Robes and the Prince of Wales!"

Everyone round the table was laughing; the laughter fluttered round Mary's head in the fumy half-light above the candles like so many moth's wings. The great log on the hearth fell in a shower of sparks and the room seemed quite apart from the frost-locked market town outside.

Mr. Blandy called Ned Hearne to mend the fire and as the door opened Mary could hear the sound of other laughter as kitchen echoed dining-room with mulled ale and a side of beef. Christmas had now been raging for three days and showed no signs of abating.

Tonight there would be no carols. The wide street was empty and caught in the ineffable silence of snow. No foot would flaw its whiteness save that of the nightwatchman. Hills, trees, roofs, fields, all lay white and still under the frosty stars. The church clock was striking the hour of eight when, in a pause in the laughter, Mary heard the ring of the front-door bell.

Something in the unexpectedness of a caller at this hour startled her. No one else seemed to have heard. In spite of the heat of the fire she found herself chilled, as though in premonition. Yet of what? What could be wrong? Here they were, all under one roof. Nothing threatened. Yet when, above the hum of voices, she again heard the sound of the bell, she found herself rising as though in obedience.

"What is it, dear?" Mrs. Blandy asked.

"The bell. The front-door bell." She started to walk round the table, past the intolerable heat of the fire, through the panel of cold air by the window, heat and cold falling on her bare shoulders like alternating blows.

"Where are you going, my dear?" her father asked.

"To answer the bell."

"I didn't hear anything."

"Nor I."

"Nor I."

She reached the door, pausing to look back at the dinner-table. It seemed to float in a haze of soft light and soft flesh and hot lush colour. I've drunk too much wine, she told herself, her heart beating quickly.

"If there is anyone there Hearne will answer it, Mary," Mr. Blandy said, but she did not seem to hear him.

The hall was cold, cold of stone floor, cold of air bandied down the wide staircase. From the direction of the kitchen she could hear the laughter of the domestics, bold and lusty, cut with an excited squeal instinct told her came from Betty Binfield.

The burnished lantern swayed a little above her head. She was conscious of confusion, as though she walked in her sleep, an automaton drawn by some force outside her control.

She was no longer certain the bell had rung; the singing in her ears bewildered her. Suppose it had rung, then she must call Ned. That was obvious. She must call Ned. Her lips moved, but no sound followed.

The bell rang again, louder, more insistent.

She started to move towards the front door, her heels tapping on the stone floor.

The chain had been slipped for the night. A little flurry of snow had crept beneath the door. It was very cold in the outer hall, and as she stooped to draw back the heavy bolt the frosty stillness at the other side of the door seemed a tangible thing.

The door swung open massively on well-oiled hinges. A man stood on the steps; booted and cloaked, his face was in shadow, a figure cut in silhouette against the snow's whiteness.

"Yes?" Mary asked, her voice faint and strangled.

"You!" the man whispered.

She drew back and light from the hall lantern, wavering in the small breeze, fell upon his face, catching at his teeth, and the dancing narrowed eyes. He pulled off his tricorne and stood hatless. Even the poor light could not rob his hair of its flame.

"It's cold," she said quickly. "Come in."

Cranstoun swung up the steps, soft-footed in his high supple boots. One or other of them—she could not have said which—shut the door, enclosing them in the privacy of the outer hall.

She drew back against the wall, staring at him. If only the beat of her heart were not suffocating her, if only the shivering that gripped her waist would cease, then perhaps she could see this meeting for what it was: the encounter of acquaintances, not—the thought shocked her—of affinities.

He was no longer smiling and he stood so still it seemed only his eyes were alive. They rested for a time on her hair, coiled darkly on the nape of her neck, then they moved over her body, dwelling on her shoulders, ivory-warm in the candle-light, and on her long throat. She found her lips parting and her limbs growing leaden. He was raising his eyes now, sliding them over the arch of brow that was her one beauty, meeting her eyes for a moment, then coming to rest at last on her lips.

Panic filled her. He was standing very close to her, so close that she could feel the chill rising up from his clothes, yet he did not move, did not speak. Even his eyes now were still. Drained of volition, an emotion quite outside her experience filled her. Without words, she felt herself bound, committed and compromised by this man who had not so much as touched her hand.

"Mary!" It was her father's voice, calling from the inner hall. "Is there someone there?"

Her voice rang out harshly. "I'm here, papa."

Cranstoun let her go. Without stepping aside or speaking a single word, he released her. As she passed him she was conscious of his eyes, bright with—what? Amusement. There could be no doubt; amusement that needed no laughter to give it expression.

"A caller," she heard herself saying, her voice ringing falsely off the stone floors.

"At this hour?" Blandy frowned slightly, his legs planted with a firmness he could not altogether depend upon.

Cranstoun saluted smartly.

"Yes?" Blandy asked doubtfully.

"This is—Captain Cranstoun, papa."

"I had the honour of meeting Mrs. and Miss Blandy at the house of my kinsman, Lord Mark Ker, sir."

"You would be the nephew——" Blandy murmured, groping among the fumes of wine for some chatter of his wife's. "You find us still at table, Captain. Perhaps you'd care to join us at dessert?"

"With all my heart, sir. But, sure—I'm intruding on your circle?"

"Not in the least. We're a company of fogies, I fear. I don't doubt my daughter would welcome someone nearer her generation."

"One moment, sir. I'll not join your party under a false flag as it were. I'm here as a messenger, not a caller."

"At this hour?"

"An unmannerly hour, I'll admit," Cranstoun said smoothly. "Blame the circumstances."

"Yes?"

"My uncle goes post to Scotland tomorrow in hopes of being across the Border in time for Hogmanay." Cranstoun drew out a packet heavily sealed. "At the last minute he recalled neglecting to instruct you about the renewal of his lease of Paradise House."

Blandy took the packet with a chuckle. "These are sober matters for such a season! I marvel he remembered anything about it. And now—no more talk of affairs." The lawyer threw open the door of the great parlour. "Come, Mary."

Mary moved swiftly across the hall without looking at

Cranstoun. He seemed to be tossing his cloak and hat on the coffer at the foot of the stairs.

"Another guest," Mr. Blandy announced. "An infusion of fresh blood. Ladies—allow me to present Captain Cranstoun."

As Mary sat down she was conscious of Cranstoun saluting in the doorway. In hot revulsion, she told herself that his bearing smacked a little of the theatre; tonight, the rôle of bold captain, tomorrow, what? The Prince of Denmark? Or, perhaps, Puck? Behind the screen of company, free of his eyes, she would watch him, watch, too, his effect on others. Her mother had on their first meeting completely surrendered to what she saw as his charm; her father would recall his lineage. What of the others? Her uncles were unlikely to resent the intrusion of a young man so obviously out to divert; Pocock was mildly drunk and wholly self-centred. She sensed that his maleness would have its impact on the other women. Lavinia's beauty seemed to overflow like a spilled cornucopia, while Mrs. Mounteney's widowhood came down like a blind drawn against a too-hot sun.

"What a long time it is since we last met, Captain," Mrs. Blandy was saying with a naïveté that was rather touching.

"Fourteen weeks, ma'am!"

"What a memory you have!"

"A man can usually remember what he wants to remember." Cranstoun's glance to Mary was no more than a raking of the opposite side of the table.

"Now, Captain, your glass!"

"Thanks, sir."

"What about some dessert? I fear my pineapple is a sorry sight, but if you'd care for a slice——?"

"Poor Mr. Blandy! His heart quite broke when it had to be cut!" his wife giggled, pressing on Cranstoun all that was left of the fruit.

"I trust Lord Mark is well?" Blandy asked.

"Well, and in the highest of spirits."

"A poor compliment to Henley, since he leaves us tomorrow!"

"We Scots draw a certain strength from our native soil, sir."

"You've been North yourself lately?"

The faintest of pauses, then, "Not since the late Rebellion."

"You fought in that, Captain?" Lavinia asked.

Cranstoun turned. "Why yes, ma'am."

The wax-lidded eyes met his. "On which side?"

"With the Duke, ma'am."

"A *Scot*! With Butcher Cumberland!"

A faint hum of protest rewarded her provocation.

"Obviously, my dear," her husband smiled, "since the Captain has not left his head on Tower Hill!"

"A very difficult affair the '45. An unfortunate affair, cutting across national and family loyalties." Mr. Serjeant Stevens's diction was a shade too perfect for a dinner-table.

Pocock laughed softly. "Some incidents of really fascinating delicacy resulted, one knows. You were not at Westminster Hall for the trial of the Rebel Lords, Mr. Stevens?"

"Unfortunately not."

"Any of you others?" Pocock glanced round, confident of disclaimers. "No? Then I'll presume to tell of just one such encounter. Old Lord Balmerino—who behaved, one must admit, with the utmost coolness throughout—was being questioned rather insolently by Solicitor-General Murray. Balmerino turned to him as though he had not recognised him before and said, 'Oh, Mr. Murray—I am extremely glad to see you. I've been with several of your relatives. The good lady, your mother, was of great use to us at Perth!'"

The laughter was almost general. Cranstoun alone lagged. It was as though he had not seen the point till it was almost too late. Only Mary noticed the incident.

"The position of the Solicitor-General must have been a little awkward," Serjeant Stevens said. "The Murrays were so deeply involved in the Jacobite interest—young Murray sentenced to transportation and, of course, John Murray secretary to the Pretender himself."

"John Murray doesn't cut a very gallant figure," Pocock commented. "I've no time for a man who sells his friends to save his own hide."

Mary continued to watch Cranstoun covertly, puzzled by his expression. There was nothing in his face of anger or resentment—emotions most to be expected when political prejudices were in question—but only of uneasiness, or—the word sprang to her mind—of shiftiness.

"I think we're embarrassing Captain Cranstoun," Mrs. Blandy said gently.

"My apologies, Captain," Pocock said coolly. "I'd forgotten you were not one of ourselves."

"From an Englishman that's tribute indeed," Cranstoun countered. It seemed to Mary his Scots accent was just a shade overplayed.

The pause that followed was broken by the cry of the night-watchman: "Nine o' the clock and a fine frosty night. . . . Nine o' the clock and a fine frosty night. . . ." The voice, echoed emptily up the silent street, seemed to bring winter into the room.

"Your glass, Mr. Pocock—Captain. What about you, John? And you, Robert?" Mr. Blandy cried. "Surely the ladies——?"

"Were you by any chance in Flanders, Captain?" the Rector asked, mistaking a change of scene for a change of subject.

"Why yes, sir, for a short time."

"You surprise me," Pocock drawled.

"How's that?"

"I understood from my acquaintance, Horry Walpole, that the English Army there consisted of something like forty thousand Dutch, thirty thousand Austrians, eighteen thousand Hanoverians, with a motley crowd of Hessians and Saxons, and—*no* English!"

"It seems Mr. Walpole is a shade out in his figures. I can vouch for at least two Britons, myself and Mr. Conway."

"You know Harry Conway?" Lavinia cut in.

"He's recently married a kinswoman of mine."

"Then you'll agree what a man of tact he is!"

"Tact?"

"In marrying *another* Caroline."

"I don't follow, ma'am."

"Sure, the whole world knows of Harry's passion for Lady Caroline *Fitzroy*, but—la! he marries Caroline *Countess of Ailesbury*!" She leaned her white shoulders over Cranstoun to add with delight, "No need to fear talking in his sleep!"

"I understand him to be deeply in love with his bride," Mr. Blandy said. "As indeed who wouldn't be."

"Mr. Blandy!" Lavinia sighed. "So I've a rival!"

Mrs. Mounteney's voice cut through the overheated air like a cool draught. "I'm afraid Captain Cranstoun must find our gossip rather trivial after his experiences in battle."

"I, ma'am?"

"Surely, Captain, you feel more in your element in the company of your brother officers?"

"You're wrong there," Cranstoun raised his glass and turned to meet Mary's eyes across the table with an air of conspiracy that took her breath away. "I'm in my element now!"

Pocock turned to him. "You say, sir, that Lady Ailesbury's a kinswoman of yours?"

"Yes."

"Then you would be——"

"The fifth son of the fifth Lord Cranstoun."

"Surely, then, your mother was the daughter of the Marquis of Lothian?"

"She is." Cranstoun's eyes danced. "Am I acceptable?"

"The man's outrageous!" Lavinia laughed.

Mrs. Blandy rose diffidently, seeking the eyes of the women. "I'm sure we should have retired long ago."

Cranstoun sprang up, holding the door for her with a smile of ineffable charm.

"Thank you, Captain," she said, a faint blush enhancing her prettiness.

Mrs. Mounteney passed him with no more than a faint nod, but Lavinia dropped her scarf. Cranstoun picked it up with something of the deftness of a fencer, his eyes on Mary as she made her way round the table. As she drew near, he said softly, his lips scarcely moving: "You know why I'm here."

"As a messenger. On urgent business for your kinsman."

"A footman could have come. As a matter of fact—a footman was instructed to come."

"Oh!" She moved to pass him, but he slipped in front of her.

"Hear me."

She glanced over her shoulder. The four men were gathered at the top of the table, isolated by laughter and the ring of glasses.

"I had to see you," Cranstoun whispered urgently.

"After fourteen weeks?"

"Because of that. To apologise."

She smiled faintly. "Then I suppose, Captain, you'll make a further opportunity to apologise for tonight's—hoax?"

"May I? When?"

"Oh, why do I pit myself against your quick wits?"

"I don't know. Why do you?"

"You give me no option."

"Flight, surely?"

"In my own home?"

"An enemy fights better on his own ground."

"Isn't enemy rather strong?"

"I don't think so."

"What makes you say that?"

"Instinct. When a man's lived as I have, his instincts develop an edge."

"Really, Captain? How odd. I've met countless officers at garden parties and balls. I've never been aware of their instincts."

"It's not at balls and garden parties that the instincts develop."

"Let me pass, please."

"I'm not stopping you, miss. You're free as air. Free as a fantail circling round a dovecot. Round and round and round." The laughter in his voice gave it a new music.

"You bewilder me," she said, with answering laughter.

"I'm outside your experience. Till now I'll wager you've known only gentlemen!"

"And what are you? Some savage from the Colonies the Army has tamed?"

"Oh no, miss, 'twould take more than the Army to tame me!"

"But as an officer——"

"—and a gentleman?" he mocked. "Come now, you wouldn't go so far as that, would you?"

"I would not indeed!"

He lolled in the doorway. "Let's compound. Let's say—an officer—and a man!"

CHAPTER SIX

THE CAPTAIN, as Mary had maliciously guessed, changed his rôle. From an elusive, rather rakish figure, he slipped unobtrusively into the character of family friend. He was everywhere. Did Mary and her mother go to the library, suddenly—dropping down at their side like a robin—there he was to carry the books and spend a morning hour over tea in the great parlour. Should it be too frosty for Mrs. Blandy to take the China Dog for his run, Cranstoun—gaily impervious to ridicule—would march the fantastic little creature up and down Hart Street. Suppose Mr. Blandy had business in town, why then, quite by chance, the Captain would have one foot on the step of the coach, eager to run the errand for him. He would make afternoon calls with flowers from his uncle's hothouses for Mrs. Blandy, a book from the Paradise House shelves for her husband and an invitation to a local ball for her daughter. Never was there a more welcome addition to a circle, as useful as charming.

Mary he approached by proxy: "Perhaps your daughter would honour me, ma'am——" and "If Miss Blandy cares for poetry, sir——" He seldom addressed her direct, never sought a moment alone with her, never, on any occasion, met her eyes.

At first she welcomed the change in his line of attack—if attack was the word. Their relations became more normal and she was no longer filled with panic or embarrassment. She could watch him almost dispassionately, conceding his charm and his eagerness to please. But to please whom? There were times when he might almost have been mistaken for her mother's admirer. "Your mama's beau", Mr. Blandy called him. It was her mother whom he flattered, for whom he held doors, picked up scissors, arranged screens, her mother whose hand he kissed. Some years older than herself, he seemed to slip easily into her mother's generation, and the little woman glowed in the sun of a St. Martin's summer.

This vicarious courtship, if indeed courtship it was, confused Mary. From a sense of relief she gradually became aware of a small nagging feeling of pique. Even at the ball, Cranstoun seemed to her to spend more of his time among the chaperones, going in to supper with her mother on his right arm, herself on his left. Her Lyons silk passed without comment and when they stood up to dance, he touched her fingertips with the professional indifference of a dancing-master.

The frost ended and thaw filled the kennels with slush, the paths and lanes with ankle-deep mud. The woods were dank as a well, grey and weeping and desolate.

For days on end, Mary found herself trapped in the house by sleet and fog. Cranstoun had formed a habit of calling in the evening, dividing his time between watching her mother's pretty fingers moving over needlework and retiring with her father to the chink of glasses in the study. More than once she had gone to bed before he left, but even this failed to draw any protest from him.

Now for three February days they had heard nothing of him: no call, not so much as a message.

The house seemed curiously empty. She found herself more acutely aware of him now than when he was present, aware not of the pleasing lackey of the past weeks, but of the disturbing man of her first impression.

The strain of their curious relationship was beginning to tell on her. There were dark shadows beneath her eyes and she had grown thinner. Mrs. Blandy, safe and warm in her own little cocoon of pleasure, did not notice the change, but her father knew, watched her with an ache of heart too complex for his understanding.

On the afternoon of the third day she felt she could not endure the house any longer. A wan sun lay on the flat brown floodwater, and in a sheltered corner she found the first snowdrops. Something in their whisper of spring brought tears to her eyes. A sense of unutterable loneliness assailed her. Where formerly she had gloried in her solitariness, seeing it as a strength, she now, for the first time, saw her defiance as a little pitiful—the long strides, the restlessness, the acid tongue, the cool, detached mind, the too-conscious prizing of freedom.

Another spring with all its mocking promise of happiness; another year. Another year gone.

She was twenty-eight, a spinster of twenty-eight. With the brief flare of a guttering candle, desire had been lit in her and as quickly snuffed out. Standing in the chill outer hall, her eyes had opened on a world of emotion whose existence she had never so much as guessed.

The memory no longer filled her with fear or shame, but only with an ineffable wistfulness as for some paradise glimpsed through a closing gate.

The meadows were filmed over with water, and her skirts were wet and draggled before she reached the woods. She drew her cloak more closely round her, pulling her hood low over her forehead. To walk on such a day was folly, but the thought of returning to the house filled her with a sense of suffocation.

The east wind whistled sickly among the branches of the leafless beech, and the grey-green boles of the trees were streaked and stained with damp. The sodden red leaves underfoot gave off a musty odour. Dankness gripped her shoulders and caught at her throat, but she hurried on up the steep path, her feet slipping now and then on its slimy surface.

A sudden crackling sound from a ragged yew startled her and she paused, listening intently.

Only a hare, she told herself, only a fox or a squirrel.

The sound returned, louder, more clumsy; too clumsy for the light feet of the wild. To her horror the branches of the tree parted and the figure of a man emerged. She cried out. The man started and swung round, swaying giddily like a puppet clumsily jerked; a queer raggle-taggle creature, all flapping coat-tails and cravat-ends and elf-locks.

She relaxed. It was only the Wargrave Fool, uneasily, disarmingly trying to stuff a snared rabbit into his poacher's pocket.

"Hello, Jack!" she called, to put him at his ease, to propitiate him, to bring normality to a situation not without its dangers.

Jack Fletcher came loping through the trees, beech-mast crunching beneath his disjointed feet. "'Afternoon, Miss Mary; lovely day, Miss Mary." The poor unlit eyes did not know how to reflect the smile the lips had learned to imitate. The rabbit banged and bounced against his knees and loose shoe buckles jingled like money.

"They're baking gingerbread," she said carefully. "Why don't you go to the kitchen and ask Mrs. Betty for some, Jack?"

"Gingerbread. Ginger bread. Bread—bread—'Cast thy bread on the waters and it shall——'" He began to intone like a curate reading the lesson. It was his trick, the one gift a niggardly Creator had conceded him in compensation for those withheld.

"My house. You know where I live. Say I sent you. Tell Betty Miss Mary sent you."

"Miss Mary. Miss Mary. Mary and Martha, Martha and Mary——"

"You'd better hurry or it may all be gone. Hurry, Jack! Hurry!"

"Hurry!" The loose lips parted again in a smile that had no meaning. To her relief he touched his hat and started to amble uncertainly down the path. She watched him until he was out of sight, then she moved on, herself hurrying to lengthen the distance between them.

The wind was stilled for the moment and there was no sound of birds. Here the tall beech formed an avenue; below, through scattered yew and holly, she caught a glimpse of the river. The sun had already left it. She should, she knew, turn back soon. Night fell so swiftly at this season. It would be wiser to return by the road. Pausing to look for a path, her heart contracted.

Footsteps. Unmistakably the sound of footsteps coming in her direction along the path she had just left.

So he was not by now safely in front of the kitchen fire. He had never left the woods. He had waited till she was out of sight, then with the terrible cunning of the insane, he had retraced his steps, hurrying, gaining on her with every yard.

Fear paralysed her, fear of the unknown, of the closed mind, of something to which there was no appeal. Suddenly the Fool was no longer pitiful, no longer funny, no longer a child to be indulged, but an elemental force, liberated from the control of human reason, yet, for all that, a male thing, invested maliciously with all a man's strength.

She started to run, plunging down the steep path, her ankles torn by brambles, her muddy petticoats clinging to her limbs, seeming intent on dragging her back. Once she caught her foot in the exposed root of a tree and fell headlong, bruising her knees and grazing the palms of her hands. The footsteps seemed still to be gaining on her. Scrambling to her feet again, she turned wildly for a moment, to catch a glimpse of a dark figure that seemed animated by the devil himself.

The path now was becoming slippery and she found herself slowed down, giving little involuntary cries of pain as she clutched at branches to steady herself.

Suddenly a shout rang out through the silent woods. A pigeon rose up, clapping noisily.

"Mary!"

She stopped dead.

"Mary!"

Faintness overwhelmed her and she leaned against a tree. There was no mistaking the voice. Gasping for breath, she waited, the blood coursing through her veins, warming her to her fingertips.

Sure-footed and nimble as a goat, he dropped down the steep path, his cloak swaying round him. "My God, what a dance you led me!" he laughed, swinging down at her side.

"Cranstoun!" she whispered. She did not ask him how he had found her, or where he had been, or why for three days she had had no word of him. He did not ask her what she was doing in the woods in the February dusk, or explain his own pursuit of her as an errand for an anxious mother. All that was at an end. Words belonged to warm parlours, to rustling silks and the rattle of teacups. Had her lips moved in this moment it would have been with the terrible cry of the vixen, his answer the eager yapping of the dog-fox.

He stared at her; at the draggled skirts and the wet, streaming hair; the grazed hands and the tear-stained cheeks. Panting, unsmiling and without words, she leaned heavily against the bole of the tree, her eyes no longer evading his.

The wind rose up high above their heads and as suddenly died away. She was no longer aware of the winter's night that waited on the edges of the sad woods, nor of the enveloping damp that crept round them, and the disconsolate dripping of the branches. She was not aware of movement, of a step towards her. There was no pain in her shoulder as it was crushed against the smooth bark of the tree. She was conscious only of a shuddering joy that racked her body as clumsily gentle hands swept away her hood to bury themselves in her thick loose hair and lips met hers in a hunger beyond appeasing, a hunger that matched her own.

Nothing that had been or was to come would transcend for her this moment in time.

PART TWO 1748-9

CHAPTER ONE

THE POST-CHAISE swayed up the lovely valley at a leisured pace. No need to tire the horses; there was all day in which to cover the short drive to Turville. The road bored its way deep into the heart of the Chilterns; the hills drew in, fold upon fold of beech-wood. Bluebells made azure pools in the spinneys at the side of the road and the air was filled with spring's ineffable sweetness. Up one of these steep lanes a Stuart king had once ridden; a humble triumphant way back to a throne.

Beyond a comment now and then on some passing incident, neither Mary nor her mother disturbed the morning's peace with talk. The little dog sat alert on his mistress's lap, his small body quivering with atavastic excitement as a rabbit hopped across the road or a pheasant rose up—its cry like the creaking of a gate—at their approach.

It was not Mary's first experience of staying with the Pococks. Turville Court was a wayward establishment; George Pocock was in town, pursuing his affairs from coffee-house to tavern, Lavinia recuperating from one season in preparation for another. She had a warm affection for Mrs. Blandy and her own invitation was, Mary knew, a courtesy one. Hours would be erratic, meals lavish and unpunctual; there would be horses for those who wanted them and dogs everywhere. No demands would be made on her company and she would have time for thought.

Cranstoun had rejoined his regiment at Southampton and would not be returning for some months. He had left Henley an accepted suitor.

Deep at the core of her mind, happiness burned like a steady sun across which doubt, pique, caution, confusion and—yes—

even suspicion passed like swift-moving clouds. Now perhaps, free at last from the impact of his presence, she could see her relationship with Cranstoun in perspective, fit him into some sort of picture.

Her mother had, she knew, no doubts. He was her 'dear Willie', the affectionate, attentive son-in-law, ready to fetch and carry, ready if need be to flirt with her in a manner that pared away the years from the pretty woman. Dear Willie was a rôle Mary could watch with unmixed amusement, catching his eye in a moment of conspiracy.

What of her father? To him he was above all else the Honourable William Cranstoun, fifth son of the fifth lord, grandson of a marquis and in consequence connected with half the aristocracy of Scotland. Her father, she told herself, saw Cranstoun much as he saw a parcel of land: one more acquisition, another step in the process of consolidation. But was that all?

Mr. Blandy enjoyed the company of the younger man. Cranstoun could talk well on a number of subjects: soldiering, the Continent, and—rather disturbingly—the occult. With on the one side geniality and on the other respect, the relations of the two men were cordial enough. Was it only to Mary's eyes, sharpened by love, that this very cordiality smacked faintly of the pattern-book? Even now she could not recall the afternoon of her formal betrothal without a touch of uneasiness. The game had been played according to the rules; her mother knew no more of her own mute concurrence in the woods than her father was to know of the tears and kisses that sealed Mrs. Blandy's acceptance of her 'dear Willie'.

Francis Blandy had called them together in the great parlour. Sending for wine to celebrate, he said quietly: "I am giving you my greatest treasure. See that you value it."

"For your years of devotion, sir, I'll throw into the scale the rest of a man's lifetime," Cranstoun had cried.

Mary found herself watching not her lover, but her father. His face, in the capricious firelight, was not easy to read as he said: "Now I suppose we shall have to permit our future son-in-law to salute his betrothed."

Cranstoun took Mary's shoulders in diffident hands, brushing her lips with his. She trembled at his touch and for a moment his fingers tightened. "This is torture——" he whispered.

Turning to her father, she caught an expression in his eyes that told her that never again must so much as a clasp of hands pass between Cranstoun and herself in his presence.

The early days of their betrothal were not easy ones. Too many eyes were on them, loving, hostile, or merely inquisitive. Littleton would hover in the hall, starting when she spoke to him; Mrs. Deane would wait for the confidences that had till now been hers; the opening of a door would surprise Betty Binfield, while old Susannah's attentions to her master had an intangible air of reproach, as though she accused his daughter of desertion. The circumspection with which Cranstoun behaved in the presence of Blandy verged on satire, while her mother was so attached to her Willie that they were scarcely ever alone together, even on their walks.

The memory of a few anguished kisses in the hanging wood was there all the time to plague them. Their moments together were too brief to bring peace or fulfilment: a kiss in a dark passage—hungry and furtive as the kiss of a passing traveller for a serving-maid; the interlacing of fingers on a riverside walk; the swooning currency of glances across a dinner-table.

Emotionally pent-up, she found herself watching with suspicion the ease with which Cranstoun carried off these subterfuges. The clarity with which she saw both his actions and his impact on others was, ironically, the measure of her love for him. Watching him in a crowd, her faculties were all the more acute for their defeat by her senses the moment he touched her. These snatched moments of cerebral excitement took their toll of her in a reaction almost indistinguishable from satiety. At times, spent in mind and spirit, she would see her love for him as a thing wholly of the body. It was then that she would catch herself listening to his voice, measuring each cadence of charm, suspecting his Celtic exuberance, questioning his sincerity. In seeking to trap him in some inconsistency, she was taking her revenge for her sense of utter subjection to him.

In all those weeks of spring, it was not until the night he was leaving Henley, that they recaptured something of the first ecstasy.

Cranstoun had gone out to the yard; by the light of the lantern above the stable door, Mary could see him saddling his horse. The night air was still chill and caught at her muslin skirts as she stood in the archway. She started to shiver. Cranstoun turned to her and, with a curious protective tenderness, enveloped them both in his cloak as Bedouins in a tent. All the trappings of talk and acquaintances, of possessions and rank and reserves slipped away from them and for a few moments they were lost together in the timeless world of affinity.

"How long, my Mary—how long?" he whispered, his lips moving against hers. He traced with his finger the line of her eyebrows and kissed her with infinite gentleness, as though there were all time in which to caress her. Their love in this moment had had a shining, ineffable beauty.

CHAPTER TWO

The great house slept. Now and then the straining of old timbers broke the silence, and once an owl shrieked from the depths of the cedar on the lawn, but for long spans of time the stillness was complete.

The bed was soft and deep, the air that moved the damask curtains was laden with the scent of flowers and new-cut grass, the sky filled with stars. The day had been spent in pleasant diversion: a drive to a neighbouring house for tea, the easy chatter of guests at supper, then, later, music in the great barn. Nothing had occurred to disturb Mary, yet, waking with a start, she lay tense and trembling, her mind paralysed by a nameless dread.

After what seemed to her a long time, there were hurrying footsteps, and the voice of Mrs. Deane, urgent with anxiety, calling her.

Snatching a wrap, Mary ran to the door. "Something's happened!"

"Madam—she's been taken ill!"

Mary gripped the door, her face pale and hollow-eyed in the flickering light of the woman's candle. "I knew——"

"How could you, miss. She's only this minute rung for me. Poor lady, she must have been lying in agony before she could reach the bell-pull——"

"I knew—I knew!" Mary repeated as, soft-footed, they hurried along the corridor. "When people are as close as we are——"

By the time they reached the gallery there were lights and voices, a coming and going of dishevelled servants, and Lavinia, a rich amorphous figure, sodden with sleep, giving orders with incoherent authority: sending a footman to Henley for the apothecary; a groom post to London for Mr. Blandy, who was attending the Courts; maids for warming pans and poultices and cordials.

Curtains were drawn across the windows in Mrs. Blandy's room, and candles made of the great canopied bed an island. Mary drew up a stool and sat in silence, her mother's fingers convulsively gripping hers as the waves of pain flowed over her.

How long would it be before her father reached them? Mary wondered. Her thoughts turned to him in a way they had not done since her childhood. The years and their trappings were sloughed off and life narrowed down to essentials: mother, father, child. It came to her with quite a shock that not until this moment had Cranstoun entered her mind.

While the women applied poultices, she drew aside the curtains. The lawns flowed away below the windows and the gentle light folded the scene in beauty. With morning, Mrs.

Blandy fell into an uneasy sleep, but by the time the apothecary arrived the pain had returned.

Mary had known Benjamin Norton since childhood, but her inherent respect did not blind her to his failure to make an exact diagnosis. Prescribing poultices, he betrayed a touch of pique upon finding they had already been applied, and criticised both method and ingredients. When Mary protested that her mother was too weak to have blood taken, he turned his back on her, calling his assistant close with the leeches.

Mary steeled herself to watch; her nerves awake to vicarious pain, she spared herself nothing. Her figure, tall and erect, the eyes sombre in the long pale face, made a curious impression on the apothecary. The memory of it would return to him years later in another place; a study in control that was somehow horrifying.

The day passed, hour after lumbering hour of it. By evening Mrs. Blandy was very weak. Mary scarcely moved from her side, the little dog on her lap. A wood fire had been lit and Mrs. Deane was asleep in a chair. Stretching her stiff limbs, Mary threw down a cushion for Dandy and moved quietly to the window. It seemed ironical that this of all nights should be the shortest of the year: she drew aside the heavy curtains so that the dawn should not be held back. With the first light a single blackbird sounded the note that was to herald the early chorus of the birds. The joyousness of their song flowed over the stillness of the June morning like cool water.

Mary leaned her burning forehead against the glass, the beauty of the day and the ineffable happiness of the birds bringing the ache of tears to her throat.

A sound came from the direction of the bed; the whisper of a name.

Mary held her breath, listening intently, but she did not move from the window.

The whisper came again. "Willie——"

No. It could not be that. Molly; that was the name her mother had used. Molly, not Willie.

Yet still Mary did not go to her.
"Dear Willie——"
There was no mistake, no possibility of mistake. Mary gripped the windowsill. Delirium, she told herself; a fever, a dream, signifying nothing.
"Come here, dear——" The voice was weak, but curiously imperative, curiously wakeful.
Mary moved across to the bed. "Yes, mama?"
"Cranstoun——"
"What about Cranstoun?"
The soft fingers pulled at the sheets. "Let him be sent for."
"Sent for?"
"I want him, Molly. Dear—did you hear what I said?"
"Yes. I heard."
"I shall get well if I see him—I know I shall get well." A faint smile played about the dry lips. "Dear Willie——"

CHAPTER THREE

MARY WATCHED her father across the wide bed. Candlelight wiped his face clean of all life had written on it: the indulgences, the vanities, the small angers, the smaller meannesses. In his rich town clothes he looked, she thought, very handsome. His well-shaped, well-kept hands were folded on his knees and for nearly an hour he had not moved; a bland figure, infinitely comforting.

He had come post from London, arriving in a flurry of white dust and sweating horses. He had made complaint neither of the fatigue of the drive nor the exorbitant cost of the post-chaise. As their eyes met across the sleeping figure, Mary thought she had never loved him more.

Of the two of them, Blandy's thoughts were the simpler. His heart was touched, but not tormented, by anxiety for the sick woman. He could not reconcile this damp pallor and draggled hair, these cracked lips, these hands that clutched and contracted, with the pretty figure that had moved so charmingly through his life for nearly thirty years. He regarded her with something of the regret he would have felt for a broken piece of Dresden. His love for her had never been profound; a tinkling bell, it was not in her to sound the deeper notes.

The distinguished Reading physician, Dr. Addington, who had waited for his arrival, had been reassuring: a colick, no more; acute, painful, but merely a colick. Mr. Blandy was confident about an early recovery; his affection for his wife held nothing of love's bitter pessimism.

Mrs. Blandy stirred. Her lips moved, seeming about to form words. Mary was at once alert, but no sounds came. Her mother seemed to sink again into a deep sleep and she allowed herself to relax.

Would Cranstoun come? She had sent for him; she could do no less. She could not be sure whether she wanted him here, nor whether anything in him would respond to the call. Conflict returned to her mind at the thought of him; no single image of him ever stayed with her long. Where he was, the waters were troubled. He stood now between her and her mother, flawing the complete candour of their relationship. She had not mentioned the matter to her father, and between them, too, an element had intruded upon this hour of shared anxiety. She should, she knew, tell him. But how? Each hour's delay increased the embarrassment.

In crisis it had been to her father she herself had turned, not to Cranstoun. Could it be that habit—the instinctive turning of child to parent—had been strongest, or was it—the treacherous thought—that she sensed in Cranstoun something less than kind?

In her feeling for him there was little either of affection or trust; only love, fierce and passionate and pitiless; an emotion that shocked her with its intensity. Such a love could bring satiety, but never peace.

Conscious of her father's eyes on her, she rose hurriedly,

afraid that he, who knew her so well, might read what was in her mind. Resting her arm on his shoulder, she whispered: "You must get some sleep, papa."

"What about you, my dear?"

"They've made me up a bed on the sofa."

Blandy hesitated. "I feel like a sentry deserting his post!" He yawned involuntarily.

"There! You see!" she smiled.

"The roads are very bad—my old bones, you know——" He rose, wincing faintly.

In the doorway, she put her arms round his neck and kissed him. "You're such a comfort——"

"My dear child." He held her close for a few moments, the anxiety of the past hours drowning in the warm tide of happiness that flowed over him at the thought that she needed him.

CHAPTER FOUR

Cranstoun came.

The letter, directed to Southampton, caught up with him in London. Mary would in time learn to expect certain discrepancies in his movements, but suffice it to know that the moment he received the letter he set out on horseback, riding post through the empty wastes of the Bath road, to reach Turville late at night.

He scattered smiles indiscriminately, smiles that opened every door to him, and swept into the sick-room like a sea breeze. Mrs. Deane started awake, Dandy ran barking in circles, Lavinia greeted him with all the confusion due to an unexpected but by no means unwelcome guest, and Mary stared at him in silence, suffocated by the beat of her heart.

Dusty of boot, rough of hair, his figure was instinct with vitality. His teeth glinted, and his eyes; his hand, catching hers, was taut as a spring. The element he brought into the foetid room was brilliant and life-giving as the sun. His body denied the existence of death and decay that had hung over the women of the house for more than a week.

This, then, was what he was. My lover, she told herself, her senses answering his nearness. My lover.

"Willie!" There was no mistaking the joy in the weak voice.

"Madam!" Tossing his hat on a chair, Cranstoun strode across the room, dropping to one knee at the side of the bed.

"It is really you?" Mrs. Blandy whispered, her eyes running over his features. She raised herself up on her pillows. "Dear Willie—I'm glad you are come." Drawing his face down, she kissed him warmly, her arms round his neck. He returned her kisses with swift affection, his lips cool and firm against her flaccid warmth.

"I'm glad you are come," she repeated, again and again, happily patting his arm and his cheek and plucking at the stuff of his cloak. "I shall soon grow well now. You see——"

"Of course you will!"

"It was so good of you to come. So good of you."

He sat on the edge of the bed, holding her hand in his. "Nothing—not Duke Cumberland himself—would have kept me away."

Mary leaned against the window-frame, outside the candle's orbit, overwhelmed by longing for him.

"You see what happens when I leave you!" he teased Mrs. Blandy. "You can't be trusted to take care of yourself! Can she now, ma'am?" He flung a bright glance round to include Mrs. Pocock. Lavinia laughed, the laugh of a careless, handsome woman. "I don't know what you were doing, Mrs. Deane, letting your lady get into mischief!"

"Me, sir?"

"Yes, you Dame Deane!"

Lavinia called for refreshments, more candles, more logs for the fire. Mary, watching Cranstoun turn the sick-room into a tavern, wondered when he would include her in his circle. When the manservant brought the wine, it was Cranstoun who filled the glasses and handed them round. He made an excellent host, she conceded wrily.

"Why hiding in the shadows, Miss Mary?" he called. "Only moths need fear the flame!" As he handed her her glass, his eyes met hers for an instant. He knows just how to keep each one of us in thrall, she thought. Filling a glass, he put it on the hearth to mull, then he cried: "Now, ladies, I'll propose a toast! To the speedy return to health of Mrs. Blandy. Of our very dear Mrs. Blandy!"

Excitement brought a surge of colour to the little woman's cheeks.

"If only Dr. Addington could see you now!" Lavinia laughed.

"Addington? Is he a party to all this?" Cranstoun demanded.

"And Mr. Norton!"

"No wonder the poor dear lady is half-dead, with so many leeches preying on her!" Cranstoun picked up the mulled wine, revolving the glass in his fingers. "This is the medicine Dr. Cranstoun prescribes."

"Willie! I dare not!"

"Who says not? Old Sawbones? Come—I know better." He crossed to the bed.

"How can that possibly be, Captain?" Lavinia protested.

"How? Because I've been nearer to death than any of you in this room. I know the best specific for the saving of life."

"What's that?"

"Something to live for!" He held the glass to Mrs. Blandy's pale lips and sat with her while she took small sips. Warmed by the wine, and by 'dear Willie's' charming ministrations, she gave the ghost of one of her conspiratorial giggles. "How fortunate, Molly, that Mr. Blandy has returned home for the night!"

Physician and apothecary arrived during the following afternoon to find a marked improvement in the patient's condition.

Since Addington had reversed most of the treatment ordered by Norton, it was difficult to apportion credit.

During their visit, Cranstoun retired to the ilex grove with the little dog. Mary remained with her mother. He had not yet exerted himself to contrive a meeting with Mary alone. Being alone with Mary was not a thing to be embarked upon lightly. Later—he told himself, making a mental note of the lie of the land. He preened himself a little on his tactical abilities. He would, he considered, have made a passable general. A moment's bitterness shot through his mind at the thought of his kinsman-by-marriage, Henry Seymour Conway, already, though his junior, with his own regiment. Everything fell to Harry Conway. Perhaps it was his looks, he thought contemptuously; the godlike Harry, carrying off Caroline Campbell within a few months of the death of her first husband. Well, she was keeping Ailesbury's name and title. One in the eye for Harry, that! Even for love of him she was not prepared to revert to a mere Mrs.! They were coming, his uncle had told him, to live in the district. Old Blandy was jockeying to sell them Park Place. No concern of his. It was doubtful if his kinship to the beautiful Caroline would be good for so much as a week's lodging. She would have other fish to fry: larger, more glittering fish; guests worthy of the delicate malice of Conway's cousin, Horace Walpole.

Cranstoun saw himself as a man with a foot in too many worlds; while not without vanity in his own versatility, he sometimes doubted whether, in the last analysis, it would serve his end. Perhaps he was too eager to please, took his colour with too chameleon a swiftness.

He paused on the fringe of the grove. The lawns flowed to the house with a grace born of centuries of care. In the distance a gardener, expert in topiary, was trimming the yews; the cubes and the globes and the pheasants and the dancing bears. Swallows wheeled high in the pale sky, their sweet mewing the only sound. The scene, in all its loveliness of setting—the sheltering woods, the hills that fell away in every direction, the trees that had stood aloof from three centuries of history, the purity of the June evening, the triumphant alliance of man and nature in the creation of a perfect whole—held for him at the moment a single message: wealth. It took wealth to buy land and conjure beauty like this from a rough heath.

The thought of his native land—poor, harsh, barren, primitive, torn by rebellion, its families ruined, its men heroically or ignobly dead—filled him with a bitterness that was not unmixed with shame that he, a Scot to the last drop of his blood, should have fought on the side of the Elector of Hanover.

In his complex nature, the desire to snatch the best that life offered warred with his innate arrogance, forcing him time and time again to pursue the line which promised easy success. Generous, with that extravagance peculiar to a race notorious for meanness, his better impulses were constantly pulled up short by lack of means. At heart attracted to the great world he professed to scorn, his was a nature that, given the means to gratify his desires, might have flowered and expanded. By birth the equal of anyone he encountered, he found the trammels of a captain's pay irksome—intolerable even. Learning young that he possessed certain social gifts, he had no scruples in using them to open doors which should have opened to him as of right. That in these very gifts lay the seed of prostitution was a thought not likely to worry an officer of Marines in a day when wit and beauty could be bought and sold as easily as peerages and commissions.

For the most part, he skated skilfully over the thin ice of his times, and sombre moods were infrequent, born often of purely physical causes. Overtired from his ride, he had slept badly. His gaiety of the night before had been quite unforced, springing to life in answer to a roomful of women, but it had taken its toll in reaction. Like a firework, it could blaze for only a brief period, to fall, spent and blackened, when the fête was over.

As he approached the house, he observed Mr. Blandy coming towards him. The two men talked desultorily for a time, but something told Cranstoun this was no chance meeting. Among his social accomplishments, the Scot had one great gift: he could always sense which way the wind was blowing. Behind a façade of recklessness, he usually knew how far to go, adjusting himself to each change of climate. Though perhaps not a very admirable quality, he had found it a useful one, smoothing not only his own way, but that of others. He baffled criticism. Among his brother officers he aroused something amounting almost to mistrust; charm such as his was always a little suspect.

Of the two, it was Mr. Blandy who appeared least at ease. "Er—Captain——"

"Sir?"

"It has been on my mind for some time to seek an opportunity for a talk with you."

"Yes?"

"Suppose we sit down." Blandy made his way to a bench on the terrace. "I could wish I were in my study. Some things come easier to a lawyer than to—a father." He took a pinch of snuff, spilling a little. "You don't indulge in this untidy habit, I know!" he temporised, slipping the box back into his pocket. "Captain Cranstoun, when I consented to your betrothal, I own I did so a little hurriedly. I allowed myself to be swayed by sentiment—the desire for my daughter's happiness."

"Sir—you're not thinking better of it?"

"Not so fast, not so fast!"

"I trust nothing in my conduct has given rise to doubts of my ability to procure Miss Mary's happiness?"

"No, no. Nothing at all, please understand that. Nothing at all. Before we go any further, however——"

Cranstoun sprang up. "Further!"

"Do sit down, Captain."

"But, sir——"

"Let me finish what I was going to say. There's no cause for alarm."

"Alarm! When my whole——"

"Sit down!"

After hesitation, Cranstoun resumed his seat.

"Now, as I was saying: before we go so far as to make

matters public, I must ask you a few—I won't say unpleasant or embarrassing, but at least direct—questions, to which I shall require direct answers."

"My life is an open book, Mr. Blandy."

"I'm sure it is, Captain, I'm sure it is. Hear me. That you're a brave soldier, I know. That you're healthy in mind and body, and upright in character goes without saying. Your social position leaves nothing to be desired. But—this is something I must ask. I should be failing in my duty as a father if I neglected to ask it. What are your means?"

Cranstoun turned to meet the lawyer's eyes. "I admit quite frankly, sir, I am not a rich man."

"Fifth sons rarely are."

"I've a small patrimony, but beyond that, in actual money, I've little but my pay."

"In actual money, you say. What of the rest? Have you land?"

"A few hundred acres of rock and heather."

"In Oxfordshire we rank a few hundred acres as an estate."

"Call it an estate if you wish."

Blandy smiled. "I like your modesty, Cranstoun. Does you credit. You understand my anxiety——"

"No one better. In your place I doubt if I should consider any suitor worthy."

"An only daughter. And, in her small way, an heiress."

"An—heiress?"

"You look quite startled."

"I confess it does come as something of a shock, sir."

"I had thought it common property in Henley."

"I'm not a Henley man."

"Then you had no idea?"

"None at all. Now, sir—you've been frank with me. If you'll pardon me, I think it's my turn." Cranstoun rose and stood, head high. "May I say that I consider it the wrong way round. A man, if he's a man at all, should be the one with the means. It goes against the grain, marrying an heiress. Puts a fellow in an invidious position."

"Your independent spirit is certainly refreshing in this mercenary age!"

"Believe me, sir, this is one of the biggest surprises I've had in a lifetime of surprises. I know Mary's home, her background, her education, all those of a gentlewoman. But wealth is different, wealth in her own right, that is. Had I known she was an heiress, I doubt if I should have allowed myself to grow so fond. No—forget that! Love at least is outside a man's control. But—to have pursued her—— You understand my feelings, sir?"

"More—I respect them. You almost make me regret having raised the matter. You will not let it make any difference—in your relations with my daughter, that is to say?"

"How can it, sir? I'd willingly sign away half my life for the right to call her mine. Can I let any petty feeling of humiliation stand between us?" Cranstoun snipped a dead rose off a bush. "Is it a very large sum, sir?"

"Gossip will tell you—if you listen to gossip—that on my death my daughter will be heiress to something in the neighbourhood of ten thousand pounds."

"So much!"

"Perhaps a little less."

"A fine enough sum, though."

"As you say."

"But no more than a pretty woman can spend on her trumpery."

Blandy rose. "And now—enough of these sober matters. I think I can hear the supper bell." He took Cranstoun's arm and together they moved towards the house. "I cannot tell you how happy this little talk has made me, Cranstoun. A load off my mind. You will, I know, forgive me when I say that it's been my abiding dread that Mary would fall prey to a fortune hunter."

"Sir! The very thought is repugnant."

"There are plenty about in this extravagant age, I can assure you."

CHAPTER FIVE

Business at the Cocoa Tree kept Mr. Pocock in town, and Mr. Blandy had his work in Henley. Cranstoun stepped easily into the breach. The lavish, careless way of life at Turville suited him admirably and he was, as he would have expressed it, in his element.

Out of danger, Mrs. Blandy resumed the silken threads that went to make up the sampler of her days. Still too weak to be moved, she yet was well enough to enjoy the small privileges, the caprices and whims of convalescence. With fresh caps, her hair laboriously curled by Mrs. Deane, her drawn cheeks delicately rouged, she would be ready to send for her Willie.

"This I owe to you, my dear Cranstoun! Your coming has given me new health and fresh spirits! Even Mr. Blandy has commented upon it. You heard him yourself last night. 'I suppose they will *both* of them be better now *you* are come!' And so we are, are we not, Molly?"

"Yes, mama dear."

Mary, herself on the edge of collapse from fatigue and anxiety, watched the little comedy listlessly; Cranstoun must be with her mother while she sipped her broth; Cranstoun must give Dandy his run; it was Cranstoun who would sit by her till she fell asleep; only from his hands would she take her medicine.

"My poor nurse must not be jealous," she smiled once to Mary. "Loving him I know is pleasing her!"

Cranstoun, his back turned to Mary, kissed her mother's hand.

"How like a ghost the dear girl looks," Mrs. Blandy said.

"Do I?"

"Yes, Molly."

"Do I? Do I, Cranstoun?" Mary's voice was harsh with weariness.

He turned to look at her. Not troubling with her hoops, her skirts drooped round her. She had grown thinner and, with her height, seemed almost gaunt. Her face was paler than usual, her eyes darkly shadowed, her hair coiled in a rope at her neck. She made no attempt to smile. As Cranstoun's eyes rested on her, she knew that here was a love owing nothing to beauty or the chance romance of time and place. Had they been alone together he would have kissed her not with pity but with passion.

"Come to me, my dears. My two dears," Mrs. Blandy said gently. As they approached, she took their hands in hers. "I want to tell you something."

"Yes, mama?"

"Do you know what was my greatest fear as I lay ill?"

"What, dear?"

"That I should die, and Willie not be here to comfort my poor girl."

Mary dropped to her knees, burying her head among the pillows as sobs shook her.

"My dear. You've been so brave." Mrs. Blandy stroked the dark head. "So brave. Willie"—tears stood in the faded blue eyes—"be good to my girl. Promise me that. Promise?"

"I promise," Cranstoun said quietly.

"Swear it," Mrs. Blandy whispered.

"On my honour, ma'am." He seemed almost to stand to attention.

Supper over, Mary left the house with Cranstoun, eagerly breathing in the fresh coolness of the air. The branches of the great cedars lay in plane upon plane against the luminous green of the evening sky; a blackbird was singing on the rooftop. Peace surrounded them, imposing its mood. As they reached the end of the terrace he paused and, leaning over the balustrade, snipped off a red rose with his thumbnail. Raising his eyes to hers, he kissed the loose petals of the flower, its scent heavy in his nostrils. Handing it to her, he said simply: "Have you ever thought how little I can give you?"

She pressed the rose to parted lips, drowning in his eyes. As her fingers tightened on the stem, she gave a little cry.

"A thorn!" he said with a flash of excitement. "Show me——" He took her hand in his and, finding a pin-point of blood, sucked her finger. Her body was close to his in a fusion she was powerless to resist. She saw his expression change: a blurring, a blankness. He did not move. Her finger against his lips, he whispered: "You know what this means."

"Means?"

"My rose. A thorn from my rose——"

"Some—superstition?"

"A very old one."

Unwillingly she said: "Tell me."

"The thorn pierced not your finger but your heart. A mortal wound—a love from which there's no escaping."

"How can you believe these things?" she cried breathlessly.

"I? You too."

"No. No, Cranstoun!"

He laughed softly. "You protest too much!"

"Superstition is for peasants—for fools!"

"So nothing has ever happened to you that you knew to be outside the run of common experience?"

"Nothing." He smiled curiously, and she repeated, "Nothing." She tried to draw away, but he held her hand to his heart.

"Think—think, Mary!"

"I tell you, nothing."

"Except——?"

"The night mother was taken ill I woke up trembling. At first I thought I'd been dreaming, but then—they came and called me to her. It—no, it was not coincidence. When they called me I was not even surprised. I knew. Knew something was wrong—I woke with a sense of wrongness. But why? Why?"

"The power of her need of you."

"Is that what you believe?"

"Yes. Wait—think back again. There's something else, isn't there?"

"Not—that I recall——"

"I see you know what I mean."

"I—I don't want to hear any more. Leave it alone. Leave it alone, Cranstoun. It's too wide and dark and deep, a deep dark river of knowledge."

He drew her closer to him, denying her identity or life apart from him. "Why did you come to the door yourself that night?"

As her head moved restlessly from side to side, her lips brushed his. "Which night?" she whispered almost in panic.

"Look at me. You know. Admit you know." She bowed her head. "Why, Mary?"

"The domestics had not heard the bell."

"You could have called them."

"They were at supper. You heard them yourself, heard their laughter in the kitchen——"

"You could still have called them. But no. You came." With his lips to her ear, he murmured: "You came to me. In answer to me. In answer to my need of you." His fingers tightened on her wrists. "You'll never know how great that need is."

CHAPTER SIX

THE POST-CHAISE was ordered; Mrs. Deane was busy packing; Dandy, as usual when journeys were in the air, had hidden under the bed; Cranstoun, with all the tactical skill of an old campaigner, had retired on Paradise House. Lavinia searched her wits for a means of paying her friend's bills without undue patronage, while Dr. Addington and Mr. Norton fumed, unwilling to see a successful treatment jeopardised by the precipitate moving of the patient.

Mrs. Blandy revealed unsuspected courage in the marshalling of her meagre resources of physical strength for the drive home, dabbing on more rouge and laughing till her throat ached. Only to her daughter did she confide the cause of the confusion: "Mr. Blandy's meanness!"

The lawyer had seen the bills: So many journeys out from Henley by the apothecary, so many journeys over from Reading by the physician, the time spent in travelling ticking away guineas as a clock seconds! Turville, Blandy protested, was an absurd place in which to indulge in a protracted illness. A man of Addington's eminence must give up half a day to a visit; it was only to be expected his fees would be exorbitant. While his wife was in danger, no expense should be spared, no promise withheld, no whim resisted; but human nature is not changed by crisis, only raised, momentarily, above itself.

The explanation, Mary thought wrily, was unanswerable in logic; where it failed was in truth.

Driving home, her mind revolved uneasily the incident which had coincided exactly with her father's change of heart.

He had arrived out at Turville in time for supper the evening before. Mr. Pocock had just returned from town, full of his winnings at faro, and the meal had been distinguished by geniality. Lavinia and Mary retired for tea, to be joined soon afterwards by Blandy and Pocock. Lavinia unblushingly encouraged her husband in all that was newest in scandal from town, laughing richly at a tale of Miss Chudleigh, "the Maid-no-more of Honour," and revelling in the fiasco of the Duchess of Queensbury's ball at Richmond for a King who had never intended to put in an appearance. While Mary was eager to hear of the triumphal progress of the Misses Gunning, who, "leagued with all the fairies of their native Ireland," were bewitching the town, her father appreciated a quip of Horace Walpole's about the peer who "purchased his ermine from the Countess of Yarmouth at twelve thousand pounds a yard". The talk was lit with sufficient malice to give it point, and it was with surprise that Mary realised an hour had already passed. Cranstoun had not joined them.

In a momentary pause, Mr. Blandy said: "Well, Mary, I suppose it's time we returned to our invalid."

She took his arm and they made their way along corridors muted by Persian runners.

The door of her mother's room was ajar, and she paused for her father to enter.

The scene that met their eyes was impressed on her mind with curious vividness.

Mrs. Deane, the dog in her lap, was asleep in front of the fire. The curtains were drawn and, after the freshness of the July evening, the room seemed unpleasantly hot. A single candle, fluttering in the draught from the open door, caught the bed in a small orbit of light. Mrs. Blandy was propped high with pillows. Cranstoun sat on the bed, her hand in his. Talking in low voices, they were unaware of the man and girl in the doorway. Before either had time to speak, Mrs. Blandy had drawn Cranstoun's head down, her arms round his neck.

The gesture, innocent and affectionate, was no different from many others Mary had watched. But at other times it had not been night; Cranstoun and her mother had not been alone together, wrapped in the intimacy of the hot curtained room. With a shock, Mary suddenly saw the incident as it must appear to her father.

Cranstoun, becoming aware of his audience, at once sensed the atmosphere. Rising, he heartily kissed Mrs. Blandy's cheek, and cried: "Now it's time for mama to sleep!" His voice rang out; a player's voice to reach the gallery. "Forgive me for a selfish wretch, sir. I mustn't monopolise your charming wife any longer!"

Mr. Blandy stared at him without speaking.

Cranstoun bowed low over Mary's hand. "Sleep well, my sweet!" With a last debonair wave to the woman in the bed, he squared his shoulders and was gone, swinging down the corridor like a piper into battle.

No, Mary thought, it was not wholly a question of 'Mr. Blandy's meanness'. Something of her old mistrust returned at the thought of the episode: had not Cranstoun been just a shade too quick-witted?

CHAPTER SEVEN

In the December, Sir Andrew Agnew's Regiment of Marines was broken, and Cranstoun arrived in Henley, a captain on half-pay.

As he stepped down from the coach in the yard of the White Hart, his kinship with half the aristocracy of Scotland did not seem particularly important.

It was raining, the chill, unremitting drizzle of December. His baggage, slung down on the cobbles at his side, held all his wordly goods. The journey from Southampton had left him with rather less than five guineas in his pocket. He was nearing forty. Although he had by now been betrothed to Mary for several months, marriage seemed as far off as ever. There had not yet been so much as a public announcement, far less any mention of a wedding day. His affairs had scarcely improved to the degree that he could press for one.

Striding into the inn with as much dash as he could muster, he called for a negus to keep the cold out.

Suppose Mr. Blandy agreed to their marriage at some early date; where would they live, and on what?

A faint pang of jealousy shot through him at the thought of his kinsman-by-marriage, Conway, negotiating for Park Place and its thousand acres.

The negus seemed no more warming than the flattery of the serving-maid's glances.

There was of course the prospect of Mary's inheritance. A lot could be done with ten thousand pounds. He had never himself handled so much as ten thousand pence. But what exactly was it, this heady sum the old boy had dangled in front of his nose? In front, come to that, of the noses of half the eligibles in the district. His own protestations of disinterestedness—overplayed, in all conscience—had been all very well for a June evening, but at the moment, with the rain splashing disconsolately into the waterbutts and the short winter day already drawing to a cheerless close, a conversation he had once had with Mrs. Blandy returned to him disturbingly.

"Mary has been brought up with great tenderness, as you know. Neither of you are cut out to live on a small fortune. I know you both so well! You, my dear, are a man of fashion!"

"Because my father chanced to be a lord?"

"Certainly."

"As mother of an only daughter you could scarce be expected to know what it means to be a fifth son."

"Your blood's the same."

"Aye and your tastes and your inclinations. The difference lies in your ability to gratify them!" For a moment a bitterness overwhelmed him that quite startled the little woman.

"Dear Willie, had Mary ten thousand pounds at her and my disposal, I would give her to you tomorrow."

He felt himself flush. "Mr. Blandy mentioned to me——"

"I know, I know! The whole town thinks Mr. Blandy will be able to give Mary a handsome fortune. But—can he? I am sure he cannot." She sighed. "But there, I was ever a stranger to his circumstances."

"If you'll only give me Mary, I'll ask nothing more of you or Mr. Blandy!" he had cried. Whether or not he could still say the same in all sincerity did not affect his future one jot.

He paid for his drinks, changing a guinea and flinging down a handsome tip to restore his flagging self-confidence.

Wrapping himself in his cloak, he strode through the yard. Dusk had fallen, and Hart Street was empty of passengers. Here and there lights from windows were reflected in the wet pavements. A farm cart, piled high with mangolds, was moving up the street, the slow clop-clop of hooves emphasising the dreariness of the scene. The Blandy's house was only a few doors from the White Hart, on the same side of the street. He had no intention of calling at this hour, or even announcing his return while this black mood lasted, but the house seemed to pull him.

The curtains were not yet drawn, and lights shone out from hall and great parlour. They would be sitting by the fire, Mary and her mother; the little dog—for whose absurdity he had an affection—would be asleep on the footstool. Mary would be reading, Swift or Pope, or perhaps Dryden—her tastes were all astringent. Mrs. Blandy, who was no reader, would be at work on one of the set of seats for the Chippendale chairs which, it seemed to him, was unlikely ever to be completed. Later, Mr. Blandy would join them, and they would talk desultorily of the day's work.

Pacing quietly up and down on the opposite side of the street, the picture his mind painted seemed infinitely desirable, and it took great strength of will not to cross the road and ring the bell, wet and travel-stained and dejected as he was.

A good dinner, together with a night's sleep and a change of clothes, was all Cranstoun needed to restore his spirits, and as he swung down the hill from Paradise House, the black mood of the evening before was of no more significance than a dream.

It was market day—the last before Christmas—and the town was full of animation, the ale-houses overflowing. Stalls in the market-place were piled high with ducks and geese and fowls; with brown eggs and white; with jars of cream and combs of honey and moulds of golden butter. There were pippins by the bushel, hazel nuts from the coppices, sacks of carrots and potatoes and mounds of cabbages. One stall was laden with mistletoe, pulled down by agile gypsy boys, and others with boughs and bunches of holly.

Cranstoun scanned the stalls for flowers to take to Mary and her mother, but there seemed none worth having at this season. As he made his way through the jostling, chattering crowd, a young woman brushed past him, staring at him for a moment in insolent recognition. It was not until she was out of sight that he recalled having seen her at the Blandys'. A cook-maid, or some such thing, she had once, when Susannah was ill, brought in the tea. Her stare then had been as bold. The incident was not sufficiently unusual to make an impression; there was that in him which provoked the advances of domestics.

After he had reached the crossroads, the crowd thinned. The Oxford coach was just swinging round the corner, its horn full of brazen life.

Suddenly, on the other side of the street, he caught sight of Mary and her mother, pausing to chat to Mr. Stockwood, the Rector of Henley. Cranstoun descended on them like a whirlwind, kissing hands, gripping hands, asking a dozen questions without waiting for a single answer.

Observing that the ladies had eyes for no one but the volatile Scot, the Rector made his adieux. Brushing aside protests, Cranstoun, with Mary on one arm and her mother on the other, carried them off to drink tea at a bun-shop. When at last he told them his news, and Mrs. Blandy said: "But my dear, what of the future?" his spirits had risen so high that he could retort: "Future? I have none, ma'am, none at all!" with the utmost gaiety.

"You must see Mr. Blandy!"

"Make a clerk of me? Not on your life, ma'am!"

"Absurd young man! You know that's not at all what's in my mind."

"Who am I to hope for anything better?" Cranstoun pressed Mary's hand to his knee, avoiding her eyes.

Upon their reaching home, Mr. Blandy's greeting—to Mary's great relief—was little less cordial than her mother's had been. His arm round Cranstoun's shoulders, he chuckled: "So you're broke, eh?"

"My regiment at least, sir."

"And I'll wager your cash is running low?" Cranstoun admitted it was. "Well, you're welcome to stay with us for as long as you care to."

"Sir!"

"Why not? Regard this as your home."

"I'll hope some day to be able to repay your goodness, sir."

"Nonsense! We shall be glad of your company. Send for your things as soon as you like. And now—what about some dinner? Since you're one of the family, I'll make no apology for the fare. The kitchen's always in confusion on market day. There'll be but a saddle of mutton and a pie, but I've a new Stilton—or rather, an old one, and we'll fetch up a bottle or two to wash it down!"

CHAPTER EIGHT

It was not often that Lord Mark Ker honoured Mr. Blandy with a call; it had in fact happened on only one previous occasion. Cranstoun, returning from a walk, recognised his uncle's coach, but decided not to intrude on what was after all a purely formal visit. Lord Mark, who had been in Scotland for some weeks, would no doubt send for his nephew when he wanted him. Joining Mary and her mother in the parlour, Cranstoun sat sprawled in a chair by the fire, expending no more of himself than a certain indolent charm. Never before had he experienced an atmosphere in which he could so completely relax. Wrapped round and sheltered by affection, his confidence in himself was complete. The little bitternesses were lulled; doubts for the future, memories of the past, all were absorbed in this compatible present. He surrendered himself completely to that strain of laziness latent in so many men. Here was the path of least resistance; a little boring, yes, but then perhaps any man who had in his day savoured the excitements of inferno would find paradise a shade dull.

The pleasant voices ran on, the firelight flickered; what more could a man ask on a February day? For diversion, there were Mary's dark eyes, embers awaiting his spark, or the heady random touch of her hand, the queer subtle game of seduction he had learned to play with her under the noses of her family.

Nothing warned him. The presence of his uncle in the house so soon after his return from Scotland told him nothing. Premonition—that force in which he believed more than he would care to admit—completely failed him.

Lord Mark had sent a footman with the message that he would do himself the pleasure to call on Mr. Blandy at noon. No mention of his business was made. He arrived punctually. Littleton was dismissed and the study door closed.

"This is indeed an honour, my lord," Mr. Blandy said.

"Wait till you hear what I've come about," the old man said wrily. "Now you're a busy man, sir. So am I, though God knows what with at my age! I'm not going to waste your time."

"I'm entirely at your lordship's service."

Lord Mark proffered his snuff-box. "I'm not here to speak to you as a lawyer, but as man to man. You've doubtless had a pretty wide experience of the world. So have I, for my sins. Now, about this nephew of mine, Willie Cranstoun."

"Yes, milord?"

"He's been staying with you for quite a time, has he not?"

"Nearly two months, milord."

"Why?"

"Why?"

"Yes, why?"

"We're delighted to have him as a guest."

"Oh, I'm not denying the fellow knows how to please. He's had practice enough in all conscience. But let's be bald. You're not a man to retain a—a sort of court jester; nor Willie a lad to waste his time. What's he after—your daughter?"

Blandy frowned, confused. "You—you mean to say your lordship has not heard?"

"Heard what?"

"My daughter Mary is betrothed to Captain Cranstoun."

"Good God!"

"That surprises you?"

"Nothing my nephew does surprises me. I will admit, though, I'd no idea things had gone so far."

"But I felt sure you would have known."

"It's not been made public, has it?"

"Not public, no. But within the family, my wife's brothers, our closest friends—I quite assumed you would have been told."

"Not a word. Nor my niece, Willie's mother, nor his elder brother, the present Lord Cranstoun."

"Doubtless the Captain has his own reasons."

"'Fore George, he has!" Lord Mark exclaimed.

"Perhaps he thought it best to wait till a formal betrothal——"

"Formal betrothal my foot! Formal divorce!"

"Formal—er—pardon me, milord, I didn't quite catch——"

"Small wonder, if you're hearing it for the first time! To be plain, my nephew will not be in a position to marry your daughter till he's free of his present wife!"

Blandy gripped his chair. "His—wife?"

"Yes, sir."

"There—there must be some mistake."

"You doubt my word, sir?"

"No, no. Of course not, your lordship. But——" Mr. Blandy rose uncertainly. "Please pardon me. I—I must ask your indulgence. You, as a bachelor—you will perhaps not quite appreciate what it means—an only daughter——"

"I understand perfectly. I had an only son."

Blandy started faintly.

"Don't pretend that's news to you—all the world knows! He was killed by the Duke of Douglas. It's an old scar, quarter of a century old. But we're getting away from the point."

"If your lordship would be good enough to explain."

"Sit down Mr. Blandy. It's a long story. I'll do my best not to make it a dull one."

Blandy resumed his seat, his good-humoured face sagging as though the bone-structure had collapsed.

"I hoped I'd have been in time to prevent him insinuating himself in here too deeply. Trouble is, I only heard the news myself a week ago up at Nether Crailing, my niece's place in Roxburghshire. The whole affair's a bit hazy. Difficult to piece the details together—politics, religion, all the usual complications. But briefly, it appears that some time in the spring of '44 my nephew married Anne Murray. Suitable enough match in its way, by birth, that is—granddaughter of Sir David Murray of Stanhope. But—here we come to the snag—*niece* of John Murray of Broughton."

"The Pretender's secretary?"

"That same Murray who sold his friends to save his own hide. All the Murrays are Jacobites. Jacobites, and Catholics into the bargain. You'll begin to see why such a marriage had to be kept secret. My nephew was only an ensign at the time. Not much chance of promotion with a Catholic wife. They lived together quietly for a time, then, when there was going to be a child, Lady Cranstoun invited Anne to stay at Nether Crailing. Like a bigoted little fool, the girl thought the Presbyterians were out to get her and her child, so she refused."

"My lord—tell me. This child—did it live?"

"Bless you, yes."

"Ah!"

"Well now, this brings us to the '45. The Murrays of course declared for the Prince and Anne's brother—who succeeded to the baronetcy, by the way—got himself taken at Culloden and sentenced to death. He was only a boy at the time, so they reprieved him and transported him instead. Now my fine nephew—fighting under Cumberland—suddenly decides to give out that the lady was only his mistress after all and that he allowed her to pass as his wife to save her honour!"

Blandy's face cleared a little. "You don't think—with all respect milord—that this is in fact the truth?"

"I'd have been only too glad to accept his word. I've a great affection for Willie, with all his faults. But with the best will in the world, I'm afraid it won't do. As you no doubt know, sir, under our Scots law, a woman can raise in the

Commissary Court an action of declarator of marriage. This is what, on the advice of her relations, Anne did."

"When—was this?"

"Somewhere late in '46."

"With what result?"

"The court declared them man and wife and the child of the marriage lawful issue. Cranstoun's got to pay the girl an annuity—I forget the exact sum. Seventy-five pounds I think—that is, with the child. Anyway, his patrimony is pretty nearly all diverted to them."

Blandy pressed his fingers to his brow, his legal mind seeking desperately for some loophole. "How long ago was this decision reached? I mean, milord, is it possible that Captain Cranstoun has not yet been informed of it?"

"Sorry, Mr. Blandy—March of last year."

"March!" Blandy's hands clasped and unclasped in his lap. "It was in the March of last year that he asked me for my daughter's hand. It's—almost incredible."

Lord Mark shrugged. "I suppose all's fair in love and war."

"And there the matter rests?"

"To the best of my knowledge." Lord Mark rose. "Not a very pretty business. But I felt it my duty——"

"I'm deeply indebted to your lordship."

"I only wish I'd known earlier. Can't find it in my heart to utterly condemn the fellow. He's a soldier, lived hard. Always was irresponsible as a boy, I believe." He paused. "I feel rather guilty myself, you know."

"How, milord?"

"Damme, I introduced them. Pretty picture your daughter made under the magnolia tree, I remember." Lord Mark chuckled. "Who am I to judge my nephew? I'd probably have done the same at his age!"

From the parlour they could hear the sound of the coach driving off. Susannah came in to put more coal on the fire. Sleet rang against the window. Cranstoun was helping Mrs. Blandy unravel a tangled skein of silk; when Mr. Blandy came into the room, he was caught, a little absurdly, with the skein in his hands.

Mr. Blandy's face betrayed him at once to his daughter. "Papa—what is it?" Blandy turned to stare at her blankly. "You're not well!"

He pressed her hand almost convulsively. "Don't look so distressed, my dear."

"But you look as though you've seen a ghost," Mrs. Blandy said.

"Not I. Not *I*."

"Is that a riddle, sir?" Cranstoun asked easily.

"If it is, perhaps you can read it, Captain." The icy derision in her father's voice startled Mary. "You appear to be adept at unravelling."

Cranstoun hastily dropped the skein into the basket and started to move across the room.

"Stay where you are, Captain Cranstoun. I've something to say to you."

"Shall I attend you in your study, sir?"

Blandy hesitated. "No. No, I think not. The matter concerns us all. It's as well we should all be present."

"Something's happened."

"Yes, Mary. Sit down. And you, my dear."

Mary and her mother sat down uncertainly. "What about you, papa?"

"I prefer to stand for the moment." Blandy gripped the back of a chair. "Captain Cranstoun——"

"At your service."

"As you may know, your uncle, Lord Mark, has just left."

"Why yes, sir. I recognised his coach as I came in."

"You did not also I suppose know the purpose of his visit?"

"I don't claim second sight, sir."

"Really? I rather thought you did."

Cranstoun flushed.

"You were the object of his call, Captain."

"Don't tell me the old gentleman has decided to alter his will in my favour?"

For the first time in many weeks, Mary was uneasily conscious of a false note.

"No." Blandy turned to Mary. "Mary, my dear, I want to try to spare you as much as possible, but that I think can best be done by getting this matter finished with in the shortest possible time. Captain, you are, I believe, acquainted with a Miss Anne Murray?"

Mary, watching Cranstoun intently, saw no more than a flicker of firelight cross his face. "Why yes, sir. I am. Or rather, I was acquainted with her."

"When?"

"A long time back."

"When, sir?"

"Let's see, now. It would be before the '45. Have you ever noticed, sir, the queer way the brain works, how the only way you can recall one thing is by remembering another?"

"Playing for time will not help you."

"Father, what is all this?"

"Quiet, my dear. Leave this to me. When did you know Miss Murray?"

"I'd say about '44. My memory's distinctly hazy."

"So hazy that you cannot recall having married her?"

Mary sprang to her feet and Mrs. Blandy cried out.

"Married?" Cranstoun said, a shade too late. "That's absurd."

"Is it? Is it, Cranstoun?"

"The height of absurdity."

"Then is your child, too, an absurdity?" Blandy demanded angrily.

"A child!" Mary whispered.

"Molly—Molly, dear——" Mrs. Blandy murmured.

"Answer me. I demand an answer, Captain."

Cranstoun looked from one face to another: the flaccid, indignant man; the faded little woman picking unhappily at her silks; the tall, still figure of the girl, her face white and, under emotion, almost plain. In the few moments that it took him to collect his wits, his eyes took in the parlour with its rather suffocating air of middle-class prosperity; the snuffling little dog on the footstool, to which he had devoted more of his time than to most human beings; the dull flat street outside, seen through a curtain of sleet. Here, he knew, was the turning point of his life; a door had opened; he had only to let this story ride and he would be free again, free to return to the life that had been his for nearly twenty years. A flash of excitement shot through him at the prospect; the temptation was a heady one. Then his eyes caught Mary's, ready even now to kindle to his glance. Their gaze, in all its subjection to the world of the senses, held for a time and he knew that there was no escape, that here, in this one woman, in this long graceful body that he had yet to possess, was excitement enough.

He turned to Blandy with a kind of despairing candour. "You have me, sir."

"Cranstoun!" Mary cried out.

"You admit this marriage, then, Captain."

"Nothing of the kind."

"But——?"

"I'd hoped to spare you. Not you, sir, as a man of the world, but Mary and her mother. I'm a soldier, with all a soldier's faults—aye, and all his temptations, too. It seems to belong to another life, that spring. The times were unsettled. I was young. No ties, no home, nothing but what the day had to offer. You see, I was not to know then that love would come into my life, love such as few ever know. Yes, I admit freely that I entered into an association with Miss Murray."

"Only—only an association?" Mary asked.

"Certainly."

"Thank—heaven."

"Mary!" Blandy gasped.

"Why, father, were all my countrywomen to reject each man who has been guilty of such acts of gallantry, few of them would ever enter the married state, I'm afraid."

"Is this my daughter speaking?"

"I've never professed hypocrisy, papa, you know that well

enough. I can't bear with over-virtuous women. I believe that if ever the devil picks a bone it is one of theirs!"

"I won't listen to you!" Blandy, drumming on the back of the chair, turned his back on Mary. "Cranstoun, this I presume is your story, your—defence?"

"Yes, sir."

"All of it?"

"Why do you ask that?"

"Do you intend to tell us anything about the Commissary Court?"

"The—Commissary Court?"

Mrs. Blandy leaned forward. "What is that, Mr. Blandy?"

"The Commissary Court has decreed Captain Cranstoun and Miss Murray man and wife. That is correct, isn't it?"

"Yes, sir. You see, I deny nothing, conceal nothing."

"Then—if legally——"

"You don't know our Scots law, Mary. A girl has only to go into court and declare she's cohabited with a man to be pronounced his wife."

"Bad law or good," Blandy said coldly, "it's still the law."

"I'd not expect you to disparage the law, sir."

"Insolence won't help you."

Cranstoun bowed quickly. "Pardon."

"Do you or do you not intend to admit you're married to this lady?"

"Yes, Willie. Nothing else matters." Mrs. Blandy insisted, "*Are you married?*"

Cranstoun turned to face her. "As I've a soul to be saved, ma'am, I am not, nor ever was married."

"You see, Mr. Blandy? You see?"

"I see only one thing; a fact. That fact is that knowing yourself to be married under the law of your own country, you brought into play every weapon in an experienced man's armoury to seduce my daughter. In this I think even you must find yourself at a loss for an answer."

"Wait! You think I lied just now when I said I was not married. Very good. According to the ruling of the court, I am married, but neither church nor priest had any part in it. Am I to be penalised all my life for the impulse of a moment? Hear me. The Murrays are, as all the world knows, Jacobites. Poor Anne—and I can assure you that pity was the emotion uppermost in my mind at the time—she was grieving for her brother, escaping the block only because of his youth."

"We're speaking of '44, Captain. Young Murray was taken prisoner at Culloden. At least get your dates right."

"That was but one of many incidents in a confused scene. As I said, the Murrays were up to their necks in the Jacobite cause."

"Which would not have stood you in very good stead with Sir Andrew Agnew, would it, sir?"

"It might have hindered my promotion, yes."

"Even if it didn't cast doubts on your loyalty!"

"My allegiance then as now was to the House of Hanover and King George."

Mary felt her heart sink as the figure of the gallant captain emerged from the wings. Of all his many moods, she liked his heroics least. What was this love of hers that it could stand outside and criticise?

"I wonder what His Protestant Majesty would have thought of the marriage of one of his officers to a Catholic?"

"But you have it, sir," Cranstoun cried eagerly, "in a nutshell! I confess quite frankly, even to Miss Mary, that when I knew there was to be a child I offered Miss Murray marriage—it was only fair she should have had the protection of my name—but—on condition she became a Presbyterian. But would she? No! She clung to her faith, her accursed Roman faith!"

"Then it was for political rather than personal reasons you saw fit to keep your marriage secret?"

Cranstoun made a desperate gesture. "I deny that I am married!"

"But the ruling of the Court," Blandy said, his patience almost at an end.

"I don't accept that."

"You—don't—accept—it."

"No, sir. It's monstrous. It wouldn't hold water in any other country."

"It happens unfortunately to be the law of your own country, and that of your wife."

"Don't keep calling her my wife."

"Govern your temper, Captain."

"I'm sorry, sir."

"Have you any plans?"

"Plans?"

"Yes. What do you intend to do?"

"Lodge an appeal."

"Where?"

"The Court of Session. Or, if need be, with the Solicitor-General himself."

"Mr. Murray?" Blandy said derisively.

"A little awkward, that, I agree! But I've no fears. Justice is on my side."

"But is it?" Mary demanded.

"Mary—should I have come to this house if there had been any doubt in my mind?"

"I must confess, Captain, that your motives are a puzzle to me."

"My motives! God in heaven, sir, my motives! Has a drowning man a motive for clinging to a spar? Has a flower a motive for thrusting its way through ice-locked earth to reach the sun? Has the Universe a motive for its great pulsing existence? A motive! A motive for loving Mary!" Cranstoun's arms dropped to his sides, and he spoke very quietly. "Life's not been so generous to me that I would lightly throw away its dearest gift."

Mr. Blandy moved slowly to the fireplace and stood staring unseeing into the flames. Mary stood very still, her face blank as it always was when she was most deeply moved.

The room was quiet save for the sound of Mrs. Blandy's weeping.

When at last Blandy spoke, it was wearily, as though he would fain shift to other shoulders the burden of decision.

"It seems to me," he said, his anger spent, "that no matter the legal aspect, the moral aspect remains."

"He was young," Mrs. Blandy faltered: "going into battle——"

"So he has told us. Mary—my daughter has led a life of utmost purity. Perhaps it's not for me to judge. This is a very enlightened age, we hear—if indeed laxity can be confused with broadness of mind. I know that in the great world little enough is thought of these things. It may be that in my ideas I am a little out of tune with the times, even a little provincial. I try to cultivate tolerance, have, I know, condoned much in others. We are all of us so sure of our philosophy in the abstract, yet when it touches us, touches those nearest us—— There is, has always been, a double standard for men and women in morals. Yet even so, Mary is so unspotted by the world, for all she may preen herself on her lack of hypocrisy. As a father, the thought of a man who, on his own admission——" Blandy wavered. "I don't know what to say."

"Would it not——" Mrs. Blandy began.

"Yes, my dear?"

"Would it not be for Molly to say. That is, if the Courts decide in Cranstoun's favour."

Blandy turned to his daughter. "Mary. You've said very little."

"No."

"What is in your heart?"

Mary turned to Cranstoun. Neither moved; not a word was spoken. Cranstoun's eyes did not for an instant waver from hers. Her senses reeled and for a moment she seemed to sway. It came to her that his will was flowing over her in wave upon wave, robbing her of all volition. She started to speak, in a curious dulled tone: "I will stay for him till his affair is brought to a conclusion."

"And suppose it goes against him?"

"Then I am willing to face my future alone. Cranstoun is my lover. My first, my last."

PART THREE 1749

CHAPTER ONE

LONDON was given over to celebrating the Peace. A simple visitor might have been justified in asking: "Peace with whom?" England had been at war for so long and in so many places: France, India, Ireland, Scotland, the Low Countries. To the simple, the spectacle of a German King of England serving Hanover's interests by fighting France in the War of the Austrian Succession in order to establish English supremacy in India and North America might have appeared a little odd. Suffice that there were to be fireworks.

This, for the people; for the quality there were other, more exclusive entertainments: balls, galas at the Opera, a water-party at the Duke of Richmond's in Whitehall, and—the most discussed event of the season—the Venetian masquerade at Ranelagh. The King would attend; this the Countess of Yarmouth had promised the Gardens' German proprietors.

The picture was one of enchantment, and as if to silence those critics who found it reminiscent less of Venice than Bavaria, there was a gondola. A kind of extravagant rusticity inspired the scene: garlands linked the old indigenous trees; alien trees intruded, thirty-foot firs, and orange trees on which each fruit was a lamp. There was a maypole, there were country dances to pipe and tabor. The illuminated amphitheatre was ringed round with enchanting little shops, shops filled with Dresden china and enamelled snuffboxes and an embarrassment of minute toys from Japan; a world of Lilliput. There were bowers and booths everywhere, booths for tea, booths for wine, booths for dancing and for gaming. On this spring night every provision had been made for the breaking of hearts and pockets.

From the early hour of five, men and women of fashion had been making their way out to the gardens, their masks a little absurd in the afternoon sunshine. It would not be till dusk fell and the countless little lights came out like so many glow-worms that fantasy would take over.

To Mary, walking through the bewitched alleys on Cranstoun's arm, the evening was isolated in its perfection from all others. In the press of one of the gaming booths, they had contrived to lose their hosts, the Pococks, and the rest of their party. Cranstoun, leaving the tables with a pocketful of guineas was, on an instant, himself as he had always seen himself; the gallant; cool and just a little insolent, aglow with the confidence that comes to a man with ability to pay his way.

Tossing down guineas, he bought wine for them both, a Dresden posy for Mary, a Battersea snuff-box for her father, and for Mrs. Blandy a Staffordshire model of a pug that was no bigger than a sparrow's egg.

Lent anonymity by masks, audacity was in the air, and Mary experienced a slackening of barriers such as she had not known since Bath. Uncritical as she rarely was, she surrendered herself completely to the night and all it had to give.

When at last the dancers were tiring and the crowd growing thin, they made their way to the gates. There was no sign of the Pococks. Cranstoun found a hackney coach. "Doctor's Commons!" he called.

It was unlikely that Mary's uncle would still be awake. A pity; he would willingly have faced Mr. Serjeant Stevens in his present mood. He was at a loss to account for that gentleman's hostility to himself. He shrugged. Who was he to grovel for a dinner! The barrister's roof served Mary and her mother as well as any for a short stay in town. Stimulated by wine and winnings, he felt able to preen himself a little on his capacity for arousing antagonism.

Ranelagh left behind, darkness came down like a cloak, enclosing them in an illusion of privacy they had rarely known. The effects were heady. For a mile or so, each sat tight-wedged in a corner of the lurching, groaning coach, then after a time, in the flare of a link-man's torch, their eyes met. The hoarded desire of months of daily contact was theirs for the taking and their emotion held in it an element almost of terror. Holding her shivering body close to his, his lips buried in her loose cool hair, Cranstoun whispered confusedly: "We can't go on like this, my Mary. We're wasting our youth—wasting a gift such as comes to few, this pure spring of passion. Week after weary week, with no more than a few snatched kisses, the touch of a hand. Banking down fires until they all but consume us. It can't go on, I tell you. It's more than a man's sanity can stand. You've seen tonight—seen what the touch of your lips does to me. Mary—Mary—for pity's sake bring this torment to an end."

"But how?" The pressure of her fingers bruised his arm. "How, my darling?"

"Marry me!"

"Don't mock!"

He silenced her edged laughter with a kiss, with a hundred kisses, until spent and tranced they drew up at her uncle's door. The dawn wind troubled the trees and for a time they could hear the sound of hooves receding through the silent streets of the city. A cat ran swiftly, without sound, keeping close in the shadow of the wall.

An old servant, dozing in a hooded chair in the hall, awoke, confused, and led the way into the panelled parlour where wine and cakes had been left for their party; half a dozen glasses and as many chairs.

"Will there be anything else, Miss Mary?"

"No, Tisdall. Nothing more."

"Very good, miss." The old man returned to his chair in the hall.

Mary and Cranstoun sat at either side of a dying fire, drinking their wine in silence. After a time he put his glass down and went over to her, stroking her hair gently. She leaned her head against his hand, her eyes half closed.

"Give me an answer," he said quietly.

"To what?"

"An offer of marriage."

She drew away. "Under what law?"

"English law. And the church." He stared into the fire. "Before a priest. For the first time in my life. You know that, Mary."

"Why do you evade my eyes?"

He gave a short excited laugh. "Is there no limit to the provocativeness of women? Why? Because we're not children, my dear."

"But—my kisses——"

"Kisses no more than whet the appetite of a hungry man. Best let me talk."

"Go on."

"If we were to marry in secret——"

"Where?" she asked with a flash of bitterness. "Mayfair Chapel?"

"Mayfair Chapel if need be. I've been giving considerable thought to this matter. I'm not speaking on the impulse of a moment. It seems to me—in regard to the affair in Scotland—a real marriage according to the Church of England might possibly invalidate a contract arising only out of cohabitation. That is, of course," he added hastily, "if things go against me with my appeal." He searched her face. "You say nothing."

"I was just thinking what it would mean."

"For us?"

"No. No, my dear."

"For whom, then?"

She hesitated. "My father."

"Your—father! You can think of him at such a time?"

"I think of him at all times. Him, and you. He would never forgive you."

"He need never know."

"Know? Know? It would be in my eyes and on my lips, in the tone of my voice and the workings of my mind and in every movement of my body!"

"You, a woman, not to be able to dissemble?"

"With anyone else, with everyone else. But not with him.

He loves me. I can see you don't know what that means. He loves me—deeply. Do you think I could keep such a secret from him? His anguish would destroy us all!"

"It's curious how little a woman is prepared to pay for love," he said coldly.

"Cruel!"

"Is it? Is it as cruel as your own petty objections?"

"Petty! God in heaven, I try to shield the two people I love, one from grief, the other from utter ruin, and you call me petty!"

"Yes, I do. Measure our love, yours against mine. A woman's love against a man's love. There's nothing I wouldn't risk for you, no sacrifice I'd not willingly make. I'd defy all the laws of England and Scotland, defy the natural law itself!"

"That's blasphemy!"

"Perhaps. Perhaps to desire a woman as I desire you is a blasphemy. I only know that were I Doctor Faustus and the Fiend himself offered me the choice between immortality and possessing you, I'd choose you!"

CHAPTER TWO

No MORE was said of Cranstoun's rather curious proposal. In its way it had a certain warped logic and was no less orthodox than many others in a decade when a Scottish duke could marry an Irish beauty at midnight with a ring off the bed-curtain.

It was an age of tolerance, the day of the recognised mistress and the acknowledged bastard, and it was not difficult even to a man of Francis Blandy's integrity to accept Anne Murray and her child, with or without benefit of Scots law. The moral issue—once the initial shock had worn off—was not predominant. For the Blandys an illicit affair was in every way preferable to a rash marriage. Cranstoun's responsibility to his child did not trouble anyone; so complete was the unassailability of the quality that the future of a girl combining the bloods of the Murrays and the Cranstouns was far from problematical; legitimacy was a secondary consideration. Any claim Anne Murray might have had to popular sympathy was invalidated on both political and religious grounds. Cranstoun—not till now noticeably devout—made much of his Presbyterian principles on those rare occasions when the subject was raised. Even on half-pay he did not altogether lose sight of the advantages of loyalty to the ruling House and the Established Church.

Mary could never be sure how deep his feelings ran. At certain times it seemed to her that policy governed his actions, while at others she felt him to be carried along on a tide of his own eloquence. Would she, she wondered, ever really know him?

The affair of Anne Murray had disturbed her in a curious way. She had accepted his word on both past and future, and no element of jealousy was involved, but her faith, not so much in him as in her knowledge of him, was shaken. For all his bouts of disarming candour, he had been able to keep this particular secret for nearly two years. What others were there?

What was he? That, in the last analysis, was the basis of the doubt that nagged at the back of her mind. She had caught glimpses now and then of elements in him which conflicted with her previous knowledge of him; notably his superstition. That this was not a pose, she was convinced. Fond as he was of raising the emotional temperature by caprices, she had an idea that in this at least he was more sincere than he would have cared to admit.

Superstition, for all the enlightenment of the eighteenth century, was still rife. It was not many years since the last witch had been burned, the last sabbat celebrated on Boar's Hill. The servants' talk ran constantly on omens and spells and predictions. She had herself as a child found a wax effigy in the kitchen hearth, all but melted away. Mad Jack Fletcher

—although it was not openly mentioned—owed much of his popularity to a confused knowledge of the occult; it was even whispered in pantries and still-rooms that he was a warlock.

Mr. Blandy discouraged talk of these things as fit only for the ignorant, but they exercised a peculiar fascination over Mary's mother, bringing to a pleasant life a delicious touch of the macabre. In her innocence the little woman could take the blackest of magic and turn all to prettiness.

Cranstoun's interest in the occult was of a different order; darker, more mature. It was in minds such as his that the germ of the Hell Fire Club was forming. Such influences were not wholly to be ignored. He did not talk much to Mary of these subjects, but he had, she knew, discussed them with her father and, she believed, her mother.

Never from their first meeting had her thoughts of him been entirely untroubled. He drew her insidiously into things she would not otherwise have condoned. Anne Murray was important less for any threat she might present to her future happiness as in marking a stage in her own moral slackening. In closing her mind to the thought of Cranstoun as this woman's lover and the father of her child, she spared herself much useless torment, but it took from her something of the fine-edged integrity that had been hers.

Coming to town in connection with a client's action in the courts, Mr. Blandy accompanied his wife and daughter home. Cranstoun had joined his family in Roxburghshire. Her visit to London had left Mary with a legacy of conflicting impressions. For diversion there were memories of glimpses caught of a season of peculiar brilliance: the Venetian fête, the fireworks, the gala at the Opera for the Prince of Hesse and the evening she had watched Herr Gluck demonstrate his curious talent for producing music out of glasses modulated with water. But these were things of mayfly life, impersonal, ephemeral and insubstantial; they were not hers as were other, less pleasant memories. For, for all its gaiety, her trip to town had not been without its anxieties.

There had been among other things her uncle's quite unreasonable hostility to Cranstoun, culminating in an open refusal to have him to dinner. "I happen not to find the gallant gentleman to my taste," was all he would say when pressed.

There the matter rested. Cranstoun, treating the episode with a contempt that was only a little overplayed, continued to call. Then there had been the encounter with Lord Cranstoun. To Mrs. Blandy's delight, his elder brother accompanied Willie on one of his morning calls, staying to drink a dish of tea with the ladies. The visit was a merry one, distinguished by the Cranstoun charm in double measure, and it was not until they had gone that Mary realised Cranstoun had not introduced her to the head of his house as his future wife. His mother had earlier in the year written to Mrs. Blandy thanking her for her kindnesses to her son, and although no mention was made of her betrothal, Mary had at the time assumed that her own position was tacitly accepted by the family. The meeting with Lord Cranstoun disturbed her.

These were however small things weighed against her dominant anxiety.

Covertly, as the coach swung over Maidenhead bridge, she glanced at her mother, sleeping lightly at her side. Her comely face bore now the unmistakable stamp of illness. Maintaining through the weeks of their stay a gaiety that was unfailing as it was pitiful, Mrs. Blandy never referred to those visits to the doctor which had been the reason for the trip. Why, Mary wondered, a London doctor? It was, she knew, on Dr. Addington's advice that her mother was seeking another opinion, but why? What could be the matter with her that was outside the skill of the Reading man?

"My little pain," was all Mrs. Blandy would say; that pain which had subtly changed the structure of her face when she was not animated and on guard.

Mary turned to her father; here at least was no cause for concern. Blandy met her eyes in a smile as confident as it was affectionate. To Mary's deep content, his attitude towards

Cranstoun had mellowed into a kind of jesting acceptance. "I'm the devil he knows!" Cranstoun had once laughed. That this complaisance rested less on any growing affection for the Scot than on the fact that her marriage to him was indefinitely postponed did not occur to Mary, nor would Blandy have admitted it to himself. For him the *status quo* could scarcely have been bettered. Both his wife and his daughter were obviously happy in their cavalier and—this was the core of his contentment—Mary remained under his roof. With the affair in Scotland still to be resolved, no decision was called for. The easy badinage with which he treated Cranstoun greased the wheels; no crises were provoked. Instinct told him that here was a situation to be let alone.

As the coach made the steep descent down White Hill and the old town came in sight, a sense of peace flowed over the lawyer; the purity of the air, the beauty of the surrounding hills, the fresh cool river; the familiar faces—plain, bucolic, stupid, even—but known and, for that reason, loved. As they rolled over the bridge there was a greeting for them everywhere; the respected citizens. A small world perhaps, but their own.

"Glad to be home, sir?" Susannah asked, bobbing on the doorstep.

"Very glad, Sukey—very glad indeed." He spoke no more than the truth; he was very glad to be home. Had anyone asked him at that moment, he would have said that life had been very good to him.

CHAPTER THREE

"Open the window, Molly," Mrs. Blandy whispered. "I like to hear the sounds."

Blinded by tears, Mary made her way to the bedroom window.

The house was quiet; quiet as a muffled knocker and straw-strewn road could make it; quiet with the quiet of whispers and felt slippers and bated breath.

As she opened the casement, life seemed suddenly to return. From the street below came all the familiar sounds: the barking of the White Hart terriers; the shouts of urchins; the jingle of martingales as the brewers' dray passed; the cawing of the rooks that flew in and out of the crevices in the soft chalk of the church tower and, high above the roofs, the sweet mewing of migrant swallows gathering in the clear autumn sky. The sun was low and the old red town stood out with edged clarity against the wooded hills across the river.

"Everything going on just the same——"

"Yes." Mary could scarcely speak for the ache in her throat.

"Let little Dandy look out. He's been so patient with me."

Mary took the dog in her arms and held him up so that he could look down on the animated scene. Beneath her fingers she could feel a small rumbling growl as his prominent eyes sighted the terriers.

She breathed deeply, filling her lungs gratefully with the clean cool air.

The third day.

It would not be long now. Tired almost to insensibility, she was no longer tormented by hope. This illness was not like the earlier one. Almost from the moment when she awoke in the wide bed, the hot racked body clinging to hers, she had seen the end. Norton had been called in, and Addington; the insensate ritual of bleeding and purging had been gone through again. She herself, with no faith in any of it, knowing it an added torture, had applied poultices every four hours through three days and nights.

Then they had sent for her uncles—John from Fawley, Henry from Culham—and for her godmother, Mrs. Mounteney. The Pococks were in Italy, Cranstoun in the North.

"So much to do," her mother had said. Her brain peculiarly clear in the intervals of pain, she had set her house in order, covering them all with her thoughts; saying to Norton: "Watch Mary afterwards. She loves me so well that I wish this may not be the death of her"; and to the Rector of Fawley: "You must help to comfort your poor niece, Jack. Never forsake her, my dear brother. All that gives me pain in death is the leaving of her behind me." She talked quite simply of death, with no thought now of recovery.

Hands outstretched to husband and daughter, she whispered: "Be both father and mother to my girl, Mr. Blandy. She is all your heart could wish for and has been the best of daughters to me. Use her with generous confidence and she will never abuse it."

Blandy, making his vow, marvelled a little that his wife should have thought it necessary to recommend Mary to him. How well he had dissembled in the daily commerce of thirty years!

Drawing him closer to her, Mrs. Blandy spoke hesitantly: "When I am gone, Francis, I beg of you—let no one set you against Cranstoun."

Her hand in his, he said with deep sincerity: "It will not be my fault if the marriage does not take place."

"I had looked to your wedding with such happiness, Molly—such happiness."

Blandy bowed his head over his wife's hand, unwilling to betray an emotion deeper than any she had ever aroused in him.

"Go now, my dear," she said, thinly; "my spirits fail me——"

He rose abruptly, averting his face. At the door he said almost brusquely: "The doctors—doubtless they will think of something——"

"Not without they can give me a new inside." A pitiful little laugh came from her parched throat.

And now they were alone together, she and Mary. The room was empty of them all: doctors, relatives, friends, servants. The sun had gone down into the hills and the afterglow suffused the room with warm light. For a time

Mrs. Blandy lay still, listening to the sounds that rose, muted, from the street below.

Leaving the window open, Mary drew up a stool by the bed, her head resting on the pillow at her mother's side.

Speaking in a whisper, Mrs. Blandy talked for a time of her faith, the faith of her brother at Fawley; simple, unquestioning, wholly sufficing; a faith that saw death as a beginning, not an end. The gentle voice had an ineffable quality, seeming to the girl instinct with that immortality her mother sought to put into words. "I want to leave something of myself behind, dear. A legacy—for you, Molly. If only I were more clever, I would make you understand. Perhaps your Uncle Jack can explain. He's so good, dear, a really devout man. A man you can turn to—but—that was not what I wanted to tell you—where was I?"

"You said—something of yourself——"

"Ah, yes. That was it. In this room. If I could leave something here—some—emanation? Is that the word?"

"Don't tire yourself too much."

"It doesn't matter—not now. If—you could come here and we could be together again——"

"Together." Mary began to tremble.

"You're not afraid?"

"I think I am a little."

"Of me?"

"Not of you. But this—this idea. An—apparition. That's not the teaching of my uncle."

"No—no."

"It has no part in our religion, the dead returning."

"Not in our religion, no."

"Then where——?"

"Where?"

Mary raised her head from the pillow. "Where did you learn it?"

"Don't look so afraid."

"Mama, please. You must tell me. What gave you this idea? Someone—who?"

"Willie."

"Cranstoun!" Mary rose to her feet. "Did you—often talk of these things?"

"More than once."

"When?"

"Out at Turville. When I was so ill."

"Do you believe in them?"

"He does."

"But you?"

"We could try." There was a child's eagerness in the suggestion that stripped it of all terror and made it wholly pitiful.

Mary dropped to her knees, pressing her mother's hands to her burning eyes.

"Will you, Molly?"

"What dear? What is it you want?"

The voice was fading, the light in the eyes growing dull. "Come to this room——"

"After——?"

"After. It may be—that we're not meant to return—but—that we shall see. We—we could try."

Mary put her arms round her mother, herself on the verge of collapse. "I'll come. I will come. I promise," she murmured.

"I only wish I could take you with me—but what would poor Cranstoun do?" The voice faded, the difficult breathing growing more faint.

Deep in the shadows closing in on her mind lay a secret shared only with a stranger—the doctor she had consulted in London; the knowledge that life carried within itself the seeds of death. She knew herself bound indivisibly to this girl whose birth had in the end cost her her life. The circle was now complete. "The Lord giveth and the Lord taketh away—" was perhaps her last conscious thought.

The birds were silent now and the lovely light was fading from the room like a receding tide.

PART FOUR 1749-50

CHAPTER ONE

With the death of her mother, Mary's life entered upon a new phase; the leaven went out of it, that leaven of kindness, of gaiety, of well-mannered inconsequence which had been Mrs. Blandy's special quality. Francis Blandy himself, for all his genial hospitality, was an inconstant element, moody and unpredictable. For thirty years the pretty woman had accepted his caprices, mildly protesting, yet never in danger of rebellion. Mary was her father's child but where Francis Blandy's emotionalism was disciplined by a strongly-developed sense of expediency, hers smouldered dully, like the core of a haystack; slowly consuming, awaiting the ultimate flare-up. With Cranstoun the heat had for brief moments touched danger-point, but the cooling rains of convention had damped the flames.

Now that affection had been withdrawn from his life, Francis Blandy was left only with love; the mild feeling he had had for his wife was no longer there to dissipate his infinitely deeper feeling for his daughter. Now, as never before, Mary was his, and he completely hers.

There was no perceptible change in their relationship; neither was demonstrative. It was in the life of the house itself that change was more apparent; there were fewer goings and comings. Mary ran the house capably, but for the first few months at least she was in a curious state of morbid apathy. A complete physical collapse had at first overwhelmed her and she had lain spent but unrelaxed in her small room, the door open to her mother's room—"She may need me."

Never at any time more than half believing in the occult, she now in her grief felt a kind of compunction, as though she had entered upon a pact. The strangeness of her last few moments with her mother had set her feet on new paths; where formerly she had rejected any ideas outside the range of rational experience, she now, sick at heart, felt herself involved in them. Her mother had, in all innocence, left her with a fatal legacy, one from which she would never wholly free herself. Where once she had been sceptical of Cranstoun's Celtic superstition, she now found herself drawn to him by yet another thread and she knew that when next they met she would be unable to offer any further resistance to his mind.

Upbringing, and the world in which she moved, would govern her behaviour; with strangers she would scoff as well as the rest, but—like an unconfessed sin—the belief would remain.

She had not seen Cranstoun now for nearly five months. He wrote to her frequently, and upon learning of her mother's death had sent a footman down from town to beg for a glimpse of her "to reassure him". Mr. Blandy had been deeply touched by the warm sincerity of his condolences and had invited him to join them—"We shall both be happy in your company."

Cranstoun's reply had been evasive: unspecified affairs had brought him to town and kept him there. No suggestion was made of a later date. Mary accepted the disappointment almost without feeling. A pall of depression had settled on her. It was November; days of fog followed close on the heels of days of drizzle. The gutters were choked with leaves and the bare branches of the trees dripped disconsolately above the ruin of her mother's borders. In her low state she saw symbols everywhere. The early days of grief had passed in a kind of amnesia; now life was returning to normal, with the difference that the house was no longer lit and warmed by her mother's presence. Cranstoun's defection was no more than a part of a disagreeable whole.

Some pretence of Christmas was made in the house in Hart Street, and the table extended to its old festive proportions.

The Pococks were still abroad, but Mrs. Mounteney came, together with Mary's uncles and two old acquaintances of Mr. Blandy's, affectionately known as the Toms—Cawley and Staverton. Cranstoun had returned to Roxburghshire. He sent Mr. Blandy a dried salmon and, in a series of impassioned sentences, expressed to Mary the hope that he would see her early in the New Year.

His next letter, from an address in Covent Garden, made no mention of visiting Henley. After some days had passed without news of him, a hurried note came, giving Mary the startling news that he was confined to his lodgings, a prisoner of debt. "Unless," he wrote, "I can raise the sum of fifteen pounds I see no hope of escape. I write only that you may understand my delay in laying my disconsolate body where already my heart rests."

Without a moment's hesitation Mary sent him fifteen guineas, nearly all that remained of her allowance. The thought of seeing him again buoyed her up all day and she was happier than she had been for months.

Quite without warning she woke in the middle of the night to the shocked realisation of what she had done. She had given a man money. At first she tried to tell herself that she had been more than glad to be able to help him, that his confidence in her was the highest tribute he could have paid her, stressed more than anything the closeness of their ties, but the voice of doubt—never long silent where he was concerned—spoke with disturbing insistence.

He had not asked her directly for the money; he had worked round to it; hinted. It had not been to his future father-in-law that he had turned, but to her, a woman. The transaction had a clandestine ring. Subtly, the intrusion of money, of being on such terms of intimacy, brought to their relationship an indefinable sordidness. As once before, she was subconsciously aware of a blunting of her integrity. In time, she thought, I shall no longer notice these things. My values will have lost their edge.

CHAPTER TWO

Spring came, and with it Cranstoun. Renewal was everywhere; in the song of blackbird on rooftop, in the fresh new green hazing the woods, in lengthening days and lilac-scented nights; in the primroses that sheltered in the writhing mossy roots of the beech and in the kingcups, knee-deep in floodwater in the river-meadows; in the crocuses at the Angel and in the coils of the Red Lion wistaria and—to Mary a symbol—in the parrot tulips that raised their arrogant ragged heads in her mother's border, quite independent of the care that had formerly been theirs.

Grief changed its dress with the season, taking on a softness, a fragrance. Mary could go now to the chancel of the church where her mother was buried with no more than wistfulness and regret, the old dry-eyed apathy gone with the dark short lifeless days of winter.

On the evening of his arrival, Cranstoun went with her to the church and they stood hand in hand above the memorial stone in the floor. She told him of her mother's last wish regarding their marriage and he made a pledge not to fail her. The solemnity of the vow and the beauty of the dim church laid a spell over them, raising them for a moment into the company of the romantics. Later, when so much was scarred and tainted, the memory of this moment would return to Mary as a thing apart, shining and high, a vindication of them both.

Cranstoun was an adventurer; he was not by any standards a good man, but like so many adventurers he had a quick understanding, was sensitive to the needs of a moment. He could rise or sink, as the hour demanded. Innately conscienceless and amoral, a moment of nobility would have no more lasting effect on him than a moment of degradation, yet—perhaps the only positive good he could have claimed for himself—with him and through him one woman at least was to touch the heights. Such a man could bring in his train tragedy or despair, but he could give happiness on a plane unimagined by characters finer than his.

Francis Blandy seemed, to Mary's relief, glad enough of Cranstoun's company at first, finding his talk stimulating. The fact that the Scot had no more than a smattering of knowledge on a number of subjects precluded any danger of boredom.

The days passed innocuously, in morning walks and afternoons of talk in the parlour, but something of the tension of their early days was returning. Now that her mother was no longer there, Mary had grown acutely aware of the intensity of her father's affection for her and her happiness in her love for Cranstoun grew increasingly edged as the weeks passed. The position with regard to his action was still uncertain, and the fact that it was tacitly ignored did nothing to ease the situation. His relations with Mr. Blandy had a thin crust of geniality that might, she felt uneasily, crack at any moment. Their talk was a shade too general, too urbane.

Cranstoun himself was conscious of the lawyer's eyes on him as never before. Instinct warned him to avoid any familiarities with Mary while Blandy was in the room. His very presence in the house imposed its own subtle censorship on their actions: the house was Blandy's, the servants his—old Susannah and Betty Binfield and the callow new footman, Harman, who had on Mrs. Blandy's death succeeded Ned Hearne. At any moment one or other of them might come into the room—to draw curtains or clear away tea or light candles. They would, he knew, carry tales. Harman could be bought with a coin, the girl from Binfield with a kiss, but Susannah—'the faithful old house-bitch,' as he called her—was beyond his blandishments. Her devotion to her master was above bribery; she was, he thought, fond enough of Mary, but himself she regarded as an intruder. None of these elements had been apparent in Mrs. Blandy's day; she had not been without her subtle strength.

"Your mother pervades this house," Cranstoun said once to Mary.

She looked at him quickly. "For me, yes. A thousand memories—everything she touched. But you——" She hesitated. "Cranstoun—you don't think——?"

"What?"

"Do you believe—— No, no, forget what I said."

"Why are you so pale?"

"A trick of light. The dusk is falling."

"What were you going to ask me?"

"Please——"

"There are no secrets between us, my dear."

The door of the parlour opened and Betty came in with the candles. Cranstoun rose to help her light them. Mary watched them uneasily: the momentary touch of their fingers as Cranstoun took the candlestick from the girl, the flush that warmed her dark cheek, the curious languor of her walk as, unwillingly, she moved to the door. It was not the first time she had seen the effect Cranstoun had on women of Betty's class, but that it should happen in her own home was disturbing.

Sensing something of what was in her mind, he caught her in his arms and kissed her swiftly the moment the door had closed, but her lips were unresponsive, her body resistant. "Why so coy? They can't be back with more candles!" he laughed.

She drew away from him and sat in the window. The roofs were red with the last of the sun, the sky a clear lilac above them. The street was empty save for the coach of one of Mr. Blandy's clients.

Cranstoun decided to change his line of attack. "What were you going to tell me?"

Swallows were circling above as they had circled the night her mother died; the sense of continuity brought a strange peace. After a pause she asked quietly: "Do you believe the dead return?"

"Your mother did."

"You talked to her about it, didn't you."

"She told you?"

"Yes. More than once?"

"I think so."

"Why?"

"Perhaps to strip death of its terror."

"But does it? Does it, Cranstoun?"

"That would depend."

"On what?"

"What the dead found on their return."

"What they *found?*"

"You've heard of earthbound spirits?"

"Yes."

"They're searching, down the ages——"

"For what?"

"The love they knew on earth." He spoke softly, abetting the peace of the hour.

She raised her eyes to his. "You mean—if they were to return, and there was no one there. If—one failed them?"

He caught her hands. "You pledged yourself, didn't you?"

"Yes," she whispered.

"When?"

"The—last night."

"What did you promise?"

"That I would be in her room, waiting. Oh, none of it was explicit. She herself only half believed."

"But you gave your word."

"Yes."

"Have you kept faith?"

"Countless times. I leave my door open every night."

"But to stay in her room, lie in her bed—have you done that?"

"Not yet."

"You're afraid."

"No. Not afraid. Not of her."

"You are—you are, Mary." His hands dragged at hers and his eyes, no longer laughing, were narrowed and strangely bright. "You are afraid."

"How could I be—of her?"

"Not of her. But of the unknown. Afraid of knowledge. Afraid even to admit the existence of the occult. I know. I know you so well, Mary. Deep in you there are powers that have never been tapped. You know them, and you fear them. Powers in you——"

"Not occult powers."

"Who am I to guess? All I know is that there's a strangeness in you."

"Tonight?"

"Tonight more than usually. Nearer the surface, shining out of your eyes, trembling at the tips of your fingers. You may damp down the fires within you. But not for always. Not for always, Mary Blandy. You're born out of your time. This sceptical age has no use for powers such as yours."

"I have no powers, I tell you. None—none." Trembling gripped her stomach like a cramp.

"You have, I tell you. You have! A century ago they would have burned you!"

"Witches!" she cried contemptuously.

"You deny their existence?"

"This is the eighteenth century!"

"What of that? Suppose I were to tell you that I spent the last night of December with a witch, watched the old year die at a sabbat!"

"Where?"

"Not three miles outside Edinburgh!"

"A sabbat! In Edinburgh!" she taunted. "And where does this witch of yours live?"

"In a wynd off the Royal Mile—a wynd where the ghosts of murdered men gather so thick you cannot climb the stair o' nights."

Mary, held by his eyes, his hands drawing on hers as though he sought to drag her down, braced herself to fight him with every weapon of superciliousness and scepticism at her command. "What it the name of your witch?"

"Mrs. Morgan."

Her laughter was high-pitched and excited. "Mrs. Morgan! Some old Welsh chorewoman living in a tenement!"

"You mean you've never heard of Mrs. Morgan?"

"Nor of Mrs. Jones, nor Mrs. Evans!"

"Mrs. Morgan is one of the most famous women of her day."

"In her own Edinburgh wynd?"

"Where better?"

"Where indeed for a qualified witch? And how does she live? By making wax dolls in the shape of Hanoverians for Jacobites to stick pins into?"

"By the infusion of potions."

"Love potions?"

"Why not?"

"Concoctions to serve drabs and ageing lechers?"

"What do you know of such things?"

"No more than can be read in bawdy advertisements in the papers." She faced him with feverish gaiety. "Are you suggesting I allow your Mrs. Morgan to prescribe?"

"Mary! This is not you, this coarseness."

"Nor is it I to believe in witches and warlocks and werewolves! Let go my hands. I'll not be seduced by your dark thoughts."

He dropped her hands as though stung and rose to his feet. Glancing through the window, he gave a cry.

"What is it?" She sprang up.

"The moon."

"What of it?" Before he had time to prevent her, she had turned to the window. Lying bright and clear above the town was the new moon. Mary stared it out of countenance.

Cranstoun, standing behind her, gripped her elbows. "Now you will believe——" She could feel the trembling of his hands.

"In what?" At the proximity of his body she felt her resistance to him weakening.

"She was right in what she told me."
"Your—witch? What did she tell you?"
"Why should I burden you with it?"
"Tell me."
"We talked of the future. Spoke of you—you and your father."
"Yes. Yes?"
"She—I could see there was something at the back of her mind. She saw—death."
"Whose death?"
"She would not say."
"An easy enough prophecy."
He rested his head against hers, speaking quietly, his lips to her ear. "Still resistant."
"Was that all she told you?"
"Just that there would be a death."
"When?"
"A matter of months."
"How many months?"
"Less than a score."
"There was something more."
"Yes."
"What?"
"The moon—the moon through glass. That was to be the sign—the confirmation."

CHAPTER THREE

THE AIR was heavy with heat; even the birds were silenced. Heat shimmered in the distances and the woods and the surfaces of the roads seemed to vibrate. Even the river was warm and lifeless and without colour as though the tide no longer ran. The brown dry reeds stood in stagnant water and the meadows were parched and tawny. Night brought little respite and roses that had been in bud at sunset were full-blown by dawn.

The little dog lay panting in the yard and swarms of flies invaded the kitchen; Harman was kept busy half the day swatting them. Betty Binfield, kerchief discarded and corselet unlaced, toiled irritably, the roaring stove an enemy. Ned Hearne who, although now sexton at the church, still came in twice a week to do the silver, slipped off his shoes, welcoming the cold of the pantry floor. Even Littleton no longer looked nipped up. Mr. Blandy conducted business in his white silk shirtsleeves. It was the first time his clients had seen him without his smoking-cap.

Mary sat on the circular bench under the walnut tree; her face was pale and damp and her ears drummed. She tried to read, wishing fractiously that Mr. Fielding could have told the history of Tom Jones in fewer words. Her eyes seemed to follow ever-descending tadpoles down the page and she constantly lost her place.

Cranstoun had been staying with his uncle for a few days. Was it any cooler behind the fifteen-foot walls of Paradise House? she wondered.

Languor flowed over her at the thought of him, and her book slid to the ground. This fret of the intellect—reading, education, thought, even—what was the use of it? Was it not possible after all that life on the plane of instinct was happier? The simple people, the ignorant, given over to purely sensual pleasures—eating, drinking, mating—how much did they miss in the last analysis? This critical faculty, this standing apart in judgment, was it a thing to be desired, cultivated? What did she herself gain by her awareness of her own faults and those of her lover? Was it not perhaps all of her own imagining, this subtle degradation of which she had more than once been conscious? Why not accept, with the blind acceptance of the pure in heart? What if Cranstoun had been over-gallant in the past? The incident was closed long before their meeting. What if he were superstitious? To a Celt these things were inherent; it was only to her English mind that they assumed an air of evil. Suppose he did now and then involve her in his financial troubles? She saw in her own reluctance to give him money a germ of 'Mr. Blandy's meanness'. Her mother would not have been so reticent, to give or to take.

Her own attitude was inconsistent in the extreme. Why, having reconciled herself to sending him fifteen guineas, should she have been so shocked when—indirectly—he asked her for a further sum? His reasons had been of the most delicate. Discovering him packing his bags one morning, she had been startled to learn that he was leaving Henley. On being pressed, he confided that the bailiffs were after him again and he would go to the ends of the earth rather than bring them buzzing like hornets round her father's house. Pressed further, he revealed that a mere fifteen pounds would stave off disaster.

Her father had recently given her twenty guineas to pay for her mourning, and going to the secret drawer of her bureau she counted Cranstoun out all but five of them. His embarrassment was obvious, but, driven as he was, he slipped the guineas into his breeches pocket. "What's yours is mine——" he quoted. On the instant, her critical mind noted that he had failed to complete the sentence.

One evening at supper he remarked to her father that his pay was overdue.

"Your half-pay, you mean," Blandy said caustically. It was not here, she knew, that either of them could turn for help.

Her own money affairs were far from satisfactory; not only were her chances of paying her dressmaker remote, but her allowance was not due for another two months. She had not inherited her mother's fecklessness about bills and the thought of them nagged at her.

No, all in all, she envied the irresponsibility of the ignorant, of good Dame Emmet and stupid Mary Banks, singing blithely in the wash-house. Emmet and Banks worked in the fields fourteen hours a day for as many shillings a week, but the roof over their heads was the responsibility of the lord of the manor and they were free of all the rabbits they could poach.

She smiled a little at herself for the immorality of her thoughts. "Heat is demoralising" Lavinia had written from Tuscany. She picked up poor Tom Jones, but the effort of stooping made the blood rush to her head.

Susannah came out to tell her that Cranstoun had called.

"He'd best come out here. It's intolerable in the house."

"If the poor master can bear it, I reckon the Captain can," the maid said tartly. Her neck and face were scarlet with heat and she waddled like an old spaniel, fat and panting.

Cranstoun, his coat slung over his shoulders like a dolman, moved with sensuous grace down the path. His hair, close to his head in damp curls, appeared almost dark against the pallor of his face. He held her fingers to his lips for a time, then sat at her side with his back to the house. They talked little, each acutely conscious of the physical presence of the other. Their heat-drugged thoughts rejected the men and women at work within a few yards of them, and they shared an illusory privacy that was infinitely exciting. His eyes rested for a long time on her lips, and he sketched them with a sensitive finger.

"This heat——"

"All my casements open," she said, "yet I could not sleep."

"Nor I."

"If only one were out in the open, in the water-meadows—it would surely be cool by the river?"

"Or in the woods." His fingers caressed the back of her neck. "In the woods there would be air to breathe."

"Yes."

"I never was up there at night."

"I have been. There's a thicket in the hanging wood where the nightingale sings—he returns every year."

"Did you go alone?" he asked gaily.

She smiled faintly. "Suppose I said—no?"

"You've no need of coquetry with me." His smile died. "Nothing you could do or say would make me desire you more than I do." She drew in her breath sharply. His fingers returned to their caress, his eyes to her lips. "And you?"

"I?" She dropped her eyes.

He laughed softly, his splendid teeth gleaming. "Hearing the nightingale is one of the few experiences I've missed."

"I could tell you the path."

"Show me."

"Show you?"

"Show me the path."

"It would be too late."

"Why?"

"The nights are so short. The whole house will be asleep before dark."

"The whole house—will—be—asleep," he whispered, raising his eyes to hers.

"No. No, Cranstoun," she said, her heart beating wildly.

"Yes."

"It's not—possible."

"Everything is possible."

"Not this. Someone would hear me."

"You've slipped out of the house before. Many times. You've told me."

"That was different."

"Yes," he said slowly, "that was different." He was no longer touching her, yet she was conscious of his will as a tangible force. Strength draining from her limbs, she knew herself powerless to resist him.

The chain slipped from its socket without a sound; the well-oiled locks yielded to her light pressure, the seasoned door closed without the faintest creak. The stairs had been solid beneath her feet, the stone paving of the hall accepted her in silence. Once out in the street, she walked like a dancer lest the tap of her heels betray her.

As she passed beneath the clock tower, the chime rang out. Half-past eleven. The moon was rising above the hill and the air now was cool and ineffably sweet. Below she could hear the churning of water round the piers of the bridge and somewhere among the rushes a wild duck laughed. The Angel, brooding low beneath the London road, was in darkness.

By the time she reached the footpath the moon had cleared the hill, flooding the meadows with light, an excess of light. Hurrying, she sought the shelter of the woods.

A woman going to her lover.

The beauty of the night and the quality of her love stripped her errand of furtiveness. Moving on swift feet through the silent woods, exaltation walked with her. The fever of the day had died down with the day's heat, leaving her calm. Here, at last, was an end to doubt. The complexities of mind, the tension, the small voice of criticism, all would resolve themselves in a single, simple act of surrender. For nearly three years now the worm of desire had eaten out their hearts; now, of her own choice, free—as she must be in everything—she was going to him. He had been patient with her, done violence to his own wild passions for her sake. Even now their meeting was no more than half of his making. Had she refused him, he would not have been insistent. He had scarcely put his wish into words; had not taken her by storm. He had given her time enough for a change of heart. Tonight, leaving his uncle's house, he would have no security; she might not keep her tryst. Even now, at this eleventh hour, she was free to go back. The thought was a heady one, not in its possibility of escape, but in the consciousness of liberty, of entity and free will it gave her. She was strong; strong to give, strong to withhold, strong to take. An excitement filled her that transcended desire. She approached him not as a subservient mate—the hen-bird, the doe; not as an abject woman dependent for her happiness upon a man's whim, but as an equal; a free woman saluting equality in a free man.

CHAPTER FOUR

The spell lay over her all through the day.

They must guess, she thought. Betty—standing at her bedside with her morning tea, insolent and inscrutable—Betty must guess. Mrs. Deane, dressing her, must guess. Littleton, brushing past her in the hall on his way to the study, thwarted and ill-at-ease as always with her, he must surely guess. Even Harman—with the instinct of clods for an accessible woman—must surely know. Her father—here her heart beat fast—of them all he, who loved her, who knew her so well, read every mood, every shadow that passed across her face and listened with sensitive ears to every note in her voice—he must know.

She dissembled for them all, was gay, brisk, pert; not till she was alone again in her room did she let so much as a random memory enter her mind lest they should read her thoughts.

A small breeze from the east had sprung up, dispersing the drugging heat of the day before, but Mr. Blandy was in dyspeptic humour, his perceptions blunted. On a morning when his tea was not to his taste, it was unlikely he would notice that his daughter had lost her virginity with pagan exultancy.

Breakfast safely negotiated, Mary returned to her room. She always did its small chores herself, dusting and making the bed. She would not be disturbed.

Standing in front of her mirror, she looked intently at her face. Her eyes were darkly shadowed but fever-bright. There was fever in her cheeks, and a new softness. Her parted lips gave her a look of sensual witlessness, as though her mind had abdicated. Her face excited her; wave upon wave of cerebral shock ran through her nerves. Morning had not brought her peace or lethargy, only a resurgence of desire.

The door behind her opened. Startled, she turned to see Betty staring at her, her arms full of red roses.

She smiled quickly. "What is it, Betty?"

"Flowers for you."

"Oh. Oh, how lovely." Mary took the roses, glad to bury her betraying face in them.

"A boy brought them."

"What boy?"

"An ordinary sort of boy." Betty continued to stare at her. "Master asked him where he was from. He wouldn't tell."

"What—what did my father say then?"

"He said it looked as though some gentleman's garden had been robbed."

"I hope not!"

"I told him you'd be bound to know where they was from."

"Why, there's no card, is there?"

"It wasn't for me to look."

Mary made a show of searching. "There doesn't seem to be one."

"Red roses. Why should he send red roses of all things?" As she spoke, the girl's eyes ran over Mary's body, then she suddenly turned and went out of the room.

Mary was on the point of calling her back, but discretion told her to let well alone.

So he had sent her flowers. Red roses. Happiness welled up in her at the grace of his tribute. He would not, she saw, call on her this morning. Delicacy in him was new, a fresh facet in his many-sided character. Never could such a man pall! My lover, she thought, burying her face in the cool sweetness of his roses; my lover!

He called for an hour in the evening to take tea with her and her father in the parlour. Devoting most of his time to Mr. Blandy, he was at the height of his powers, sending up squibs and rockets of bright talk. On taking his leave, he bowed low over Mary's hand, and asked if he might have the honour of her company the following morning. As a comedy of manners, the thing was delicious.

The heat wave had broken and they set out early, calling at Saragossa House for a dish of tea with Mrs. Mounteney, then striking in behind Phyllis Court to walk in Fawley meadows. A breeze ruffled the surface of the river and the willows swayed like the skirts of dancers. There were great purple banks of loosestrife and willowherb and the air was filled with the scent of meadowsweet. Water-lilies, smooth as porcelain, floated on the flat surface of the water, echoing the yellow of the iris above them. A heron stood on the bank, immobile as bronze, and they discovered the precarious nest of a moorhen. Cranstoun, with a swagger, stuck a posy of cowslips in his hat and carried Mary over the small streams that intersected the meadows.

They paused to sit on a fallen elm and suddenly his gaiety left him. "Mary——"

"Yes, my dear?"

He drummed nervously on the bark of the tree. "There's something I must tell you. It's queer the tricks a man's conscience plays him. You might ask why I should think of this now, why have I never told you before? Do you know I could answer in complete honesty that the thing's slipped my memory till now. All these years. No accounting for it." He took off his hat and adjusted the posy, giving the action his full attention. "Everything's changed——"

The colour drained from her cheeks. "Since——?"

"Since"—he raised his eyes to hers—"since you became my bride."

"Is that how you think of me?"

"Last year in town I asked you to marry me in secret. You have. You have married me, Mary. As surely and as solemnly as in a church. The woods were our church, with the song of the nightingale for choir and nothing but the trees above between us and God."

Tears stood in her eyes. "Thank you for that."

"My dear—my very dear——" He buried his face in her

hands. Neither spoke for a time, then he raised his head. "That's why I have to tell you——"

"I don't know what's in your mind, but there's no need to tell me," she said earnestly.

"There is. Every need."

"I've no wish to pry into your life before we met."

"Maybe not. But you've the right. A wife's right."

"I don't think I want to know."

"You must."

"Why? Why, Cranstoun?"

"My conscience is plaguing me."

"You should turn Catholic and rid yourself of your burden in the confessional!" she cried, her gaiety sharp-edged.

"You're not to say that."

"Why not?"

"You're not to suggest I might ever renounce my faith."

"But I was only jesting."

"A queer kind of wit!"

"Willie!"

"Forgive me. You see—too much of bitterness is involved in this question of religion. It brings to mind things best forgotten by you and me."

"I'm sorry."

"Not your fault. How could you know how the thought of the unhappy event in Scotland preys on my mind."

"Indeed, sir," she laughed, "your conscience is very active this fine morning!"

"I think it is. Mary, hear me." He hesitated, then spoke very quietly. "I have a child."

She looked puzzled. "I know."

"You don't understand. We—we're not thinking of the same thing. I have a son."

"But—I thought Miss Murray's child was a daughter."

"It is."

"What—what are you trying to tell me?"

"I have a son. A boy of"—he calculated quickly—"a boy of four years."

"Miss—Murray's son."

"No."

She gasped, afraid for the moment to ask: "By whom?"

"A Miss Capel."

"Where?"

"Southampton."

"When—did this happen?"

"I told you. The boy is nearly four."

"I mean, before we met?"

"My dearest, you surely don't think——"

"How do I know what to think?" she cried, her voice harsh with agitation.

"You must at least know that from the moment my eyes fell on you——!"

"Is that what you told Miss Capel of Miss Murray?"

"Mary! That was unworthy of you!"

"Who are you to speak of worthiness?"

"I know, I know. Nothing you can say will equal what I think of myself. I'm a wretch, a miserable, unspeakable wretch! But how was I to know?"

"Know what?"

"That you were in the world," he said simply.

She did not reply.

"You know what? There's been but one woman in my life. A single love."

"Don't!" She sprang up.

"What have I said?"

"To talk of love at this moment! It's a sort of blasphemy!"

"But all this belongs to the past."

"Does it? Does it, Cranstoun? How do I know that's true?"

"Your heart knows."

"My heart knows that you've concealed this Miss Capel from me as you concealed Miss Murray. How many more are there? In God's name, how many more?"

"If that is your attitude——"

"My attitude!"

"Trust a woman to bring vulgarity to the issue." His face was sullen.

"Vulgarity! How dare you!"

"I repeat. Vulgarity. I had no need to tell you. I confessed of my own free will. Without me you need never have known."

"Why did you confess?"

"I've already told you. Because you had the right to know."

"Was it that? Or was it because you were in danger of being betrayed, as you were betrayed before?"

"No one knows of this, not even my brother officers."

"Not even Miss Capel? Not even your son?"

"For pity's sake, Mary. I wish to God I'd never raised the thing."

"Why did you?"

"How many more times must I tell you?"

"I don't think I believe you."

"What do you believe?"

Her eyes narrowed and she breathed like a runner. "Why should you choose this day, our first morning together since I gave myself to you? Was it that——"

"Yes—yes?"

"Was it that you're devil enough to want to humble me, to drag me down to the level of a garrison drab?"

"Mary!"

"It's true. It's true. I was too proud in my love. Too arrogant!" Her hands came to her mouth and she looked round her wildly.

Cranstoun stood taut and erect, but he was trembling. "If that's what you believe," he said slowly, "then perhaps it's true."

She moaned softly, her body rocking to and fro.

"If you see yourself as a drab—if you've the mind of a drab, then perhaps it is true." He moved towards her, a host of little flowers dying beneath his tread. "If you say it's so, then it is so." There was a note in his voice she had never heard before. Suddenly he caught her to him and, dragging her hands from her mouth, kissed her savagely. For some moments she struggled against him, then an emotion took possession of her that was akin to panic and she found herself returning his terrible kisses.

CHAPTER FIVE

CRANSTOUN had gone north. His appeal was, he said, down for hearing at the next sessions and his presence in Edinburgh was necessary.

"I hope to return a free man," he announced at the dinner-table in Hart Street; adding jauntily, "You'll have to be talking to the rector soon, sir."

Mr. Blandy paused, his glass half-way to his lips. "I?"

"About putting up the banns."

The lawyer put his glass down. "That, I think, is for my daughter to say." He turned to Mary. "You're very quiet, my dear."

"You know my feelings, papa."

"What man ever knows a woman's feelings?" Blandy said smoothly.

"It occurs to me, Mary," Cranstoun said, "would you prefer to be married by your Uncle John?"

"Quite out of the question," Blandy said.

"Why sir?"

"Think of the horses! That steep drive up through the woods! A most inaccessible place, Fawley. I always tell my brother-in-law it's more suited to a monastic retreat from temptation than to a parish church." Mr. Blandy leaned back, sipping his wine comfortably. "A curious idea when you come to think of it—escape from the world. One wonders how many of its sins can be cured by a few men turning their backs on them! In the old days—the so-called Dark

Ages—there's no doubt the monastic houses did a fine work in keeping learning alive. Our culture might well have perished without them. But with schools and universities one sometimes wonders if the monks find their occupation gone. Unless, that is, we accept intercession as the supreme good. For myself, I should say each man must fight his own devil. A vicarious salvation is surely not acceptable to the Almighty?"

Cranstoun caught Mary's eye. As so often before, they saw their own urgent affairs drowning in a sea of philosophical generalisation. "I've no particular wish for Fawley, sir, if it's not to your liking. Henley would suit me well enough, if that pleased you? And you, Mary?"

"A fine old church," Blandy said. "Beautifully situated. Have you observed how the Church followed the river? Marlow, Bisham, Hurley, Medmenham, Remenham, Henley, Wargrave, Shiplake, Reading—one could go on indefinitely."

And you'd like to, you old fox, Cranstoun thought. "I believe, sir," he cut in, "that her mother would have been happy to think of Mary being wed in the same church as herself. It would be hard to find a happier augury."

"You speak as though no impediment exists," Blandy said ironically.

"By the time you see me again, sir, I'm confident none will."

"You're very sanguine. Youth! Ah, youth!"

"If a man's will is strong enough, all things are possible," Cranstoun declared.

Cranstoun was to take the morning coach for London. His bags were already in the hall and his cloak buckled, when a small crisis arose. He found, upon searching his pockets, that he had not left himself with enough money for the long journey to Scotland. "But I'll not take a penny from you, Mary. Not a penny more!"

Searching her bureau, she tried to press on him her two remaining guineas, but he remained adamant. "Not a groat. I've already trespassed on your generosity too much."

"But where will you get the money?"

"I'll find a way."

After a moment's thought, she cried, "Mother's watch!"

"What about it?"

"She would have been happy for you to have it, I'm sure!"

"Come to think of it, she did make some mention——" he said, without looking at her. "Naturally I refused."

"But if it was her wish——"

"Under no circumstances. It's a pretty bauble for a woman. What would I do with it?"

"I know it would have made her happy to think you'd accepted it in the end. You will? Say you will?"

"No."

"Please." Mary unpinned the watch, a delicate piece of blue enamel set with thirty pearls. "With her love. With my love!"

"You make it difficult for a man to refuse."

"Don't." She held out the watch to him. "Don't refuse!"

He took it in the palm of his hand and kissed it lightly. "My two dear loves!" he whispered, then he slipped it into his pocket.

Francis Blandy came from his study to see Cranstoun off, pressing on him at the last moment a silver flask. "I can assure you it's not empty!" he smiled. He was in the best of spirits. He could always find it easy to like his future son-in-law when he was going away.

Mary watched the coach ride the crest of the bridge and swing out of sight up the steep London road, then she wandered about the house, unable to settle to anything. In a few days, she told herself, the impact of him would have worn off, the spell abated. But as the days passed she found her restlessness increasing if anything. She was thankful for a respite from the demands his presence made upon her nerves, yet his going brought her no surcease.

Surrender had not given her the peace she sought. There was, she now saw, no peace. The emotional tension had heightened, not slackened. She had learned the lesson that every major step in life is a beginning, not an end.

Words—her own? some poet's?—came into her mind. "Judge no man happy till he dies." Ecstasy she had known, and a certain wild exultancy; but not happiness. Looking back on the past three years, she wondered if she had known a moment's happiness with Cranstoun, that happiness which comes quite at random in a country lane in June—larks singing above; in response to sunlit water glimpsed through trees, or to the soaring loveliness of boys' voices in a cathedral; that abstract, insubstantial, impersonal, almost baseless joy which is happiness at its most pure. This she had forfeited in exchange for—what? A thing wholly of the senses, obsessing, engrossing, but never satisfying, a thing so powerful that once its fire had entered into her, all lesser suns paled.

It was as though she had made a Faust-compact with the devil, only to find herself quibbling at the cost.

He put too much on her, burdened her with too many frailties. His love for her was never in doubt, but could she in her heart depend upon him in anything else? Every train of thought led her to an uncertain end. Desire fought a battle with upbringing that exhausted her physically and spiritually. She no longer felt candid in her dealings with people. Chance condemnations of domestic sluts, odd phrases in church stabbed her. Their love would have been a wonderful thing could it have held its head high, but close on the heels of ecstasy came the furtive return home by separate paths, the silent slipping of a bolt, the fear that Betty would see the night's mark on her waking face; Betty, with whose origins she now shared a dark link of knowledge.

The weeks passed with almost daily letters from Cranstoun, full of love for her, and she would feel ashamed of the complexities with which her woman's mind invested their relations. Then, the letter once read and locked away in her bureau, the doubts would return, memory fastening not on what he had said, but what he had omitted; the date of his return, the progress of his action; plans for their marriage.

She slept now in her mother's bed, vulnerable to any influence. She dreamed a lot. But only of Cranstoun. Waking, startled, she would tell herself that here was the message she waited for; a projection of her mother's wishes concerning them, but in her heart she would know the dreams for what they were—evidence only of Cranstoun's dominion over her senses.

CHAPTER SIX

THE FIRST week in September brought a brace of grouse from Cranstoun, together with a note to say he would be returning to Henley in a few days' time. Mr. Blandy was fond enough of game, but something in the note's insolent assumption of a waiting lodging in Henley sent him out to the coffee house, with consequent damage to health and humour.

To Mary, the confidence of the note was a good augury; although it made no mention of his action, it was surely the note of a man legally free to presume on his welcome? On the other hand, her father's attitude was disturbing. Cranstoun had, she was forced to admit, strained hospitality to the limits permitted a future son-in-law. Generous as he might be, with his patrimony sequestered to Anne Murray and her child, his half-pay did not leave him with the means to make any substantial return to her father. The thought that he might make further demands on her was an uneasy one. She snatched rather pathetically at every small gift of fish or fowl to bolster up her sagging pride. The least mercenary or ambitious of women, there was at times something humiliating about her penniless lover that all the aristocratic connections in Scotland could not counter.

In this, as in much else, she had learned to accept, to compromise, stilling the small voice of disillusion with the memory of a few red roses filched from an uncle's garden. She came to see all life as a compromise; a shedding of dreams, of ideals, of hopes, of certainties; a choice between the nothing of integrity and the tarnished gifts of a lowered standard.

My lover, she told herself, her senses awaking. Was that all he was to be, a lover—no more, no less; compound of hands and eyes and lips and a limitless demanding fund of passion?

Had she, with her reading, her critical detachment, come to him too late for perfect happiness? Would love at twenty have been a simpler thing than it was at thirty?

Preparing the hall chamber which her father—with a contemptuous "Since the fellow's coming, he might as well have the best room"—had decided was to be Cranstoun's, she felt curiously cold and detached, yet when, an hour later, he held her in his arms, all doubt was at an end and she had surrendered herself completely to that joy which his presence alone could bring.

Dinner was not an easy meal. Cranstoun's spirits were pitched a little too high, Mr. Blandy's eyes and ears a shade too keen. When the meal was over, the two men retired to the coffee house, returning later.

It was not until the next afternoon that Mary was alone with Cranstoun, and then only on the steep London road, with countless opportunities for the making of diversions.

"Cranstoun," she said tentatively.

"My sweet?"

"The Courts——"

"Later. Let's save our breath for the climb for the moment."

"But I've waited all these weeks——"

"Now, Dandy, now! That's no rabbit on the bank. That's a stoat, a little foxy-faced miniver!"

"Your letters told me nothing."

"All in the proper place at the proper time. That chalk-cliff yonder—I've seen it often from the coach. Is it a fault, or a quarry?"

"A quarry. The parishioners of Remenham have the right to take what chalk they need."

"And, having taken chalk, what can they do with it?

Write 'Death to the Elector of Hanover' on walls?" he laughed.

She paused. "Please tell me. No matter what your news is, I must know it."

"I've no news."

"None?"

"Not as news goes."

"But your action was heard?"

"Heard, yes. But no decision reached. Now, Dandy, you'll hang yourself on that cord of yours if you spin round like a whirligig!"

"Cranstoun!" she said sharply.

"Yes, miss?"

"Will you answer me?"

"I thought I had."

"What was the result?"

"You, a lawyer's daughter, expect results so soon?"

"Soon! It's months."

"Seven weeks to be exact."

"Well?"

"Six months passed before any ruling emerged from my previous encounter with our Scottish Law."

"You mean there's no decision yet?"

"Now should I have kept you in suspense if there had been? Should I—I ask you—be panting up White Hill were I free to be down in the town engaging choristers and putting up banns?"

"No. But suppose you're not free?"

"Would you find me in such high spirits?" he demanded bluffly.

"Who am I to know?"

"Ah, Mary, Mary!" Glancing round, he gave her a little kiss.

A token payment, she told herself helplessly, an earnest of more to come. All there was to come; the single gift, the single good; all she could hope from her lover.

The tale of the law's delay was later retold to Mr. Blandy with less provocativeness. Mary watched her father's face curiously. She had wondered before; now there was no doubt: he was glad. While the possibility of favourable news had existed, anxiety had pinched the corners of his lips, but with news of the indefinite postponement of her marriage, all his geniality returned and a fresh bottle of Burgundy was brought up from the cellars.

Cranstoun himself skated easily enough over the delay, and for a few weeks no crisis arose between them. The golden days of early autumn set their own pace and their love slipped into a mellow, mindless contentment which was as near peace as such love as theirs could be. No questions were asked, no answers volunteered. Francis Blandy's attitude remained the only uncertain factor. His relations with Cranstoun oscillated between the over-genial commerce of their early days and a new-found scepticism that brought a note of ironic humour to his comments on the Scot's more florid tales.

The intimacy of the household was frequently diluted by guests. Lavinia Pocock had caught a fever in Venice and remained in town, together with her husband, but there were other, less vivid figures to fill their places at table: the Reverend John Stevens, Mrs. Mounteney, and the Toms—Cawley and Staverton.

The first ripple in the calm was entirely, almost wantonly, of Cranstoun's making. At the time the incident made little impression on Mary, but later, taken in conjunction with others, the memory of it was disturbing.

It was their custom to drink tea in the parlour each evening. On one occasion Mr. Blandy had not joined them by the time Susannah brought in the tray. When she had gone, Cranstoun—with an absurd little air of mystery—had taken out a white packet.

"What have you got there?" Mary asked.

"A love potion!" he teased. To her surprise he tipped a little of the powder into the large Rockingham cup that was special to Mr. Blandy. "Let's see if this will make the old gentleman more fond of me!"

"Cranstoun! No!"

He kissed the top of her head gaily. "I insist. He's not said a civil thing to me this se'nnight!"

"He's been dyspeptic!"

"Exactly. Here's the cure!"

"But what is it?"

"A harmless enough concoction, but, we hope, effective!"

"Let me taste it!"

"Are you in need of a philtre, miss?"

"An antidote, if anything!" she laughed. She sniffed a little of the powder. It was white and quite without scent. "We must tell him first."

"Heavens, no! The essence of the cure is that he should be in the dark."

"Why?"

"If we tell him what we expect of the powder, he'll imagine a cure and nothing will be proved!"

"So you've turned apothecary now! Lord, what a man!"

Mr. Blandy drank his tea without comment and, to Cranstoun's delight, seemed in excellent spirits for the rest of the evening. The experiment was not, to Mary's knowledge, repeated.

The next episode was of a more perplexing kind. Mary had been aware of Cranstoun's air of excitement during breakfast one morning, but it was not until her father had left them that he spoke. Closing the door carefully, he drew a chair up to her side. "Did you know this house of yours is haunted?"

"Really?"

"It is. I swear it. Did you hear nothing in the night?"

"No."

"Well, I did. Heard, and saw. Well? You don't appear very interested!"

"Nothing has ever happened in this house. Nothing."

"Until now."

"Not——?"

"Your mother? No, my dear."

"What, then?"

"Your father."
"My—father!"
"I think so."
"But——"
"It's just occurred to me. Has he ever walked in his sleep?"
"Never to my knowledge."
"You would have known."
"How did he look?"
"Much as he looks by day."
"How dressed?"
"A nightshirt, slippers—a long white stocking cap with a tassel."
She stared at him. "That is how he sleeps. Tell me more clearly what you saw."
"I'd been asleep some hours, I suppose. When next I heard the clock it was striking the hour of three; anyway, I woke suddenly. It was quite light——"
"The moon shines full into that room."
"He was standing in the doorway."
"What did you do?"
"What any sentry would have done. Challenged him."
"What happened then?"
"He vanished."
"How—vanished?"
He shrugged. "He was there. Then he was gone."
"Was the door closed?"
"Who can say? The next thing I knew the clock was striking eight."
"I—see." Mary paused. "You don't think——"
"Yes?"
"You're sure it was an apparition and not——"
"—your father himself?" She nodded. "Why should he come to my room?"
She met his eyes. "I've no need to tell you."
"God knows he's got no cause for suspicion!" Cranstoun cried bitterly. His respect for a sensibility that denied him so

much as a kiss under the parental roof was beginning to wear a little thin.

"He watches me," she said sombrely. "Watches both of us."

"He loves you." Cranstoun spoke slowly. "To excess."

She started faintly. "What makes you say that?"

"A lover knows love when he sees it." His expression changed. "Aren't you just a little—afraid?"

"Afraid?" Her heart began to beat quickly.

"I too have watched." He ran his hand gently down her arm. "Aren't there times when you feel yourself—caught in the web of such a love—suffocated—stifled by it?" When she did not reply, he added, "I see there are."

She dropped her eyes, drawing away from him. "Suppose there are? What then?" she asked harshly.

There was a curious note in his voice as he answered: "I don't somehow think it will arise. The—choice for you."

"Why not?"

"This—apparition or dream or vision of mine—surely you've read it?"

"How—read it?"

"As a portent."

"Of what?" she faltered.

"You know without my putting it into words, my dear."

There were other diversions.

Subtly, by a word here, a whisper there, Cranstoun began to weave a spell of superstition among the servants. Why? Mary wondered uneasily. No matter how deep-rooted his own belief in the occult might be, there seemed no possible justification for subverting the ignorant, always only too impressionable. The house was an old one, rambling and dark; a rat in the wainscoting, the straining of old timbers, a trick of moonlight, a snatch of music on the night air from a ball at the Catherine Wheel, and a whole cycle of legends could be built up. Even Ned Hearne mentioned a rumour of 'unearthly' music that was going the rounds. "The

Captain's a very superstitious gentleman, isn't he, miss? I mean, for one who's been in the wars, that is."

Once she had caught Cranstoun in the yard with the Wargrave Fool. Jack Fletcher was showing him a ferret, its ruby-bright eyes peeping out of his poacher's pocket. She caught the word 'familiar'. Her appearance silenced them both, and Jack slipped easily into one of his chaotic sermons, mimicking the Rector of Henley in what seemed to be a parody of the marriage service. He made no attempt to show her the little animal. Cranstoun was unmistakably excited.

Cranstoun's was, she knew, a nature incapable of inaction; even a state of bliss would in time pall on him. He had been accustomed to a life of excitement, and the daily round of a country town provided little outlet for his restless energies. For a time the risks attached to their love affair had, she believed, contented him. Now, it seemed, he must find other waters to trouble. On the face of it, peopling her home with ghosts appeared a rather puerile exercise for such a man. But was it puerile? Was it merely a diversion? Or could it be that he genuinely believed in his apparitions and potions and ghostly sarabands?

And what of herself? If he was overplaying a little, was she not herself underplaying? Was she in her heart so sceptical, or could it be that her superciliousness was a defence raised against a thing in which she more than half believed?

CHAPTER SEVEN

THE WORK-ROOM was at the top of the house, with a dormer window looking down on the long range of red roofs of the White Hart. The room was very hot in summer and very cold in winter, but the seasons seemed to have little effect on the quality of Mrs. Deane's needlework; the bed-linen and the table-linen, Mary's cambric petticoats, Mr. Blandy's silk shirts, the maid's aprons, all were paid the tribute of almost invisible stitchery. Sometimes, as a diversion, the woman would make a cap for Mary, or continue the set of chair seats started by her mother; humming softly at her work, straining her excellent sight, Mrs. Deane asked nothing better than the opportunity to express her one talent.

It was quiet up here under the eaves, a refuge from the coarse talk and steamy heat of the kitchen. Mrs. Deane was a lady's maid, in her element among ladies; her memories were of balls and garden parties by proxy, visits to Culham and Turville, seasons in Bath and town. Mary was a good mistress, unexacting and courteous, but she could not feel for her the affection her gay little mother had inspired. Also, Mrs. Deane was forced to admit, life had been very dull since Mrs. Blandy's death. It was curious a young woman should have so few desires; Mrs. Blandy had been fond of change right to the end. If only Lady Cranstoun would invite Miss to Scotland, or the Captain propose a trip to town! How she would revel in the preparations, the sewing, the packing, the scrutiny of fashion-plates. But no: Henley it was and, it seemed, Henley it was going to be to the end of time. For change, there were Mr. Cranstoun's things to mend in addition to the family's; shirts torn by impatient arms, unmatchable buttons lost from embroidered waistcoats, lace handkerchiefs burned by ash from his pipe, buckles adrift from shoes kicked off under the bed. A wild, reckless man; she had never fallen victim to his charm. Miss could, she thought, have done better for herself.

The hall chamber was, as usual, in a state of disorder. Cranstoun never troubled to put out the things in need of mending and Mary had got into the habit of searching among the motley in chest and cupboard, on chairs and under chairs, draped over the bed or tossed in a corner. She went methodically through his possessions. A service she had always done for her father, its intimacy made no particular impression on her, and with so careless a man she had no sense of prying.

Searching among the linen in the press, a note fell to the floor, a scrap of paper covered with sprawling handwriting. Picking it up to return it to its place, a word caught her eye.

She sat back on the floor, the strength draining from her limbs. Her hand was trembling so violently that she could scarcely read.

The address at the head of the letter at once struck a familiar chord; it was one to which earlier in the year she had sent the fifteen guineas. The date—17th October 1750—was of four days ago.

The note was short enough, but it lacked nothing. In a few lines, lewd in their intimacy, it told her all she needed to know. The words danced in front of her eyes, and the window seemed to vibrate in intolerable lightness. She leaned back weakly against the press. She was not angry. Tears had never been further from her eyes.

This is the end she told herself; this is how it is to end. Humiliation overwhelmed her, a sense of degradation beyond anything she had ever conceived, and for a moment she thought she was going to vomit. Her brain was numbed, a machine to repeat 'This is the end, this is the end, this is the end,' insensately. She had no idea what she was going to do. The note had dropped from her fingers as though it carried a contagion, and she stared at the neat pile she had made of Cranstoun's possessions. They, too, were unclean. There was nothing among them that was not familiar to this Covent Garden drab; these same possessions had littered *her* room; an element of her hung about them still in all the horror of intimacy bought and paid for. Bought and paid for at the rate of fifteen guineas for—how long? Sordid images crowded her mind.

For the moment self-disgust overwhelmed her. I—where am I better that this creature? What has she given that I have not gladly, eagerly, hungrily given, panting like a spaniel bitch! Memory of her own emotion shocked her more profoundly than that of surrender; it was not in the giving that the shame lay, but in the taking.

A desire to plunge into the river, cold and swift and cleansing, possessed her.

I can't face him, she thought, can't look at his hands, his lips, see his eyes on my body, full of knowledge.

Through the singing of her ears, she was aware of footsteps on the landing outside. His tread had always been soft. As the latch was raised, she struggled to her feet, swaying a little.

"Hello, sweet!" he cried. Pausing in the doorway, his gay smile did not flicker, but he sensed at once that something was wrong. "Why so pale? Another ghost?"

She drew back, steadying herself against the wall.

"Well, what is it? Has the spectre robbed you of speech?" He was still smiling, but his voice had a hollow note.

"Stand away from the door," she whispered. He stepped back. She moved swiftly across the room; as she passed him he caught her wrist and pulled her towards him. She cried out and sprang free. Slipping in front of her, he closed the door. She stood in panic, shudders running over her body.

"Shh! Quiet, Mary. Someone will hear you."

"Let me go."

"Not till you tell me what's wrong."

"Let me go."

"No, Mary." He leaned against the door. "What's happened?"

"There—on the floor."

He glanced down at the note, then swung across the room and picked it up. "Oh—that!" he said smoothly. "Imagine my keeping such trash!" He turned to her. "Why, Mary, you didn't let this rigmarole upset you? I own it's a thought coarse for your eyes, but——"

"—but good enough for yours. All you're fit for."

"You—you surely don't think——"

"Think what?"

"That there's anything—personal about this?"

"Go on. See if your wits are quick enough this time."

He glanced down at the note. "Frankly, I've scarce read the thing. Poor creature! One certainly encounters all sorts in lodgings."

"Go on."

"A chance meeting on the stairs now and then. At risk of immodesty, I must be frank. I'm afraid the trollop was rather taken with me. Admittedly the language in which she expresses her sentiments is not of the nicest——"

"Is that the best you can do?" she said contemptuously.

"The truth, no more, no less."

"Read the note again."

He looked at her sharply. "By George, Mary, I'd no idea you could be such a fury!"

"Read it again. Carefully."

As he read the letter, his expression changed.

"There's no argument, is there?" she demanded inexorably.

Screwing the note tightly, he tossed it on the fire. His hands dropped to his sides. "I'm sorry," he said with deep sincerity.

"To degrade me so," she whispered.

"Degrade you?"

"To condemn me to share——"

He winced. "How dare you say that!"

"I—dare!"

"Yes. How dare you compare a man's random wenching with what I've given you!"

"What have you given me that this whore hasn't had?"

"Love."

The word hung in the room for a moment, silencing them, then Mary hurried on. "Your love! A thing wholly of the senses, something countless women have enjoyed, women everywhere, of every class——"

"I won't listen to you. I won't have you drag our love in the kennels with your jealous woman's tongue."

"Jealous! God in heaven! You think I'm jealous of the nights you spend in the bagnios—jealous of the bastards you bring into the world——"

Sharp as a whip, his hand flickered across her face. "Quiet. Quiet, I tell you." She gasped and drew away from him. "You don't know what you're saying—you don't know what you're doing to me. What do you think it is for me, this wretched half-life of ours? Eyes on us all the time, never alone save for some furtive encounter. Do you think it's only on these terms I want you? If there's never to be the chance of anything better, yes. Yes, Mary, on any terms. I love you too much to despise the poorest crumb of happiness a grudging destiny lets fall. But for you! Don't you think it's torture to me to see our love condemned to secrecy and lying? D'you think I don't want you to be able to hold your head high? Can't you guess how much I want a home for you and a free honourable life at your side? Don't you know it's my dearest wish to hear you called by my name? Mary Cranstoun . . ." He repeated it softly, "Mary Cranstoun . . . You accuse me of betraying you. My poor Mary, how little you know of men for all your intelligence! These women are a thing apart, forgotten as soon as seen, a necessary evil, no more. Some men drink, some game, some drab. It's in a man's nature. But you—you I worship with every breath of my body. Longing for you consumes me every moment we're apart. Even now, when you're standing in judgment over me, I'd not have you other than as you are. Your very anger is dear to me. Believe me—you must believe me, Mary. Never from the moment I saw you standing there under the magnolia tree have I wavered in my feelings for an instant. Forgive me. Say you forgive me."

"Don't touch me."

"Must I go on my knees?"

"Don't touch me. Your touch is horrible—contaminated!"

"For God's sake!"

"Horrible—horrible!"

"But after all I've said——"

"Words, words! You've broken my life with your words! Drugged my mind as you've drugged my senses——"

"And shall again. And shall again, Mary!"

"Never. Never again."

"Yes—yes!"

"Never. This is the end."

"You don't mean that. You're only saying it to punish me. Tell me what I must do. Anything you ask."

"There's nothing you can do. Nothing more you can say——" Her voice died away and for a moment she thought she was going to faint. "This is—the end."

Cranstoun stared at her, conscious at last that she had gone beyond his reach. Until now his feelings, though genuine enough, had been facile, the easily-aroused emotion of an undisciplined nature. He had not for an instant been seriously alarmed. Even while most distressed, half his mind had stood outside, telling him this scene would end as so many before it, in a renewed cycle of passion. But now something in her—cold, withdrawn, finely-poised on the brink of faintness—frightened him. "Mary——" he faltered.

"This time you've gone too far."

"But—you can't mean what you say. Never—never to see you again, to match my wits with yours. Never again to feel the touch of your hands, the touch of your lips—the coolness of your hair." Tears sprang to his eyes and his voice grew thin. "Is this what you mean? Answer me, for God's sake. Is it?"

"Yes."

He gave a cry and flung himself down on the bed. The sight of his hysteria, the insensate rocking of his body and the clutch of his fingers on the pillows, the ignominious sight of a man in tears, filled her with a kind of panic. "Stop it!" she demanded. "Stop it! I can't stand it. Do you hear? I can't stand it. Stop it! Cranstoun—stop it!"

He dragged himself from the bed and dropped to his knees, burying his face in her petticoats. "Mary—forgive me," he sobbed, his face streaked with tears, his hair rough above his damp forehead. "I won't be answerable for my actions. You mustn't forsake me. You cannot. You're my bride—my wife. All the hope of happiness I have in this world or of salvation in the next." He snatched at her hands, kissing them, blundering after her on his knees as she tried to move away from him.

She looked wildly round, resisting the answering hysteria that welled up in her. "Let me go. Let go my knees. For pity's sake stop crying—it's hideous—hideous—Cranstoun!" She caught his head in her hands and tried to drag him away.

Through hysteria, through panic, through disgust and horror and contempt for his abject figure, her hands recalled his hair, crisp to her touch, and instinct with vitality. His head was warm beneath her fingers, and the eyes that sought hers, wet and swollen, yet were a wild blue, the lips—bitten to master their sobbing—lips whose touch was all she had known of love.

Rising uncertainly to his feet, her hands still clasping his head, Cranstoun knew with a moment's exultancy that the tide of battle had turned.

In the fusion of her mouth with his, she thought: This is the end.

CHAPTER EIGHT

THERE was nothing more to be resisted. She had tolerated everything, surrendered every principle, accepted every deceit, every betrayal. She no longer doubted that he was married to Anne Murray; she had condoned not only Miss Capel and her child, but his concealment of them; she had given him money; she had allowed him to involve her in superstitions alien to her; she had surrendered to him heart and mind and body and spirit with undemanding generosity. Each gesture had stripped her of a little more of her integrity, weakened her resistance to him until she was ready for the ultimate depth of degradation: the realisation that his dominion over her senses was stronger than pride, than shame, decency or self-respect. The hysterical wretch sobbing at her feet had filled her with a repugnance bordering on nausea, yet at the touch of his hand she had known herself ready to take him back on any terms.

She was not unhappy; it was simply that life now was lived on a lower plane. She no longer regarded Littleton's abject worship with contemptuous pity, and when her father implicitly criticised Betty Binfield, she diverted the talk from a path that might lead to Cranstoun. She had no real cause for suspicion, yet, she asked herself, why not? Why not with her own domestics under her own roof? And suppose she once again found him out; what then? He knew her now, knew he had only to touch her.

She began to walk again in the early morning, through the sad autumn countryside. She tried prayer; lay awake in her mother's bed seeking some guidance from that innocuous spirit; everything failed her. He had brought her low. But he remained. And here she touched bottom; Cranstoun remained. He was there for the taking. No sense of disgust could rob her of the ecstasy she could still find with him. In stripping her of all the things that had gone to make up her self-respect, he had bound her more completely to himself.

With heightened sensibility, she was aware of a shifting of relationships between Cranstoun and her father; on the one side, an anxiety to please, on the other a slackening of pretence. Most of the servants, she knew, sided with their master. Meals were uneasy, poised always on the edge of unpleasantness.

One morning at breakfast, after what seemed to her an uncomfortable silence, Cranstoun, with a burst of charm, said: "Did you know, sir, that this house of yours is haunted?"

"Indeed, Mr. Cranstoun? If by that you mean that the hall chamber has been occupied now for a considerable—I might even say, an unconscionable time, then I agree heartily. My house *is* haunted."

Mary dropped her eyes, but Cranstoun blundered on. "Not only the hall chamber, sir. The corridors, and, indeed, the fabric of the house itself. Miss Mary will abet me."

"What nonsense is this? I thought you'd more sense, Mary, than to prattle of things fit only for the lower orders."

"Why, sir, we've compared notes many times, have we not, Mary?"

"We've talked, yes. But only of the things you insist *you've* heard."

"Don't tell me I'm the only psychic member of the household? You must all be very heavy sleepers if you didn't hear the music in the night."

"What sort of music, Cranstoun? Scotch music?" Mr. Blandy said derisively, pushing back his chair.

"You don't believe me, sir?"

"I don't doubt you thought you heard music. Time must hang very heavy on your hands in this quiet household of mine." The lawyer paused in the doorway. "I suppose a little music—even spectral music—would enliven so protracted a stay!"

Even a month ago this could not have happened, Mary thought, wearily rising from the table. "I must see to my chores," she said dully.

Cranstoun was staring out of the window. In the morning mist he could scarcely see the houses opposite. "Shall I give Dandy his airing?"

"If you will."

"You've no wish to come?"

"It's my day for counting linen."

"As you like."

She closed the door quietly. The mist had seeped into the house and no sounds came from the deserted street outside. Calling to Susannah, she went slowly up to the landing and opened the linen press. Susannah waited in silence while she counted out the bed linen; fine, lavender-scented, monogrammed by Mrs. Deane.

"Miss?"

"Yes?"

"There's something I think you should be told."

"Three, four—how many pillow-slips have you there?"

"Two, miss. It's about Mr. Cranstoun. Has he said anything to you about——"

"—music and apparitions?"
"He has, then."
"Yes, Sukey, he has."
"And to the master?"
"Yes."
"How did master take it?"
"With derision."
"Quite right, too. I only wish he'd have a talk to them in the kitchen."
"Who?"
"Harman and Mary Banks—Dame Emmet. Jack Fletcher, too. Him, particularly. Starting to gossip outside. You'll pardon me, Miss Mary, I've got to speak my mind. I've been with your father since before you was born. He's a proud man, always held an honourable position in the town. There's few gentlemen in Henley wouldn't be glad to visit Mr. Blandy in his home. There's never been a breath, not so much as a breath of gossip till this fellow came sponging——"
"Susan!"
"I'm sorry, miss, but there it is and the sooner you know the better. Everybody else does. Not content with starting the tongues wagging whether he's going to marry you or not, he must needs spread it about that Mr. Blandy lives in a haunted house!" The old woman held the linen tightly, her voice shaking. "No one could ask a better master than I've had, and if you take it amiss me speaking out, I can't help it!"
Mary closed the press carefully.
"Are you angry with me, miss?"
Mary absently pressed her arm. "As well be angry with a good housedog, Sukey."
The rest of the morning passed in small duties: filling the caddy with her father's favourite Hyson, dusting her room, making out a list for the grocers and checking the tradesmen's books.
Cranstoun stayed out all the morning, returning for the midday meal with a few bronze chrysanthemums from his uncle's hothouse. He was at his most charming, playing subtly on

the chord of Mr. Blandy's snobbery. "My uncle was wonder
ing if you and Miss Mary would care to drink a dish of te
with him some evening, sir?"

"That's very civil of Lord Mark, very civil indeed."

"He tells me my cousin Caroline—Lady Ailesbury, that is—has great plans for Park Place."

"To judge from the land she's buying, I can well believe it.'

"Not content with a rustic bridge to carry the Wargrav road, Grecian ruins, and caves cut from the chalk-hill, sh must needs follow Horry Walpole's taste for the Gothic an build a little tea-pavilion, all cloisters and flummery!"

"Milady Ailesbury is as energetic as she is beautiful, i seems," Blandy said. "A happy dispensation that. Mr. Con-way should be in all ways worthy of her."

"Were you ever up at Park Place, sir?"

"Only in my professional capacity. In His Royal Highness' day."

"We must change all that! If Cousin Caro cannot be per-suaded to invite my future father-in-law——"

"Aren't you being a little precipitate?"

"In what, sir?"

"Or have you on the instant received news of your divorce?"

Cranstoun rose abruptly. "If you consider my position equivocal, you've only to say so."

"Isn't—pique a rather shallow emotion in the circum-stances?"

Neither Mary nor Cranstoun moved until they heard the sound of the study door closing.

Mary sat staring into the fire, her eyes filled with tears, her back aching with weariness. Seldom had she felt so des-pondent. Cranstoun—her father—herself, three people bound inescapably by ties of love, three people in closest daily contact; each alone, isolated in dull-eyed mistrust.

"Mary." Cranstoun was standing over her.

"Yes?" She did not look up.

He touched her hair with infinite tenderness. "Nothing is worth your tears." She leaned her head against his hand.

"My dear——" He dropped to his knees. "What has gone wrong?"

"With us?"

He nodded. "Where has it gone, our delight in every moment together?" He took her face in his hands and very gently dried her tears.

"Everything seems so sad and sere and worn," she said thinly, "as though we're grown old."

"Grown old in waiting."

"Is that it?"

"Oh, Mary—my own sweet Mary." Resting his head against hers, he kissed her wet cheeks and swollen eyelids. "We're asking so little of life, you and I. Only the right to love, proudly and freely, the right fate concedes the humblest ploughman, the very scavenger in the kennel! Forgive me, my dear. Forgive all my failings and my follies and remember only that I love you. With all my heart."

"Perhaps the fault has been in me. I don't know. There's so much darkness in a woman's mind; fear and suspicion and doubt. When mama was alive—her goodness and her innate happiness, the happiness of a bird, innocent and unthinking——"

"If——"

"Yes?"

"Mary." He drew a little away from her. "It seems to me we've reached a crisis in our lives."

"You feel it too?"

"Yes. Deeply. Suppose—how can I make you understand? The thought's only just come to me. Could it be that the power of thought is strong enough—the need imperative enough—the desire for guidance intense enough. Is it possible that by reaching out, reaching up—through the veils and levels of existence—you could——"

"Yes?" she said quickly.

"—summon her."

"You *do* believe!"

"I was never sure till now. When you mentioned her

name, it was as though some emanation—an aura of peacefulness——"

"But I've tried. Even these past few weeks. Night after night, lying there——"

"But not in such need of help as now." He caught her hands. "She loved you, Mary. You were so strangely close to one another. If it were ever possible for the dead to return, surely it is now?"

"I wonder," she said, in awe.

"You're not afraid?"

"Of that quiet spirit?"

"What if——"

"Go on. Tell me what's in your mind."

"I think she loved me too—as a son."

"She did, my dear. I know that."

"Her last thought was for us. Together."

"Yes."

"Suppose we were to call on her—not you alone, but—as she would have wished. Together."

CHAPTER NINE

WITH NIGHT the fog became impenetrable. Absorbing the clock tower, it clung in rags to the tombstones that stood at random among the yews as though thrown up by some subterranean disturbance. The shutters of the almshouses were fast closed against the fog, against the tombstones and the sad dark yews and the owls and the hibernating bats. The night-watchman, coughing on his rounds, moved warily, his lantern no more than a glow-worm's effulgence in the night. Silence came down on the town like a pall; the very rats in the cellars were stilled.

'On such a night as this——' Mary thought, lying, her faculties acutely awake, on her mother's bed. The fire glowed and flickered, throwing monstrous shadows among the timbers above her head. She could hear the level breathing of Mrs. Deane, already asleep in her chair, and the little eager yaps of Dandy, deeply involved in a dream-chase.

The clock started to strike the hour of eleven; the very chimes were muffled and laboured. Cranstoun would not be coming yet. He was to wait till the house was asleep.

She lay outside the coverlet, shoes and corselet already uncomfortably tight. She sought to empty her mind of thought, leaving a vacuum for the forces of the night to fill. She surrendered herself completely to belief in the possibility of miracles, and a peace she had not known since her mother's death began to flow over her.

When, shortly after midnight, Cranstoun came, she saw that he, too, was in a state of quiet exaltation. Mrs. Deane awoke and for a few minutes the three spoke in whispers, then Cranstoun drew a chair up beside the bed and sat down, taking Mary's hand in his. Neither spoke, yet each was aware that a new element had entered their relationship; a tranquillity, a spiritual nearness that had been absent before. The frets and follies of the past slipped away and Mary knew that here, without any further manifestation, was the answer they had been seeking; this unquestioning, undemanding happiness in each other's presence, this affinity that nothing could take from them.

Hovering on the borderland of sleep, she was aware that Cranstoun's head had dropped to the pillow at her side. Should they keep awake? she wondered. Or should they surrender themselves wholly to the peace of the hour?

The fog had penetrated the curtains and it seemed to her that the room, the house, the very town itself was suspended in cloud; a nebula. The fog had set it free of the world.

Free of the world, she thought. And slept.

Hands were drumming on the door, insistent, impatient.

She woke confused, her ears singing. Cranstoun sat up abruptly and Dandy gave a single short bark.

"Open the door!"

She struggled off the bed, her heart racing. Cranstoun sprang to his feet, gripping her hand. Terror silenced them.

"Open the door, Mary. Open the door, I say!"

There was no mistaking the voice, no mistaking its anger.

Mary stifled a cry and Cranstoun made a swift panic movement in the direction of the dressing-room. She clutched his arm. "No——" she whispered breathlessly. Fuddled with sleep he looked wildly round.

The little dog began to bark, bouncing against the door on which a fist was banging frantically. Mrs. Deane rose giddily to her feet, and all the time Blandy's voice demanded admittance.

"Coming, sir," the maid said, automatically, moving without thought to the heavy bolt.

"God!" Cranstoun whispered, as the door swung open.

Francis Blandy stood in the doorway, a candle held above the level of his head. He was flushed and plethoric. In a single glance his eyes recorded the entire picture; a conversation-piece of guilt: the dim room, the maid, dazed with sleep, the face of his daughter, white and startled in its setting of loose dark hair, the man—the lover, arrested in the motion of flight.

For a moment the lawyer faltered. "As I thought!" Closing the door with a clumsy hand he stared in horror from one to another.

Cranstoun was the first to recover his wits, crying, lamely: "I can explain everything, sir."

"I don't doubt it, Mr. Cranstoun, I don't doubt it. Years of experience in similar situations must have brought your explanations to perfection!"

"As I've a soul to be saved, I was never in a situation like this before—sitting up with two women waiting for the spectral visitation of a third!"

"More witchcraft?" Blandy jeered bitterly.

"Certainly."

"It's true what he says, sir," Mrs. Deane cut in. "We was waiting, all of us."

"What for? Bagpipes?"

"Please, father—I beg you. This is too sacred for mockery."

"Sacred! How dare you use such a word! Lie as you please, Mary, but at least don't descend to blasphemy."

"I was never more reverent."

"Hear her, sir, please. Miss feels it deeply. We all do. There's not one of us didn't love madam——"

"My—wife! You bring her into this—invoke her as—as a chaperon!"

"I swear to you by God, sir, on my honour as a soldier, that we're speaking no more than the truth. I—I've no wish to mention such matters—but Mary, perhaps you——?"

Mary spoke very quietly. "I've lain in mother's bed—hoping for guidance—that perhaps, if my wish was powerful enough, she might reach out to me—from the world beyond this one."

"And what, then, has Mr. Cranstoun to do with it?"

"Mama loved him—it was her wish——"

"I don't need to be reminded of her wishes. All I ask of you, Mary—if you've a remnant of sensibility—that you will keep your mother's name out of this."

"But she's the core and heart of it—the reason for our being here."

"I discover you in circumstances obvious to even the dullest of minds and in defence you trump up superstitious lies that violate every instinct of decency!"

"Father! That's not true! I insist you accept my story!"

"You—insist!" Blandy put the candle down. His face was bloated and dark. "You, Mary, with your education, your upbringing, your home. With the example of your mother, with the teachings of the church to guide you and myself to advise! Surrounded by affection, born into an honoured family, sheltered and indulged in every way—God give me patience, for I have none! The very trulls would have more pride, more dignity, more decency than to indulge their lusts under their own parent's roof!" Mary cried out, but Blandy hurried on, anger tightening its grip on him, blinding and deafening him, numbing his reason. "You're no better than an animal, a bitch or a doe or a cat howling on a roof-top! I've caught you this time—but how many times have you escaped? Answer me that! No wonder this man presumes so much in my home! He knows himself to possess its greatest treasure! No wonder his stay has been protracted beyond all conventional limits! No wonder he is in no hurry to marry you!"

"God in heaven!" Cranstoun cried out. "Do you think I'd not have made Mary my wife before now if the courts hadn't decided against me——" He stopped dead.

"What—what did you say?" Blandy asked softly.

Cranstoun floundered. "My tongue ran away with me——"

Mary groped for the bedpost, swaying uncertainly.

"What did you say?" Blandy asked. His voice was a whisper, icy, inexorable. "Repeat what you said, sir. Repeat what you said."

Cranstoun hesitated a moment, then he squared his shoulders, met the older man's eyes. "Very good, sir. You shall have the truth. When my action came up for hearing, judgment was not deferred." His voice dropped. "The case went against me."

Mary sank on to the bed. There was no sound but the dripping of tallow from a guttering candle and the sigh of a log, collapsing among ashes.

"I've nothing to say. No plea to make, no excuses." Cranstoun's shoulders sagged, his arms swung limply at his sides. "I lied. Once more. Lied to you again, Mary. It's open to me to appeal to a higher Court but"—he shrugged desperately—"God knows if things will go any better there. I came back to you under a false flag. Knowing I was not free, knowing I had no right to—to waste any more of your time."

Mary's head slumped forward on to her hands and she began to rock to and fro, moaning.

"The final betrayal," Blandy said.

"Say what you will, sir. I'd almost welcome your condemnation. I've lived so long now under the scourge of self-contempt. I want you to believe one thing, sir. I've wished you well. I've known my only real happiness under your roof, and God is my witness that I have most truly loved Mary." Mastering his emotion, he went on: "It seems it was my doom to bring suffering to you both that I'd have given my life to save you. There's nothing to be said for me. I'm not asking your pardon. But just one thing—a single request. I ask you to accept my word for what took place in this room tonight. For Mary's sake. It's a question of the highest principle. Her respect for the integrity of your home is as great as your own. I leave in the morning. I shall, I know, never again set foot on your step—I hope in all sincerity that with time, anger and bitterness will be spent—that you and Mary can return to the old candour and companionship so dear to you both." For a moment his voice faltered. "Believe me, sir, I envy you with all my heart. If fate had willed it I could have been the happiest man on earth. But it seems it was not to be." He turned, taking a step towards Mary. "Don't think too ill of me, my dear—my very dear. Try only to remember—my love for you——" His voice broke, and turning on his heel, he blundered out of the room.

PART FIVE 1751

CHAPTER ONE

WINTER came to the house in Hart Street, the winter of age, of loss of expectancy. No sap of hope rose.

The surface pattern of life was unchanged; nothing now could happen to alter it, this daily existence of an old man, an old maid. For Mary, as for her father, the days were drawing in. The shadows were lengthening and the robin's song was a song out of season, infinitely nostalgic.

The fires glowed cheerfully as before, mahogany and silver were as bright, beds as soft, the table as good. Now and then guests came, but muted: two uncles uneasily skirting awkward topics, two baffled old friends and a godmother all unexpressed sympathy.

Lavinia Pocock was dead, she who had been the most fully alive of them all. The little dog was growing old—suddenly, unmistakably.

It seemed to Mary that age had swept over her home like a scythe. In this she was not alone. Mr. Blandy's friends, the faithful Toms, tentatively mentioned it to her: "Being with him all the time it may not strike you so forcibly as it does an outsider, but I confess to the feeling that—— But there, I musn't distress a daughter."

"Please go on, Mr. Cawley."

"I've had the feeling for some time that my old friend was—well, failing."

"Failing!"

"Too strong a word, no doubt. Anxiety robs us of tact. But tell me, Mary, in confidence, has he seen a doctor lately?"

"Mr. Norton attended him just before Christmas. A heavy cold, no more."

"Norton mentioned visiting him, I recall. Yes, I remember very clearly now. He told me some fantastic tale about—apparitions. He said Mr. Cranstoun confessed to having seen your father's ghost! I admit quite frankly—and I hope I'm not offending anyone—I heartily share the good apothecary's scorn for such nonsense! Now your father mentioned something about his teeth, about their having grown loose in their sockets of late. Strikes me they're more likely to be at the root of the trouble than any of your hauntings and visitations!"

Mrs. Mounteney expressed anxiety about Blandy's deterioration, and Susannah would question Mary now and then, always on a note of reproach, as though she were failing in sympathy.

But what could she say to them, she who alone knew that his illness was wholly of the spirit? How explain that springs which had flowed unfailingly for more than thirty years had dried in a matter of minutes?

Blandy's love for his daughter had not been killed; he was not, could never be free of it. Reversed, turned in on itself, it was perhaps stronger now than at any time, but as a torment, not a delight. He watched his daughter as closely, listened with heightened acuteness to every note in her voice; his vigilance increased; but now all he saw and heard was distorted and his mind endowed her with subtleties of which she was incapable. The things he had loved best in her—her grace, the poise of her head, her fine pale skin and the beauty of her brow, he now saw through the eyes of another man; a man who had possessed her.

To his love for her he had brought the idealism of a boy. He had scarcely seen her as a woman, with all a woman's faults and emotions. He had subconsciously shied away from the thought of her marriage; it was always as a daughter that he saw her, never as a wife. He had, unreasonably, assumed Cranstoun's love to be of a similar quality to his own; Mary was too fine, too aloof for the ordinary commerce of love. His illusions had been very dear to him, close and secret as his love. The brutality of the awakening had been a shock from which his spirit had never recovered. The flagrancy of the situation as he saw it—its innate furtive vulgarity, its lack of sensibility and pride—had filled him with horror. Never himself a passionate man, the world of the senses was curiously repugnant to him. Mary had brought it within measurable distance.

For all his professional skill and even subtlety, he was innately simple. He did not condemn; he could not cease to love, but disillusion had so completely shaken the foundations of his world that an apathy descended on him which nothing—not tears, not protestations, not devotion—could penetrate.

To Mary he was courteous, as he would be to a stranger. For him she was a stranger, a woman given up to passions which set her in his eyes on the level of an erring cook-maid. She had brought him down. Although, to the best of his knowledge, the happenings of a night were known only to Mrs. Deane, he no longer held his head high. The fabric of an honourable life—so assiduously built—had collapsed, and with it his confidence in his dealings with others.

And so January passed, and February, and all the slow cold spring when the blossom on the trees hung back week after week as though in prescience of late frost. May was cold and overcast and there was little enough of promise to mock the empty of heart.

Of Cranstoun, Mary had heard nothing. Once, encountering Lord Mark in the churchyard, her heart had beat wildly at the thought that he might pause and give her news of him, but he passed on with no more than a cry of, "Foul weather, Miss Blandy!"

Where was he? she wondered. What doing? Had he returned to Scotland or—let torment have its word—to Covent Garden? With no pivot left, what would become of him?

For days at a time her thoughts of him would be wholly bitter, a tale of deceit and betrayal from first to last, then, quite without warning, she would recall some small incident—a moment of gaiety and gentleness—and suddenly the memory of all that was best in him, all that had been happiest in their love, would return to her. There was infinite sadness in these moods, but she welcomed them, giving herself up to them. She would recall his ineffable tenderness when he shared his cloak with her, the spendthrift gaiety of a night at Ranelagh, little absurdities with Dandy, small kindnesses to her mother, his hand in hers as they waited—linked in spirit—on the last fatal night; all would combine to build up a picture that was wholly good.

For more than three years he had been in her life, filling it. Emptiness now was everywhere; there was not a room, not a lane, not a tree that did not hold some memory of him. If only, she told herself, she could get away for a time; not to London or Bath—they, too, had their ghosts—but somewhere fresh. Yet all the time she knew she would not go, knew that without her memories she would be lonelier, more completely lost than now.

In the first weeks after his going she had lain awake night after night, hypnotised by the chimes of the clock. 'I must be asleep before it strikes one . . . before the quarter . . . before the three-quarters . . . before two . . .' The quarters seemed to rush past, beating through her brain until her only thought was of morning, of the first light, the start of another day.

She tried not to think of him, throwing herself into small duties, closing her mind, but the thought would take on the shape of a fear; if she slept, it was only to dream of him, waking again to the fear.

Some nights her longing for him would narrow to a single point of desire, but not for long. Free of his physical presence, her senses lost their insistence and she learned that the body's memory is shorter than the heart's.

Sometimes, even after months, she would torture herself with the hope that he would return, that he might one day be free, but in time this too faded and she grew wholly unexpectant.

Winter had come to the house and neither the scent of lilac nor the song of a thrush could dispel it.

CHAPTER TWO

AND THEN, quite without warning, he came back into her life.

Not to Henley, not even to England, but to her. It was as though she were convalescent and everything she touched and saw and heard came fresh to her; or as though a long frost had broken; or as though a film had lifted from her eyes and all colours were more brilliant. Never had the old town seemed so orderly, so warm; never had the trees in the surrounding hills been in such full leaf; never had the river flowed among such enchantment of forget-me-not and iris; never had the brewer's horses been so glossy, the chaffinches in such bright livery, the air so fresh, the sun so brilliant.

Carried on a tide of happiness, she no longer cared if winter still held her home in its grip. The bantering gaiety with which she treated her father did not for a moment falter. Let Susannah reproach, let Betty sulk, let poor Littleton sigh in corners, let her father shut himself away from the affection she was so eager to give; nothing mattered; Cranstoun was back in her life.

His return had been staged with dignity and subtlety; concealed from the public eye in a gift of linen from his mother. The box had arrived quite openly, addressed to *Miss Blandy*. On top of the gleaming pile was a note from Lady Cranstoun: "I must crave your forgiveness, my dear Miss Blandy, in delaying so long this small gift. My excuse is of the best: I have been waiting for it to be woven! Do please accept it as a token of my gratitude to yourself and to your father for the great kindness you have shown my son. It is my dearest wish that we may one day meet, when I can express my thanks in person."

This, for the world; the treasure lay buried deep among cool white layers: a flat case containing a collection of Scotch pebbles, set to form bracelet, necklace and brooch. With them was a small packet inscribed: "The powder to clean the pebbles with."

No need to look twice at the packet before concealing it; the writing was unmistakable.

A Pandora's box, in which half the blessings were imponderable. For Mary there was a return to life with all its fine-drawn bliss, and for Francis Blandy a complex of emotions in which self-respect and vanity and suspicion played equal parts. Lady Cranstoun's graceful gesture, with its implications of respect and recognition of equality, was of inestimable value to him. That his friends knew nothing of his humiliation had done little to mitigate it. Although the past was not cancelled by Lady Cranstoun's courtesy, the thing had been put, subtly, on a different footing; pride at least could be salvaged. When next Tom Staverton and Mrs. Mounteney came to supper, he was able to draw attention to the napery: "A gift to my daughter from Lady Cranstoun."

"Together with these Scotch pebbles," Mary said boldly.

"The height of fashion!" Mrs. Mounteney commented.

"And, what's more, they become you!" Tom cried gallantly. "It's a long time since I've seen her in such spirits, Francis!"

Blandy turned to Mary. She was, he saw, radiant. Pride fell like a pricked balloon and suspicion overwhelmed him. Radiance, because a man's mother had sent her a trifling recompence for hospitality, Mary who for six months had moved on leaden feet, dull-eyed, her skin filmed over with the greyness of insomnia? Mary with her nerves stretched tight as a bowstring? Mary who had let spring slip through her fingers, to be so revived by some baubles and a few table-napkins?

When the guests had gone, he brought himself to question her. Questions implied an intimacy their relations had lacked for long, and in his mind two fears conflicted: the fear that she might lie and the fear that he might learn the truth.

She was moving along the supper table snuffing the candles.

"Mary."

She paused, her face, in the half-light, inscrutable. For all his love, he had never really understood her. "Yes, papa?"

"There is something I want to ask you."

"What is it?"

"About—Lady Cranstoun's gift."

"Yes?"

"Was there—anything else in the box? A note, for instance?"

"Only the one from Lady Cranstoun."

"Nothing to——" He hesitated to voice his fear. "Nothing to give you the impression Mr. Cranstoun might be returning to Henley?"

"No, sir. Why?"

"I—I confess I've been perplexed by your mood these last few days. You saw for yourself how Mr. Staverton commented upon your looks."

"Mr. Staverton was always gallant."

"I am not gallant, Mary. It's with no desire to flatter you that I say: since Lady Cranstoun's gift arrived you've been a changed woman."

"May I say, father: you yourself have been greatly improved in spirits. Why, tonight at table you were quite your old self!"

"We're not discussing my moods. For reasons I've no need to go into, Lady Cranstoun's gesture has done something to restore that pride of which I had been all but stripped."

"Please!" she cried sharply.

He flushed. "The last thing I want is to revive—certain memories." He paused, as though faced with a decision. Life, now that a semblance of self-respect had been restored to it, would be tolerable enough. Something told him to let well alone, avoid change. Strained as his relations with Mary had been—would in some ways always now be—she was his; his alone. His hatred of Cranstoun had in it an element of fear, never acknowledged even to himself—the fear that he might even now take Mary away from him. He faltered: "Perhaps it would have been wiser not to raise this matter again."

Mary snuffed another candle. "On the contrary. I'm glad you did."

"Glad? Why?"

She turned to him. "We've lived in silence too long. It's been poisoning our life together, destroying the frankness of our relations."

"There was little enough of frankness on your side at any time, it seems to me."

"Father—please let me speak. If you'll hear me now, I give you my word never to mention this again. You've watched me all these months. No one could say I haven't paid for my deceits and my follies. I don't ask for forgiveness. What's done is done. Don't think I haven't felt for you, suffered with you." She came towards him. "Don't draw away from me. Please—don't withdraw yourself from me." She spoke now with a kind of desperate courage. "The past is past."

"I cannot accept that. It's too easy, too false. You're no longer the same. I am no longer the same."

"One thing between us is unchanged," she said quietly: "our love for each other."

"I would rather we did not speak of love. It seems to me the word has suffered too much degradation in this house." His voice was hard with emotion he would not show.

"But it's of love I wish to speak. You shall hear me. You must. I've asked nothing of you all these months, but I do ask something now. Listen to me. The past is over—but the future remains. Our future together. We may both of us live for many years. Are we going on like this—in enmity?"

"Enmity! What nonsense!"

"No, father. Oh, our manners are good enough, we don't give ourselves away in front of the domestics, but in truth—the deep, underlying truth—we do live as enemies, always on watch, always on the defensive, always guarding our tongues!"

He was beginning to tremble. "What do you suggest?"

"Can't we come closer to each other?" she pleaded. "Recapture something of the old happiness?"

"I've told you," he said wearily, "we're changed. Our happiness was based upon things that no longer exist."

"But is that true? For me nothing is changed where you're concerned. I may have failed you in myself, but never in my loyalty to you."

"Your loyalty to me! When you can bring shame to my house!"

"That I deny. Now as always."

"And I reject your denial, now as always," he said bitterly.

A sense of irony overwhelmed her and she faced him angrily. "Very good. Suppose it had been true? Where is the betrayal? To your love? Or your pride?" Blandy gasped. "Is it of me you're thinking, or only of your house? Of what am I accused? Of giving myself to a lover, or of giving myself to a lover *under your roof?"*

"How dare you!"

Her anger on an instant spent, she dropped her head. "That was unforgivable of me." She spoke in a low voice, almost humbly. "You will never know how I denied myself—denied Cranstoun—in order to spare you."

"Spare me? In what?"

"Do you really think I don't appreciate the quality of your love for me, your—ideal of me? How can you believe me so lacking in sensibility as to take a lover in my mother's room."

Blandy sank into a chair. "How do I know what to believe?"

"That, at least."

"This man—this unspeakable Scot—it was an ill day for both of us when he came into our lives." She was silent. "Mary—come here." She moved to him. "Look at me. I want you to tell me something. The truth. No matter what it is. Will you promise?"

"I swear."

"If Cranstoun were to return a free man, would you, knowing all you know of him—his vices, his deceit, his treachery—would you still be willing to marry him?"

This is the crisis of my life, she thought. A second chance. I've been given a second chance. On what I say now will depend our future, my father's and mine. As surely as I've destroyed him I can restore him. A word—one word from me——

Neither moved. As the moments passed anxiety turned to fear in the eyes of the old man.

When at last she spoke, it was in a whisper. "Yes."

"Mary!"

"With all my heart."

He rose to his feet, gripping the chair for support. "Then there's nothing more to be said."

"And you, father? What would you say?"

"I?" He stared at her, the colour draining from his face.

"Yes. What would you say?"

"That I would rather die. More, that I would rather see you dead."

"Even if my life's happiness depended on it?"

"Happiness? With such a man?"

"You would never give me up to him?"

"Never. I would use every weapon in my power to prevent such a marriage."

"I could marry without your consent."

"Then I would pursue you to the ends of the country. I would not rest till I had had the marriage set aside."

There was a new note in her voice as she said: "You never wanted me to marry Cranstoun, did you?"

"Certainly. Until he was shown up for what he is."

"No, father. You never wanted me to marry him. Month after month passed and no mention was made of our wedding. I see now. I see a lot of things that were obscure before. When Lord Mark came here, you were not really shocked. You were relieved. News of Cranstoun's former marriage came to you as an answer to prayer——"

"What are you saying?"

"You condoned it too easily. It was not in your nature to be so complacent. It suited you admirably. Promised to

Cranstoun, there was no danger of my marrying another man. No danger of your losing me."

"God forgive you for that!"

"You say you would never give me up to him. Would you have given me up to any man?"

"Anyone worthy of you."

"I doubt it. What of my other suitors?"

"Which other suitors?" he demanded angrily. "A hare-brained ensign and a Bath apothecary? You ever aimed too low. And where has it brought you? Down to the level of a slut beneath a hedge!"

"I've known love. No one, not even you, can take that away from me!"

"Love! What do you know of love? Have you watched and planned for thirty years, given all your thoughts, all that is best in you to a single object? Suffering agonies of fear when she so much as coughs, wincing at every slight to her, seeking to surround her only with what was beautiful? A love so deep that the very mention of her name seemed a blasphemy? What have you understood of such a love, that you were willing to throw it aside for the first wretch who stirs your senses! You say I've never welcomed the thought of your marriage. Very well. Perhaps not. Perhaps I rated you too high for marriage!"

"But what was my life to be?" she cried, on the verge of hysteria. "What kind of love was it that would condemn me to loneliness?"

"What of my loneliness?"

"Yes. Yes. What of your loneliness? What of it, father? You say you've watched me for thirty years. Perhaps I too have watched—watched you spinning your web round me—closer, finer, more subtle all the time. When Cranstoun left this house for the last time, the web was complete. My only chance of escape had gone and you knew it. Yes, escape! Why do you think I used to walk, walk, walk, till I was ready to drop? Because I was being suffocated—stifled by you and your house!" The thought was not hers, the words and the voice were wild, but they did their work.

Blandy swung round on her, plethoric with rage. "Leave me! Leave me alone! Get out of my sight before you destroy me utterly!"

CHAPTER THREE

It was as though the house held its breath and every keyhole had its listener. The veneer of good manners was so thin that at any moment it might crack, the tension so acute that even the daily women—Banks and Emmet—were aware of it. The very Wargrave Fool was conscious of something in the air, sniffing it as an animal sniffs danger.

The thing that had come into the house was intangible. Betty and Susannah had heard angry voices, but loyalty to their master imposed discretion on them.

Mary got away from the house as often as she could, but for Mr. Blandy there was no escape. He sought refuge in work, but his work was too closely bound up with his life; the very deed-boxes with their distinguished names mocked his pride. Subconsciously, everything he had done had been bound up in his daughter: the amassing, guinea by guinea, of a fortune for her; the purchase of land in her name; the standing of his clients, the fine furniture, the dignity of their way of living, all had been part of a mosaic in which she was the central motive. When he had warned her not to destroy him utterly, he had scarcely exaggerated. He could not have conceived on a November night six months earlier that she held it in her power to hurt him further; suffice that she had.

Human nature had suddenly become for him a thing of terror with its bottomless well of passion and bitterness and cruelty. Shocked too profoundly to see that words may reveal more, not less, than exists, he watched Mary with a kind of dread, wondering what fresh blows she would deal him.

They met only at meals, eating in silence when possible, evading even the smaller courtesies. He no longer enquired where she went. She should not, he told himself miserably, feel herself suffocated.

For Mary the days passed in a trough of unhappiness all the more profound for her brief resurgence of hope. Regret for her own fatal words warred with the despairing realisation that Cranstoun's freedom, if it came, would come too late. She knew her father too well to delude herself that his words had been as thoughtless, as unrelated to conviction or deep feeling as her own; he had not, as she had herself, spoken in anger. His attitude was set; nothing would change it. She did not understand the law sufficiently well to know how far he could carry out his threats, but she had lived long enough in the world to realise how small her chance of happiness with Cranstoun would be if he chose to hound them.

Life then with Cranstoun was not to be hoped for. What of life with her father? The silent old house, the whispering—perhaps hostile—servants, the suspicion of her every action, the small duties no longer undertaken with love. Cranstoun gone, and the hope of him; her mother dead, Lavinia dead, even the little dog nearing his end; and herself, a spinster of thirty-one, with, perhaps, more than half her life ahead of her in a day which held little but marriage for a gentlewoman; with no love, no hope, nothing but a few memories, intolerably bitter now in their nostalgic sweetness. Walking always with the thought: 'This time last year I had Cranstoun in my life; the year before I had mama as well. I had a season in town, a season in Bath! How young I was, dear God, how young! How rich in illusion and hope. Surely—surely I was not restless then? Not discontented? Why used I to walk in the woods at dawn? Surely only for zest in life, only because the days were all too short, the sights and sounds and scents too precious to be missed? Was it really I who walked in the alleys at Ranelagh on my lover's arm, a Dresden posy in my hand? Was it I who danced—actually *danced*—with the heir to the throne? Was it to me a lover sent red roses? Was it I who had the daily companionship—quivering always on the edge of ecstasy—of such a man as Cranstoun? Was it I who was surrounded by love—mama, my father, my lover—cosseted and sheltered and ringed round with love?'

Nostalgia for the things that had been hers overwhelmed her. No day out of the past seemed so dull she would not have wished it back. The very griefs of the past took on a certain beauty and dignity. One, two, three, four—no matter how many years she chose to look back—each seemed infinitely desirable.

She tried now to forget herself in books. She had for too long neglected her mind. Surely the habit of it would return if she persevered?

Choosing a quiet hour, she would spend some time in the library, wandering along the shelves, taking down now this volume, now that. One afternoon in early summer she was aware of the rather unexpected figure of a footman, also studying the books diligently. Out of the corner of her eye, she recognised his livery as that of Lord Mark Ker. So milord entrusted his reading to the taste of his domestics!

She had chosen a book and was considering a second when the footman began to move steadily in her direction. Taking down a small volume from one of the higher shelves, he paused at her side. Bowing low, he said: "If I might presume to recommend this, Miss Blandy, madam. I understand it is very fine." Meeting her eyes for a moment, he bowed again and left her.

Uncertain whether or not to be annoyed at his presumption, she glanced down at the book. Shakespeare's *Sonnets*. Running through the pages, she closed the book abruptly. Between the leaves there was a note. Her heart started to beat wildly. Looking round to make sure she was not observed, she slipped the note into her pocket. Had the choice of book been a random one, or was the servant not only literate, but an artist among go-betweens?

There was no one in the hall as she entered the house and she reached her own room unobserved.

Her name was printed discreetly: MISS BLANDY. The paper was hand-made, the hairy grey of Lady Cranstoun's letter. She opened the note clumsily, her eyes blurring with excitement. It was very short:

"My Mary,

"If you say the word I will come South. It would be better for your reply to be directed to me in a man's hand. Initial it M.C. as I believe us to be married by solemn contract before God. If I do not hear from you then my prayer will be for death to put an end to this torment of longing."

"Your C."

Happiness welled up in her and she read the note through and through until she had memorised every word.

Directed to me in a man's hand.

But what man? Whom could she trust? Who, for that matter, would undertake it?

She would not implicate Ned Hearne. Harman was illiterate. Her father's friends were out of the question, as were her uncles. Who? Who? She could not go to a stranger; nor to the Rector or the apothecary; not to the mercer or the corn-chandler or the butcher. Lord Mark's discreet footman? How reach him, even supposing him to be able to write, which was doubtful. Who? Who? A legible hand; neutral, not too pronounced in style; a neat, clerkly hand. Clerkly! A clerk!

Why had she not thought of it before? Littleton. Poor Littleton who had shown himself so pathetically anxious in the past to do her small services.

She would ask him. He was her friend. She would have to dissemble a little; he must on no account guess that the note was more than formal. It should not be difficult to think of some plausible tale.

Her reply was discretion itself:

"My dear Willie,

"The suggestion you make is perfectly agreeable to

"Yours,

"M.C."

Nothing there to betray either of them if it should fall into unfriendly hands.

She ran down the stairs. "Mr. Littleton!" she cried, catching him as he moved, a gaunt shadow among shadows, across the hall.

"Miss Mary!" He still flushed when she spoke to him.

"Come here a moment." He followed her into the parlour. "Close the door."

Shutting the door, he waited diffidently.

"I've a favour to ask."

"Of *me,* Miss Mary?"

"Only a small one."

"Nothing would give me greater pleasure, you know that," he jerked. "What is it?"

"I want you to address a letter for me in your best clerkly hand."

"A dozen letters if you wish."

"Not a dozen. One." She found herself slipping into the mannered archness which uneasiness always aroused in her. Littleton was not a young man with whom she had ever felt at ease. Ned, yes; or the Prince of Wales; but not Littleton. "I have a pen. Or perhaps you prefer your own?"

"Anything of yours——" he stopped abruptly, setting little waves of embarrassment in motion. Sitting at the table, he dipped pen in ink. "To whom is it to go, Miss?"

She moved about the room light-footed as a dancer, distracting him, creating a diversion. "To Captain the Honourable William Cranstoun——"

Littleton paused, pen arrested. "Captain—Cranstoun——"

"Yes, Mr. Littleton. Captain Cranstoun."

"But——"

"A small account he left outstanding on his last stay. A

purely formal thing, or of course I should have written the address myself."

"In that case——" he said uncertainly.

"If you'd rather I asked someone else——"

"No. No, please. Don't ask anyone else. It's so rarely you give me the opportunity of serving you. There's so little I can do—so little you let me do——"

"Then write: To Captain the Honourable William Cranstoun, Nether Crailing, Roxburghshire, Scotland."

"He—he remains in the North?

"Certainly."

"Perhaps as well——" he murmured with a flash of bitterness.

"I'm afraid Mr. Cranstoun's views *are* a little strong. For my father, certainly," Mary said smoothly. "In politics, that is. He had the courage of his convictions to excess in these matters."

"Is that the reason——?"

"Yes?"

"Forgive my presumption, but—Mr. Blandy will not allow the Captain's name to be mentioned."

"Alas, no. That's why"—she drew nearer the clerk, giving him one of her rare inscrutable smiles—"I'd rather you made no mention to him of your kind service to me."

He raised his short-sighted eyes to hers. "Thank you, Miss Mary," he said softly. "I'll never forget that you honoured me with your trust."

CHAPTER FOUR

CRANSTOUN'S next message, slipped among the pages of *Hudibras,* was printed as a child prints: "The hanging wood midnight." Falling into the wrong hands it could equally have referred to a ploughman's tryst or a poacher's cache.

From experience he had learned not to entrust many of his secrets to any one person and he hesitated to employ his uncle's footman again, but the Blandy's servants were out of the question, and the man had proved his discretion and resourcefulness.

In the Scot, intrigue, philandering and duplicity were so inextricably mixed with romanticism, superstition and passion that his emotions would have been difficult to dissect. Most generous, even kind, where his worst motives were involved, he could use tortuous means to an honourable end. Neither so good as he believed himself nor so bad as he appeared to the world, few men of his day made a more distracting lover. Incapable of behaving either wholly badly or wholly well, he could dupe a friend or keep a woman in thrall longer than the most accomplished rake. Loving Mary, he could yet betray her at every turn; generously giving his name to Anne Murray, he had yet compelled her to sign a declaration that they were not married. Enjoying Francis Blandy's hospitality and, up to a point, his friendship, he had subtly worked to undermine his daughter's love for him. Even his affection for Mrs. Blandy had not been entirely innocent of both vanity and self-interest.

Learning young that charm is a useful substitute for money, he had exploited his gifts with a lack of compunction that amounted almost to innocence. While resenting a lack of means with which to bolster up his rank, he yet made good use of his birth. Certain things were to his credit: in a day of gamblers, his losses in play were small; his vitality owed nothing to wine, his debts—though pressing—were not large, and he had not chosen as a young man to sell himself in marriage. He would up to this time have said he could make out quite a good case for the Recording Angel.

But the sands were running out. Making his way down the hill from Paradise House, he knew himself committed to a game in which the stakes were higher than ever before. The balance was a fine one; winning, he told himself, he would play no more; losing—but here his heart beat a little too fast for his liking. He must not--dare not lose. There was even at this late hour still the chance that he would not be called upon to play his last card, that that luck which had not yet failed him in an extremity would still hold. God knew he was in need of luck now as never before. He had traded too long on his meagre capital of birth and charm and the doors were closing with ominous finality. At forty-two, Cranstoun had reached the end of his tether.

With London out of bounds as though the plague raged, he had left the coach on the northern outskirts to make his way cross-country to Henley; the bailiffs could not trace him to Paradise House for some days, by which time his mission would have been accomplished, for good or ill.

The clouds were moving rapidly, and by the time he reached the woods, the moon had gone. The darkness disconcerted him. It was nearly a year since he had been there and the path was difficult to trace. A rare feeling of apprehension began to fill him. He had no idea what the night was going to bring forth. The thought was a disturbing one. From inception to outcome, the venture was perilous in the extreme; at any one of a number of points it might miscarry, with incalculable consequences.

He started as a pallid shape crossed his path on silent wings. A moment later the cry of a screech-owl tore the silence to shreds. Here and there along the path the wan greenish lamps of glow-worms shone, and in the moment that the clouds parted he saw the small fluttering form of a bat.

Nature was at its most eerie, the mood of the wood in tune with his own. When, he wondered, was Walpurgis night?

From the distant town he could hear the sound of the church clock. He paused to count.

Midnight. She should be here soon, if she had understood the message; if she had ever received it; if it had not been intercepted; if she had been able to get away from the house; if she wanted to come.

As the minutes passed and there was still no sound of footsteps, the uncertainties which hedged the adventure began to lose their charm and he wondered whether perhaps he had loaded the dice too heavily against himself.

The moon cleared the clouds again and he thought he recognised the fallen tree which was their meeting place.

How long would he give her? And supposing she did not come? What then? A return to his uncle's house, a few more days lying low in Henley, another message, and then——?

His heart sickened. Why, why in God's name had he been brought to such a gamble?

Suddenly he stiffened, straining his ears. The sound was uncertain, no more than a rustling of dry leaves; a small breeze, perhaps, or a hare.

But no. There was no doubt now. She was coming. She—or someone.

The drum of blood in his ears deafened him to all other sound. The moon slipped wantonly in and out of the racing clouds, but by its light he could recognise her. Darkly cloaked, a hood drawn low over her face, there was no mistaking the grace of her movements. "Mary!"

She did not come to him for a moment, but stood at arm's length, her eyes—accustomed now to the dimness—searching his face. "Is it really you?"

He caught her to him and for a time emotion overwhelmed them. "You came, my darling—you came!"

"Adding folly to folly," she cried exultantly.

As she threw her head back, he caught avidly at her hair, desire for her momentarily driving thought from his mind. "This endess mindless waste without you——"

"Not a word from you—no proof even of your existence until a few weeks ago—nothing! Cranstoun, why, why?"

"It was too dangerous."

"You call this safe?"

For answer he kissed her laughing mouth, then drew her to his side on the fallen tree. "No one saw you leave the house?"

"Not so much as a cat. Even the bridge was empty. The silence everywhere was so complete I thought the beat of my heart must wake the town!" Outlining his face with her finger, she whispered again: "Is it really you?"

"Why do you say that?"

"I live among ghosts. A world of ghosts. Reality and illusion change places as swiftly as the moon slipping among the clouds. The things I touch seem real enough—cups and glasses and chairs. The faces are the same. Or, no, not quite the same. There have been changes."

"What do you mean?"

"Wait—remember I've lost the habit of speech. I say 'Good morning, father', and 'Good morning, Mr. Littleton'. No more. My tongue has grown stiff and my mind is packed away in the lumber-room. The church clock marks the quarters—some long, some short. But its note is not the same. It's muted. All sounds are muted and all colours dim. Do I begin to make you understand, my darling? I live entirely in the past—and since you're no more than a memory, why not doubt that you're really at my side? How do I know that I shan't soon wake to find Betty standing beside my bed with the morning tea?"

"How?" he demanded excitedly. "So!" The hunger of his kisses belonged wholly to the waking world. He let her go as abruptly as he had seized her, laughing with a boy's triumph. "Now you may go on talking nonsense, miss."

"And you? Where have you been?"

"In the North."

"I—see."

"You don't ask me my news."

"No."

"Why not? Have you grown indifferent?"

"Don't laugh at me."

"Sweet!" He held her fingers to his lips. "Suppose I were to tell you——"

"That you're free?" She drew away from him. "It would come too late."

"Mary! Mary, look at me. What are you trying to tell me?"

"Your freedom no longer matters."

"You——" Brushing back her hair, he searched her face. "Something's wrong."

"Need we talk of it? It's such heaven—to be near you, to hear your voice. Let me forget—for one night."

"With all my heart. But can *you* forget?" She did not reply. "Your father?"

"Yes."

Cranstoun shrugged. Now was the moment to play his first card. If it was a winning one—as God send it might be—that other, the last card, need never be played. "He was angry that night. And, come down to it, can you blame him?" He chuckled richly. "I'll admit the old man jumped to conclusions, but who wouldn't have done in the circumstances? Ironical, when you come to think of it—being punished for one of the sins we didn't commit!" Playing his hand, he did not notice the shock in her eyes at his lack of sensibility. "All the same, I'll wager he'll be glad enough for me to make an honest woman of you!"

"Cranstoun!" she said faintly.

"Don't look so startled, sweet! It's the way any man of the world would see it. A fellow would be a fool not to drive as good a bargain as he can!"

"But—there's no question of bargains." She pressed her fingers to her brow. "We don't seem to be talking about the same thing." She spoke in an awed whisper. "He hates you."

"Probably. None the less, he'll be glad enough of me as a son-in-law."

"Haven't you understood anything I've said?"

"Sure I have."

"He hates you. With a terrible icy hatred. He would rather die than see me marry you."

"An easy enough figure of speech."

"No. No, Cranstoun. He would rather see *me* dead."

His confidence, never great, began to waver. "He—said that?" She nodded. "When? The night I left?"

"No. Later. Much later."

"When?"

"A few days after your mother's gift came." She shuddered. "There are no words for it—we both said things that nothing can wipe out. We spoke in a moment of madness, but the words are there. Burned in acid." She faced him, speaking with infinite sadness. "There's no future for us."

"We could elope," he cried, but the ring in his voice was off-key.

"He would hound us to the ends of the country."

"We should still have each other."

"For how long?"

"Is this what you've lived with, my Mary? This knowledge?"

"Yes."

He drew her head to his shoulder and they sat in silence. After a time she was aware of a whisper, but the words were indistinct.

"Did you speak?"

"I was thinking——"

"Yes?"

"Nothing. Nothing for your ears."

"Tell me what you said."

"I—was thinking—there is a way. But not one you'd take."

"How can you know?"

"I know you."

"You—want me to come to you now. Is that it?"

"No, not that."

"Why not?"

"A half-life is not for you. Our love must hold its head high—remember? That's what we've always said."

"What's in your mind then? You—Cranstoun. You came here tonight with an idea of some sort." He evaded her eyes. "What is it? There is something?"

"Suppose——Mary, why are you shivering?"

"I don't know. Suddenly, for no reason, I felt afraid. I can't explain it. Nothing tangible. As though—there were wings—in the air, agitating the air——"

"An owl, perhaps. Mary, are you listening?"

"I'm listening."

"Suppose I were to say there is only one way out for us."

"Yes?"

"Would you take it?"

"How can I say without knowing what it is?"

"Would you? Would you be prepared to make an experiment?"

"An experiment?"

"How can I explain what I mean? To—interfere with the chemistry of human affections. To tamper with the fine balance between love and hate?" His voice dropped to a whisper. "To challenge the natural law."

"What are you saying?" she asked breathlessly.

"You're not wholly ignorant of the powers that lie outside the pale of ordinary life—beyond the confines of orthodox knowledge. I've never been certain how much you knew, how much you accepted."

"Very little."

"I'm not sure I believe that."

"Very little," she repeated dully. She was growing aware of a feeling of oppression.

"But something. At least you admit the existence of forces?"

"Dark forces?"

"Call them dark. Who are we to judge? We're taught that light is good and darkness evil, yet we know that the sun can blind and kill and drive mad and that darkness brings restoring sleep. A maze of paradoxes! Suppose——" He drew near her and in the uncertain light she could see that his eyes were very bright, glittering like an animal's. "Suppose that by some means you could—bring about a change of heart in your father?"

"Towards you?"

"Yes."

"The powers that could accomplish that would be strange indeed."

"They are." There was a curious note in his voice and he gripped her wrists. His eyes sought and held hers. Suddenly she understood her earlier sense of oppression; he was exerting his will.

"What are they, these powers of yours?" A feeling of faintness robbed her words of the derision she would have given them.

"Who am I to presume to know? For all the learning of this Eighteenth Century, how much do any of us really know? The sum of what dead men have written is ours for the taking, yet what simple question does it answer? Can it give a formula for the elixir of life? Can it so much as trace the springs of love and hate?"

"The path you tread is too dark for me to follow."

"Yet follow you must if we're to find our way through the trackless forest that is the world. My dear"—he took her hands—"here in these woods we've touched ecstasy—something that comes to few. At our first meeting I saw in you my destiny—my affinity." Hypnotised by time and place, and by his own words, he whispered: "Without you I've no future."

"Nor I."

"Then listen to me carefully." He drew her hand to his side. "Do you recall a powder I once put in your father's tea?"

Her laugh broke on a high note of hysteria. "The love philtre?"

"He was in the most genial of moods afterwards."

"I remember."

"Have you had occasion to clean your Scotch pebbles?"

"Not yet."

"The powder I sent you——"

"Not more of your Mrs. Morgan's work?" she mocked shakily. Beneath her fingers she could feel the wild beat of his heart. Why? Why?

"Yes. Yes. You still drink tea at night?"

"A ghost drinks tea with a ghost. Every detail of the ritual is preserved, down to the last spectral teaspoon. Even among wraiths we have our conventions." She spoke at random, confused by the racing of the heart beneath her fingers which seemed to have no connection with the banality of his words.

"No more than a dusting of the powder—tea would do. Or gruel. It might mix better with gruel."

"What is it, this powder?"

He hesitated for a moment, then he began to speak hurriedly, drawing her close to him, his lips to her ear. "The philtre of itself is nothing—vervain, perhaps, and mandragora—stripped of the belief we bring to it all magic is meaningless. To expect of some concoction of herbs a change of heart is folly—folly. But—the philtre does not stand alone."

Drugged by his physical nearness, her critical faculties slept. The words that fell on her ears were one with the strangeness of the night and she gave no more than an involuntary cry as a small bat brushed against her hair in blundering random flight. This was its element as it was the element of glow-worms and screech-owls and toads. The hands that held hers were trembling, the voice in her ear was no longer steady, the words no longer coherent. "—an agent of forces potent beyond all imagining. This is the root of necromancy. Belief. An infinity of belief that transcends all our sceptic learning and breaks free of the trammels of possibility!"

"But how?" she found herself asking. "How can I be sure that my belief, my will are strong enough?"

"I shall be at your side. In spirit."

Words, words, she told herself, rhetoric without sense or meaning, but his lips were brushing her cheek and his grip on her was tightening and desire for him was draining from her all power to resist his mind.

"You don't doubt the existence of these forces?"

Yes, yes, her mind cried out, but the words fainted on parted lips and she was filled again, as so often before in these woods, with an emotion that brushed the verges of panic.

"You don't doubt, Mary?" The grip of his fingers on her wrists sent shocks of pain through her nerves. His mouth was close to hers, yet withheld. "Say it—say you accept their existence?"

"Why—why do you demand this?" she pleaded.
"Because you must choose."
"Choose? How can I when my brain is drugged and numb?"
"Choose—choose, Mary."
"Help me."
"It's not for me. I've made my choice, the choice between annihilation and salvation."
"Salvation! That dark spirit!"
"Dark, but yet a spirit. Bedraggled, yes, but still an immortal soul for better or worse. Incapable of escape or oblivion, with all its apprenticeship for good and evil yet to be served. Eligible yet for heaven or hell, part—a single warped part—of the pattern of life."
"The pattern—but——" She groped for words. "If all we are and all we're to become is part of a pattern, predestined—how then can we talk of will and choice?"
"Because choice is part of destiny. What is it the Chinese say? 'The journey of a thousand miles starts with but a single step'. The choice of that step is ours."
His voice flowed on. A kind of lethargy began to steal over her and she knew that her resistance to him was ebbing, that no matter what he demanded of her the answer would be the same.
"Where is it to end, this journey of yours?"
"Not here, with so much unresolved between us, Mary."
"Hold me," she pleaded; "give me a little of your strength. Let your splendid strength flow over me." She was conscious now of a merging, a fusion of mind and spirit and body that transcended anything she had ever known with him; a complete submission.
"Your choice?" he whispered.
"There is no choice."

CHAPTER FIVE

Betty Binfield was standing at the side of her bed watching her. Her first thought: So it was a dream. Her second: Would to God it were.

In the moment before the fumes of sleep cleared from her head, she saw in mindless panic the hatred in the eyes that met hers, raw, animal, implacable. The moment passed; mistress and maid assumed masks. The scene slipped into perspective: muslin curtains fluttering in a southerly breeze, shafts of sunlight discovering rainbows among the glass on the dressing chest; her petticoats, with their goffered flounces, tossed on a chair, her shoes at the foot of the bed, her cloak hanging from a hook; everything where she had left it.

Betty's lips parted thickly. "Good morning, miss."

"Good morning, Betty."

The girl handed Mary her tea, but she made no attempt to go. In the bright light Mary was conscious of the blurring of her good looks, the coarsening of skin, the thickening of shoulder, the sagging of the plump lips. A warmth emanated from the maid's body that filled her with uneasiness. How much longer, she wondered, was Betty going to stand there, the hot blue eyes running over her in insolent appraisal; eyes full of brutish female wisdom.

"How did you come to hurt yourself, miss?"

"I?"

"Your wrists."

"My—wrists?" Mary looked down. Her wrists were ringed with sensitive blue bruises. "How—odd," she said breathlessly.

"Very."

"I—I can't think what it can be."

"Can't you?"

"Unless it's—rheumatism. It must be that. It leaves a mark sometimes."

"Does it hurt to touch?"

Mary pressed the blue marks gently. "A little."

The girl sprang forward, catching Mary's wrists in her strong servant's hands. "Does it hurt—like this?"

"Let go. Let go my wrists. Let go, I tell you, you're hurting me!"

The pressure relaxed abruptly, but Betty continued to stare. "That's not rheumatism."

"Why should you know? If I'm in need of advice, I'll consult Mr. Norton."

"Not with marks like that. He might ask questions."

"Will you go please."

Betty did not move. "What about your cloak?"

"My—cloak?"

"Shall I give it to Mrs. Deane?"

"What for?"

"Mending." The maid tossed the cloak over the bed. A jagged tear ran across the back.

"How can I have done that?"

"A bramble. Or maybe the branch of a tree."

"How careless of me not to notice it when I came in yesterday."

"Too dark."

"But no—I got back long before dusk." Mary's voice came uncertainly. Her eyes rested, fascinated, on a pulse in the girl's throat, throbbing thickly. Then, with a curious cry, Betty turned and rushed out of the room.

Mary drew the bedclothes close to her shuddering body.

So Betty knew. Knew, and hated her. Five years of hostility had crystallised at last in consuming physical jealousy; the hatred of a frustrated bawd.

The girl's knowledge established a bond between them that was infinitely degrading; sisters in concupiscence. But among a crowding host of fears, the cook-maid's figure was a small one.

The night's exultancy had left Mary with a sick legacy in mind and spirit. Waking always in the past to a moment of shame and revulsion, she knew that this last meeting was of a different calibre; its passions were less simple. Giving herself to Cranstoun she had seen their love hedged round with a dark mysticism, as though love were no longer enough. Subtly, intangibly, evil had become a part of it. Until now she had known a sense of guilt, but never of evil. Their love for each other had been wrong only in common law, not in natural law. The evil which troubled her was wholly of the mind, yet so fundamentally was it intermingled with her love that love itself took on a new complexity. The bruises on her wrists were the mark of Pan. She had surrendered herself more wholly to his will than ever to his desire. He had violated her mind, her faith, her innermost integrity. Lying in the borderland between sleep and waking she had been assailed by the thought: I've sold my soul to the devil.

Was it possible? she wondered, crouching under the bedclothes? The belief was as old as time. Beside it the spite of a cook-maid seemed peculiarly wholesome.

And it was not over. It was only just beginning. She had a task now; an exercise in necromancy. She was no longer in a position to mock. She was committed. She had made a compact. He had drawn her into the net of his will, compromising her spirit as inescapably as her body. She looked curiously round the room: the room of a young girl.

The powder to clean the pebbles with.

The packet was locked away in her secret drawer in case the writing on it should betray the sender.

The powder to clean the pebbles with.

She opened the packet. Would it be effective? Would it, in fact, clean Scotch pebbles?

The powder was white and fine without scent. The powder had had no scent the night Cranstoun put it in her father's tea. He had not noticed anything unusual about his tea and had, as Cranstoun said, been in the most genial of moods for the rest of the evening.

The most genial of moods!

Could it be——? For a moment hope welled up in her. Suppose the philtre could accomplish its end——

But dark thoughts ran on parallel lines. It was as though she heard her own voice saying: "He was in the most genial of moods," while all the time her thoughts were quite other. A sensc of duality was beginning to take possession of her.

Breakfast passed without incident. By ten o'clock she was at the window of her mother's room to see the London coach swing out of the White Hart yard. Cranstoun would, she knew, be on it; she was to write to him to lodgings in the Haymarket when the experiment had been made.

The day was a curious one. Knowing what she must do, she found herself seeking excuses for holding back. There was after all no hurry. A day more or less——

Littleton was away, staying with his family in Warwickshire, and her father, under pressure of work, remained in his study later than usual that night. Shortly before nine o'clock Susannah brought the tea-tray into the parlour. Mary asked her to let her father know.

The elderly maid went out of the room, leaving her alone. The fold of paper containing the powder was in her pocket. Now, she thought sickly. But she let the minutes slip through her fingers. Such an opportunity might not recur for days: Littleton might be back, acquaintances might have called, or Susannah waited to draw the curtains. Yet something held her, some hope—no more than half-formed—that even now, at this eleventh hour, she need not fulfil her bargain, that the end she sought could be accomplished on the normal plane of life.

Hearing Mr. Blandy's step in the hall, the thought clarified: an appeal, a last appeal to reason, to sentiment. In the moment that he raised his hand to the latch she closed her eyes in swift mute prayer: Let him listen. Dear God, let him hear me. Save me, dear God from what I must do.

The door opened and Francis Blandy came into the room. In the grey light of dusk he seemed perceptibly to have aged.

His cheeks had sagged and their ruddiness was revealed as a massing of hair-fine veins. His legs—always a source of mild vanity in their black silk hose—were bent and faltering. He sank into his chair by the window as though he had come a long journey.

"Tired, father?" Her voice was thin with pity, affection for him tightening her throat.

"I suppose so." He picked up the book he had left the night before and began to search for his place. He was not sure he had any stomach tonight for Dean Swift's bitter advocacy of cannibalism. "Has that tea stood long enough?" he asked sharply as she started to pour it out.

"Too long, I'm afraid." She handed him the large green-rimmed cup with its posies of summer flowers.

"Thank you."

They drank in a silence broken only by the ring of cup on saucer. Dusk was falling rapidly and the maids came in with candles, drawing the curtains before they left. Mary took up her needlework, but her hands were trembling so violently that she could not thread her needle. Putting the basket away, she paused outside the circle of light. "Father." In the quiet room, the word had a sharp disturbing ring.

He frowned, ostentatiously keeping his place with a finger that trembled little less than her own.

"I must speak to you." Her face had a luminous pallor.

He raised his eyebrows. "*Must?*"

"Yes."

"I cannot think of anything left unsaid between us."

"Please." She came towards him. "You've got to listen to me. I beg you. I'll never ask you again, I promise." She sat on a low stool, her eyes searching his face. The mark of suffering on it made her throat ache and she spoke with quiet urgency. "We were happy together, you and I. Happy and close as two people could be. Wait! Hear me. We cannot go on as we are, playing out this pitiful travesty of our lives together. The trappings are unaltered. That's what's so horrible. We take our meals together, drink tea together, keep the same courtesies and customs and habits. There's nothing missing, nothing but the spirit—the essential meaning in all we do. The silence between us is so complete it drums in the ears—drum, drum, drum, like the beat of two cold hearts. I sit here night after night with my needlework, waiting for you to turn the pages, and I say to myself: 'This can't go on. It can't—it can't—it can't!' "

Blandy's grip on his book tightened. She was beginning to speak with a kind of rhythm, infinitely exacerbating to the nerves. "Have you—finished?" he said tensely.

"No. One minute more. Just one minute out of life. Give me your thought for just that single minute."

"What more can you say than you've already said?"

"Believe me, I'd give all I have to call back that night. I was mad—mad."

"Nothing can recall the word once spoken. You see, the spell—such as it was between us—is broken." He spoke with infinite bitterness. "You showed me my illusions for what they were. It was, I confess, a shock to me to find my—affection was wearisome to you. But I shall recover. Have no fear that I'll trouble you any more. I willingly set you free of the—web."

She sprang up. "For pity's sake! In what am I free?" she cried desperately.

"I make no demands on your affections."

"Am I any the less trapped for that? Trapped as surely by your bitterness as your love. Perhaps we're both trapped, caught in this house with its memories. Father, haven't you seen the irony of it?" She gave a wild laugh. "You opposed my marriage because you were afraid of loneliness, and what have you gained? What is this? God in heaven, what is this but loneliness?" She wrung her hands, her body swaying. "For the last time—I'm your daughter. Myself, still myself. For all the love you've given me over the years I do most humbly beg you to forget a few demented words. Words cannot cancel the past, the shared past. Father—dear father—it's not much to ask. Say you'll forget all the things in which I failed you——"

Blandy rose uncertainly to his feet. Her grief moved him almost to desperation and for a moment his love for her overwhelmed him. He half-raised his hand, then a thought came to him, poisoning the springs of pity. "And—Cranstoun?"

"What of him?"

"As you say, what of him?"

She spoke so softly he could almost have deluded himself he had not caught what she said. "For good or ill—I believe for ill—I shall love him till I die."

He began to walk towards the door, stumbling a little. Steadying himself with his hand on the latch, he said: "I'm going to bed. I am very tired. I shall leave you to snuff out the candles."

When the door had closed, she moved like a pale moth from candle to candle. The little lights died one by one, leaving a faint rancid smell. When the last of them was extinguished, she stood for a time by the open window. The night air was soft, carrying music from a ball at the Catherine Wheel. The last greenish light was dying in the west and swallows wheeled high. It would be another lovely day tomorrow.

CHAPTER SIX

On Sunday Mary and her father went to church as usual, sitting in the Blandy pew. After evensong they talked for a time with the rector, then, nodding to acquaintances, returned home. Pleading a touch of heartburn, Mr. Blandy asked Susan to make him some water-gruel and retired to bed. Mary made a pretence of eating, then sat in the parlour with a book until about ten o'clock. In all she did, the sense of duality walked with her; the parallel behaviour.

She moved according to the habit of a lifetime: bowed to acquaintances, chatted to domestics, sang hymns, knelt on her hassock, folded her clothes, went to bed, rose the next morning, came down to breakfast with the usual enquiry about her father's health, received the customary formal reply; and all the time, in the numbed core of her brain, she was conscious of obedience to a will stronger than her own, of a love half desire, half fatality, of a sense of dedication, of predestination.

When the door of the study closed and the first client of the day drove up to the door, her heart began to beat sickly.

The moment had come. As she opened the door of the common pantry, she thought: It was for this moment that I was born. She could not have said what prompted the thought; her conscious mind rejected it. Yet the words remained, unforgettable.

Even now, alone and unobserved, the duality must be preserved; never for a moment must behaviour slacken. Like a guardsman trained in bravery, so she too would know her paces. Her muscles would do their duty, and her vocal chords. Her feet were light as ever on the stone flags, her hand, stirring the water-gruel, as firm, her face as inscrutable. Meeting Susannah in the passage, her voice was only a shade too friendly as she said: "I've been stirring my father's water-gruel and eating oatmeal off the bottom of the pan. I declare if I had to choose any one thing on which to live it would be oatmeal."

Over-candid, perhaps, to mention stirring the gruel. No one had seen her. The window of the pantry looked out on the wall of the adjoining house and the door was closed. The pantry was used by the entire household. She could have gone there for a saucer of milk for Dandy, a scrap of suet for the tomtits or to taste Betty's syllabub. No need to mention gruel, none at all.

Even when she was alone in her room, she continued to dissemble, taking bundles of letters from her bureau and sorting bills before she slipped the flat packet of white paper among them with the deftness of a pickpocket.

Tying her wide straw hat carefully and changing her kerchief, she took the little dog for a walk, adjusting her swift stride patiently to his jerky gait. In the churchyard she paused to chat to Tom Staverton, aware all the time of ears and eyes at the almshouses.

"And how is your father?"

"A little dyspeptic, I'm afraid."

"What was it I heard from Mr. Cawley? Some curious tale —forgive me if I misquote—something about—apparitions?"

The eyes that met his lay deep in shadow, the voice was cool. "Mr. Cranstoun mentioned more than once during his stay that he had heard music in our house."

"And what is that supposed to portend?"

"According to the superstitions of his country—a death."

Staverton chuckled. "Bless my soul! I'd no idea they were so primitive north of the Border! Lucky for us we won the day at Culloden, eh, Miss Blandy?"

"Indeed, yes!" Her laugh was only a shade too merry.

She returned home, shutting the door on a life in which, for the moment, she had no further part to play.

A Monday morning in August, a day like any other: the new red brick houses, bland in the hot sun; terriers barking at a departing stage-coach; prinked brewer's horses moving majestically from inn to inn; ladies chatting at corners, ladies matching ribbons and cheapening salads; rooks flying in and out of crevices in the church tower and swans congregating in slack water and swallows wheeling high in the clear air; leeches stirring in sub-life beneath the perforated lids of their jars; Lady Ailesbury—at the zenith of her beauty—driving up Hart Street with Mr. Horace Walpole and the child, Anne, who was to become heiress of Strawberry Hill; an old man leaning over the parapet of the bridge whose father had watched Prince Rupert enter the Lion, and a boy holding a horse's head who was to see Victoria come to the throne. A day like any other. . . .

Francis Blandy again retired early to bed. Through the open door of the parlour, Mary watched Susannah climb the stairs, a lumbering figure, pausing for breath on the half-landing. As she returned to her chair, Mary found her mouth dry; she could not have trusted her voice, but her mind was curiously empty. It was as though the centre of her brain were the still core of a whirlpool. She sat for an hour with a book. She could not have said what she read, yet when, months later, she opened the book again, the evening returned to her with terrible clarity.

At ten o'clock she went up to bed. She would sleep tonight in her mother's room; tonight should be given wholly to occult influences. She was committed now to dark ways. There was a certain intoxication in such complete surrender.

Will.

She would open her mind to Cranstoun's will.

I shall be at your side in spirit.

She lay in the stifling darkness calling upon him; evoking him. Evoking. Something in the word horrified her. To evoke. Surely—surely——

An infinity of belief that transcends all our sceptic learning and breaks free of the trammels of possibility.

Belief. But in what? What were these powers? Never till now more than half believing in them, she had been free from awe. But who had set the clock? Why, because the century was sceptical, had the natural law changed? It was little more than a decade since witchcraft had ceased to be punishable with death; had it, because the law of the land had changed, lost its power? Did a thing in becoming legal become impotent?

Terror gripped her. What had she done? What forces was she calling on? What was this course upon which she was embarked? Where would it end?

It was for this moment that I was born.

Why? Why?

Breaking the habit of a lifetime, she did not pray. Prayer had no part in this night. To call upon God now would be a blasphemy.

She was in a curious state of mind. When at last she slept, her dreams were no more confused than her waking hours.

The night was close and airless and not long before dawn heavy drops of rain fell, presage of a short sharp thunderstorm. The rooks were restless and a dog in a New Street yard started to howl.

Waking with a start, Mary lay on her back, staring at the arrows of lightning that sped the sky.

Above the sound of the storm she thought she could hear another sound and her heart contracted. She lay trembling, waiting for it to be repeated. When it returned, she sprang out of bed, moving on swift bare feet to the door.

There was no possibility of doubt. The sound came from the direction of Francis Blandy's room; the sound of moaning.

She opened the door quietly and went out onto the landing. Her father's room was at the back of the house, up a short flight of stairs. Moving without a sound, she crept to the foot of the stairs. The moaning did not return, but after she had waited for some time, a fresh sound took its place: the sound of retching.

She relaxed. Years of good living had left Francis Blandy with an uncertain digestion and such attacks were by no means unusual.

She returned to bed, to sleep until her normal hour.

The atmosphere at breakfast was no more strained than usual. Littleton's early arrival, refreshed by his holiday, relieved the tension, but Mr. Blandy, picking at his food, complained of his tea.

"Isn't it to your liking, sir?" Mary asked.

"Liking! Give Mr. Littleton a dish. I ask you, Littleton, is it to your liking?"

Littleton took a few sips. "Very nice, sir, if I may say so."

"Your manners do you more credit than your palate. What tea is this, Mary? You filled the caddy, I presume?"

"The same as usual, sir—your favourite Hyson."

"Nonsense! This tastes more like that black stuff—what do they call it? Bohea?"

"Perhaps it's stood too long. Let me pour you another dish."

Blandy turned to the clerk. "Take notice, Littleton, of an example of woman's logic. The first dish of tea, having stood too long, is bitter. The second, having stood twice as long will be half as bitter!"

Littleton flashed a look to Mary, ashamed of his own lack of courage in her defence. Susannah came to say the barber had arrived and Mr. Blandy followed her out to the kitchen.

Littleton clasped and unclasped his bony hands. "Don't let Mr. Blandy distress you, miss. He's not himself this morning."

She pressed her fingers to her eyes. "Perhaps I'm not myself either—the storm—I slept badly."

Going out to the hall, she paused uneasily, listening to the voices that came from the direction of the kitchen. Old Sam had come to shave her father at this hour for more than thirty years. There was something inexorable about habit.

The kitchen drew her. It was as though she must be where her father was, hear what he was saying, study his face.

The big room with its roaring stove and rows of shining plates and hams smoking in the chimney corner, seemed, as usual, full of people. Betty was setting crocks of dough in front of the fire to rise; Susannah stood near the door with Mrs. Emmet, sprinkling linen ready for ironing, Harman was scrubbing the great deal table and Ned was sorting knives for cleaning. Seated in a chair drawn up to the window, Mr. Blandy had given himself up to the barber. Without his smoking cap, he was quite white. Every now and then the light caught the blade of the razor. The shaving done to his satisfaction, he asked the barber to trim his hair. It did not, he knew, need trimming, but the man's attentions were soothing and he sought to prolong a pleasant moment.

Above the snip of scissors and the scouring of Harman's brush Mary heard her father ask: "Betty, did you make my tea this morning?"

"Yes, sir."

"Then your hand is losing its cunning, girl."

"I'm sorry, sir, if it wasn't to your taste."

"Anything but."

Sam wagged his scissors: "Mend your ways, young Betty, or you'll have the master thinking you're trying to poison him!"

Harman gave a loud guffaw, but Mary noticed Betty did not join in the laughter.

"Remember that tale I once told you, Sam?" Blandy asked.

"About yourself and the other gentlemen at the Lion? Very well, sir, very well indeed."

"What a memory you have!"

"Need it in my profession, sir. Wouldn't do to forget the whims and fancies of my gentlemen."

Mr. Blandy spoke reminiscently, with something of his old geniality.

He was in the most genial of moods—— Mary pulled her mind back to what he was saying.

"—A foolish affair. I cannot recall where the suggestion originated, but once the idea had entered our heads, nothing would persuade us that the wine had not been poisoned! I do remember we were all three very ill afterwards!"

"If I may say so, sir, I'll wager it was more like to be the quantity than the quality of the wine drunk that was to blame!"

Blandy chuckled. "Perhaps you're right, Sam, perhaps you're right. Poor fellows—one was to die within a year anyway, and the other's dead now, so the result would have been much the same in the end!"

The day passed without event, and at about nine o'clock Mr. Blandy went up to bed. Mary was aware of footsteps on the stairs a short time after. Had he, she wondered, asked for more water-gruel? The conflicting emotions of the night before had left their reaction in a kind of dejected indifference, in which neither hope nor fear had a place. Her back ached as after another evening spent in silent dissembling—playing a part with empty rooms for audience—she went to bed.

She woke with a start to the sound of a voice calling Susannah and the sound of footsteps on the attic stairs. Snatching a wrap she dashed out onto the landing, grey and shadowed in the first light.

Clinging to the door of his room, his body looped in pain, was her father. She gave a cry and ran to him. With Susannah's help she got him back to bed, where he lay gasping for breath, his face damp and contorted. She stayed at his side while Susannah roused the other servants. Recurrent fits of vomiting weakened him, but seemed to bring relief from pain. With poultices and a cool towel for his head, he appeared more comfortable, but as soon as it was morning, Mary sent Harman for the apothecary.

Benjamin Norton arrived with his shoes unbuckled, cravat untied and periwig awry. Mary was standing in the shadow of the bedcurtains. She seemed scarcely to be breathing. Norton looked at her curiously for a moment, memory stirring. Then, with a brief greeting, he asked her to leave him alone with her father.

She sat outside on the stairs. In the twenty minutes the examination took, she did not move. When at last the door opened, her face, white against the dark wainscoting, startled the apothecary.

She rose uncertainly to her feet. "Yes?"

Norton took her arm and led her down to the lower landing. He spoke in a whisper. "For the moment I do not know what to make of his condition."

"Did he give you any idea—of his feelings?"

"Yes."

"Well?"

"They mystify rather than enlighten. He complains most of what he described as exquisite prickings, both internal and external—rather as though he had been scourged with nettles. Then there's the difficulty in breathing—not of the lungs, but rather of the throat. A thickness of utterance quite unlike his familiar clarity of diction. As though the tongue were swollen." Norton seemed to hesitate.

"That's not all, is it?"

"I don't know what importance to place on it, but—he compared himself to a rabid dog that dare not drink." Mary seemed to sway and he caught her arms. "I'm saying too much. We grow so accustomed to these things in our profession, we don't realise how they shock."

"Forget me, Mr. Norton. Think only of my father. Tell me one thing—the pain, is it easier?"

Norton nodded. "He may sleep for a time, I think."

"Thank God," she whispered. "Have you given him any physic?"

"I am sending some round."

At the head of the stairs she caught his arm. "I've no need to beg you—take every care of my father."

"Rest assured of that, Miss Blandy."

"Just one thing more. If—if you think there is any—danger let me know, that I may send for a physician."

"I will."

"Promise?"

"I give you my word."

When Norton had gone, she dressed and coiled her hair into a cap, then she paused in the doorway of her father's room. He appeared to be sleeping peacefully. Unwilling to disturb him, she went downstairs, finding small tasks in the hope of distracting her mind. Susannah was busy ironing linen washed on the Monday; old Dame Emmet was with her, folding the things neatly and hanging them over the horse by the fire to air. When Mary came out to the kitchen with her instructions for the day, Susannah asked her if she should make some more gruel.

"Leave it for the moment, Sukey. He's sleeping now. I don't think he will require any."

"It would be no trouble, miss."

"I don't want to take you away from your ironing."

"As you say, Miss Mary. There's plenty of the other left in the pan if he wanted it in a hurry. I just thought it mightn't be fresh enough."

"Fresh enough for me!" the washerwoman hinted when Mary had gone.

"You're very welcome to it, Dame," Susannah said. "You can finish it up if you can stomach the stuff. That's more than I can."

Mary returned to her father's room, sitting near the window watching the bed in silence. Dozing lightly, he did not for the moment appear to be in any pain.

Shortly after noon, Susannah came quietly into the room and beckoned to her. Mary went out onto the landing without a word.

"Will you come to the kitchen, please?" The woman's agitation communicated itself to Mary as she followed her downstairs. As they neared the kitchen, Mary was aware of a sound that filled her with dread, a sound too fresh in her ears for mistaking: the sound of moaning.

Anne Emmet was crouched in a chair by the fire, her head between her knees, rocking to and fro in agony. Mary was dimly aware of other figures in the kitchen: Harman, carrying a bowl of water, and, standing motionless with her back to the window, Betty Binfield.

"Dame!" Mary cried. "Oh, my poor Dame!" She dropped to her knees and took the old woman's head in her arms. "Sukey—get some pillows from one of the beds, and a coverlet. We must make her more comfortable. You—Harman, go at once to Mr. Norton and ask him if he can come. Poor Dame." Holding Anne Emmet's head to her shoulder, she asked quietly: "When did this start, Sukey?"

"No more than half an hour ago, miss. I can't think what it can be. She was right as rain when she come this morning."

The old woman tried to govern her cries, but now and then a moan escaped her that distressed Mary deeply. She had a sincere affection for the washerwoman. "This is not like you, Dame." She tried to rally her. "You, always so merry! Try to tell me—are you in a fever?" Mary pressed her hand to the woman's forehead. Her skin was damp, but cool.

"It's—the pain—miss."

"We must get something to soothe it—some broth, I think Betty?"

The cook-maid did not reply.

"Betty, I want you to make some broth for Dame. As soon as possible. Wine-broth."

The girl made no attempt to move, and suddenly Mary realised she had not moved since she came into the kitchen had not spoken and had not for a moment taken her eye off her.

"Did you hear what I said?"

"Yes, miss."

"Then——"

"You seem to know the cure, miss. I suppose you would knowing the cause."

Mary rose slowly to her feet, facing the girl. "The cause! What do you mean?"

Betty spoke very softly. "Water-gruel."

CHAPTER SEVEN

Mrs. Mounteney sat erect on a wooden-seated chair in the parlour of Saragossa House, the almost featureless austerity of the room echoed in her long-backed rigidity. There was nothing in her pose to betray that she was disturbed, more disturbed perhaps than at any time in her life.

No matter which way she looked she was aware of an objec that violated the dignity of her parlour: a gruel-pan, it burnished copper seeming to draw to itself every beam of the hot morning sun. Its presence was an affront. An affront too, the kitchen gossip to which she had been compelled to listen. Knowing Susannah Gunnel a devoted servant of he old friend, a sense of duty had made the interview unavoid able, but she could not recall it without embarrassment; neve had she thought to listen to a tale of what Binfield told Gunnel of Emmet.

"Has your mistress seen the gruel-pan?"

"No, ma'am."

"Why bring it to me?"

The old servant had dropped her eyes. "It's my belief, ma'am, Mr. Norton should see it."

"The apothecary? Why?"

"He might be able to say if it's poison."

When Susannah had gone, Mary Mounteney stood for some time staring curiously at the sediment at the bottom of the pan—so starkly, so unnaturally white against the creamy oatmeal.

A monstrous element had suddenly entered her life, disturbing to her innate integrity. She was experienced enough to discount the gossip of kitchens, but the fact that such an accusation——

Accusation? Her breath caught. Against whom? As she returned to her straight chair by the bureau she was trembling.

Loyalty would impose its rules for her conduct, but for the moment she would give rein to thought, a train of thought that had waited to be followed from the instant she learned that Mary had not been shown the gruel-pan. Small, disturbing incidents returned to mind. She had neither liked nor trusted Cranstoun, for all his facile courtesies to herself. Something in his relations with Mary had filled her with uneasiness whenever she was with them. Since his going she had more than once caught a glimpse of the atmosphere of strain between Mary and her father; the girl's dutiful behaviour had seemed to her to ring a little false.

She had loved her goddaughter from childhood with the love of a good woman for a girl of high principles. It was not a love that could easily compass disillusion. Herself living apart from the laxity of her day, she could neither comprehend nor condone the frailties of others.

She was a woman of reasoned judgment, swayed neither by impulse nor sentiment. On the delicate walnut table in her parlour was a kitchen pot which might contain evidence of a crime. That the victim and—her heart misgave her momentarily—perhaps even the instigator were people she had known and loved all her life would not for an instant sway her.

Her voice was cool and firm as she instructed her footman to go for the apothecary.

CHAPTER EIGHT

THE BOWLING green had been cosseted and wooed and pandered to until it resembled a bolt of Lyons velvet stretched tight.

Against its vivid colour the figures of the players were thrown into relief; there were buff coats and coats of tobacco brown; coats of Lincoln green and Watchet blue; sad-coloured coats and gay; here a flash of military scarlet and there a note of clerical grey. A warm breeze bellied the sleeves of silk shirts, and silken hose gleamed in the sun. Among the spectators—sprawled on benches in the shade—moved the bright prints of the serving maids with their clutches of pewter tankards, spilling over with cool ale.

In the yard of the Bell, glossy hides of chestnut and sorrel and bay jostled piebald and roan, and sparrows hopped among polished hooves for the corn that fell from brimming mangers. A couple of hounds—pensioners of a local hunt—lay panting in the shade of the tap-room wall.

Now and then the placid morning was enlivened by a sober cry of congratulation as one of the gentlemen bowled a cunning wood.

Standing a little apart, the apothecary waited for the game to finish. The Rector of Fawley was skip of his team and it was unthinkable to make his presence known to him till the last head had been played.

Seen against this familiar background, his business was preposterous, and Benjamin Norton found his earlier conviction wavering. The interview with Mrs. Mounteney; the retold tales of the servants, Binfield and Gunnel; the symptoms of the old washerwoman, Emmet, all of which had yesterday seemed so complementary, so consistent in their evidence, now, in the stability of this masculine world, became the gossip of a coven of malicious females. Had it not been for the gritty, scentless, insoluble powder at the bottom of the pan and the suspicions his own training told him were correct, he would have been inclined to finish his ale and return to his galleypots. But the powder remained, a sediment in his mind. Best to see the business through. He would be failing in his professional duty if he allowed his natural scepticism to influence his judgment.

What a monstrous regiment they were in all conscience: Mrs. Mounteney with her too-conscious uprightness, the maids with their ignorant prejudices and their patent jealousies, the poor old creature Emmet, too inarticulate to explain her own sufferings intelligibly enough to permit him to prescribe an antidote. Then Miss Blandy herself, riddled with superstition, for all her schooling! Among such unreliable witnesses anything might be true. Or, for that matter, nothing.

Well, the least he could do was to inform Mr. Blandy's brother-in-law of the position, passing his own burden of doubt to the unworldly wisdom of the Rector.

The implications of the affair were too outrageous for credence; such things did not happen among educated people. Even the law—lagging ever behind popular opinion—had at long last reduced witches to the level of the illiterate crones they had always been, and as for the rest—why, this was mid-eighteenth-century England, not the Italy of the Borgias!

The last bowl came to rest and, the decision reached, the gentlemen began to move away from the green. As the apothecary approached the Reverend Mr. Stevens, he was conscious of an acute feeling of embarrassment. With a member of the medical, or even the legal profession, he would have been on sure ground, but, he told himself irreverently, the cloth was the very devil!

CHAPTER NINE

THE HOUSE was quiet, but not at rest. An atmosphere of uneasiness hung about it, intangible as the first exploratory fingers of mist, but there all the time, an uneasiness that did not spring wholly from anxiety. It was as though there were eyes at every keyhole; the opening of a door would surprise a silence, and servants paused just a shade too long before accepting an instruction.

Even Mr. Blandy, sheltered by illness, was aware of the atmosphere. In the intervals between bouts of pain and nausea, his sensibilities were curiously alert. For two days now he had made no pretence of dressing or attending to business. Other pretences had gone, too. He no longer deluded himself he was getting better. His body was tormented by such a complexity of ills, some of which he knew without the apothecary's word to be irreparable. Pain had drained him of strength to resist further pain. Futile to talk, as Mary did, of sending for Dr. Addington. Send for his lawyer, make his will and set his house in order, yes; send for his brother-in-law to instruct him in his conduct on his last journey, by all means; but incur further expense and endure further questioning and prodding and bleeding and purging from another leech, no. If, after all, he agreed to Addington, it would only be to please Mary.

To please Mary. For a moment tears clouded his eyes. The phrase, with its ring of childhood, was infinitely sad. The years slipped away and he was a man in his early thirties again, walking down Cheapside, a pair of tiny green slippers in his briefcase. He recalled the incident as though it were yesterday. He had always liked his little girl to have pretty things; it cultivated the taste. Taste was important. Even when you reached the end of it all, it was pleasant for the eye to rest, as his did now, on the gracious lines and tones of a walnut tallboy, on Persian runners and mellowed wainscoting. Even physic was a little less unpleasant taken from a Bristol glass.

Mary brought him fresh flowers every morning from his wife's borders, setting them on a line with his eyes. She rarely spoke to him, or he to her. There was no need. Words were a mistake. Words had all but destroyed their relationship. She would sit at the window by the hour, doing her needlework. Mary had come back to him. There was no doubt in his mind. She was closer to him now than at any time since——

His thoughts came to a barrier; beyond lay a prohibited country. No matter. Suffice that Mary was his once more.

It was curious how wrong the living could be about life; when you reached the end you knew how few things really mattered. He must try to pass on his new-found wisdom to Mary. She would be in need of wisdom when he was no longer there to protect her.

The past was past. He could find in his heart no trace of bitterness towards her. How, when she had been his only love? With her at his side he would face death with the utmost tranquillity, knowing a single regret: that he must leave her. The small ambitions, the little indulgences, the petty vanities shrank into insignificance and love alone remained. No need for words—words were dangerous.

Here at the back of the house the Saturday sounds were muted; a certain clatter from the yard and the murmur of voices from the kitchen below told him that the morning was well advanced. He had sent Mary out for a walk. It was not right that her eyes should rest only on sickness. He thought wistfully of the fresh cool river as it flowed below the wooded hills. It had been pleasant riding out to Culham Court to woo his pretty Miss Stevens, very pleasant. Taken all in all, life had not been too grudging. . . .

Susannah closed the door softly and came towards the bed on silent feet.

Francis Blandy opened his eyes. "No need to creep, Sukey," he said with his laboured articulation. "I was not asleep."

The old servant pulled nervously at her apron.

"What is the matter?"

"Sir—I——"

"Come a little nearer. I cannot hear what you're saying. Such a clattering in the yard."

"That Harman!"

"A clumsy fellow. I miss our excellent Ned sadly."

Susannah came to the side of the bed. "Are you feeling any better, sir?"

"Much the same, Sukey."

"The pain?"

"Abated a little for the moment."

"Thank God for that, sir."

"Is there—something you wish to say?"

"Not *wish*!"

"Must, then?" She nodded. "What is it?"

"Concerning your health, sir. And—and your family."

"My—family?"

"Sir—I beg you not to put yourself in a passion, but hear what I have to say."

"Passion and I are long since strangers," he said gently. "Go on."

"It's a matter of life and death, or might be, and—well, the Reverend Mr. Stevens wrote me——" Her voice was unsteady, her manner confused. "Sir—I believe—that something in your water-gruel did you an injury."

"My water-gruel? Surely there's nothing more innocuous?"

"Not the gruel itself, sir. Something added to it."

He stared at her, puzzled. "Added to it?"

"On Monday morning she came to me—Miss Blandy, that is, and said she'd been stirring your gruel. It was kept as usual in the common pantry. I made it, the way you like it, sir. Why should she stir it?"

"I've no idea, Sukey, unless from solicitude."

"Sir, haven't you understood what I'm trying to tell you? Haven't you, sir?"

Blandy pressed a trembling hand to his brow. "My wits are

not so sharp as they were. My head is not right—not as it used to be, nor has been for some time. Bear with me—I get confused. Try to be more clear. What is this you say—something about my gruel?"

"A powder, sir."

"What powder?"

"We found some. In the bottom of the pan. A white gritty powder, standing apart from the oatmeal. Mr. Norton's seen it, sir."

"Mr. Norton? But how does he come into this?"

"I took it round to Mrs. Mounteney. She was to show it to him."

"All these people, these outsiders—and I not consulted——"

"I didn't want you troubled, sir."

"You troubled me far more by drawing strangers into my affairs, and then, when all has been bandied about, presenting me with the public verdict."

"I'm sorry if I did wrong, sir, but I thought it my duty."

"After all these years, Sukey, I suppose it's too late for me to point out what your duty is to me. Very good, then. What does Mr. Norton say?"

"He can't make out what the powder is while it's still wet."

"Norton not know! And so much used to drugs!"

"He said: 'Let it be what it is, it ought not to be there.' He thinks it proper that Miss be searched, her pockets, and her keys and papers taken away from her."

Blandy gasped, a pain gripping his heart. "My daughter——" He closed his eyes as the room seemed to sway in front of them. "What has this to do—with her?"

"I've told you, sir. Or leastwise, I thought I had. It's my belief she stirred some powder into the gruel!"

He could not find strength to speak for a time, then he asked:

"Even supposing—this powder, whatever it may be—where could Mary have got it from?"

"Him."

Blandy gripped the coverlet. "Whom?"

"Mr. Cranstoun," the old woman whispered.

"But——" He could scarcely breathe. "She has not seen him this year."

"Betty says——"

"I'm not—interested in what—Betty says."

"But, sir——" The whiteness of his face and the faintness of his breathing silenced her.

When at last he spoke again, she knew he had forgotten her. "He—a long time since—when he was here—we talked of such things. He mentioned some poison they have—in his country——"

Susannah hesitated, then she said: "Her papers. She should be searched. And her room."

"It's unthinkable. I cannot shock her so much. I cannot."

"But suppose there were letters. I'd do it, sir, only I've no right. She's your daughter. Tell her you must see all her papers. You've the right. You and no one else."

"I never in all my life saw a letter that came to her—from any person."

His pitiful wan dignity made her drop her eyes. "As you say, sir."

"Go now."

She walked in silence across the room. As she was closing the door she thought she heard him murmur: "That villain—that he ever came to my house——"

CHAPTER TEN

He was not well on Sunday night. He complained of heartburn. Susannah would agree to this. It was because he was not well that the water-gruel was made. His illness was the reason for the gruel, not the result of it. If he had not been suffering from one of his recurrent attacks of dyspepsia there would have been no question of gruel.

And so on: variants of a single thought, revolving in the surface of Mary's mind, expressed always in words; as a sentence, clear-cut and reasonable; an answer.

In the beginnning there had been duality, the being and the seeming; then, called forth by a cry in the night, pity, anxiety pure and simple and disinterested, the anxiety she would have felt for a loved parent at any time, an instinctive emotion quite separate from the dark numb core of her brain. And now, after three days, the numbness spreading outwards until there was nothing but the single thought, revolving all the time: *It was not the gruel, it was not the gruel.*

She walked like a woman pursued, her hair damp on her brow, her linen clinging to her body, hurrying in the humid heat of an overcast day up the hill to Harpsden, taking paths and lanes at random, asking only that they should hold no memories. It was so small, her world; one road led up to Paradise House; another to an uncle at Fawley, a third to an uncle at Culham, a fourth to a dead friend at Turville, while over the Wargrave road and the towpath to Shiplake brooded the hanging woods. The surrounding hills, heavy with the past, seemed to her to be drawing in on the town, a trap. Useless to walk; there was no escape. Her strong young body was tireless; it was not through exertion that she would find sleep.

He was ill, she told herself, *he was ill. He had been failing for a long time; even his friends remarked it.*

Striding, unseeing, through the Saturday crowds that thronged the pavements, she returned to the cool dim listening house. There was a letter for her on the hall table. For a moment she did not recognise the handwriting and her eyes blurred in apprehension. It had been agreed that any letter of Cranstoun's should be addressed in a borrowed hand. Once safe in her own room, she realised the writing was that of her uncle John, but less firm, less neat than the Rector's usual crabbed academic script.

The note, obviously written under stress of emotion, was almost incoherent: through a fog of scriptural allusions, prayers that God in His wisdom and mercy might show her the way of expiation, self-reproach for his failure in guidance of his niece, and for his lack of moral courage in delegating to an old servant what he knew it to be his duty himself to communicate to his brother-in law, its meaning became clear.

The letter dropped from her nerveless fingers as panic gripped her.

The house: the whispering, listening, spying house: the servants, hushed whenever she came into a room; Betty Binfield, her eyes never leaving her; Harman's sullen insolence; Susan's hostility; the apothecary's evasions.

Instinct took over; the primitive instinct for self-preservation. With swift silent movements she locked her door, slid open the secret drawer where Cranstoun's letters were concealed. They were few in number and innocuous to a degree, but among them was the packet of white powder. Very little of it had gone. Very little—— As she took the bundle of letters from the drawer, a few brown petals fluttered to the ground. Once they had been crimson. A musty odour hung about them. Thrusting the bundle deep in her pocket, she unlocked the door and, glancing round, walked steadily down the stairs. At this time of year only one fire was kept going: the kitchen.

She opened the door, her face prepared to meet any scrutiny. By chance the kitchen was empty. With a single swife movement she stuffed the packet between the bars and poked it in firmly. Fresh coal had recently been put on the fire and it burned dully. The papers, tight-packed, were slow in catching. She raked vigorously, a shower of ashes falling redly to the hearth, but no more than the edges of the packet smouldered. On her knees, frenziedly working the bellows, she became aware, without turning, that she was being watched. Her legs withered beneath her and she found herself unable to move. Someone was coming towards her, walking softly as a cat. Paralysed with fear, she crouched over the fire, no longer strong enough to hold the bellows. It was, she knew, Betty Binfield.

Suddenly the papers caught and little flames licked round the tight-wedged packet. On an instant the cook-maid dived forward and, plunging her hand among the dead coals, snatched at the blazing fragments, stamping out the flames with her foot. No more than a scrap of paper remained but, Mary saw to her dismay, the writing on it was still legible.

"Only—some old bills—of mama's," she heard herself saying lamely. "No use keeping them."

Betty was standing over her. This was her hour. Nothing could take it from her.

"Give me that paper," Mary cried, struggling to her feet. "Give it to me. Do you hear? I insist you give it me."

The girl drew back, holding the scrap of paper high above her head as though teasing a child. "Sukey!" she called. "Come here!" Still clasping the paper, she ran to the yard door shouting: "You—out there in the washhouse, Ann James and Mary Banks. Come here! Come here, your mistress wants you!"

Mary stood with her back to the fire, unable to escape as her servants gathered round her.

"Sukey, you read what it says!" Betty cried.

"You know I can't read."

"Can either of you?"

"No."

"Nor me neither."

"Then I'll read it myself." Betty took the fragment to the window, smoothing it carefully. "'The powder—to——' Wait—it's scorched. Yes. Yes. Listen, listen carefully all of you. 'The powder to—clean—the pebbles with!'" She laughed wildly. "And in his writing, too! In the Captain's own hand!"

"Betty!" Mary cried. "What are you saying?"

"Listen to her! Listen to her voice! Look at her face, look at the way she's shaking! What am I saying? She knows, she knows all right!"

"I insist you tell me and the others what I am accused of!"

"See? Out of her own mouth! Digging a pit for herself with every word she says! A pit filled with quicklime!"

Mary cried out.

"Control your wicked tongue, girl!" Susan shouted. The two charwomen clutched each other, shivering with excitement.

"Me? Not any more. I've kept silence long enough about her and him, and she knows it. That's why she can't send me away. She daresn't—I know too much!"

"I can send you away!" Mary cried angrily. "I'm sending you away now. It's nothing to me where you go or what lies you tell. I'm sending you away!"

"You won't be in a position to send anybody anywhere by the time a week's out!" The girl began to lose her head, floundering now among a dozen petty jealousies, climbing up out of the gutter of her own inferiority, scarring and smirching and degrading everything she touched, seeing in every kindness a bribe; goaded on to fresh outrage by the thought that in addition to all its other boons, life should have given Mary the only man ever to touch her own wanton heart. Twisting and betraying and distorting, she yet never for a moment lost her grip on the thin thread of truth; wounding blindly and ignorantly, she was never too wide of the mark.

The room was in an uproar, but still the voice went on, relieving a common soul of the resentments of five years. When at last she paused for want of breath, her face distorted with passion, Susannah cried: "How dare you speak so of Mr. Blandy's daughter!"

"Mr. Blandy's daughter! Mr. Blandy's daughter! God damn her, I say. God damn her for a black bitch!"

The two charwomen screamed.

Betty whipped round. "Why so queasy? *I* should be glad to see her go up the ladder and swing!"

CHAPTER ELEVEN

DUALITY was at an end. The parallel lines had converged in a single point of horror.

Horror would not leave her now. It was nothing to her that the servants knew. She knew.

Stumbling up the stairs on feet her brain had ceased to control, she hid in her room as an animal hides. The blood was singing in her ears like a high-pitched shriek.

She had no idea how long she lay there with her horror. Through open casements the afternoon sounds rose to her from the street below, but she was shut off from them; a woman set apart.

After what seemed a long time she was aware of voices outside on the landing. It would be Mr. Norton on his evening call.

She must see him. That at least was clear. She must speak to him. Struggling to her feet, she caught a glimpse of her face in the mirror; the face of a stranger. Without troubling to push her hair inside her cap, she waited in her doorway until at last the apothecary came from her father's room, then she stepped out of the shadows, catching hold of his arm as he came along the passage.

Norton started, staring at her terrible face as though he too had difficulty in recognising her.

"Well?" she whispered.

"Well, Miss Blandy?"

"How is he?"

"Worse."

She gave a moan.

"What did you expect?" he demanded roughly.

She faltered. "When I was with him this morning he—he said he was feeling a little better."

"He wanted to spare you pain." Norton did not attempt to conceal the irony in his voice.

"What about Dr. Addington?"

"He is still against consulting him."

She held her head high, swaying a little. "Then I'm afraid we shall have to override his wishes."

"You want me to send to Reading?"

"I insist you send. Or, if you prefer, I will take the responsibility."

"It's not a question of responsibility, Miss Blandy. I am answerable only to my own conscience when a patient is in danger."

She gasped.

"Very grave danger, miss," he said icily.

"Then why did you hesitate to send for Dr. Addington?"

"I had no hesitation myself. I just thought it a little curious *you* should be so eager to call him in." Norton turned quickly and, hurrying down the stairs, let himself out of the house.

CHAPTER TWELVE

THE RING was closing; soon now there would be no one left outside. Susannah, Betty, Harman; Mary Mounteney, Benjamin Norton; John Stevens; Francis Blandy himself. By the Sunday morning Dr. Addington, paying his second visit, had joined the circle, drawn in by a charred scrap of paper thrust into his hand by a servant and a sample of powder from the bottom of a gruel-pan. These things, the material evidence, came late, serving only to corroborate what medical knowledge had already read in the patient's symptoms. It needed neither Binfield's malice nor the apothecary's laborious analysis to show him where the wind stood.

An expert in mental diseases, Addington would one day be called in to attend the King, George the Third; between that day and this August morning lay over thirty years of experience, yet never would he encounter a stranger situation than this. His acquaintance with the Blandys was of the slightest, he neither liked nor disliked. Sentiment was not in any way involved, yet the implications of the affair shocked him. Here were people of a similar social status to his own, not effete, or debauched, not, on the other hand, ignorant. Yet he was presented with almost incontrovertible evidence that the daughter had made an attempt to poison the father. The thing was monstrous, yet—here was the disturbing thought—it could happen. The human mind was indeed a terrible thing.

It was with the utmost embarrassment that he suffered Mary's anxious enquiries. With the fragment of paper—its writing still legible—in one pocket and Norton's sample in the other, he promised to drive over again the next day, to do everything in his power to ease pain, save life. Watching the long pale mask with its shadowed eyes, he asked her carefully: "Has your father, to your knowledge, given offence to anyone lately?"

"Offence?" Mary's voice came, toneless, from a throat dry with fear.

"To servants—clients—anyone who might wish him ill?"

"My father is at peace with the world and the world at peace with him."

"I—see." He paused for a moment, hesitating still to strip away the last lying decencies good manners demanded, then, meeting her eyes, he said: "You realise, Miss Blandy, that if your father dies you will be irretrievably ruined?"

Not so much as a shadow crossed her face. There was, he thought, something less than normal in such self-control.

When he had driven away, she went up to her room, walking as a somnambulist walks, or a woman in the thrall of a hypnotist. Taking her pen, writing methodically, conventionally, as though accepting an invitation to a garden-party, she began a letter to Cranstoun. The note was written from the heart; a cold heart, a heart stilled by terror. Even as her hand moved over the paper she saw it, this, her last effort to save herself, as futile and—more—ignoble. Yet she signed it and sealed it, and, with a discretion little short of grotesque, sought out Littleton, and, with some thin excuse of forwarding a receipt, asked him to address it for her. On this occasion Littleton made no demur. His complacency should have warned her. He did not even query the London address. He queried nothing. Obligingly he offered to see the letter posted. She thanked him with wan effusiveness. The incident was over, that unworthy moment when the instinct for self-preservation was stronger even than remorse.

Left alone in the study, Littleton stared at the note uncertainly. Compunction, instilled by a lifetime of training, stayed his hand. Spying was for servants. For a short time the young man was shaken by emotions more complex than any he had known in his narrow existence. Industrious, loyal, pure, life had been niggardly to him. His love for Mary had been selfless and undemanding; a starveling love. He had asked no more than a word, a glimpse, the chance to perform a small service. Cranstoun he had mutely accepted as a being of different clay from himself; undependable, perhaps, but a man of birth and charm. Now, suddenly, he found himself prey to a jealousy he had never known when Cranstoun was under Mary's roof.

She could think of him. With her father dying and the house ranged against her, it was to Cranstoun that she turned.

He flushed unhappily at the thought of himself as go-between. She had, he saw, used his selfless worship without scruple.

His hand was trembling as he picked up the paper knife.

It was, he saw, his duty to intercept the letter while there was yet time for the doctors to save Mr. Blandy.

He spread the sheet out flat on the table. The words seemed to stand apart from the paper.

"Dear Willie,

"My father is so bad that I have only time to tell you if you do not hear from me soon again, do not be frightened.

I am a little better myself and lest any accident should happen to your letters, take care what you write. My sincere compliments. I am ever yours,

"M.C."

Methodically, in his neat clerk's hand, Littleton copied the letter and walking up the empty Sunday street, delivered the copy to Mr. Norton.

He returned home reluctantly. There was no breeze and the sun beat through his fustian clothes, his footsteps echoing. In the distance he could hear a dog barking at the water. On this brilliant afternoon the house, with its sickness of body and mind, filled him with repugnance. It was not in him to revolt, but a certain dulled unexpectant wistfulness penetrated the layers of his mediocrity, and youth flickered in him for a moment, a wan candle in the August sunshine.

His footsteps on the stairs were diffident, his tap on Mr. Blandy's door too soft for first hearing.

The interview did not last long. No longer than was needed to read the four lines of a letter. Returning to the study, the clerk carried with him the memory of the smile that washed the old man's face clean of pain as he whispered: "What will not a girl do for the man she loves!"

CHAPTER THIRTEEN

Night waited. Through the day there had been subterfuge, the need to dissemble; behaviour and the exercise of wit; a constant vigilance over tongue and muscle lest in an unguarded moment she should seem to accept the suspicion with which the house was instinct. But now the door was closed and the candle snuffed. Here in the darkness she was alone with her fear.

Fear tied a ligature round her head and dried her throat

and cramped the muscles of her stomach. Fear had become an end in itself. It had been to this that all which had gone before had led. It was not a constant thing, her fear—it ran through many mutations, now of this, now of that, but she knew it integrated by a single thread; fear of the moment when she could no longer blind herself to what she had done.

That moment had come. She was alone with it, with a horror that transcended remorse or anguish for her father's suffering, transcended regret or self-condemnation. Lying on her bed in the airless darkness, she traced with pitiless clarity the steps in her own degradation; the subtle undermining of her integrity—condoning here, accepting there—the growth in her of an uneasy smirched tolerance, the lowering of standards. "The journey of a thousand miles——" he had said. Which, then, had been the single step? A kiss, perhaps, in the February woods. From such a starting-point the rest was easy. Easy enough for the woman who had accepted Anne Murray to accept Miss Capel. From there, why quibble at a Covent Garden bawd? For the woman who had taken a lover so hungrily, the acceptance of the occult would be no more than a titilation of the senses. Corruption was only a matter of degree; it would not be possible to say at which precise point the rot set in. Suffice to say that an essay in the occult, with all the dark emotion it implied, would not have been possible to the girl who had looked out across the Thames Valley on a summer morning and thought the world fair.

The journey of a thousand miles—— And this, then, was where it ended; to lie alone with horror.

Alone.

I shall be at your side in spirit.

But he was not at her side. Never in all the years she had known him had she felt more apart, more wholly forlorn.

Where are you? her heart cried out in anguish. But she could not evoke even so much as the lines of his face, the timbre of his voice. The night was empty of him.

Where are you? her heart cried, but with a fainter voice now. A thought was shaping, as a picture shapes among embers.

Tossing wildly, she tried to shut her mind to it, but it grew in clarity until resistance was useless.

He had known.

God forgive him, Cranstoun had known what was in the powder, known what its effect would be.

On an instant the fabric of necromancy and witchcraft and faith and will and all the powers of darkness that he had so patiently built over a long period began to crumble. There were no dark powers; there was no will; nothing beyond, behind, beneath; nothing to invoke, no devil in the market for souls. He had hypnotised her, not through any supernatural power, but through her consuming love for him. His dominion had been over her senses, not her spirit.

With the full realisation of what he had trapped her into doing, she slipped to her knees in a frenzy of prayer for forgiveness, incoherent, chaotic: "Almighty and most merciful Father—Father—— My father—have pity on him. Do with me what you will, only spare him further suffering. Our Father which art in Heaven—we have strayed—like lost sheep, and there is no health in us—health. Restore him to health—give him health—give him life. Gentle Jesus—gracious God, forbid it not. Let the punishment fall on the guilty, not the innocent. Oh, God—dear God, forgive me—God, help me——" Rocking to and fro in anguish, her face distorted with tears, she slept at last, but that night something left her never to return: the power to feel deeply. In all that was to follow, nothing would more than brush the edges of her mind. With the realisation of Cranstoun's guilt and her own complicity, the limit of human suffering was reached.

CHAPTER FOURTEEN

Dr. Addington arrived early on the Monday morning. The change in his patient shocked him. Mr. Blandy's pulse was intermittant, he breathed and swallowed with difficulty and appeared to be in considerable pain. From experience in similar cases, Addington knew that the chances of pulling him through were slight; the damage to tissues and organs was irreparable.

Francis Blandy had abandoned his rather pitiful jocosity and seemed very weak. It was not without diffidence that Addington asked him whether he had any idea as to the cause of his illness.

"Yes. Oh, yes, doctor."

"You mean?"

"Poison," Mr. Blandy whispered painfully.

"Have you any suspicion of the giver? Let me say at once, that I have formed an opinion of my own which it would take a lot to sway."

Tears stood in the old man's eyes, but he smiled faintly. "A poor lovesick girl—not—not to be blamed——"

Inured as he was, Addington found himself curiously moved. He had made arrangements to stay in Henley all day. The case was disturbing in more than a medical sense. If—as seemed tolerably certain—his patient did not recover, the affair might come before a court of judicature. Little as he desired it himself, he could see no way of avoiding it. Too many people were involved: a host of gossiping men and women. Professionally the thing was unpleasant; a distribution of responsibility was desirable. Norton was a capable enough fellow on his own level, but—an apothecary! He decided to send to Oxford for Dr. Lewis, a man whose writings on the *Pharmacopœia* he held in respect. He could have wished he had never been involved in the affair. His job was to save life, not take it. The hounding of a young gentlewoman—however guilty—was a distasteful business.

He had already felt it his duty to take the step of refusing Mary her father's room. The girl's grief and anxiety appeared genuine enough, but for all his learning he knew himself a novice in the inscrutability of women.

Mary, livid and draggled, hung about the passage, sitting

on the stairs outside her father's door, or standing against the wall waiting for Addington to go in and out.

"Miss Blandy."

"Yes, doctor?"

"Come here a moment." He noticed her gait was faltering and uncertain, as though some conduit between brain and muscle were faulty.

"Yes?"

"I think it only right to tell you—your father is sinking."

She swayed, and for a moment he thought she was going to faint.

"If you have a wish to speak to him——"

"I was afraid to seek your permission."

"It can do no harm. Nothing can do very much harm now. Or very much good."

"Tell me something——"

"He knows," Addington said quietly.

"Ah!"

He opened the door for her and watched her walk with her strangely disintegrated gait towards the bed, then he closed the door without a sound.

Susannah was sitting by the window watching her master. It seemed wrong to be sitting there with her hands in her lap. Her eyes followed Mary across the room with something of the vigilance and distrust of an old dog's. Mary did not even see her.

"Mary!" Blandy's ravaged face lit up.

"Father!" She dropped to her knees at the side of the bed, taking his hand. For a time neither spoke.

"How are you?"

"Very ill I fear—very ill, my dear."

She dropped her head to his hand. "How can you so much as look at me——"

"Love is a strange thing, my Mary—as I think you've learned."

She raised her head. "There's something I must tell you."

"I know."

"You don't. Not everything. Not the inner truth. I—I want you to hear me. To believe me when I say—as to your illness I'm entirely innocent."

"Not—*entirely,* Mary."

"No. That was wrong. But innocent of any desire to cause you suffering."

"Go—on," he whispered.

"The powder—this deadly, terrible thing—it was given me with another intent."

"What—intent?"

"To procure your love."

"For—*you,* Mary?"

"No. No. To—make you kind. God forgive me that I should ever have dabbled in such things, but I did honestly believe the powder to be an innocuous thing." She looked into his face, holding his hand in both hers. "It would be useless to lie to you now. You're—on the threshold of knowing everything. Oh—your poor eyes are blank with pain—pain of my causing. Father—papa, dearest papa—I do beg you most humbly—forgive me. Forgive my wicked folly."

He stared at her in silence, waiting for the moment when the pain would relax its hold and allow him to speak, then he whispered, his voice no more than the rustling of frozen leaves: "I forgive thee, my dear—and I hope God may forgive thee——" Unconsciously he had slipped into the older mode of speech, using little words she had not heard since her earliest childhood. "Thou shouldst have considered better than to listen to that man. Such a villain. To come to my house—eat and drink the best my house could afford—then—to take away my life and—ruin my daughter." With a supreme effort he rallied his failing strength. "Oh, my dear—thou must hate the ground he treads on—thou canst not help it——"

"No blame for me?" she murmured. "None, father?"

"My child—my little girl——"

"You—believe me?" He nodded faintly. "It's like a knife piercing my heart, your tenderness to me. I think anger would have been easier to bear."

As a spasm of pain caught him, she cried out: "You must curse me for what I've done. Curse me—I ask you to. On my knees. Curse me!"

"I? Curse you? You, Mary, my daughter? How could you think that I could curse you? My dear—I bless you. I hope God may bless you too and—and amend your life——" The effort of speech was draining him of the last remnants of strength and it was in the faintest of whispers that he said: "Go now, Mary. Out of this room. Say no more—lest you should say anything to your own prejudice."

CHAPTER FIFTEEN

Dr. Lewis arrived by postchaise from Oxford at about eight that night. Addington had not left the house. Betty brought a supper of cold meat and ale to the parlour and hung about in the hope that one of the doctors would question her, but neither was in the mood for such answers as hers. Now and then footsteps passed by the window, but no one looked up at the house. Addington concluded from this that the matter was not yet common property.

"A rather curious situation," Lewis said. "The two of us sitting here waiting for a crime to be, as it were, consummated."

"One feels monstrously impotent." Addington poured out some more ale. "You confirm my opinion?"

"About the cause?"

"No. The outcome."

"Inevitable."

"Nothing more to be done?"

"Nothing. The damage to organs and tissues is, as you suggested, quite irreparable. It puzzles me a little that he should have held out so long."

"A man of spirit."

"So I should guess. An unpleasant business."
"A tragic business."
"This girl——" Lewis said. "The daughter——"
"Yes?"
"What was your idea?"
"I've taken no action, if that's what you mean."
"With a magistrate?"
"No action of any sort."
"She's still at liberty?"
"Yes."
"Isn't that rather dangerous?"
"I've forbidden her her father's room."
Lewis went over to the window. "That's not what I was thinking of."
"You mean——?"
"What is her state of mind?"
"I should say—desperate."
Lewis looked down the street to the river. "And it hasn't occurred to you she might do herself some harm?"
Addington started faintly. "I confess it hadn't."
"She could, I feel, be confined to her room, a guard placed on her door."
"One rather hesitates to take so much on oneself. I could find it in my heart to pity the creature. I should tell you—her father believes her innocent."
"Poor old man."
"Not innocent of the action. Of the intent."
"Are you sure of this? He's not merely trying to shield her?"
"He's passed beyond any possibility of—dissembling. He sincerely believes her to have given him this powder in ignorance of its qualities."
"Perhaps it's a consolation to him."
"If ever a man was in need of one——!"
"What's your own feeling, Addington?"
"I? Defend me from the workings of the feminine mind!"
"I thought minds were your speciality," Lewis said drily.

"Diseased minds I can deal with. It's seeming normality that baffles me."

"Where is Miss Blandy now?"

"In her room I expect. She hasn't stirred since morning."

"Then it would be quite simple—the turn of a key."

"I suppose so."

"I think a guard of some sort, do you?"

"As you say."

"Have you any ideas?"

"I was just trying to think. There's a fellow—Heane, Hearne—some such name. Sexton at the church; comes in now and then to do the silver, I believe. He was sometime servant to Mr. Blandy. I think he would be a reliable man."

Lewis looked at Addington shrewdly. "So the suggestion is not a new one?"

"Not entirely. One rather likes—a second opinion."

As the key turned in the lock, Mary threw herself on her bed, crouching against the wall. Addington stood a little apart, coolly waiting for her hysteria to spend itself. An emotional bleeding would do her good.

After a time her sobs died away and she lay exhausted, seeming unaware of the tall figure at the window. "When you feel yourself able to talk, Miss Blandy——"

She sat up, staring at the doctor. "What now?"

"A few questions." He drew up a chair to her.

"Does it need any words of mine to describe the horror—the agony of mind——"

"Don't distress yourself, miss. I'm not your confessor. Repentance is no concern of mine."

"I can think of nothing else. A lifetime is too short——"

"Yes, yes, I understand," he said calmly. Then, crossing his elegant legs, he asked: "Tell me something. This powder—you put it in your father's gruel?"

"Yes," she said faintly.

"Which he drank—when?"

"On the Monday and Tuesday nights."

"Only then?"

"Isn't that enough?" she cried out.

"Not on any earlier occasions?"

"No."

"Where did you get this powder?" He watched her fa through narrowed eyes. It seemed to him subtly to chang

"From Mr. Cranstoun."

"Have you any idea where he obtained it?"

"It might be from a Mrs. Morgan, in Edinburgh. Ho do I know? How do I know the truth of anything? H told me the powder was harmless, that it would make m father kind to him. Told me he had taken it himself, man times."

"And you believed him?"

"Yes."

"Surely you should have known better?"

"I knew nothing—nothing. Only that—I loved him."

"I—see." Addington changed his ground. "Suppose possible to prove what you say. Would you endeavour bring this Mr. Cranstoun to justice?"

She leaned forward, staring at the floor, her chin in h hands. "Adding guilt to guilt?"

"Pardon me—I don't follow."

"Isn't that what I should be doing? I'm fully conscious my own part in this. Nothing can wipe that out. Wouldn it be adding guilt to guilt to take any step to his prejudice"- she raised her head—"to the prejudice of a man I consider m husband?"

"Your—husband?"

"In all but ceremony."

Addington rose abruptly.

"Is that all, doctor?" she asked wearily.

"Not quite all. I believe Mr. Cranstoun described this powder to clean Scotch pebbles. Why, if it was merely philtre?"

"This is not a day for witchcraft. He was afraid derision."

"A curious thing to fear in such an enterprise," Addington murmured ironically. "Tell me—if you thought the powder to be harmless, why did you not try some yourself?"

"I was never asked to. There was no useful purpose to be served."

"What prompted you to throw the packet into the fire?"

"I wanted to destroy all evidence that I had been in touch with Cranstoun."

"Why, at this particular stage?"

"I was hedged round with suspicion—the servants, Mr. Norton, even my own uncle."

"Very well. Your father was taken ill on the Monday night."

"Only a slight attack. He—he had been complaining of heartburn on the Sunday. That was why he asked for gruel."

"How did you know he was ill on Monday night? Did he rouse the house?"

"No. He told no one, to my knowledge."

"Then how did you know he was ill?"

"I heard——"

"Heard what?"

"The sound of moaning."

"His room is some distance from yours. You must sleep very lightly, Miss Blandy."

"I was awake."

"Why?"

"The storm woke me."

"Very good. We now come to Tuesday night."

"Then the house was roused. I called in Mr. Norton as soon as it was light."

"Wednesday morning. And I was not called in until Saturday. A man in such a grave state is left to an apothecary. Why?"

"I wanted to call you. Mr. Norton will tell you—I begged him to call you immediately he saw any danger. My father opposed it. In the end I went against his wishes."

"If you were in such distress, why, when at long last I was

consulted, did you keep me in the dark?" He stood over her. "Why did you not tell me the cause of his illness?"

"How could I be sure? I was blind—blind——"

"You still maintain you did not know the powder to be poison?"

"Not till I saw its effect, no. No, no, no! I've told you everything I know. Must you go on? Isn't it enough to you that I should be locked up in my own house like a felon? Isn't it sufficient punishment that I know now what I've done? Isn't it torment enough to be separated, on your orders, from the only person in the world I love? Must you go on and on and on? Are you a doctor, or my prosecutor?"

"Control yourself, Miss Blandy. You will make yourself ill."

"Ill! Ill! I wish I could die—I wish I could die! Why don't you allow me to die now? Or would that be letting me off too lightly?"

CHAPTER SIXTEEN

The next day and night were so many hours cut out of life; dawn came, sounds rose from the street below, then at last dusk fell and the sounds ceased. The house was quiet but sleepless. Now and then the silence would be broken by a footstep on the landing, or the opening and shutting of the door of Mr. Blandy's room. Mary had asked to be allowed to sit on the stairs below her father's door, but Addington had refused her. At midday, and later, just before dusk, Ned Hearne brought her some tea and a few slices of bread and butter.

"Tell me, Ned. How does he?" she whispered.

"Badly, miss."

She seemed scarcely to hear him. She did not speak again, but he stayed with her for a time, unwilling to leave her alone. He felt his position keenly, thankful only that he and not some stranger had been made her gaoler. Her kindness to him over a long period of years bound him to her and it saddened him he could do so little to repay it. A simple man, he could not reconcile this distraught woman with the tall girl of thirteen he had known when he first came to the Blandys. He did not for a moment think her guilty; Miss Blandy could not be guilty. The treachery and insolence of her other servants—with the honourable exception of Mrs. Deane—disgusted him.

When Ned had gone, Mary lay down on her bed. She did not sleep, but amnesia lay over her exhausted mind like a drug. When at last the light returned to the sky she thought: Another day. What day? She no longer knew.

The moaning that had punctuated the silence through the night had ceased and the house was quiet. Perhaps pain had ebbed away; perhaps life——

She had reached the nadir of suffering. Death, when it came, would scarcely touch her.

The doctors told her, Addington and Lewis, breaking the news with dignity and sensibility.

"Thank you," she said quietly.

The door closed on them and the key turned again.

Ned brought her food and sincere, unspoken sympathy, but no one else came near her. That night she slept, the first time for ten days, waking to the sounds of market day in the street below. Refreshed by rest, her mind was a little clearer. She began, listlessly, to dress herself in a half-sack and a petticoat without a hoop. Her garters and shoe-buckles had been taken from her, together with her keys and, on the orders of someone—Addington, she supposed—she had been denied the services of Mrs. Deane to attend her in the common decencies. Washing with cold water from the little ewer, she rolled her hair tightly inside a plain cambric cap.

Shortly after nine, Ned brought her some tea.

"Well, Ned?"

He made a tentative move to the door, seeming unwilling to be drawn into conversation.

"You've some news."
"Well, yes, Miss Mary."
"What is it?"
"The—coroner's inquest sits today."
"That means—questions."
"Yes, miss."
"To whom?"
"The doctors; Susannah; Betty. They've called me, too."
"I—see." She poured herself out a cup of tea. "Who is holding the inquest?"
"The Mayor, Mr. Miles. Before a jury."
She looked at him. "That's not all, is it?"
Ned dropped his eyes. "I—I hardly like to tell you."
"Why should you spare me? No one else does."
"Oh, Miss Mary!"
"Please, Ned. Tell me."
"The master—Mr. Blandy—the doctors are to open him."
She covered her face with her hands and he thought he heard the word 'violation'.
He did not speak until she had recovered her composure, then he said: "In case you should wonder, Miss Mary—I shall be away this afternoon."
"Away?"
"Church duties," he said. No need to tell her he was going to dig her father's grave.
"Who will take your place as turnkey, Ned?"
"That I don't know." He hesitated, then said: "It's not work I'd have chosen with you, Miss Mary."
"Since it had to be, I'm glad it was you and no one else."
"I—I hope you'll not take it as impertinence, miss—but—I don't believe a word of it. Not a word."
She gripped his arm, deeply moved. "Thank you—dear Ned."
He turned abruptly and went out of the room.
The morning passed without incident. From below she could hear the roll of farm-carts going up the street to the market-place, and once the cries of a drover and the pattering of

hooves as a calf broke loose and ran among the crowd. The terriers gave chase and some girls screamed excitedly.

Looking down, she saw a chaise draw up and a man enter the house. She recognised him as the Henley surgeon, Edward Nicholas. Lewis and Addington had, she knew, already arrived. So two doctors were evidently not sufficient.

Horror overwhelmed her. Were not the sufferings of the living enough that they must subject the poor corpse to such indignities? What more could they hope to find than they already knew? Confirmation? Of what? Of their diagnosis; or their suspicions? Their skill had proved useless to save; what could be accomplished now?

In an instant the mist of amnesia cleared and her nerves were fully sentient.

The old house with its legacy of suffering—the very walls whispering against her, the very timbers moaning in remembered pain—seemed to be closing in on her. A panic feeling of suffocation seized her. For four days now she had been a prisoner in her room, the life of the town coming to her at second hand. What lay outside—the woods, the clean river, the bright meadows, birds, dogs, cattle—called her irresistibly. She felt she must plunge in the river, walk beyond the limits of exhaustion, tire her body, cleanse her mind of the horror of the past week.

With a movement that was purely instinctive, she turned to the door.

It swung open.

It was not until she was halfway to the head of the stairs that it occurred to her: the door had not been locked.

The passage was empty. From the direction of her father's room she could hear the murmur of the doctors' voices as they performed their terrible task. Slipping off her shoes she ran down the stairs.

The hall, too, was empty. The servants would be gathered in the kitchen, raking dead ashes for the last malicious spark. Pausing in the outer hall, she stepped into her shoes. Stripped of their buckles, she had difficulty in keeping them on. Her hoopless petticoats dragged in the dust at her sides, and her hair, loosely coiled, tumbled down her back as she began to hurry, drawn by the river.

People stood to stare at the swift passage of the scarecrow figure, then a whisper started, running from mouth to mouth up the crowded street.

"Mary Blandy . . . Mary Blandy . . . Mary Blandy . . ."

The whisper swept like flames over brushwood; up Hart Street, round the market-place, among the stalls and in and out of the alehouses: "Mary Blandy's escaped . . . Mary Blandy the poisoner . . . While the inquest's sitting . . . She's out . . . She's got away . . ."

At first only a few followed her. Aware of them, she tried to accelerate her pace, but her unbuckled shoes pulled her back and once she stumbled over her dragging petticoats. Reaching the bridge, she glanced quickly over her shoulder.

Still keeping a distance of a few yards, the crowd was growing. It seemed as though the whole street were bearing down on her like a pack of hounds. The murmuring swelled and here and there a shout rang out. The crowd was subtly changing, losing its local quality and degenerating into a mob, any mob, any gathering of faceless insensate men and women in pursuit. This was no longer Henley, these were no longer shopkeepers and domestics and farmers and artisans; she was no longer Miss Blandy, the girl they had known all their lives; they were the pack and she the quarry.

Swarming over the bridge—market forgotten, entity lost, decency abandoned—they began to gain on her, shouting taunts and accusations and obscenities. In this mood they would willingly have displayed her head in front of the Town Hall, these men who had until a week before touched their caps to her.

Soon now they would close in on her. A short distance ahead she could see—below the level of the London Road—the Angel Inn. Was it, she wondered, a refuge? Or would good Mrs. Davies join the pack? She could not go much further: turning back was out of the question. Her heart was beating wildly, but never for a moment did her walk degenerate into a run, never for a moment did she relax that dignity which had always been hers.

Hearing the indeterminate, menacing roar of the mob, the innkeeper's wife glanced through the tap-room window, fearing a herd of cattle, runaway from the market. She did not for the moment recognise the girl, but sensing at once the mood of the mob, she ran to the door. No matter who she was or what she had done, the young woman should find sanctuary.

"Miss! Miss!" she called.

With a cry of relief, Mary flung herself inside and Mrs. Davies hastily barred the door.

"Why, Miss Blandy! Where were you off to?"

"To get some air—they are opening my father. I can't endure the house—it's horrible to me!"

Fists battered against the door and angry voices demanded it to be opened.

"Poor lady!" Mrs. Davies cried. "I never saw such an ugly sight."

"I think they would have killed me, Mrs. Davies." Mary leaned panting against the wall.

"They're gone mad. Come to the parlour, miss. You'll be quiet there. The rabble!"

Still breathing painfully, Mary allowed herself to be led to a small, dim room at the back of the inn.

"Sit still and get your breath, Miss Blandy. I'll send you in something. A nice dish of tea?"

"You're so kind. I can never thank you."

"It's a pleasure, miss, I'm sure."

Mary sank into a chair. As her eyes became accustomed to the gloom, she found that she was not alone. A middle-aged man—a traveller, apparently—was sitting on the bench in the corner sipping a glass of wine. She gasped. He rose, with an apology for startling her. Distraught and confused still, she slipped, unthinking, into the convention of another life. "Sir, —I have not the pleasure of knowing you."

The man stared at her, uncertain whether or not to laugh at the formality of this raggle-taggle doxy. Best humour her, he decided. Bowing ironically, he said: "No, madam, I am a stranger to you."

Through closed doors she could hear the clamour of the mob. She paused, listening, then she turned to contemplate the man; the sober elegance of his dress, the composure of his face were reassuring. "You look like a gentleman, sir."

"Robert Lane of North Court."

She rose to her feet, swaying a little, but head high. "I am Miss Blandy. Miss Blandy of Henley," she said clearly.

He started faintly. "Your servant, Miss Blandy."

"I see you know who I am."

"I'm afraid the gossip of small towns—even when one is only passing through——" he apologised.

The door opened and a comely woman came into the room.

"My wife," Lane explained. "This is Miss Blandy, my dear."

Mary did not seem to hear. "Mr. Lane, what do you think they will do to me?"

"It's not for me to say, ma'am."

"If you have any idea, please tell me."

He looked to his wife for support, but finding none, said, with a touch of embarrassment, "I should say you will be committed to the County Gaol and tried at the Assizes."

"Ah—and if my innocence is proved?"

"It follows that you will be acquitted."

Mary steadied herself on the arm of her chair. "And if—the verdict goes against me?"

"Then—in that case, ma'am, you will—er—suffer according to the law."

To the Lanes' dismay, Mary's uncanny self-possession slipped from her like a cloak and she started to pace the room like a woman demented, stifling her sobs with a clenched fist. Shut their ears as they would, they could not avoid hearing much that she said. "That damned villain—to bring this on me—on my father. Why did I spare him? why, why, why? My honour to him will be my ruin." She seemed quite oblivious of the presence of strangers, and the Lanes were uncertain whether to leave her alone. Suddenly she paused in her frenetic walk and stared out, her face terrible in its grief. "But why should I blame him?" she whispered. "It is I—I—I gave it him and know the consequences—God have mercy on me—I know, I know. I've seen——" She collapsed sobbing on a bench and Mrs. Lane signed to her husband to find the innkeeper's wife. Mrs. Davies brought Mary hot tea and bathed her face gently. Under the influence of kindness, the girl's hysteria gradually died away.

The potman came to the door, catching Mrs. Davies' eye. "The Town Serjeant's at the door, ma'am, asking for Miss."

"Oh." Mrs. Davies rose. "I suppose he'll have to see her. Very well, Joe. Ask Mr. Fisher to step in."

"Yes, ma'am."

The potman returned with Richard Fisher, who stood, hat in hand, in the doorway. "I'm very sorry to hear of your misfortune, Miss Blandy," he said courteously. He was too much a man of habit to lose his respect for the Town Clerk's family on an instant.

"Thank you, Mr. Fisher."

"You should have known better than to run off like that. I was going up Hart Street to market—I could scarce believe my ears when they told me Miss Blandy was gone over the bridge. I don't know what you could have been thinking of to come from home."

"Is the inquest over?" she asked dully.

"Yes, miss."

"And—the rest of it?"

"Yes, miss. Would you—now the doctors have gone—would you be glad to go home?"

"With all my heart. But what can I do? You saw them, Mr. Fisher. They're still there, aren't they—the rabble?"

"They are, Miss Blandy. An uglier sight I never saw, or thought to see in this old town. They'll not trouble me, though."

"Perhaps you could get me a postchaise—a close one?"

"I'll do my best." Fisher hesitated in the doorway. "You——"

"I shall not run away again," Mary said.

By the time the Town Serjeant returned, the mob had tired and only a few stragglers with nothing better to do remained. Bringing the chaise round into Remenham Lane, Fisher hurried Mary out through the back of the Angel.

The sun was low, throwing a golden path down the river, and the willows, weeping at the water's edge, swayed gently in the evening breeze. The swans had congregated below the lawn of the Lion and swallows mewed sweetly in the clear air. The church clock was striking seven.

It was the last time Mary Blandy would cross Henley bridge.

There would be other bridges to cross that night: the long bridge at Dorchester; Magdalen Bridge, lying in the shadow of its gracious tower; then—lumbering up the High and down Paradise Street behind tired horses—Quaking Bridge. The journey was at an end; the coach drew up and the gates of Oxford Castle closed on her.

PART SIX 1751–2

CHAPTER ONE

THE CIRCLE widened, sending out rings to Oxford, to London. The depositions of the witnesses at the inquest were published and a plague of pamphlets descended on the town. Grub Street was in full cry, and *The True Life of Miss Mary Blandy* appeared in many forms, prejudging the trial which still lay months ahead.

It was rumoured in the gutter that she had friends—some in high places and some in the nether regions—and would in consequence cheat the hangman.

Her name was coupled with that of Elizabeth Jeffries, who, together with her lover Joseph Swan, was accused of the murder of the uncle who had debauched her, an affair of the utmost squalor.

With the Misses Gunning and the Misses Blandy and Jeffries to divert it, the town was in high spirits.

A whisper—no more—rose about Cranstoun's part in the business, and various dukes-in-office exchanged letters pointing out to each other the complications entailed in bringing any charges against the Honourable Willie.

Their delaying tactics gave Cranstoun just the time he needed.

Groppty was there to oil the wheels; Francis Groppty, Esq., of Mount Street, yet, somehow, no more than Groppty in the minds of the fashionable, one of that curious band of 'creatures', attached to society by threads of services discreetly rendered at the right moment.

With so many peers behind him, Cranstoun was not a man to be refused much.

An autumn dusk was falling soft-footed on Mayfair as a chair drew up at Groppty's noncommittal door and a cloaked figure expansively tossed the chair-men what was in fact his last crown.

By the unrevealing light of candles, Cranstoun explained in some distress that he had been robbed of his purse on the coach coming South. Groppty, in equal distress, found himself without so much as a groat in the house. A footman was dispatched to a kinsman of Cranstoun's with all sorts of protestations and compliments and apologies and guarantees, to return from Pall Mall with a loan of twenty guineas—just half the sum requested.

By this time a postchaise was drawn up in front of the house and all Cranstoun's worldly goods—consisting largely of sprigged waistcoats—stowed in front. The night air held a rumour of winter and neither postillion nor horses were patient of delay.

Cranstoun paused for a moment before stepping into the chaise, savouring with a swiftly-stifled pang the ineffable air of the city—sweet for him with its sights and sounds and scents, with all it had held and had seemed to hold. Then, with a nod to Groppty to follow, he stepped into the carriage and gave the signal to start.

The lights of linkmen pricked the dusk as so often before, and the silence was broken here by the pad of chair-men's feet, there by a snatch of music from an open window.

St. James's fell behind, and soon, with the crossing of the river, London.

Traversing the dangerous waste of Blackheath, Cranstoun sat silent in his corner, borrowed guineas in his pocket, a borrowed companion at his side. Lent privacy by darkness, he could drop at last his mask of gallantry and gaiety and charm and, through the weary hours of the drive—posting inns half-seen, soon forgotten as tired horses were replaced by fresh—he examined as he had never examined before and would perhaps never examine again, the balance-sheet of his life.

His final, his most reckless throw had failed, that single card upon the turn of which had hung on the one hand the heiress to ten thousand pounds and on the other—now, with the margin of safety lengthening with every mile, he could admit it—the gallows. A heady enough gamble for the most desperate of men! He could scarcely have said what extremity of passion, of despair, of resentment against a niggardly destiny, what soldier's familiarity with the cheapness of life or what blind faith in the guidance of some dark star had brought him to an action cowardly as it was cold-blooded. From earliest boyhood his life had been a tale of betrayal, great and small; the desertion of the woman whom he had in all sincerity loved was no more than the apotheosis of what had gone before.

Behind him lay a familiar scene; vivid, uncertain, filled with intrigue and excitement, precarious, but infinitely dear. Behind lay the whispers against him, the possibility of the constable's knock on the door, the hand on his arm; behind lay the law, lay retribution, lay, perhaps, the supreme penalty. Behind lay his home, his family, his country, his wife and child; behind lay the woman he had loved above all others and betrayed beyond all hope.

Ahead down the Dover Road lay the packet to Calais; Flanders, and exile. What lay beyond the grey Channel was for the moment hidden in the mists of the future. Could intuition have served him he might perhaps have chosen a loyal assumption of guilt and a quick death by the rope in preference to the empty shoddy furtive existence of debt and false flags, and the protracted bloated agony that was to end it before a year was out; a death mitigated—with crowning irony—by absolution and a grand mass according to the rites of the Catholic Church into which, inscrutably, he was to be received.

Of all the actions of a baffling life, Cranstoun's conversion was, perhaps, the most esoteric. To his daughter by Anne Murray he left his patrimony of fifteen hundred pounds; to the world he left the curious assurance that he had legally married Mary Blandy before her mother's death, but to posterity he left no word to elucidate this final enigma.

To what end had he embraced a faith so antipathetic to his family and political convictions? Was it merely that, escaping punishment in this world, he was making sure of salvation in the next? Or did he see in this all-demanding, all-engrossing faith the possibility of a penitence unknown to the milder, colder creed of his youth?

Or could it be that he had in the end turned to God, this man whom the Devil had failed?

CHAPTER TWO

THE HORSE gone, hands in high places hastened to shut the stable door. Signing themselves the "Noblemen and Gentlemen in the Neighbourhood of Henley on Thames", a group of men—among them the Lords Macclesfield and Cadogan—addressed to the Duke of Newcastle a petition assuring His Grace that "no endeavours shall be wanting on our part to render the prosecution successful and bring to condign punishment not only the unnatural daughter of that unhappy gentleman, but also the wicked contrivor and instigator of this cruel design".

A little belatedly, Mr. Fox of the War Office wrote to Mr. Pitt, the Paymaster-General, directing that "a reduced first-lieutenant of Sir Andrew Agnew's late Regiment of Marines" should be struck off the Establishment of Half-Pay.

Some rumour of the outside world reached Mary Blandy as she walked in the Keeper's gardens at Oxford, pacing up and down, up and down as the shadow of the immemorial Castle Mound lengthened and the leaves fell from the gallows tree.

Various concessions had been made to her. Lodged in reasonable comfort in the Keeper's House, she was allowed to have Mrs. Deane in attendance; and if the ageing maid saw a certain irony in this answer to her prayer for a break in the monotony of her mistress's life, she said little.

Mary read and sewed, and found in the prison chaplain, ohn Swinton, a man of wide culture, not wholly theological.)uring the early weeks of her imprisonment, she lived, in a estricted way, the life of a gentlewoman. Drained of emotion, he recovered something of her old inscrutability, calling on ll those reserves of self-control inherent to her class. No ne—not even the shrewd and experienced chaplain—knew er inner feelings. She behaved impeccably, setting up a arrier of courtesy between herself and her daily associates.

The manifesto of the Noblemen and Gentlemen made a con- iderable stir in Henley, and it was from the humble lips of Ned Hearne that Mary heard of it. "You see, Miss Mary! There's many believes in your innocence!"

"Not in my innocence, Ned. Only in Cranstoun's guilt." 'or a moment she betrayed emotion, but only for a moment. 'Do you think they will take him, Ned?" she asked quietly.

"It's hard to say. Once a man's out of the country——" Tentatively he added: "Would you wish him taken?"

Her eyes rested on the barred windows. "He is the author f all my misfortunes—and yet——" The well of her bitter- ess at Cranstoun's desertion was too deep for so much as a ipple to come to the surface.

Stimulated by the petition, sympathy for Mary grew. Lady Ailesbury—refusing to believe her lawyer's daughter capable f such barbarity—began to exert her considerable influence n the girl's cause. Mary's own conduct made, as Horace Walpole expressed it, "a sort of party in her favour", and for few weeks in the late autumn of 1751 it almost seemed as hough the tide of conviction-before-trial had turned. But very good has its attendant ill. Without any foundation in act, the rumour began to circulate that an attempt was to be nade to rescue Mary—a romantic storming of the castle at east two centuries out in probability. But although unlikely nough at that time of day, the story could not entirely be gnored and the old laxity was at an end.

Removed to a stone-walled cell with a table and two hairs as her only concessions, she was put in irons. She did not share Mrs. Deane's tears. "All mine are long since shed."

The irons dragged at her steps and after a few days her ankles became swollen and inflamed. For some weeks she could not walk. The spiritual effect was considerable. "Now at last I know myself a felon."

With the New Year, Grub Street embarked on a fresh chapter in Mary's history: her life in prison; one of the wildest debauchery, in which, foul-mouthed and drunken, she was abetted in occult practices by the worldly and disgraced chaplain.

John Swinton allowed her to see a few of the more innocuous sheets. "It is as well you should know something of the public temper before you face your trial." Exercising particular vigilance, he kept from her the most cruel of all the libels; that she had been her mother's murderess.

In the case against her, much play had been made of the ten thousand pounds Mr. Blandy had in his vanity rather pathetically conjured. Dying as he had intestate, his affairs were in some confusion, and it was not until the January that the last of the complications had been cleared away. He was found to have left estate—including the Hart Street house, the parcels of land and his holdings in the Funds—to the value of just over four thousand pounds.

The irony was not lost on Mary: "My accusers might not have considered a mere four thousand motive enough for my crime!"

The attendant thought—that Cranstoun might not have considered the sum motive enough for *his* crime—was no more than the reopening of a spiritual wound already mortal.

The date of her trial had been provisionally fixed for the beginning of March, and with the aid of the Chaplain she wrote an answer to some of the calumnies against her. Witnessed as it was by two clergymen, members of the University it carried little more weight than the libels of the hacks.

The Reverend John Swinton was insistent that she should prepare a defence, since her counsel—as the law stood—would ıot be allowed to address the jury. But she expressed her ntention to answer her critics from her heart.

"The heart plays little part in our legal system," he pointed ›ut, but she refused to be persuaded.

In all she did, a sense of fatality dogged her. She seemed o John Swinton to have gone beyond feeling. Even the ›rimary instinct of self-preservation burned low. He tried o rouse in her a desire to vindicate herself, only to be met vith a murmur about predestination that baffled him com- ›letely. He sought to convince himself that her supineness vas a Christian submission to the will of God, but he knew n his heart this was not the answer. Her figure to him was vholly enigmatical. Administering the last sacraments in his, 'Newgate's golden age', he had had a wide experience ›f men and women at the gallow's foot. The majority had ›rotested their innocence to the end, but he had grown wise to he undertones of guilt and his conscience had rarely been roubled by fears of a miscarriage of justice. With Mary he vas at a loss; her very assertions of innocence were so cold, so ndifferent that at times he wondered if suffering had destroyed ıer sensibilities. Her intelligence in the ordinary commerce ›f life was acute enough—seldom had he derived such pleasure rom a prisoner's company—but she seemed to him emotion- ılly stunned.

Her case had been placed in capable hands, but it surprised ıim a little that neither her uncle in the Church nor her ıncle in the Law had rallied to her. It was sad to see a young voman so forlorn, and the chaplain saw in the defections of ıer relatives and her abandonment by her lover a possible xplanation of her negative attitude. Could it be, he won- lered, that she had no intention of fighting for a life that ıeld so little?

CHAPTER THREE

On Monday the second of March, 1752, a Bill of Indictment was found by the Grand Inquest for the County of Oxford against Mary Blandy, Spinster, for the murder of Francis Blandy, late of the Parish of Henley-on-Thames, in the said County, Gentleman.

The Town Hall being in process of rebuilding, another venue had to be found for the Assizes. The Sheldonian Theatre was suggested, but the University authorities resisted, raising no objection, however, to the use of the Divinity School.

Cloud hung low over the city this March morning, greyly roofing the grey streets. An east wind raked the quadrangles and roughened the surface of the narrow rivers. Sighing round the spires, it irreverently bandied senior gowns and insinuated chilly fingers beneath sported oaks. The water meadows were filmed with crackling ice and men hurried in the shelter of ancient walls. None but the poor and the over-zealous were abroad at this hour.

The wind seemed to blow with special malice down Brasenose Lane, making wretched as well as ridiculous the little procession hurrying away from Radcliffe Square as from temptation. An odd enough group in all conscience: full-bottomed horse-hair wigs flapped against learned faces, legal robes hobbled judicial legs, blue fingers of sober clerks gripped vital documents, King's Counsel jostled Prisoner's Counsel in the same kennels, and all, from Barons of His Majesty's Court of Exchequer down to the humblest scribe, ruled out of court by the quip of the youngest of young members of the University.

For the door of the Divinity School could not be opened.

That was all. No last-minute postponement of the trial, no reprieve, no divine or demoniacal intervention, but merely a small wedge, inserted in the lock by a mischievous hand. A pigeon, roosting on a perpendicular pendant, cooed derisively.

To stand, in all the panoply of the Law, while a carpenter

was summoned and a crowd collected, was unthinkable. A retreat to lodgings was decreed, through the raw emptiness of the windy streets while all the bells of Oxford stressed the hour of seven.

The bells were at their work again—booming, tolling, singing, tinkling, carolling—before the learned group returned, picking its way painfully over the cobbles in narrow buckled shoes.

At eight o'clock the door opened ceremoniously and the lovely Perpendicular hall began to fill as it had seldom filled in three centuries. The beauty of its lines lent a certain mitigating grace to proceedings which, for all their legal dignity, were to prove as tedious as sordid. The ten years spent by the craftsmen carving *in situ* the stone monograms of the hall's benefactors had not passed more slowly that the thirteen hours which were to be given to the trial of Mary Blandy. High on a cornice, among the wheatsheaves and cardinal's hats, sat a single jester—quip of some medieval mind, irregular and unexpected as the door known as 'Wren's Mistake'—that same jester who two centuries earlier had looked down upon the trial of the Martyrs, Latimer and Ridley.

Mary Blandy was placed at the bar.

Arrayed against her were the Honourable Mr. Bathurst, Mr. Serjeant Hayward, the Honourable Mr. Barrington, Mr. Hayes, Mr. Nares and Mr. Ambler, Counsel for the Crown. They could call on Dr. Addington, Dr. Lewis, Apothecary Norton, Mrs. Mounteney, Robert Littleton, the Lanes and a motley group of hostile servants. Against this phalanx Mary could pit her own counsel, Messrs. Ford, Morton and Aston, none of whom, though they could examine and cross-examine, would be permitted to address the jury. As witnesses she had a washerwoman, a charwoman, two old acquaintances of her father's, the landlady of an ale-house, a member of the coroner's jury and the sexton of the church.

There was not—could not be—a single open mind in the Court. Fresh in every memory were the published depositions of the inquest witnesses and a score of libellous pamphlets.

This, then, was the trial of Mary Blandy.

Mrs. Deane dressed her with great care. Her irons had been removed the night before and the maid had wrapped her swollen and inflamed ankles in soft cloth so that she should not be seen to wince. She was no paler now than she had been for six months. Her eyes were heavy and dark-ringed and her face seemed intangibly to have lengthened. Nothing could destroy the line of her brows, but there was little else of beauty in her. A poet might call her the Fair Parricide, but fair was a loose term, embracing an entire sex. The mark the irons left on her had robbed her of that grace which had been her special quality, and suffering had dulled her skin, her eyes, her hair—even her voice. She had attained that calm which is the recompense for loss of hope. She would listen carefully, tax her tired brain for a defence, but all the time she would know she must not cry out in protest, must accept all that was said of her—every lie that malice could invent, every truth the Law could twist, every misconstruction every hoarded-up memory of an indiscretion. She must hold her head high, comport herself with the dignity and reserve expected of a gentlewoman. In this, the supreme crisis of her life, she must use only those weapons proper to a spinster of this parish. She had no influence in high places, no beauty to sell; nothing but cold dulled courage and the stubborn assertion and reassertion of her own innocence.

The Court rose to its feet as the Judges—the Honourable Heneage Legge and Sir Sydney Smythe—entered.

The Clerk of the Arraigns spoke first: "Mary Blandy, hold up thy hand." Mary raised her hand. "You stand indicted by the name of Mary Blandy late of the Parish of Henley-on Thames in the County of Oxford Spinster daughter of Francis Blandy late of the same place deceased for that you not having the fear of God before your eyes but being moved and seduced by the instigation of the devil and of your malice aforethought contriving and intending him the said Francis Blandy your said late father in his lifetime to deprive him of his life and him feloniously to kill and murder on the 5th day of August in the 25th year of the reign of our Sovereign Lord George the Second now King of Great Britain with force and arms at the Parish of Henley-on-Thames aforesaid——" The passionless voice ran on, unpunctuated, clearly articulated, neutral; negation in essence, an expression in sound of the scales of justice. The words carried no meaning to Mary. Her eyes, resting a few feet above the Clerk's head, did not waver, nor did her colour change. Here and there a phrase or a word freed itself from the soporific repetition:—"deadly poison to wit white arsenic . . . that you Mary Blandy might more speedily kill," and "Francis Blandy of that poison died . . . did kill and murder against the peace of our said Lord the King his crown and dignity." The voice paused as though now, at last, it could draw breath. The Clerk turned again to Mary. "How sayest thou, Mary Blandy, art thou guilty of the felony and murder whereof thou standest indicted, or not guilty?"

"Not guilty."

"Culprit how wilt thou be tried?"

"By God and my country."

"God send thee a good deliverance. Crier, make a proclamation for silence."

The Crier's voice rang through the lovely hall. "Oyez, Oyez, Oyez! My Lord the King's justices strictly charge and command all manner of persons to keep silence on pain of imprisonment."

A conscious hush descended on the hall. A number of men now filed into the Court.

"Oyez you good men, that are empanelled to try between our Sovereign Lord the King and the prisoner at the bar, answer to your names and save your fines."

The Clerk of the Arraigns accorded Mary the formal privilege of challenging any member of the jury before they were sworn.

One by one the gentlemen of the jury took the oath: Anthony Woodward, sworn; Charles Harrison, sworn; a pause, while one was challenged, then Samuel George Gaze, sworn; John Haynes the Elder, sworn.

Mary was reminded of the sheep and the goats: the sheep, sworn; the goats, challenged; sheep, goats, sheep, goats—— She forced herself to curb her wanton imagination and concentrate her weary resources on face and name, but she was so tired, so helpless, so friendless and without hope that already, before her trial had begun, her nerves were crying out for a verdict.

The jury were sworn, counted, proclaimed; the Clerk meticulously reread the indictment: "If you find her guilty, you shall enquire what goods chattels land or tenements she had at the time the felony was committed. If you find her not guilty you shall enquire whether she fled for the same. If you find she did fly for the same, you shall enquire of her goods and chattels as if you had found her guilty. If you find her not guilty and that she did not fly for the same, say no more."

Her chattels; the accumulated treasures of thirty years: the hair brushes and pin-cushions and handkerchief sachets, the scraps of lace and ribbon; the Dresden posy Cranstoun had bought her in another life; her work-box and the sampler she had once made ('Mary Blandy, aged 9, her sampler'); the tiny green shoes her father had bought her in Cheapside. What, she wondered, would the jury make of such trumpery?

The Honourable Mr. Barrington opened the indictment, then Henry Bathurst rose. He had, she recalled, been Solicitor-General to the Prince of Wales—'Poor Fred', as the hacks called him now he was dead. For a moment, incontinently, the gracious Assembly Rooms swayed in memory's eye. A harvest moon had silvered the fair city of Bath that night, she recalled.

Bathurst attacked. The ears were assailed, the emotions assaulted, the nerves bludgeoned, the heart carried by storm; there was no note of anger, of sentiment, of righteousness, shame, horror, disgust, no gamut of drama he did not exploit to serve his end. As a *tour de force* the opening speech for the prosecution would stand unexcelled for a considerable time. He was not, he declared, surprised at "the vast concourse of people collected together to see the trial and catastrophe of so execrable an offender as she is supposed to be". Good. So be it. He would give the concourse a run for its money. Garrick himself could not have bettered his performance. "Her crime, if she proved guilty of it"—the parenthesis was contemptuous —"will justly render her infamous to the latest posterity and make our children's children when they read the horrid tale of these days blush to think that such an inhuman creature ever had an existence. . . . Whoever beheld the ghastly corpse of the murdered innocent weltering in its blood and did not feel his own blood run slow and cold through all his veins? Has the murderer escaped? With what zeal do we apprehend? And when the dreadful sentence of death is pronounced upon him, everybody hears it with satisfaction and acknowledges the justice of the Divine denunciation that: 'By whom man's blood is shed, by man shall his blood be shed.'" Proceeding to outline the affair, he cried: "I trust I have such a history to open as will shock the ears of all who hear me." Mary he described as "genteel, agreeable, sprightly, sensible". He dwelt on the stories of her ten thousand pound fortune, "that pious fraud", as evidence of her loving father's anxiety to see her settled. As proof of her excellent upbringing he conceded that "she was from her earliest youth received into the best company and her own behaviour made her afterwards acceptable to them", but these admissions were no more than the high lights a painter uses to stress his shadows.

As he turned to Cranstoun, there was a curious rustling sound in the court as though a small wind had arisen and as suddenly dropped. Even here, Mary thought dully, he has his dominance. She listened, with a renascence of emotion, to the derisive words: "hearing she was to have ten thousand pounds, he fell in love—not with her, but with her fortune."

The hanging wood returned to her, sighing and weeping in winter, sweet with the song of nightingales in summer. She recalled for a moment something of the quality of their love, a love that transcended desire, deeper and higher than anything she had thought possible. Instinct—older, more fundamental than intelligence—told her that no matter what else might be a lie, the final truth lay in the thing they had shared.

"Ten thousand pounds," the mannered voice drawled, "ten thousand pounds—he fell in love with ten thousand pounds."

Her heart cried out. Cranstoun had destroyed her beyond all hope or help, but love remained, pure, complete; a thing apart from what he was or what he had done to her. The gallows-tree itself could not cancel the memory of the ecstasy she had known with him nor any crime falsify its truth.

Bathurst now took up the curious happenings of those nights when Cranstoun was under their roof: the music and the footsteps and the apparitions; these, not as proof of Mary's credulity but of her cunning, the elaborate preparation of the servants' minds for her father's coming death. Now followed a series of statements: "In August 1750 they both agreed on the horrid deed. . . . One of the effects of poison was the teeth dropping out of his head whole from their sockets. Yet what do you think, gentlemen, the daughter did when she perceived it? She damned him for a toothless old rogue and wished him at hell."

Mary began to tremble with anger. *They agreed.* Who said they agreed? Who knew what passed between them? *His teeth dropping out.* Yes. But what proof was that of poison? *She damned him for a toothless old rogue.* When? In whose hearing? Not once in the long savage indictment did the learned gentleman say "It is thought" or "It is alleged". Conjecture and hearsay and the malice of a dismissed servant were presented to the jury as unanswerable fact. The opening speech for the prosecution ran like a summing-up. Based as it was on the depositions of witnesses yet to be called, Bathurst presented not so much a case as a *fait accompli*.

Mary's body sagged. A feeling of lethargy overwhelmed her. There was nothing to hope from this man. Useless to waste her small reserves of energy in concentration on what he was saying. It would be futile to attempt to refute it; as well try to stay the tide.

For a time the lines of truth and hearsay converged. Listening unwillingly, Mary lived again the last few days of her father's life, her emotion wholly one of regret and inconsolable loss.

Her mind was brought sharply back to the voice of her prosecutor; the indictment had suddenly plunged into the realm of fantasy: "Upon his death the prisoner, finding herself discovered, endeavoured to persuade a manservant to go off with her, but he was too honest to be tempted by a reward to assist her although she told him it would be five hundred pounds in his way."

Great heavens! What nonsense was this? Five hundred pounds to Harman—she who had never been able to pay her dressmaker the twenty pounds owing to her!

"The next morning she dressed herself in a proper habit for a journey and while the people put to take care of her were absent, stole out of the house and went over Henley Bridge."

Draggled petticoats and flapping shoes a proper habit for a journey! And on foot, away from the Lion and the Bell—the only places where a postchaise could be hired, even had she been possessed of the necessary guineas! Something of her old derision came to her aid, stiffening her.

The opening speech for the prosecution was drawing to its end on a note of solemnity: "And let me here observe how evidently the hand of Providence has interposed to bring her to this day of trial that she may suffer the consequence. For what but the hand of Providence could have preserved the paper thrown by her into the fire and have snatched it unburnt from the devouring flame? Great God! How wonderful are all Thy ways and how miraculously Thou preserved this paper to be this day produced in evidence against the prisoner in order that she may suffer the punishment due to her crime and be a dreadful example to all others who may be tempted in like manner to offend Thy Divine Majesty." For a moment the court was hushed in the presence of an avenging Jehovah, but the learned gentleman recalled in time that temporal things also have their value: "Let me add, next to Providence, the public are obliged to two noble lords—Macclesfield and Cadogan—whose indefatigable diligence in enquiring into this work of darkness——"

The spell was broken; place and interest had raised their heads and the flaming sword spluttered like a roman candle at a fête.

It might have seemed that there was little left to be said, but Mr. Serjeant Hayward stepped, the second lead, onto the boards. His methods were quite different; while the side boxes might have admired his cooler reasoning, the gallery would have felt itself cheated by his lack of fire. He was, in short, an anti-climax, not, unfortunately, the farce that rounds off the evening, but as it were a sixth act, repeating with diminished effect what had been so well done before. Sensible of this perhaps—for he was no fool—he took advantage of the venue by addressing himself to the young gentlemen of the University: "—earnestly beseeching you to guard against the first approaches of and temptations to vice. See here the dreadful consequence of disobedience to a parent." A statement from which much amusement would later be derived in junior common-rooms, for surely, among the delectable temptations Oxford life had to offer, parricide scarcely seemed the most seductive.

"Could a man," Mr. Hayward demanded, labouring the moral line, "could a man that had a wife of his own and children, really be in love with another woman? Such a thing cannot be supposed!" A faint titter greeted this assertion. The Serjeant was surely a little out of period? There were few homes, from the Royal household downwards, where such a thing could not be supposed with the minimum of imagination.

Feeling his grip on the audience slipping, Mr. Hayward now followed his leader in sweeping statement. The Court was told that, Mr. Blandy becoming ill, no physician was sent for. How, then, would the evidence of Norton, of Addington and Lewis be explained?

The circumstances of Mary's attempts to bribe not only Harman, but Betty, together with her flight, were offered as irrefutable evidence of her guilt. "Innocence—celestial, virgin—dares look the frowns, the resentments and the persecutions of the world in the face . . . while guilt, the baneful fiend makes use of unjustifiable means—bribery and corruption are the defenders of her cause, she flies before the face of the law and justice and shuns the probation of a candid and impartial enquiry."

The blood drummed in Mary's ears. Why go on with it all? What defence could she make, what witnesses call that could purge the mind of the Court of distortions which by their insidious repetition built up, drop by drop, their stalactite of guilt. Useless to hope for an impartial jury, listening with open mind to the evidence. If she were ten times guilty, surely *this* was a travesty of justice?

Evidence for the prosecution was now called.

Dr. Addington was first to go into the box; an impressive figure, he did not glance in the direction of the prisoner at the bar. His duty was an unpleasant one, but he would, he hoped, acquit himself well. "I attended Mr. Blandy in his last illness."

"In what condition did you find him?"

The medical evidence now followed in all its wretched detail, together with the attendant tortures to which the poor old man had been subjected by his medical advisers.

Addington recalled his encounter with Mary on the stairs and her insistence that he should visit her father the next day.

Mary relaxed a little. Here at least was the truth.

"When I got downstairs," the doctor continued, "one of the maids put a paper into my hands, which she said Miss Blandy had thrown into the kitchen fire. Several holes were burnt in the paper, but not a letter of the superscription was effaced. The superscription was: 'The powder to clean the pebbles with.' I opened the paper very carefully and found in it a whiteish powder, like white arsenic."

A sigh escaped from the Court.

"As soon as the maid had left me, Mr. Norton, the apothecary, produced a powder that, he said, had been found at the bottom of that mess of gruel which, as was supposed, had poisoned Mr. Blandy."

The Court, bludgeoned almost into insensibility by the prosecution was now fully awake again. Here was no rhetoric, no invoking of Divine approval; here was fact, stated fairly and without motive. In dealing with matters outside his province, Addington might be no less prejudiced than the next man, but in the field of medicine his integrity was beyond question. A man might have his loves and his hates and his loyalties, but he would not have described white arsenic as anything but white arsenic to save the life of his own son.

He outlined faithfully the events that led up to Mr. Blandy's death. A nerve throbbed in Mary's temple as he described the pitiful scene between himself and her father—"A poor lovesick girl"—but she betrayed no emotion.

Coming to the morning of the fourteenth, he said: "Mr. Blandy recovered his senses and told me he would make his will in two or three days, but he grew delirious again, and, sinking every minute, died about two o'clock in the morning."

He would make his will in two or three days. The words seemed to Mary an arrow of light. He would make his will. He had not already made it. How then was she assured of her inheritance? In a single sentence, surely, the motive supplied by the prosecution collapsed? She glanced quickly to her counsel, to other faces in court. All were impassive. Had none then, on either side, seen its significance?

But no. Minds were attuned to Addington's answer to the next question: "There was no doubt in my mind as to the cause of death: poison." Unflinching, in a resonant voice, he read his report of the autopsy. Its details were not sufficiently horrible to bring nausea to a generation that flocked to Tyburn.

After Dr. Lewis had confirmed the medical evidence, Mary's counsel, Mr. Ford, rose to cross-examine Dr. Addington. "Did you first intimate to Mr. Blandy or he to you that he had been poisoned?"

"He first intimated it to me."

"Did you ask him whether he was sure he had been poisoned by the gruel he took on Monday night, August the 5th, and on Tuesday night, August the 6th?"

"I do not recollect that I did."

"Are you sure that he said he was disordered after drinking the gruel on the Monday night?"

"Yes."

"Did you ever ask why he drank more gruel on the Tuesday night?"

Addington hesitated for the first time. "I believe I did not."

The cross-examination now turned to the experiments made by Addington: "Why did you believe the powder to be white arsenic?"

The doctor described in detail the five tests to which he had subjected the sample in his possession, together with five parallel tests made with white arsenic. It was in this moment that history was made; never before in a murder trial had convincing scientific proof of poisoning been given.

Benjamin Norton was now called and the prosecution returned to the attack. At first question and answer were rational enough, dealing only with the apothecary's professional calls on Mr. Blandy over a long period of years, but suddenly the examination plunged: "Did you ever hear Miss Blandy talk of music?"

"I did. She said it had been heard in the house and she feared something might happen in the family. She did not say anything particular because I made light of it."

"Did she say anything of apparitions?"

"She said Mr. Cranstoun saw her father's apparition one night."

"How long before his death was it she talked about music?"

"It might be three or four months before."

The subject was dropped as suddenly as it had been raised, and the issue—credulity or cunning—left to the discretion of psychics and sceptics.

The examination now returned to the powder, and a packet was produced bearing the seals of Providence's envoys to the Court of St. James, the Lords Macclesfield and Cadogan.

Mr. Ford rose again.

"Had you any suspicion of poison?"

"I had not. Nor did Mr. Blandy mention any."

"Did Miss Blandy show a dislike to her father having physic?"

"No. None at all. She desired when I saw any danger to her father I would let her know, that she might have the advice of a physician. She begged that Dr. Addington might be sent for. Mr. Blandy was for deferring it."

"How had she behaved to him in any other illness of her father's?"

"I never saw but at such times she behaved with true affection and regard."

Mary found herself warming with gratitude to Norton. In a few words he had brought into Court something of the reality of her background. That his words could in any way affect the verdict was not, for the moment, important. Dignity had returned; for a few brief moments she had become Mr. Blandy's daughter, Mary; not a fury, not a felon, not a name with which to frighten children yet unborn, not a quarry, not the epitome of all evil. The moment was already past, but it had in a small way restored her faith in human nature.

The cross-examination was droning on. "How came you to suspect that at the bottom of the pan was poison?"

"I found it very gritty and it had no smell. When I saw the old washerwoman, knew that she had tasted the water-gruel and was affected with the same symptoms as Mr. Blandy, I then suspected he was poisoned. But I did not tell either him or Miss Blandy so, because I found by the maid that Miss Blandy was suspected.

Mary folded her arms, trying to still the trembling that gripped her at the thought of Betty Binfield. So with Norton, too, the seed had been sown by that same hand!

The apothecary's evidence was at an end. How long she wondered, would her trial last? In two hours little enough had emerged. Could the brain remain alert through all these hours, clear and balanced, fresh enough to arrive at a just verdict?

There was a rustling of stiff silk. She gathered her thoughts and raised her eyes to the witness-box. Mrs. Mounteney, her hand trembling a little on the Testament, was taking the oath. Something in the familiar figure, so intimately linked with her childhood, moved her as nothing else had done. For the earlier witnesses she had felt little, but here was someone for whom in another life she had felt affection, an affection ending abruptly in all the anguish of betrayal. That her godmother should have been, even unwittingly, one of the instruments of her downfall was bitter enough, but that she should be a witness for the prosecution was all but unendurable.

The eyes of the two women did not meet. Watching the erect figure in the box, memory awoke with a mocking picture of a dinner-table, rich with the wrack of Christmas. This same figure had even then sat a little apart. Mary Mounteney would not, on oath, permit herself the smallest tempering of the wind to the shorn lamb at the bar.

Yes, she had sent for Mr. Norton when Susannah Gunnell brought the pan of gruel. Yes, she had locked up the sample of powder the apothecary found at the bottom of it. No, she had never seen Miss Blandy otherwise than dutiful to her father—as far, that is, as she saw. No, she had made no mention of the powder to anyone until Mr. Norton took it away to show to Dr. Addington. No she did not mention it to Mr. or Miss Blandy.

That was all. Her evidence at an end, Mrs, Mounteney knew herself free to turn in the direction of the prisoner. Neighbours all their lives, for nearly seven months they had not spoken. For half a year she had thought of Mary only with horror, forced by the weight of evidence and gossip to believe her guilty of the most inhuman of all crimes. The thought of giving evidence against her had not troubled her conscience unduly, but now, when she saw again the girl she had known since earliest childhood—tall and pale and beyond hope—an emotion stronger than any she had ever felt welled up in her and, blinded by tears, she made her way to the bar. Catching Mary's hands in hers, she whispered; "God bless you!"

Mary clung to her hands like a drowning woman, and for a moment the court was stilled.

Susannah Gunnell was making her way to the witness-box. The oath in her Oxfordshire dialect had an unfamiliar ring. Prejudiced, illiterate, stubborn, passionately loyal to a dead master, it would be on her evidence and that of the vindictive girl who was to follow her that the case for the prosecution would stand or fall, for in the last analysis two things hang a man or woman: motive and opportunity. The King's Counsel with his reiterated ten thousand pounds had supplied the motive; the doctors had described the means; it would be the domestics—living under the same roof, watching, partially or impartially, the everyday actions—who would prove the opportunity.

The old woman gave her evidence convincingly; the ground she trod was sure, the questions never beyond her limitations; "The gruel was made for Mr. Blandy's use on the Sunday seven-night before his death. I made it. I put it in the common pantry where all the family used to go. Miss Blandy told me she had been in the pantry—I did not see her—stirring her father's gruel and eating oatmeal out of the bottom. I gave Mr. Blandy a half-pint of it on the Monday evening for him to take before he went to bed." And so, on and on; fair enough, truthful enough, and only a little wise after the event; "I then recollected I had heard tell poison was white and gritty."

Counsel for the prisoner raised an objection to the admission of hearsay evidence, but withdrew it when assured that Betty Binfield would be called. Words through keyholes were magnified and distorted, the gossip of servants used to place the ladder more firmly against the gallows-tree.

Counsel for the defence supinely watched the case for the

prosecution being built up brick by brick. Given a preliminary assumption of guilt, he realised there was scarcely a loophole in the evidence. His client's case, such as it was, rested solely on a plea so fantastic at this time of day that he was thankful the law precluded the possibility of his addressing the jury. His tongue would, he felt sure, have stumbled on the word 'philtre'. Given a plea of insanity, or justification, even of stress of passion, Mr. Ford could, he knew, have put his back into the case, distasteful as it was—but magic! He would have credited the frigid—to him rather repelling—figure at the bar with more woman's wit!

Mary tried to shut her mind, her ears, as Susannah—her memory kept fresh by devotion to her master—described his last talk with his daughter. All the old ground was trodden and retrodden, the servant adding for good measure the sore throat which in the light of later knowledge, she attributed to drinking from her master's cup.

Among the brighter spirits in court, a picture was beginning to form of an establishment where the domestics were continually lapping up, like dogs, the dregs of their master's dishes, and where arsenic enough to kill an entire household was left accessible to all in palatable form. To more critical minds, the very clumsiness of the crime appeared to be a vindication. Here was an educated young woman living a highly civilised life, not a distracted peasant in a Shropshire valley experimenting with sheep-dip. The evidence, piled on so heavily, was beginning to spill over.

Mr. Ford rose at last to cross-examine, reverting to Mary's last meeting with her father; "Did Miss Blandy say with what intent the powder was given her?"

"With another intent, she said."

"Did she say with what intent?" he persisted.

"He did not ask that."

"Was it not explained?"

"It was in no ways explained."

Mr. Ford paused, then he said slowly; "Did he treat her as if she herself were innocent?"

Mary held her breath. Here, and here alone, lay her defence. Susannah's answer could tip the scale.

"Did he treat her as if she herself were innocent?"

"He did, sir."

"As to the ruin of his daughter, did he think it was entirely owing to Cranstoun?"

"Mr. Blandy said he believed his daughter entirely innocent of what had happened. He said: 'Poor unfortunate girl. That ever she should have been imposed upon and led away by such a villain to do such a thing.'"

A kind of sigh drifted through the hall. It seemed to Mary that in a few words her trial had changed course. It was as though a window had been opened on the world. Could it be that, by the most tragic of ironies, her father's love for her would be strong enough to reach out from beyond the grave to which she herself had sent him?

King's Counsel rose. "What did he mean when he said: 'Poor unfortunate girl. That she should be led away by such a villain to do such a thing'?" Bathhurst paused. "What do you imagine he meant by *'such a thing'*?"

"By giving him that which she did not know what it was."

Tension found relief in a little titter at the involved honesty of the answer. The Crier called for silence, but the spell was broken. In that moment, Mary sensed, the door to the world had closed.

"When she told you the water-gruel would serve her father on the Wednesday, did she know her father had been ill by taking water-gruel on the Monday and Tuesday nights?"

"She knew he was ill, but I cannot tell whether she knew the cause of it. She did not oppose my making fresh for any other reason but that it would hinder my ironing."

Washing-day intruded in court, and for a moment a few of the best legal intellects in the country considered not life and death and good and evil but the ethics of interrupting on Wednesday the ironing of linen that had on Monday flapped in a Henley yard.

Susannah's evidence was at an end.

Mary found herself growing cold with fear. The shivering returned to her body and she felt the blood draining painfully to her heart.

Betty Binfield was taking the oath.

My enemy, Mary thought.

The years had blurred the good looks the girl had brought with her to Hart Street, hardening the fresh colour to an apple redness and thickening the plump body, but her animal vitality had not diminished and she was still a disturbing element.

The examination began: "Did you ever hear Miss Blandy talk of something in the house that presaged her father's death?"

"I often heard her say he would die before October."

"Did she express herself glad or sorry?"

"Glad, for that then she should soon be released from all her fatigues and soon be happy. I heard her say: 'Who would grudge to send an old father to hell for ten thousand pounds'!"

In the gasp that swept the court, Mary's cry was submerged.

Gratified by her effect, Betty added: "Exactly them words!"

Bathurst raised his eyebrows faintly but betrayed no other emotion. "How was this conversation introduced?"

"She was speaking of young girls being kept out of their fortunes."

"Who was with you at the time?"

"It was to me, and nobody else."

There was no indication that Prisoner's Counsel had even heard, much less realised the implications of the admission. Mary found herself beginning to watch, with a kind of fascination, the opportunities slipping by. There was something inexorable about the mildness of her defence, as though destiny did not intend her case to get a hearing.

"Did you ever hear him say anything about having been poisoned?"

"I was in the kitchen when my master came out to be shaved—I stayed there till he went out again. Miss Blandy was there. He said how he was once at the coffee house or the Lion and he and two other gentlemen had like to have been poisoned by what they drank. He said: 'One of the gentlemen died immediately, the other is dead now and I have survived them both, but it is my fortune to be poisoned at last.' He looked at her very hard during the time he was talking."

"What did he say was put into the wine?"

"I remember he said it was white arsenic."

Was it only to Mary's ears that the glib answer rang so false?

"When he looked hard at her how did she look?"

"She looked in great confusion and all in a tremble."

The course changed again: "Did you sit up with Miss Blandy the night after her father died?"

"I did till three o'clock. She said to me: 'Betty will you go away with me? If you will go to the Lion or the Bell and hire a postchaise I will give you fifteen guineas when you get into it and ten guineas more when we come to London.' I said: 'Where will you go, then? Into the North?' She said: 'I shall go into the West of England.' I said: 'Shall you go by sea?' She said: 'Some part of the way.' I said: 'I will not go.' Then she burst into laughter and said: 'I was only joking.'"

Mary's heart beat wildly at the monstrousness of the evidence. Could anyone in Court seriously believe that she would attempt to bribe this girl who of all her servants had been her enemy throughout? If this were evidence of anything, it was evidence of lunacy! Was the Court so ignorant of geography that it would accept an illiterate tale that in order to get to the West Country she would take a postchaise thirty-five miles to the east and board a ship? Confusion drew a tight band round her head and her thoughts lost coherence.

The cross-examination now resumed its mild activities, eliciting that Mr. Blandy had had a bad cold the year before and that Mary was fond of the washerwoman.

"Have you any ill-will against Miss Blandy?"

"I always told her I wished her very well."

Prisoner's Counsel then asked, in his perfectly-modulated English: "Did you ever say 'Damn her for a black bitch. I should be glad to see her go up the ladder and be hanged'?"

"No, sir, I never did in my life."

At this point Mr. Ford appealed to Dr. Addington: "Did not Miss Blandy declare to you she had always thought the powder innocent?"
"Yes."
"Did she always declare the same?"
"Yes."
Sensing that the quarry was drawing away from the hunt, King's Counsel interposed to say he had not intended to mention what had passed between the prisoner and Dr. Addington, but that since her own counsel had been pleased to call for a part of it, he desired the whole might be laid before the court.
Addington told, in all fairness and in great detail, his interview with Mary after he had decided to place her under guard in her room. For a little while Mary appeared through the fog of calumny as her father's daughter, her refusal to implicate Cranstoun echoing something of the old gentleman's generosity of spirit, each, in their turn, refusing to avenge themselves on a destroyer, each valuing love higher than life itself.
"Was anything more said by the prisoner to you?"
"I asked her whether she had been so weak as to believe the powder she had put into her father's gruel so harmless as Mr. Cranstoun had represented it; why Mr. Cranstoun had called it a powder to clean pebbles if it was intended only to make Mr. Blandy kind; why she had not tried it herself before she ventured to try it on her father; why she had flung it on the fire; why, when she found it hurtful to her father she had neglected so many days to call proper assistance to him; and why, when I was called at last, she endeavoured to keep me in the dark and hide the true cause of his illness."
"What answers did she give to these questions?"
At this point Addington's memory—till now so remarkable—failed him. Six questions he could recall with accuracy, but of the answers: "I cannot say, but very well remember that they were not such as gave me any satisfaction."
Mr. Ford rose again. "Let me ask you, Dr. Addington, this single question: were the horrors and agonies which Miss

Blandy was in at this time, in your opinion, solely owing to a hearty concern for her father?"

"I beg, sir, that you will excuse my giving an answer to that question. It is not easy, you know, to form a true judgment of the heart and I hope a witness need not deliver his opinion on it."

"I do not speak of the heart; you are only desired to say whether those agitations of body and mind Miss Blandy showed at this time did not seem to you to arise entirely from a tender concern for her father?"

"Since you oblige me, sir, to speak, I must say that all the agitation Miss Blandy showed at this time, or any other when I was with her, seemed to me to arise from the apprehension of unhappy consequences to herself." Dr. Addington was a man of integrity; he would not be deflected from what he believed—in light of subsequent events—to be the truth. Compassion would not deflect him, nor charity, nor the thought that by being a little less than scientifically positive, one insignificant life might be saved. Mary was no longer Miss Blandy, heiress to one of his most reputable patients, but the prisoner, the parricide, butt of Grub Street with her legs in irons. Addington believed implicitly in the law, in the right side of the law. He was not a Messiah to touch pitch and save, he was an ambitious physician. He would go far; this he knew; his road lay clear ahead. That Francis Blandy with his last breath had tried to save his child made no appeal to this man whose own child was to become Prime Minister of England.

Addington left the box with an air of conscious rectitude. He had, it would be agreed in legal circles, been a model witness.

It was with a numbed brain that the Court greeted Littleton. The clerk took the oath in a voice high-pitched with nervousness, his bony hand raised like that of a spell-binding Methodist. In his formal black he was gaunt as a rook. The attorney's clerk approached a court of law with far greater awe than the medicos and domestics. He evaded Mary's eyes; he would, he knew, have enough to do giving satisfactory answers to these gods of his own profession without having to deal with the passions she could still—from beyond the pale—arouse in him.

His evidence dealt mainly with Mary's last letter to Cranstoun.

"Had you ever directed a letter for her before?"

"I had. To Mr. Cranstoun." On being shown a letter, he said: "This is one."

"Did you put it in the post?"

"I did not. I opened it, having just before heard that Mr. Blandy was poisoned by his own daughter. I transcribed it and took it to Mr. Norton, and after that I showed it and read it to Mr. Blandy."

"What did he say?"

"Very little." A muscle twitched in Littleton's cheek and he spoke as though the words were being extracted under torture. "He smiled and said: 'Poor lovesick girl. What won't a girl do for the man she loves.'"

Mary covered her eyes with her hand.

"Have you ever seen her write?"

"I have. Very often."

"Look at this letter. Is it in her own handwriting?"

Littleton took the slip of paper, his thin fingers contracting a little in the memory that her hands had touched it. "I cannot tell," he said, reddening. "It—it is written worse than she used to write. But—it is the same she gave me."

Wearily, beating on numbed minds, the cross-examination returned once more to ghostly music and presages of death, then, adroitly, to family bickering, so terribly significant when seen through the eyes of a criminal court.

The footman, Harman, now went into the box: "I was servant to Mr. Blandy at the time of his death. That night Miss Blandy asked me to go with her. I asked her where she was going? She said it would be five hundred pounds in my way and no hurt to me if I would go. I told her I did not choose to go."

"Did she want you to go away at that time of night?"

"Then, immediately."

The bizarre story was disposed of in a few words. Perhaps more would have spoiled it.

The Town Serjeant, together with Mr. and Mrs. Lane, reconstructed faithfully in their evidence their encounter with Mary at the Angel.

"She wrung her hands and cried: 'But why should I blame Cranstoun?' " Mrs. Lane said. " 'I am more to blame than he, for I gave it my father and know the consequences.' "

Bathurst struck like a cobra: "Did she say I *know*, or I *knew*?"

"I really cannot say, sir," Mrs. Lane said earnestly; "I did not expect to be called to be examined here and will not take it upon me to swear to a word. She was in a sort of agony, a very great fright."

With excellent timing, Mr. Bathurst wound up the case for the Crown with the reading in court of the letter Littleton had intercepted:

"Dear Willie,

"My father is so bad that I have only time to tell you if you do not hear from me soon again, do not be frightened. I am a little better myself and lest any accident should happen to your letters, take care what you write. My sincere compliments. I am ever yours,

"M.C."

The evidence for the prosecution was at an end.

The hunters had taken seven hours in proving their case. What of the hunted?

CHAPTER FOUR

With aching backs, cold feet, dry eyes and brains numbed by repetition and sensation, the court, fidgeting and coughing, settled down to hear the other side—if another side could be said to exist.

The moment had come for Mary to address the jury. Tired in body and mind, her spirit failed her at the prospect of finding words with which to meet the complex of accusations made against her, and now that it was too late she bitterly regretted her failure to prepare a defence.

Rising to her feet, she stood very erect. Her height, her pallor and the sober elegance of her clothes gave her an air of aloofness which aroused a certain amount of antagonism. Her poise—so widely interpreted later as lack of feeling—was based on that ultimate courage which comes to some women in a crisis; the deep chill calm when anguish and terror have been transcended. She had so little to hope for that she had gone beyond fear. Kindness might have broken her down, but she knew herself among enemies, and to enemies she would not show her heart.

"My lords," she began, her voice as cold and disciplined as her body, "it is morally impossible for me to lay down the hardships I have received. I have been aspersed in my character. In the first place it has been said that I have spoken ill of my father, that I have cursed him and wished him at hell, which is extremely false. Sometimes little family affairs have happened and he did not speak to me as kind as I should wish. I own I am passionate, my lords, and in these passions some hasty expressions may have dropped; but great care has been taken to recollect every word I have spoken at different times, and to apply them to such particular purposes as my enemies knew would do me the greatest injury. These are hardships, my lords, such as you yourselves must allow to be so. Your lordships will judge the difficulties I laboured under. I had lost my father; I was accused of being his murderess; I was not permitted to go near him; I was forsaken by my friends; affronted by the mob; insulted by my servants. Although I begged to have the liberty to listen at the door, where he died, I was not allowed it. My keys were taken from me, my shoe buckles and garters too—to prevent me from making away with myself as though I was the most abandoned creature. What could I do, my lords? I verily believe I must have been

out of my senses. When I heard my father was dead, and th
door open, I ran out of the house and over the bridge and ha
nothing on but a half sack and a petticoat without a hoop
my petticoats hanging about me—the mob gathered about me
Was this a condition, my lords, to make my escape in? A goo
woman beyond the bridge seeing me in this distress desire
me to walk in till the mob dispersed. The Town Serjeant wa
there. I begged he would take me under his protection t
have me home. The woman said it was not proper, the mo
was very great and that I had better stay a little." She pause
for a moment, taking a sip of wine and water. What next
Playing for time to marshal her thoughts, she descended t
a note of grievance. "I was locked up with only an old servan
of the family to attend me. I was not allowed a maid for th
common decencies of my sex. I was sent to gaol and was i
hopes that there, at least, these usages would have ended. Bu
was told it was reported I was frequently drunk, that
attempted to make my escape, that I never attended the chapel
A more abstemious woman, my lords, never lived. Upon th
report of my making my escape, the gentleman who was High
Sheriff came and told me, by order of the higher powers, h
must put an iron on me. I submitted, as I always do to th
higher powers. Some time after he came again and said h
must put a heavier one upon me, which I have worn, my lords
till I came hither. I asked the Sheriff why I was so ironed. H
said he did it by command of some noble peer on his hearing
I intended to make my escape. I told him I had no such
thought and would bear it with the other cruel usage I had
received." Launched now on a blind alley of grievance, sh
seemed unable to retrace her steps. "The Reverend Mr
Swinton, the worthy clergyman who attended me in prison
can testify that I was very regular at the chapel whenever
was well. Sometimes I really was not able to come out, an
then he attended me in my room."

The court listened with growing confusion; the prisone
seemed in her defence to have lost sight of the charge agains
her.

Gripping her handkerchief tightly in her right hand, Mary appeared for the moment to be floundering. "They likewise have published papers and depositions which ought not to have been published in order to represent me as the most abandoned of my sex and to prejudice the world against me." She paused; then, returning at last to the salient point, she began to speak in a clear, firm voice. "I submit myself to your lordships and to the worthy jury. I can assure your lordships, as I am to answer it before the grand tribunal where I must appear, that I am as innocent as the child unborn of the death of my father. I would not endeavour to save my life at the expense of truth. I really thought the powder an inoffensive thing, and I gave it him to procure his love. It has been mentioned I should say I was ruined. My lords, when a young woman loses her character, is not that her ruin? Why, then, should the expression be construed in so wide a sense? Is it not ruining my character to have such a thing laid at my charge? And whatever may be the event of this trial, I am ruined, most effectively."

Mary sat down. Not a clever defence, not, perhaps, a very wise one, seeming unduly preoccupied with petty grievances rather than with the single, terrible accusation. She had made no appeal to sentiment, nor had she at any point touched it. Her sufferings seemed, to a prejudiced Court, those of a proud woman; indignities, rather than sorrows. Her speech had the ring of truth, but it did not go deep enough. Her self-discipline, her almost contemptuous courage were cold weapons with which to fight such a battle as this; the weapons of Miss Blandy, spinster of this parish. Her class, her background, her upbringing inhibited her from showing her heart to strangers. Of woman's wiles she had none; not a tear would she permit herself to shed in order to excite the emotions of the men ranged against her. She would have scorned to emulate a weakness she was far from feeling. As the defence of an innocent woman, her speech had the merit of moderation; coming from a felon, convicted in all but the final verdict, it failed. And so, head high, enunciating perfectly, she threw away, in her intelligence, the chance that instinct would have shown the most abject illiterate infanticide how to seize.

Her friends in Court—and they were few enough in all conscience—felt their hearts sink, while her adversaries found in her address just that element of detachment that set the seal on their appraisal of her character.

The weakness of the defence was perhaps epitomised in the first witness it called: Ann James, a washerwoman. She took her place with a little bob, her red hands clasped over her best apron, her merry face shining below her best cap. With her broad dialect, she brought a note of rich low comedy to the scene; a delicious character, town and gown agreed.

"I remember the time Mr. Blandy grew ill. There was a difference between Elizabeth Binfield and Miss Blandy, and Binfield was to go. I heard her say: 'Damn her for a black bitch I shall be glad to see her go up the ladder and swing.'"

"When was this?"

"It was before Mr. Blandy died."

Betty Binfield, recalled by the prosecution, denied ever using the words Mrs. James had quoted.

The next witness for the defence was the charwoman, Mary Banks. Complete stupidity gave her face a youthful comeliness. My friends! Mary thought. As well call the Wargrave Fool!

"Did you hear Elizabeth Binfield say she should be glad to see the black bitch go up the ladder to be hanged?"

Like a child repeating a lesson, Mary Banks said: "She did say she should be glad to see the black bitch go up the ladder to be hanged."

"When was that?"

Into the charwoman's mind sprang the memory of the most exciting event of her life. "It was the day Mr. Blandy was opened," she cried with innocent relish.

Mary closed her eyes.

"Are you sure it was that day?"

"I am sure it was." Mrs. Banks repeated obediently. Her

examination at an end, she left the box quite unaware of the value of her evidence—to the prosecution.

Hearne now took the oath. Poor loyal Ned, Mary thought, what further service can you give me? Save my life? The ranged wigs, the scarlet and ermine on the dais, the inimical faces of the twelve just men rose like a wall in front of her eyes, shutting out the future.

"I formerly was a servant in Mr. Blandy's family. I went there eighteen years ago."

Eighteen years ago! Just before my fourteenth birthday, Mary thought, in the wonderful summer of 1734. Or was it only to her the summer had seemed so wonderful. It was then that suddenly after her mother's patient years of guidance, the world of books had opened to her and she would spend long hours by the river reading. Even now a fallen elm in Fawley meadows recalled to memory Pope's *Elegy to the Memory of an Unfortunate Lady*.

"I left Mr. Blandy's employ about two years last November, but have been frequently to the house ever since—that is, maybe three or four times a week."

"What was Miss's general behaviour to her father and the family?"

"She behaved according to what I always observed as well to her father and the family as anybody could do—an affectionate, dutiful daughter."

"Did you see her during the time of Mr. Blandy's illness?"

"I did. The first time I went into the room she was not able to speak to me nor I to her for ten minutes."

"What was that owing to?"

"The greatness of her grief."

"When was that?"

"It was the 12th of August. She was put into my custody that night."

"Did you ever hear her speak ill of her father?"

"I never heard her swear an oath all the time I have known her, or speak a disrespectful word of her father."

King's Counsel rose. "What are you?"

"I am sexton of the parish."

"How came you when she was put under your care to le her get away?"

"I was gone to dig a grave."

Mr. Ford continued his examination: "Did not th prisoner at some time declare that as to herself she was totall innocent and had no desire to hurt her father?"

"She declared that when Cranstoun put some powder int tea no damage came and she apprehended no damage woul come to her father when she afterwards put powder herself." In answer to a further question, Ned spoke with emotion: "She thought if Cranstoun should be taken and brought t justice it would bring the whole thing to light, he being th occasion of it all, for she suffered by being in prison and wa innocent and knew nothing that it was poison, no more tha I or any person in the house."

As Ned stepped down from the box, Mary caught his ey with a mute whisper of gratitude. The sexton's plain goo face was transfigured for a moment.

Mr. Blandy's old friends, Tom Cawley and Tom Staverton followed each other. The first: "I have known Miss Bland twenty years and upwards and her father likewise. I wa intimate with the family and frequently drank tea there. never saw her other than dutiful."

The second: "I have lived near them five or six an twenty years and was always intimate with them. I alway thought them two happy people, he happy in a daughter an she in a father, as any in the world."

The prosecution was quick to blur the impression: "Di you observe that he declined in health?"

"I do not say as to his health, but he seemed to shrink, an I have often told my wife my old friend Blandy was going." Tom Staverton smiled wistfully. "He was a handsome man."

The landlady of the Angel now took the stand: "I remembe Miss Blandy coming over the bridge. She was walking alon and a great crowd of people after her. I, seeing that, asked he where she was going. She said: 'To take a walk for a littl air, for they were going to open her father and she could not bear the house.' The reason I asked her to go to my house was the mob followed her so fast."

"Did she walk fast or slowly?"

"She was walking as softly as foot could be laid to ground. It had not the least appearance of her going to make her escape."

The constable, Robert Stokes, was now examined: "I told her I had orders from the Mayor to detain her. She said she was very glad because the mob was about."

"Did you think from her dress and behaviour that she was about to attempt to make her escape?"

"No. It did not appear to me at all."

Prisoner's Counsel addressed the Judges: "As very unjustifiable and illegal methods had been used to prejudice the world against Miss Blandy such as, it is to be hoped, no man will have the boldness to repeat—I mean the printing and publishing of the examinations of witnesses before her trial—and as very scandalous reports have been spread concerning her behaviour ever since her imprisonment, it is to be desired that the reverend gentleman who has attended her as clergyman may give an account of her conduct while in gaol, that she may at least be delivered of some of the infamy she at present lies under."

A pause ensued, hanging on the stale air like a presence. There was no movement in Court. Mr. Bathurst's eyes rested in space—rested, perhaps, on the shadowed figure of the jester, poised on his cornice.

It was only a matter of a minute or so before the ruling was given that it was needless to call such a witness as the jury was only to regard what was deposed in court and entirely to disregard what papers had been printed and spread about, or any report whatsoever.

Then she knew.

From the moment when, dressing by candlelight in her cell, she had set out under the low March sky, Mary had never allowed herself more than the most tenuous hope of acquittal,

but up to this point she had believed that out of a mountai
of calumny some poor molehill of justice might emerge; tha
at least if she was to pay the supreme penalty for a single sin
a shred of virtue would be conceded her. It was perhap
strange that a woman on trial for the most abominable crim
conceivable, forced to accept the impossibility of proving he
innocence, should have been jealous of her reputation in smal
things, could, in her address to the jury, recall "a petticoa
without a hoop"; could, charged with parricide, wince at th
suggestion that she had neglected chapel. Yet why so strange
when love or hate can be born of a mannerism, a statesma
made or broken on a single phrase and a king's lampoon on
courtesan plunge great nations into war?

For Mary the refusal of a small indulgence told her all sh
needed to know of the larger tolerance. What followed now
would flow over her, leaving no mark on memory. All had
been said, all decided. The prosecution would cross the t'
and dot i's of its unassailable case; no more would be allowed
from the defence.

It was with the dream sense of having heard it all befor
that Mary listened to the closing speech for the prosecution
"Gentlemen, you observe it has been proved to a demonstra
tion that Mr. Francis Blandy did die of poison. It is as clearly
proved that he died of the poison put into his water-grue
upon the 5th of August and that the prisoner at the bar pu
it in. For so much appears, not only from her own confession
but from a variety of evidence. The single question, therefore
for your consideration, is whether she did it knowingly o
ignorantly."

Bathurst paused. "She says she gave her father this powde
to make him love her. After having heard of the great affectio
with which the poor dying man behaved towards her, can you
think she wanted any charm for that purpose?"

In turning against her her strongest defence, the prosecutio
made, perhaps, its most brilliant stroke. The rest was easy.
The damning facts slipped into their places like the numbered
pieces of a mosaic as Bathurst told in broad, incontestable

outline the story of the last ten days of Francis Blandy's life. Even in its shoddiest aspect—the testimony of Betty Binfield—the case did not falter; evidence of her malice had rested wholly on the testimony of servants whose dates did not tally. Supremely confident, the prosecution could afford a gesture: "I will in justice to the prisoner add—what has already been observed by Mr. Ford—that the printing which was given to the evidence before the coroner, drawing odious comparisons between her and former parricides, was a shameful behaviour towards her and a gross offence against public justice. But"—here the screw of mockery was given a final turn—"you, gentlemen, are men of sense and upon your oaths. You will therefore totally disregard whatever you have heard out of this place. You are sworn to give a true verdict between the King and the prisoner at the bar according to the evidence now laid before you. It is upon this that we (who appear for the public) rest our cause. If upon that evidence she appears to be innocent, in God's name let her be acquitted; but if upon that evidence she appears to be guilty, I am sure you will do justice to the public and acquit your consciences."

As Mr. Bathurst sat down, Mary rose to her feet, speaking very quietly. "It is said I gave it my father to make him fond of me. There was no occasion for that—but to make him fond of Cranstoun."

The trial was drawing to a close; nothing remained now but the charge to the jury, and the verdict. Mr. Baron Legge began to sum up. Covering the ground for the fourth time, his address was to take more than seventy minutes. Scrupulously fair, he did not miss a point, but so unbalanced was the weight of evidence that less than a quarter of that time was given to the case for the defence, and that at a point when most that it sought to refute seemed immaterial.

"A very tragical story it is, gentlemen, that you have heard, and upon which you are now to form your judgment and give your verdict. The crime with which the prisoner stands charged is of the most heinous nature, attended with considerations that shock human nature—the murder of her own father.

But the more atrocious, the more flagrant the crime is, the more cleanly and satisfactorily you will expect that it should be made out to you. In all cases of murder it is of necessity that there should be malice aforethought, which is the essence of and constitutes the offence; but that malice may be either express or implied by the law. Express malice must arise from the previous acts or declarations of the party offending, but implied malice may arise from numbers of circumstances relating either to the nature of the act itself, the manner of executing it, the person killing, or the person killed. . . .

"Thus far is undeniably true and agreed on all sides: that Mr. Blandy died by poison, and that that poison was administered to him by his daughter, the prisoner at the bar. What you have to try is reduced to this single question—whether the prisoner at the time she gave it to her father knew that it was poison.

"If you believe she knew it to be poison, you must find her guilty. If, on the other hand, you are satisfied, from her general character, from what has been said in evidence on her part and from what she has said herself, that she did not know it to be poison, nor had any malicious intention against her father, you ought to acquit her. But if you think she knowingly gave poison to her father, you can do no other than find her guilty."

The jury did not retire.

Mary sat motionless; death, when it came, could add little to what she now experienced in mind and body and spirit.

The Court was still with the pent stillness of held breath.

Exactly five minutes passed before the Foreman of the Jury rose.

"Gentlemen," the Clerk of the Arraigns asked, "are you agreed on your verdict?"

"Yes."

"Who shall say for you?"

"Our Foreman."

The Clerk turned to Mary. "Mary Blandy, hold up thy hand."

She complied. "Gentlemen of the jury, look upon the prisoner. How say you, is Mary Blandy guilty of the felony and murder whereof she stands indicted, or not guilty."

"Guilty."

A single swift pang of horror shot through her, but not by so much as the throbbing of a nerve did she betray herself.

"Hearken to your verdict as the Court hath recorded it." More reiteration, more raising of a hand that no longer seemed part of her, then the final: "What have you to say for yourself why the Court should not proceed to give judgment of death upon you according to law?"

Her pale lips seemed to move, but no sound came, nor was any expected.

"Oyez!" the Crier called. "My Lords the King's justices do strictly charge and command all manner of persons to keep silence whilst sentence of death is passing on the prisoner at the bar, upon pain of imprisonment."

Mr. Baron Legge's eyes rested on the pale, blank face. He spoke quietly, unwillingly, as though the thing were infinitely distasteful. "Mary Blandy, you have been indicted for the murder of your father and for your trial have put yourself upon God and your country. That country has found you guilty. You have had a long and a fair trial, and sorry I am that it falls to my lot to acquaint you that I am now no more at liberty to suppose you innocent than I was before to presume you guilty. You are convicted of a crime so dreadful, so horrid in itself that human nature shudders at it—the wilful murder of your own father. A father by all accounts the most fond, the most tender, the most indulgent that ever lived. That father with his dying breath forgave you. May your heavenly Father do so too," he added in a whisper, then continued: "It is hard to conceive that anything could induce you to perpetrate an act so shocking, so impossible to reconcile to nature or reason. One should have thought that your own sense, your education and even the natural softness of your sex might have secured you from an attempt so barbarous and so wicked. What was your intention is best known to your-

self. With God and your conscience be it. At this bar we ca
judge only from appearances and from evidence produced t
us." He spoke sombrely, moved by real emotion. "But d
not deceive yourself; remember you are very shortly to appea
before a much more awful tribunal, where no subterfuge ca
avail, no art, no disguise can screen you from the Searcher c
all hearts: 'He revealeth the deep and secret things, H
knoweth what is in the darkness, and the light dwelleth i
Him.' Let me advise you to make the best and wisest use o
the little time you are likely to continue in the world. Appl
to the throne of Grace and endeavour to make your peac
with that Power whose justice and mercy are both infinite."
He paused for a moment, the colour draining slowly from hi
face. "Nothing now remains but to pronounce the sentenc
of the law upon you: That you are to be carried to the place o
execution and there hanged by the neck until you are dead—
and may God, of His infinite mercy, receive your soul."

A sob somewhere at the back of the hall broke the awe
silence that had fallen. The terrible words of the deat
sentence touched off the springs of a mass emotion pent fo
thirteen hours, and there were tears in many eyes.

Mary rose to her feet for the last time, her voice no les
steady, her head no less high. "My lord, as your lordship ha
been so good as to show so much candour and impartialit
in the course of my trial, I have one more favour to beg, whic
is that your lordship would please allow me a little time ti
I can settle my affairs, and make my peace with God."
Devoid either of fear or bitterness or servility, her manner wa
that of a gentlewoman craving a courtesy from a gentleman

His lordship answered in kind: "To be sure, you shall hav
a proper time allowed you."

PART SEVEN 1752

CHAPTER ONE

WRITING to Sir Horace Mann on the 23rd of March, Mr. Horace Walpole said: "There are two wretched women just now that are as much talked of (as the Gunnings), a Miss Jeffries and a Miss Blandy, the one condemned for murdering her uncle, the other her father. Both their stories have horrid circumstances; the first having been debauched by her uncle; the other so tender a parent that his whole concern while he was expiring and knew her for his murderess, was to save her life. It is shocking to think what a shambles this country is grown . . ."

One among many footnotes to a twice-told tale.

Lady Ailesbury made a final effort to save Mary, and the Countess of Huntingdon—energetically raising chapels for Mr. Wesley to preach in—wrote her a warm letter of sympathy, but the end would be the same for her as for Elizabeth Jeffries, already cut down from the gibbet in Epping Forest.

With the aid of the chaplain Mary composed an appeal, ending with the words which had more than once entered her mind: "Remember the instability of sublunary things and judge no man happy till he dies." The appeal would become an historic document—perhaps as a record of woman's duplicity, perhaps—in the minds of the few—as a *cri de cœur* from beyond the grave.

The date of her execution had been postponed, as a hanging was considered unsuitable to Holy Week. March ended and even to her cell a rumour of spring penetrated, infinitely nostalgic.

In the time conceded her she had to the best of her ability set her affairs in order. Had she, she wondered, made her peace with God?

It was very quiet now. Through the open window she could hear the cooing of pigeons on the castle roof and the distant rush of water, then later, borne on the wind, the bells, speaking with such a babel of tongues that the hour of seven was lost. Below their carolling a single voice tolled, deeper, more portentous than the rest.

She sank to her knees and prayed; the prayers of childhood. In her months in prison she had recaptured something of the old simplicity of her family faith; she no longer felt herself dedicated to darker altars and unfit for worship. Except for a short period when the inflammation of her ankles spread to a general fever, she attended chapel regularly and, praying alone in her cell, found some release from the remorse that numbed her brain.

The slow insidious degradation of her years with Cranstoun had slipped from her like a sloughed skin; convicted parricide, wise in all the ways of love, tainted by the occult, she was yet what she had always been: spinster of this parish. It could not be said that she had found peace; even now at the end of the journey she had her moments of anguish, but for the most part she accepted her fate not so much as a punishment for crime but as the price demanded of those who choose to live fully.

"This world is a comedy for those that think. A tragedy to those that feel." Where had she heard that? Lavinia, surely, quoting Horace Walpole? Well, she had felt, most deeply. Few women had known such love as hers.

The ironies of love were beyond her comprehension: her father had given her a rare selfless love, and she had been born to take his life; Cranstoun whom she had herself loved with transcendent passion had in his turn destroyed her.

She no longer asked herself: Why did I make of my life

what I did? For her, she now accepted, there had been no choice.

And now the lock was turning in the door of her cell—the chaplain. He had never before visited her at so late an hour. As the door closed quietly behind him she said: "So it is to be tomorrow."

He took her hands in his. "I want you to pray for courage."

"Courage——" she repeated. In the flickering light of the candle, he could not read her face. "Courage. I wonder what that means?" As she drew her hands away, he knew she did not expect an answer. "Can you tell me what truth is? What is loyalty—innocence? Once I thought I knew. Now I'm not so sure. Range them all against a single factor; man's justice. There they sit, judge and jury, weighing souls like St. Michael! 'This soul,' they say, 'shall go to heaven, and this to hell!' They weigh the spirit of man in their scales, and what do they find? That there is nothing to weigh! Only material facts count with them, things they can read and hear and handle. The only truth they accept rests in a chemist's analysis. They knew what they were about when they blindfolded their Justice! They were afraid she might recognise innocence and starve the mob——!" Her voice broke and she stood trembling, startled into silence by the realisation of the deep well of her own bitterness.

Swinton sat down wearily. "Still thinking in terms of the world, Mary."

"Forgive me, sir—I suppose our roots are strong."

"That's why I'm here. To try to help you."

"One of my good friends——" Recovering her poise, she paused for a moment in thought, then she said: "I had intended to speak at—at the tree—but—I'm only a woman. The ladder seems very high. I was ever afraid of ladders. Suppose I were to falter at the last——" Moving to the table, she picked up a pen. "There is something—something I ask of you."

Swinton looked at her keenly. "A—confession?"

She met his eyes. "A declaration of innocence."

After a moment he said: "Very good." Drawing his chair up to the table, he asked: "Would you prefer me to write it?"

"If you will, sir." Handing him the pen, she moved out of the orbit of the candle's light. Speaking slowly, her voice was firm and clear. "I, Mary Blandy, do declare I die in full persuasion of the excellency of the Christian religion and a sincere though unworthy member of the Church of England. I do likewise hope for pardon and remission of my sins by the Mercy of God—through the merits and mediation of our most blessed Lord and Saviour, Jesus Christ——"

Coming to the end of the sentence, the chaplain looked up. "Yes?"

Only now did her voice begin to falter. "I do further declare that I did not know the powder, to which the death of my dear father has been attributed, had any noxious or poisonous quality in it." She pressed her fingers to her eyes. "I—I had no intention to hurt—much less to destroy him——" She came into the light, speaking strangely. "He forgave me. You knew that? I told you? Or—no. He forgave me—his voice—his poor voice——Yet he forgave me."

"At least you have that consolation."

She looked at him in wonder. "Consolation? It was then that my heart died."

The chaplain dropped his eyes, the pen trembling in his fingers. "Is there—anything more you wish me to write?"

She frowned in confusion. "More? Oh—yes. Please go on. I did honestly believe it to be an inoffensive thing and I gave it him to procure his love. All this is true, as I hope for eternal salvation and mercy from Almighty God in whose—in whose most awful presence—I must so soon appear." For a moment fear gripped her, fear of a step into the unknown.

"Is that all, my dear?"

"No. Wait. There was something more. What was it? Yes. Yes, I know. I die in perfect peace and charity to mankind and do from the bottom of my soul forgive the person who has been instrumental in bringing me to the ignominious death I am so soon to suffer." She turned to Mr. Swinton. "This is my last declaration and I do most earnestly desire that it may be published after my death."

The chaplain handed her the pen and Mary leaned over the table, writing:

"Mary Blandy.
In the Castle of Oxford,
April 4th, 1752."

"So much for the world," Swinton said. "And now—what of God?"

"God?"

He rose to his feet. "The time is short, Mary. Do you intend to face your Creator with a lie on your lips?"

"You, too," she said in a low voice.

"It's not for me to judge you."

"But you are judging me! You who know me so well!"

"The human mind is a strange thing, Mary. Stranger even than the human soul. This is a defence, consistent enough, true enough for a court of law—but—is it true enough for the ultimate tribunal?" He spoke gently, almost persuasively. "I've heard so many confessions in my time—more than anyone knows. Believe me when I say—the relief is immeasurable."

"But how can I confess to a guilt that is not mine?"

"You're too young, Mary Blandy."

"Too young to die?"

"Too young to die unprepared."

"What more can I tell you than I've already told?" she demanded.

"The truth."

She stared at him, drawing away a little.

"Are you forgetting your own words of a moment ago?" he asked quietly. "'What is truth?' What is it—the inner truth? Search your heart, that's all I ask. I accuse you of nothing. I think you honestly believe what you say. But is it the truth? My dear—the time is so short. Is it not possible that you, even you yourself, have missed something, some link between the semblance and the reality? I don't know. I only wonder. Think, think back—is there a point, some moment in time when your judgment was blurred by emotion—when the dividing line between innocence and guilt was no more than a hair's breadth?" He spoke in an awed whisper. "Think—think, Mary Blandy."

She made her way to her narrow bed and sat staring out, staring back into another life; into the mind of another woman.

A moment in time. A single moment in time when judgment was suspended, a moment of surrender to a will stronger than her own, a moment of surrender of body and mind and spirit. A hair's breadth; a suspension of judgment. A single moment in time.

Think, think—like mist shifting and changing form, so the form of her thoughts changed intangibly.

A sense of wrong; a sense of evil. But in what? Accepting evil, had she questioned in what evil lay? Had her eyes been too blurred by passion to distinguish the half-tones of darkness? Was it in this mindless submission to the will of another that guilt lay?

I had not intention to hurt much less to destroy.

Nothing could strip her words of the truth. But was that enough? What had been the intention? What had been *his* intention? Had she for a moment asked herself, asked Cranstoun? Projecting herself into that other woman who had been herself, she knew that she had not, and that in those few hours of somnambulent impulsion her guilt lay. Her sin—inexpiable—had been in the last analysis a sin of omission.

She raised her head slowly. "I see now—with pitiless clarity—that in listening to the man I loved above life itself I was made the fatal instrument of death——"

What, then, was the answer? Was it possible that as the years passed and the clouds of prejudice cleared, someone, in some day remote from her own, might know the answer to a question she could only ask herself: guilty, or guiltless?

CHAPTER TWO

Mrs. Deane dressed her as though for a ball, coming to her early to brush her hair until it gleamed. She had been saving a fresh muslin cap for just such a morning as this. There were ribbons of black paduasoy to tie her mistress's hands and arms, and a sack of black crape to fall over hooped petticoats.

When she was ready, Mary stood at the open window watching the sky change from grey to rose. She had been awake since four, spending most of her time in prayer, and she drank in eagerly the ineffable freshness spring lent even to the air of a city. A blackbird was singing somewhere on the Mound, and as the light grew stronger she thought she could see for the first time a hazing of green over the branches of the gallow's tree.

Closing her eyes, she gripped the iron bars. "I have so loved the dawn——"

Mrs. Deane drew the girl's head to her shoulder and stood at her side in silence until the moment of weakness had passed.

As the many bells of Oxford were striking eight, the key turned in the door.

The chaplain came first. Mary had received the Sacrament the night before and there was little more to be said. By the time the Sheriff entered the cell she was standing erect; a tall pale gentlewoman dressed to meet death in impeccable taste.

Her own attorney joined them, and after half an hour in the chapel they led her out to Castle Green. The crowd was hushed as she appeared. She walked with curious dignity to the foot of the tree where the Sheriff's men waited for her. Her grace as she handed him his fee of two guineas would remain in the memory of her executioner.

The gallows was high; a ladder of twenty rungs or more ran up to the pole laid between the two trees.

The chaplain prayed with her for a few minutes. Looking into her calm face, he told himself she had at last made her peace with God.

In a day of public executions, the crowd, drawn from every phase of the City's life, was awed by her superb courage. Some among them had an uneasy feeling of intrusion, some wept silently, as though an open display even of sympathy would be an affront.

Pausing at the foot of the ladder, she said: "Do not hang me high, gentlemen, for decency's sake." Her hands were trembling a little as she started to ascend. Even as a child she had been nervous of ladders. At the fifth rung she paused, hoping she would not have to go any higher.

Below her lay a sea of faces: bright colours and drab, with here and there the black gown of a member of the university. The silence now was so complete that she could hear the sound of the blackbird, welcoming an April morning. For a moment the thought of all she was leaving behind overwhelmed her; this spring which would give place to summer, the wooded hills, the river and all the dear known sights and sounds and scents.

I had not thought to die so young——

The moment passed and she ascended two more rungs. Drawing the handkerchief down over her face, she raised her hand in the signal for which the crowd waited.

They carried her home through the night: through the lovely sleeping city and over Magdalen Bridge; across the long bridge at Dorchester and through the deep forests of beech. As they entered Henley, the clock was striking one, yet Hart Street was as animated as though this were market day.

The flickering glow of a hundred candles lit the church, and the Rector performed the funeral service to the greatest concourse ever assembled below its roof.

They buried her at the side of her father:

ALSO

HIS DAUGHTER

MARY

WHO DIED

AT OXFORD ON 6TH APRIL 1752

AGED 32.

Mr. Horace Walpole commented: "Miss Blandy died with a coolness of courage that is astounding, and denying the fact, which has made a kind of party in her favour. As though a woman who would not stick at parricide would scruple a lie!"

Wyndham Books are obtainable from many booksellers and newsagents. If you have any difficulty please send purchase price plus postage on the scale below to:

Wyndham Cash Sales
P.O. Box 11
Falmouth
Cornwall

OR

Star Book Service,
G.P.O. Box 29,
Douglas,
Isle of Man,
British Isles.

While every effort is made to keep prices low, it is sometimes necessary to increase prices at short notice. Wyndham Books reserve the right to show new retail prices on covers which may differ from those advertised in the text or elsewhere.

Postage and Packing Rate

UK: 30p for the first book, plus 15p per copy for each additional book ordered to a maximum charge of £1.29. **BFPO and Eire:** 30p for the first book, plus 15p per copy for the next 6 books and thereafter 6p per book. **Overseas:** 50p for the first book and 15p per copy for each additional book.

These charges are subject to Post Office charge fluctuations.